Saga of Dead Men Walking

Insanity's Rapture

Book II of the Auramancer's Exorcism

Joshua E. B. Smith

© 2020 Joshua E. B. Smith

Published: December 29, 2020

ISBN-13: 978-0-9990590-6-7

ASIN: B08P61MNVN

Imprint: Independently published

Publisher: Joshua E. B. Smith

josh@sagadmw.com

DEDICATION

You've made it to Book II of the Auramancer's Exorcism.

This book is dedicated to you. You, the survivor. You, the fighter. You, the person that bought this book. You, the person that looked 2020 in the eye and said, "You know what? I'm gonna take the time to read a book right now."

When I put together the plot of Respite through 2018 and 2019, the underlying plot of, "Let's tease a potential apocalypse-level supernatural plague! That hasn't been done in a while!" came to mind and I went with it.

Then 2020 arrived and said, "Hold my wineskin."

In my defense, I really had no idea. By the time I did, Respite was well on its way to print and that plot point was effectively etched in literary stone.

So, here we are.

2020 came, and it'll go.

For all of you that faced the challenge of this year, I applaud you. If you're reading this after 2020, I'm sitting here going, "Really hope that we've seen the worst of it."

One way or another, we made it through it. We made it through 2020.

This book is dedicated to you. However you came through it, and with the memory of those that didn't, this book is dedicated to you.

And now it's time for the rapture. That's on point for things, isn't it?

I mean... Rapturous Insanity.

OH. AND HEY. AND OTHER LOUD EXCLAMATIONS TO GET ATTENTION:

Make sure you sign up for the email newsletter! Get free things, news on upcoming releases, and more!

http://email.sagadmw.com/

CONTENTS
Acknowledgments

	Prologue	1
I	Of Healers and Thieves	5
II	Return to the Repository	28
III	Refugee of Insanity	46
IV	A Secret Rage	59
V	Rime and Punishment	89
VI	Hunting Truths	102
VII	Enslaved to Lies	116
VIII	Failure of Faith	135
IX	What Lies in Vines	158
X	Landing's Loss	175
XI	Embers of Honesty	191
XII	Dreams of Damnation	211
XIII	Of Rapturous Insanity	239
	Epilogue	255
	Compendium of the Damned, the Divine, and All Things In-Between	264
	The Saga of the Dead Men Walking	278
	Welcome to a World...	280

ACKNOWLEDGMENTS

I don't know where to begin. Seriously – I have absolutely NO idea where to begin. I wrote the acknowledgments for Respite on February 27th, 2020. It's now October 19th, 2020. In the last seven, nearly eight months, my life has been bizarre and truthfully, probably worth a book of it's own.

So who do I say thank you to? Who made the biggest difference in my life?

My mom, my girlfriend, my cat, the wonderful people at the hardware store that helped me with some roofing projects, the staff at my mom's nursing home, the webinar marketing hosts that I've watched all spring, summer, and fall long? The mechanics that have worked on my car, my healthcare providers, the people working at the local super-center to keep the shelves stocked and the toilet paper flowing? The vet's office, my editor, my cover designer?

My friends who helped me keep my sanity? The other authors I've interacted with as I network my way across the... well, the network? The local paper for doing an interview with me, the blogs and podcasts that hosted me? My web host provider?

I can't begin because I can't say. Because I can't say, I can't tell you.

What I can say is, "Thank you and I love you."

I love my fans. I love my family. I love my cat. I love my girlfriend. I love all the people in my life that have helped me survive and keep sane to write this book the last few months. The people that have helped and that will help edit and design aspects of this book. The people that provided inspiration and aid and more.

Thank you.

And in some way (or in many ways!), I do love and cherish all of you. All of you listed, all of you not, and all of the things you have done. I hope that you know – all of you! – what your impact on my life was, is, or will be.

I hope that this book, and the things I do in your lives, helps to entertain you as much as you've helped me – and if I don't know you? I hope it entertains you all the same.

~Josh

PROLOGUE

Pridis, the 19th of Riverswell, 513 QR

*Had I realized that the drugs were not the only demon
vying for supremacy in his flesh, much would have been different.*

*If I had known how deep his dependency on cocasa had grown,
I would have intervened himself.
It was, as most fights are with such things,
a demon that had to be slain from the inside out.*

*Had I realized that Basion City was not the safest place…
Had I realized that his suffering was being exploited…
Had I realized what game was truly at play…
But they didn't know. Thus, I didn't know.*

*A few murders. A terrible thing, but not uncommon.
A few missing. A distressing thing, but in a city the size of Basion?*

*A priest suffering a crisis of pain no prayer could reach?
The city holds one of the largest outposts in the Order of Love!
Where else would I send him to find peace but a place
designed to grant it, designed to study the faults of the broken,
and to put them on the road to well-being and health.*

*The only saving grace, if any were to be had,
was that he was both in the worst place I could have sent him,
and the best person to see where others were fractured, battered, and lost.*

*And while that may not be enough of a grace to let me sleep
without guilt and a crisis of my own conscience,
there was one thing that filled my heart with pride.*

*It was not that he held his faith. It was not that he held his morality,
no matter how much he bent it as he needed to ease his pain.
It was not the Love in his heart. It was not the relief offered by his Words.*

*It was that in the darkness, he found forgiveness,
and granted it in a way that only he could.*

*~Sir Steelhom
Office of Oversight
New Civa*

He played with her. Almost every night, he played with her. With each stroke of his claws, he played. With each agonizing rake of his fingers, he played. With each touch, each twist, each gouging thrust of his nails, he played a symphony of pain in her soul.

It didn't matter how much pain he inflicted. How much damage he did. Nobody noticed. Nobody saw it. Nobody saw the handiwork he left behind nearly every night – nearly every night, except for the nights he had to feed. Those nights, he stayed away.

No, he was much better than that. He wanted to play. He wanted to make her suffer. He wanted a measure of revenge. He took it in the shadows.

He took it *with* the shadows.

No matter how often they sliced through her soul, his claws never once split her skin. They traced down and over every inch of her flesh and left rivulets of pain coursing through her spirit with every long, agonizing stroke. Though no matter how many times the shadowy claws raked just under her skin, they never flayed flesh from bone.

He could have. He could have left her body tattered, shattered, a testament to his skill at weaving exacting carnage on the unwanting and unwilling. He could have severed tendons and wrapped them around his fingertips as he pulled them free of her arms and legs one after another. He could have plucked the bones from her fingers out through the tips one after another. He could have twisted her tongue until it tore from her howling mouth with just a single nail.

He could have done that. All of that, and more. He knew he could.

She knew he could.

He'd done it before. She'd seen it. She'd cleaned up after it.

He chose not to. He chose, instead, to set her spirit on fire. He chose, instead, to pluck at her being in ways that you could not see unless you knew where to look – or how. He slipped his ethereal claws through her flesh and into her body and coaxed whimper after whimper, cry after cry, and tear after tear from her bloodshot, exhausted eyes.

Each time she asked why, the response was the same. "You know why."

She did. "Squistal."

"That is a place. That is not a why. You know why."

She whimpered in pain as he twisted something under her breast and sent fresh electric agony down her arms. "She wasn't… wasn't human. Wasn't… wasn't natural. Had to… she had killed. Had to… had to stop her."

Her answer made him do it again. Another slash of shadow against soul. Another twist of long black claws that plunged from the shadows under her bed to slice at her legs through the straw-filled mattress as if it wasn't even there. "*I'm* not human," the whispered, gravely voice snarled, "and she was *mine*. Zilyph. That was her name. You. You took her. You took my heart. I take yours."

"My… my heart doesn't belong… to you," she whimpered again as moonlight began to shine through the window in her room. For a moment, it made the shadows go away. But not for long.

Never for long. "Yes, it does. Your Goddess hasn't saved you. She won't. She had Her chance, and your heart belongs to me now," it purred. "*You* belong to me."

"Punishment," the exorcist whimpered as she covered her mouth to hide the scream she knew he was about to force from her lips. The staff at the Manor didn't like it when she screamed. Some of them were nice. Others weren't. It was easier just to muffle herself. He'd only be angrier if he was interrupted. She'd learned that lesson years ago. "This is a test. I will be... be rewarded. Test... test of faith."

"Be rewarded with blood," he promised. "You'll draw blood for me. Be with me. You cannot give me back what I lost but I will make you into what she was."

She closed her eyes and screamed into her hand as his shadowy nails ripped into her womb and *twisted* in a way he'd perfected long before he met her. "It's... not... not just... my test."

His shade moved up between the bed and the wall and leaned down over her as she thrashed under his touch in her nightgown. "It's no test. You're believed by none. You're wanted by none. You've earned only me."

The broken priestess looked up at his towering menacing form and weakly shook her head. "Faith... faith includes... trust. Induces belief. Trust when... trust when blind... is its own... reward... and its own battle."

"Lost your battle," he mocked.

"No," she replied with the thinnest of smiles, "but I have seen. Heard. Heard the ether."

He reached down and placed the tip of his index finger just to the side of her nostril. She knew what was coming. He loved to do this. The nose, the eyes, the ears. She'd learned – even before they'd 'met' – that he loved to remove the senses. He wasn't doing that with her, but he relished the way it made her cry when he pushed through her spirit. "The ether doesn't care. The Gods don't care. The only one that cares for you is me."

"Those not believed... they must... must have the most faith in what they know is true."

"But that isn't you," he mocked. "None will believe you. They believe what they see. What they know. They know that this is a place that I cannot be, so they don't believe you."

She sucked in a slow gulp of air. "Another's belief will... will... become their faith. His... his trust will... be my truth. And you? You..." she whispered as even more shadows began to dominate the walls. They blocked out the window. They hid the moonlight.

Annix, a monster born of darkness and shadows, a monster with more blood on his hands than she had in her veins, pulled his claws back and lorded over her as if he owned her. He thought he did. He believed he did. "What,

Bistra? What will I receive?"

"You'll have… you'll have more than you… think you deserve."

He sliced down through her chest and ripped into parts of her soul she never knew she had. He laughed so loudly that the rest of the Manor should have heard it. His magic was the only thing that stopped the caregivers, the helpers, or the healers from rushing to her aid.

For the first time, as he laughed, so did she. She laughed, because she *knew* from what she could hear in the ether, she *knew* that someone's nightmares were coming true. She knew that *those* nightmares would bring the end of this one. *Those* shadows would *hate* this one.

She knew, because she was the Auramancer Exorcist. And the aura of the exorcist interred just a few rooms away was one that screamed for all those who could hear. Who would hear. Who would bother to listen. Bistra screamed. Annix laughed. Someone else cried.

His tears would end her suffering, in time.

Another slice. Another scream.

Even if now was not that time.

I. OF HEALERS AND THIEVES
Staddis, the 20ᵗʰ of Riverswell, 513 QR

"*Do you see it?*" the dead woman whispered in his ear, "*do you see what you missed?*"

He struggled fitfully in her arms, but her ruined flesh had him in a vice-like grip and wouldn't let him go. If she did, he thought was going to die – they were floating over frigid waters full of crashing waves and twisted shapes moving under them. She had one hand around his naked waist, and another wrapped in his dirty-blonde hair to force his eyes forward.

Being dead might have been an improvement.

What he saw was almost worse than being held tight to a corpse ravaged first by flames at the end of her life and then by flames from a stint in the Abyss. While she had been beautiful in life, death offered no such kindness. Exposed and splintered ribs pressed against his naked shoulders while her remaining breast obscenely pressed against the side of his head.

And yet...

The boat was another story. He saw crewmen in Dawnfire attire fighting each other on the deck under the midnight sky. Someone was trying to light a fire in the middle of it; at first he thought it was to see. Then he realized they were desperately trying to set a barrel of pitch ablaze. The shipman was panicked and he carried the barrel like a desperate madman. A few other sailors were attempting to guard him as the rest of the crew tried to attack. Others threw themselves onto their own blades, and he watched as one man hung himself off of the mast.

"*Don't see it yet, do you? Shouldn't need two eyes to see. Just one should work. Listen to them, look at them,*" she commanded.

He knew what it was. He knew what they were fighting. He obliged anyway. He didn't have a choice. She'd made sure of that. The sailors didn't have a choice, either.

Thick, black, oily tentacles started to rip out of one body after another. They thrashed on the desk and wildly knocked down anything and anyone in reach. When the mast collapsed, the defenders quit trying to fight back, and started to take their own lives.

The man trying to light the pitch almost made it.

Almost.

A tendril of black fog the size of an ox reared up from the center of the ship with a multitude of faces writhing just under its surface and all along its length. It crashed down on top of the silvery-haired officer with the force of an avalanche – which obliterated him and destroyed the barrel at the same time.

A few minutes later, and the dying was effectively done. Blood flowed down the side of the ship, and loose limbs tumbled overboard. Slowly, as she held his head locked forward, as she slowly carried him over the boat – he couldn't make out the name on the side despite his best efforts – he watched as the central tendril plucked body after body out of the water. He watched as it collected each corpse, and dropped them into the belly of the ship.

He watched as the creature cleaned up its mess. After what felt like an hour, the boat was clean of broken and bloodied sailors. Once the last one fell into the hold, the tentacle vanished behind them and all was left in utter silence.

"*You know what it is.*"

"I destroyed it."

"*You know what it is,*" she repeated.

"I watched it get ripped to shreds. The Abyss consumed it. It didn't belong here. It wasn't supposed to be here. I sent it to the pit, and every corrupted soul it owned found release."

"*I didn't,*" she replied with a slow hiss.

"Daringol lost its hold on you. You earned the one the Abyss has."

"*Did it let me go? Did it truly?*" she countered as she turned him around in her arms and lifted him slightly. She grotesquely licked what remained of her melted, distorted lips and gave him a mockery of a seductive smile. "*Why do you think I force you to see?*"

When she pressed her lips to his, he screamed in fresh terror…

…and didn't stop until Seline pulled his head into her lap and quieted him with a finger placed to his lips. "Ah. There you are."

The world spun around his head. Crashing seas faded and were replaced with wooden slat walls; a derelict ship turned into an old bed and bear-fur blankets; and the dead woman turned into a very calm, very soft, and very tired blonde-haired woman only a couple of years his senior. "Seline? I…? What? What… how'd I get back in my room?"

"Carried here, by cot," she replied as she wiped his face off with a small cloth, "five days ago. We weren't sure how long you were going to be out, in all honesty. We've been talking about what to do with you if you were asleep much longer."

He tried to lift his head up from her thighs but couldn't do more than weakly struggle before he gave up entirely. "Five da...? I was just in the atri...?"

"You were in the atrium on Wundis. Today is Staddis."

"But I just...?"

She placed her finger back on his lips and shook her head slightly. "After what you did in the garden, you went straight to surgery. After – Keto sends his regards, by the way, and said that it's easier to work on you when you're not thrashing about – you went straight to an examination from Lady Ridora and then Maiden Prostil. Lexcanna had final say over you before you were brought back here, where you've been ever since."

He blinked and tried to rub at his forehead before he realized that his hands were tied to each other. "What happened? *Why am I tied up*?"

"Let's start with your leg," she began. "When you fell, you tore it open. You were right to be complain about pain, it turns out. You had an abscess. Keto had to scrape it out. Never seen anything like it before, he said."

He struggled to remember the last few things he could. He had been looking at the statues of Isamiael, Solinal, and Niasmis in the garden when he'd seen a glimmer behind the edifice of Love. He'd reached for it and there was a flash of light and... burning. A lot of burning.

Then an eye that peeked out of the side of his leg. The eye that belonged to the fog that belonged to a spirit he had personally sent screaming into the Abyss. "Wasn't... infection. I saw it," he mumbled as he began to struggle against her grip a little more. He kicked at the blankets on his lap and couldn't get his legs to move either – and realized that they had tied his ankles to the bedposts, too. "Daringol, saw it, saw the tentacles, I –" he ranted as he tried to twist his leg under the covers before he let out a pained cry.

The healer stopped him with a gentle squeeze of his cheek and waited for him to settle down. "No, Akaran. No tentacles. No demons. Just an infection."

"It's not a demon," he countered, "it's a spirit. Angry. Wraith, nesting wraith. An *arin-goliath*. I saw it, it was there, it's there. Let go, I –"

"No, Akaran. You screamed about it a few times in a few very brief lucid moments. Catherine was so worried she personally worked on you to make sure that there was nothing there. You're okay. I promise."

He shook his head as much as he could (and ignored how nice it felt to lay on her lap). "No I'm not. I don't remember what happened. Just that I saw it." That's when he realized that there wasn't anything he could remember after. "What... what DID happen?"

Seline sighed softly and went back to work cleaning his face off. "You fell, and you banged into the wards in the atrium. They had an... um... an *adverse* effect on you."

His eye went as wide as his face went pale. "On *me*? What kind... what kind of *adverse effect*?"

"From what the ladies said, whatever is wrong with your aura caused all of the wards to react as if you were... what was the word? Oh yeah. 'Inimical.' Like your soul was hostile to them," she said as she continued to soothe him with the cloth across his stubble-covered cheeks. "On the other side of the coin, you did demonstrate that they still worked."

The horror in his eye sunk to new levels as she talked. "They treated me as... defiled?"

"Yes, I am afraid that they did."

Akaran sank down into her lap and gave up struggling against the ropes. "I'm... defiled..."

She shook her head and dismissed the dejected tone to his voice. "No, you're not. Your aura is a little unusual. That's all. It's hard to say *what* magic will do to you right now, given your state. Even before that."

"Nothing good, apparently," he muttered with a defeated sigh. "What did the wards do?"

"You'll have to speak to Ridora for a full breakdown, if she offers to give it," she returned. "But to watch it? First, you banged into Solinal's statue. It made you glow blue and you froze the grass. Then I... I accidentally knocked you into Isamiael's."

"I... froze the grass?"

"Solid. The caretaker is *pissed* at you. I'd keep away from him for a while."

He grunted in vague annoyance as he tried to imagine what could've happened. "Yeah well, Yannis doesn't like me anyway."

"Likes you a lot less now," she warned, "though Keto was *really* interested in what happened after you triggered the ward from the Lady of the Hand."

"What did it do?"

Seline cleared her throat and started to count the effects off on her fingers. "Let's see. First, you suffered minor burns around the scar on your upper arm – from the wound you had when you first got here. There's matching burns on that mess on your chest, several other scratches. More or less, any injuries you had when you arrived at the Manor blistered like someone poured hot soup on them."

He tilted his head down and for a brief moment, was grateful that he was swaddled up in the blankets. "That's first...? Is there a second?"

"Yes, actually. Not only did you suffer burns, Keto thinks it turned the mass in your leg into a solid rock. Said it looked like charcoal when he pulled it out. Also, you may notice that a couple of your scars are simply *gone* now. Said he'd like to start experimenting with directly touching patients wounded by magical means against the statue in question." Seline blanched and looked out the window. "I've never heard Ridora say 'no,' so forcefully before..."

Meekly, he found the courage to ask, again, "What else? I have a feeling there was an else."

"Well. I'd like to say that good things happened when you activated the Niasmis ward. Do you remember telling me that the spell read more like a threat than it did a warning?"

"I... think so? *'Trespass against the lost and Love will trespass against you,'* wasn't it?"

"Yes."

Akaran swallowed slowly. "Did it think I was the lost or the trespasser?"

"There's a charred imprint of the back of your head in the dirt now," she slowly replied. "Yannis is *really* pissed at you."

"Fisk."

The blonde-haired healer nodded understandingly. "As for what *actually* happened? How the magic worked on you? I don't really know. I don't know if Ridora will tell you."

He frowned up at her. "I'm the one that set them off. I think that gives me the right to know," he retorted as he struggled against the bonds a little. "Do you mind taking these off?"

"I suppose you're lucid enough. You start moving around in your sleep again, and expect to be chained down every night."

"Start moving...? You said I was unconscious?"

Seline started to carefully work the linen cords off of his wrists, one knot after another. "You have a habit of being insufferable while you're awake. When you're asleep, you're an outright pain in the ass. You fell out of bed once, and nearly knocked Abbagail's head off when she was trying to feed you."

He sunk even lower into her lap and mouthed a quiet, "Oh."

"Oh, indeed."

"But the wards...? Why don't you think Ridora will tell me? It's my body. If I caused them to activate, I should know what happened."

"Oh, you did indeed set them off," she replied as she finished untying his hands. "The ladies are not happy with you for doing it. Regardless of fault or intent, you caused... a situation."

She guided him upright and he trepidatiously looked down at his still-covered knee. "What do you mean by situation? Please Seline, tell me what in the name of the Goddess happened already."

The healer took a deep breath and caved. "To hear them curse about it – and they've been cursing about it – triggering all three spells at once caused some kind of feedback loop that amplified the effects that each of them felt. Instead of a simple tingle or noise in the ether, they –"

He tensed up and interrupted her before she could finish. "A feedback loop? Oh no. How bad? Tell me it wasn't bad."

"Ridora was taking a well-deserved nap when you did it, and she kicked her puppy off the bed and into the fireplace," she replied with a cringe. "The dog is fine but her bedroom has an odor now."

He slammed his hand over his mouth as his eye went wide all over again. "Oh Goddess. I'm so sorry."

Seline went on as she scooted away from him and began to work on the knot holding one of his feet down. "They say that Lexcanna passed out in the middle of service, and a room full of worshipers thought that the halo that appeared around her head was a sign from the Pantheon. Figured she was either ascending to the Divine or had done something heretical that she was being punished for."

"Oh. Oh dear. Were they appropriately mollified?"

"Yes, but the members of the Odinal delegation she was preaching to were unimpressed."

A mental vision of a bunch of armed barbarians standing around a service grumbling their displeasure in the middle of the Ellachurstine Chapel flashed in his mind. "Pits…"

"The one you must apologize to the most would be Maiden Prostil," she warned.

He cringed and painfully stretched his good leg once she had the ropes undone. "What happened that was worse than charbroiled puppy?"

"The feedback caused her to throw up."

"Oh. Well that's not so bad, is it?"

Seline brushed a lock of hair from her eyes and shook her head. "She was holding her niece's daughter when she did it. Her two-winters-old daughter."

That image was worse than the barbarian one. "Oh… my Goddess. Oh no. Oh no."

"None of them felt too sympathetic to the sounds you made while Keto was operating on you," she added. "I'm not sure they will be too sympathetic to your current state now."

"Oh… no. No I don't… imagine…"

"Suffice it to say that the three did as you said they were designed: the Solinal ward attempted to calm the disturbance in your aura, the Isamiael ward attempted to heal you, and the Niasmis ward attempted to purge you of the effects that ravaged you."

He took a deep breath as she finished the knot on his bad leg and slowly pulled the blankets away. "Why didn't they ever do it before?"

"I asked the same question," she said. "Catherine assumes it's the same reason that the wards in the Repository have yet to have a negative effect on you – you never physically touched them, thus the otherworldly magic infesting you directly came into contact. Whatever *was* wrong with you is bottled up inside your flesh, much like Adept Lolron pointed out."

Thankfully, his leg was bandaged. Even better, he hadn't bled through it. "No, if it reacted to the energy then it should've worked even if I wasn't touching it unless…" he replied as he thought on it for a minute. "Oh! I served as a direct conduit. Connecting the spells directly to me and bridging the gap… they haven't reacted to me before now because the magic from Tundrala isn't mixing with the ether in this world and as long as it's just in me it's contained and not spreading… and if it isn't spreading then the wards won't work," he rambled.

"I do hope you understand I don't know what you mean."

"Well, like you said. What Lolron said. It's like… oil and a glass jar. You can press the glass against something, and the oil won't do anything… you can put the glass in a fire, and it'll just make the oil hot until the jar breaks."

"In this example, should I assume the magic inside you is the oil?"

He nodded. "While the wards were the fire."

"And your jar broke when you touched it," she added.

"I broke when I touched it," he agreed with a frustrated sigh. "If it wasn't so terrifying to *be* the damn jar right now, I'd be excited that I think I just figured out a new metaphysical concept that could have some implications on how the Order handles exorcisms."

Seline shook her head at him, desperate to understand how he could go so quick from 'deeply embarrassed' to 'lost in discovery' so quick. "Nothing is new in this world Akaran, we're all old souls."

He rolled his shoulders and stretched his neck. "Fairly sure I'm new."

"No, just rare," she countered. "You've told me as much with your studies."

The priest just sighed and tried to work a kink out of his neck as he thought about his reply for another few moments. "I'm fisked over a barrel is what I am. Can't coat that any other way."

"We can't as long as you have that attitude," she argued. "What it *does* mean is that you are restricted from entering the atrium again, under any circumstances. Same with any of the shrines in the city or places where someone might've set up warding. Maiden Prostil has her own new rules for you, and I imagine that Ridora has a few suggestions on how you should spend your time now as well."

"Fisk. Just... fisk me."

"The circumstances don't really present themselves for certain acts of dalliances, I have to admit," she muttered in vague disappointment.

"Why should now be any different than any other point in my life," he grunted.

Seline caught herself blushing as she raised an eyebrow at him. "Are you suggesting you –"

"What happens to me now?"

"Not fisking, apparently," she started to say before she caught herself. When he began to protest, Seline quickly cleared her throat and replied before he could utter any indignancies. "For now, you rest. I'm sure Ridora will be in to see you tomorrow. Nothing else you're doing right now is, or will, matter."

That made Akaran shake his head a little too vehemently. When the room quit spinning, he put words to his disagreement. "Wait. No. In the garden, there was something behind the statues. That's what I was reaching for when I fell."

The healer frowned at him and tilted her head a little to the side. "No? There wasn't anything there."

"Yes there was," he argued. "Looked like a necklace of some kind. Silver chain."

"No, there wasn't anything. I promise. I went back to look after."

He shook his head again and immediately felt worse for Lexcanna's nausea. "I'm *telling you* that I saw something. I think it's important."

"In your state, I imagine you saw a lot of things," she replied as she gave him a reassuring little smile. "Don't let it trouble you."

"Fine," Akaran grumbled. "Then Bistra. I need to speak with her."

That earned a more forceful condemnation. "No. There will be no speaking with anyone. There will be no more of your investigation. Catherine and Ridora had a very animated chat about that – you are no longer to do it."

It also went over like a herd of dragons. "Wait, what? Why not?!"

Seline pointed a finger at him. "We can ignore the fact that for an exorcist that *can't*, you've been waving your sigil at anyone that might pay attention to it. A person with your fragility has no business being around *anything* that might have a relation to magic."

"It's a magical world out there. For the sake of the Pantheon, even *this* place is steeped in magic!"

She nodded at that, and pointed out a flaw in his argument he hadn't considered. "Yes. It is. Be happy that they decided it was still reasonably safe to allow you to stay. They could have easily determined you'd be best off in a monastery, or a hermitage."

"They wouldn't."

"They nearly did," the healer warned. "*I'm* the one that talked them out of it."

The realization sunk onto his shoulders and made his head sag. "Piss."

She reached over and placed her hand on his good knee. "Please don't make me regret that choice, Akaran. While I realize that it isn't your fault for what happened with the wards, you've proven to be a very dangerous patient – all other things set aside. Your *intention* may not to be to harm those around you, but *unintentional* harm is still harm. There are many people here that are weak and innocent that need to be protected from threats."

"The wards treat me as defiled and the staff now thinks I'm a threat," he lamented as he scrunched his eye closed. "Isn't all of that wonderful."

"*Please* don't make me regret it," she implored a second time.

"Fine," he reluctantly assented. "Fine. What do I have to do for now?"

Seline let out a breath she barely realized she'd been holding. "For now, rest. Ridora wants you active and stretching your leg as soon as you regained your senses. You can expect a long conversation with Adept Lolron and others in your near future as we figure out what exactly has to be done with you. Waiting for things to change does not seem to be the wisest course of action to follow."

"No. No I guess it doesn't," he said after a brief internal debate. "At least it means I'll get back to normal soon. Can deal with that damn malignant specter on my own terms."

She tensed up and squeezed his leg a little harder. "There's *no* specter, Akaran. No wraith, no ghost. It's in your head," she reiterated. "I'm going to assume you had the same dreams while you were out of your head?"

"Bit different this time. She was showing me a ship. I didn't get the name.

Hull... something. Dawnfire colors. Daringol was there, too. Ripped the crew to shreds," he said. "It was... bad. It felt real. I thought it was."

"That's the demon you have to battle then. Don't worry about any others. Defeat your mind, the rest will follow."

"It's real. It's in me."

"It's in your head," she clarified. "The demon is the trauma you're fighting. Whatever damned soul that you took a blade to *is* gone. Long gone, I promise," Seline added with an encouraging smile. Then, unexpectedly, she added: "You *will* get through this. You *are* strong. I have faith in you."

"Thank you. And... Sel?"

"Yes?"

He looked down at his hands and rubbed his fingers together absentmindedly. "In the Academy, we were told one thing, one little bright lining that was supposed to work in our favor. It's not. I don't understand why."

Perplexed, she straightened up a little. "What isn't?"

"Abyssians," he replied. "They're not like this. The one that took Liv? It's an aberration."

"An aberration?"

"It's *smart*," he complained. "Yeah. Some of them are sentient. Some are intelligent. Upper-end daemons? The Fallen? Beyond comprehension. Beyond understanding. Those things though? They're all *in* the pit. They're not up *here*."

She bit down on her lip and silently begged him not to say what she thought he was thinking. "I don't know what you're trying to get at."

He started over at the door and refused to meet her eyes. "Something from the dark has figured out how to hide in the light. Figured out how to circumvent the wards here at the Manor. Figured out how to kill with impunity. Figured out how to hide," he answered. "Yeah. They hide. They want to stay here. Survive. Avoid the pit. But that's *hiding*. This bastard... he's hiding. Still doing it."

Seline took a deep breath and squared her shoulders back. "Akaran, no. It's not pitborn. For all the reasons you said it can't be. It's just a man, doing what men do. Killing other men."

"Has to be," he retorted. "It *has* to be. Makolichi figured out how to de-power wards. He used Daringol's nature to do it so he could act with impunity and hide from judgment. Now this thing. Whatever this thing is. I don't know what it is and I can't find it and it's going to kill again."

She reached over to him and made him turn his head to face her. "The Garrison will find out who did it. It's not your worry. It's not your fault. It's not some boogeyman. It's just a man," she said as she stood up and handed him a cup of water. "You need to rest. I'll be back soon with food. I promise."

"Not a man," he grumbled. When she slipped out of the room he tossed the cup into the corner with a clatter and shouted at her. "IT'S NOT A MAN!"

The only thing that greeted him was silence.

"These things aren't supposed to be smart. We are. I have to be smarter than it. All of it," he growled as he tried to get comfortable on his bed. "I'll be smarter than you, I promise," he grunted as he squeezed his thigh just about his knee so hard it left marks. "Gonna kill you before you kill anyone else ever again... and then I'm going after the rest..."

That wasn't to say she didn't hear him. It was more to say that she found her attention focused on someone else: the Lady of the Manor herself, Ridora Medias. "Are you alright, m'lady?"

The obvious answer to that question was 'no.' Normally, she presented herself as regal as regal could be without owning a crown. You almost never saw her wearing anything other than a linen maroon robe with gold trim stitched down the center. You almost never saw her without her auburn hair pulled up into a bun, and you almost never saw her with anything but firm conviction and compassion in her pale-blue eyes.

You also never, ever saw her showing signs of weakness.

So when Seline saw her resting against the wall, holding her head in her hands, it came as a shock. "It's just... I have this splitting headache," she half-groaned through clenched teeth.

The healer reached over and tried to touch her forehead, but Ridora flinched away before she could. "I'm sorry, m'lady. Is there anything I can do?"

"Nothing touches it," the much older woman lamented. "Comes and goes. I swear it gets worse whenever I get near him."

Seline frowned and tried to pull her disheveled strands of hair away from her elegant face. "Is it from the feedback? Or is it that he's a stubborn mule?"

"Yes to both, I am afraid, but it's not just that," she replied with a pained sigh. "It was even before his experiment down in the garden. Do you know the feeling when you hear people talking? But you can't tell what they're saying? It's like that. But not. And it's making my head simply pound."

"Like that, but not?"

Ridora ignored her confusion and went on like it made perfect sense. "Yes. It's not 'people' talking. It's just one. A woman. She's screaming. Angrily. Almost like... well. Not to brag about my experiences in such matter, but the last time I heard that tone, I was expressing to my husband what a necessity he should find it to keep his manhood away from the maid."

"Maybe you've been spending too much time with some of our patients, m'lady," the healer slowly suggested. "Should I have Prostil come back and –?"

The Lady gave her a withering glare. "One headache is enough. I do *not* need that witch to come give me another one. Listening to him right now only compounded it."

"He is showing more signs of delusions," Seline sighed as she looked back over her shoulder. "I am very concerned for what being cut off from the natural order of the world is doing to him."

"There is no shortage of that causing him grief, I am sure. I also think the cocasa is compounding matters."

"It might be. It's a poor sign that we had to continue to administer it while he wasn't in his right mind. I'm grateful we were able to find a way to feed him…"

"As am I."

Seline sighed and ran her hands through her ponytail. "Well. At least now that the abscess is cleaned out, he should be able to have his daily dosage reduced."

The older woman nodded in agreement. "Yes. When he leaves the Manor next, go through his room with a brush and make sure that he doesn't have any stashed."

"You think he's been getting it off-grounds?" she asked, then paused before adding, "Oh, and you're thinking of allowing him to continue to wander outside in the city?"

Ridora rubbed her temples and glared over at his door. "When he's here, my head starts throbbing. I can't afford to *not* have him go out and about. As far as the other," she continued, "I do not know. Yet, it is a truth that addicts always find a way to hide a supply."

The healer pursed her lips and had to agree again. "Unfortunate, but true. Lady – I really am concerned for his nightmares. A man like him shouldn't be left to his own devices if he's terrified of sleep. He might start trying to find drastic measures to stay awake."

"We will address that soon enough. Now is not that time, I am afraid."

"No, not with… everything else. Soon, hopefully."

"Yes, soon," Ridora replied. "Did you tell him about his friend?"

Seline couldn't stop herself from cringing. "No. He'll find out sooner than later. He doesn't need to know right now."

Her boss nodded in complete agreement. "Hopefully a great deal later. I can't imagine how he'd react in the state he is."

"That his friend has been accused of multiple murders? Including Lexcanna? That Raechil is missing and they think he had something to do with it? I'm still amazed that Hender hasn't had him hung already."

The Lady bowed her head at the name. "Raechil… I am terrified for her, I truly am. As far as the Lieutenant-Commander goes, he spoke to me this morning. Executing the mage has been forbidden."

"Forbidden? By who?"

"Paverilak," she replied. "As far as Maiden Sanlain's Betrothed is concerned, the culprit being arrested and out of sight is good enough. A public execution of one of the Queen's men could be seen as a weakness in the eyes of the midlanders."

Seline couldn't hide the shock on her face. "Surely you'd think that they'd be more impressed to see justice carried out swiftly?"

"One would," the Lady agreed. "I suspect if it was anyone other than one of her soldiers, a pyre would already be lit. And an officer of the Crown, no less?" She paused and shook her head. "They haven't even bothered taking him before a Justiciar or a tribunal. Ordered held without companions, for now."

Seline glanced back at Akaran's room and leaned in close to the lady of the manor. "Do you... do you think he did it?"

She started to rub her temples again and finally shook her head no. "It isn't my place to assume either way. I don't... I don't know. With blame being foisted onto the shoulders of the Mother Eclipsian at the same time? It is... it's hard to imagine that our city would be home to murders at all. Let alone someone like her plotting them."

"She's well-loved, too."

"So was Lexcanna," Ridora pointed out. "Jealousy between the light and the dark is not unheard of."

"If she wasn't hiding, maybe we could make sense of it. Not that I blame her. Half of the city wants her head and the other half wants her vindicated. It'll be a nightmare once she's found, either way. But Raechil... has he found *anything* that might give a clue? Anything at all?"

The Lady closed her eyes and felt her shoulders slump. "No. Henderschott told me he had gained nothing from interrogating the mage. As far as anyone can tell, she's vanished with no trace."

"Another one of Akaran's alleged disappearances, do you think?"

"I don't want to think anything that may prove him right," Ridora tersely retorted, "so come join me in prayer that he isn't."

***

Of the numerous Guilds that worked in, out, and around Basion City, there was one above all others that was respected, revered, and cherished. They worked in secret, they lived in shadows, but if you ever crossed them – you'd not wake until you were safely on the other side of the Veil. They were not to be trifled with, and those rare days when their entire council convened, you'd be best off if you not uttered a word out of place or time.

They didn't bother with lofty titles. One of them didn't bother with a proper name at all. Most never admitted their real or their names, though everyone on the council knew them. It was the nature of their business, and the nature of their game. Their business was in knowing everything that could be known at any time it could be, because simply, one couldn't make a profit unless one knew from where to steal.

Each district of Basion was represented by their own local leader. Yuchin sat patiently, a graying man with wrinkled, leathery skin and calloused hands. He hailed from the District of Piapat, where tradesmen and Guildsmen from all around worked tirelessly every day. Across from him, Bantia sat straight up with her hands daintily crossed over each other and her white robe with gold trim flowed across the tabletop. "I don't see the necessity for all of us to meet today," she demurely muttered to none of the other managers present, "for there are other things that I must do in preparation for the day of worship in the morn'."

Yuchin gave a dirty snarl at the pristine (on the outside, at least) woman from the Chiadon district. "Can't peddle whores to the faithful as they march up and down the streets if you ain't there pushin' tits out to 'em, eh?"

She let it slide even as Rodric, dressed in the finest attire that a mere goldsmith could afford retorted with a guffaw. "Like you'd know," the trader from Akkador West accused with a sly smirk. "Only whores you do business with are the ones that pay me."

"Gold's gold," Yuchin countered, "an' my boys make their livin' doing more honest work than yours."

"My 'boys,' as you call them, sell to everyone. What good is a city of commerce without a firm hand guiding its center?"

"No good if that hand don't have a sword in it," one of the other guests interrupted. That was Raes – a former Huntsman-turned-enforcer. His holdings were reflected in the darkened shadow of Akkador East, and not a single mercenary or soldier looking for a little bit of *extra* income made a deal near any gate without him knowing all about it.

That earned a soft rebuke from Bantia, though it was the self-proclaimed 'Lady' Aldeina Hessmage who countered his blunt assumption. She was one of the few of the Guild that made sure that her name was known everywhere it could be heard, and she made a point to make sure it was heard often. "You say that as if you don't respect the edicts of the ruling class of the city," she scoffed. "A sword is no good unless the hand that it's in can be claimed as coming from the hand of the Crown."

"You'd be surprised what good a sword can do," one of the two remaining souls yet to speak up interrupted. "Come talk to any of the sods that keep my caravans up and running and they'll tell you all about how important the Crown is or ain't."

"Oh, Hammer," she scolded, "your sods are the same sods that answer to Raes. Truly the worst of us, they are, for they get taxed twice over."

Before Hammer, or Raes, or any of the others could add their two crowns to the discussion, the woman that had the distinction of owning the fine establishment they were whining and not dining in spoke up after slamming a heavy copper tankard down on the oblong table they sat around. The basement of the *Drunken Imperial* offered many things for many people – and the representative of both Upper and Lower Naradol found it a useful nexus to hold the occasional meeting of the Fleetfinger's Guild. Not that she had any authority to call one on her own, of course.

Or hadn't, before recent events.

The last person that could – Liona Reanage – had been butchered at her day job, though everyone else in the city had known her as Livstra Oliana. For the Fleetfingers, she'd been known as the Gambling Mind. Or as otherwise known, the Boss of Basion City. Her death at the hands of a murderer (or *murderers*) unknown threatened more than most people would know. "Alright. That's enough shit outta all you. Didn't bring you all here for us to piss about," Celestine 'Cel' Navarshi growled out as loudly as she could.

"Don't think you needed to at all," Hammer grumbled from the door.

"No, she was right to do so," Bantia interrupted. "As grim a task as it may be, the Gambling Mind has moved to a place of rest. We would be advised to replace her rank, though we can never replace her spirit or place in our hearts."

"You grift the shits on temple row, woman, you aren't one of them," Raes retorted, "so don't go tryin' to talk to us like you do. The city's been doing just fine with us leading our own districts and you know it."

Yuchin shook his head. "You know as well as I do that won't last. Never does. Even if *we* work out together, once word gets out that this city lacks a Chairwoman? We'll be fighting for our lives."

Rodric snorted and flipped a golden crown into the air. "You say that but be honest now: nobody's dumb enough to move in and try to stir shit up with the way that the Guard is acting."

"Yeah and what about *after* the Guard calms down?" the extortioner-of-tradesmen challenged.

"Then we'll pay them off," he replied quickly. "Like we've *always* done."

Aldeina ran a hand through her platinum-blonde bangs and rolled her eyes. "Which one of us? They do not tax our holdings the way Liona did. We have no combined fund to pay them with. You all know as well as I that if they come for one of us they will come for us all. The Mind took care of all of that."

"Liona was a businesswoman," Yuchin retorted. "We just... do what she did. It isn't as if we don't all know our way around a ledger. Or a banker."

"She was more than that," she replied with a sad smile. "She was *fair* and *understanding*. She settled our disputes – in and out of the council. Before she came in, things did *not* run so smoothly. My predecessor learned that the hard way."

Cel sighed and took a drink. "An' now she's gone. She's gone and I ain't got a lick of trust for any of you to abide by the decrees of a dead woman."

"The innkeep's got a point," Bantia replied. "No disrespect to anyone here, of course. But do any of you trust *me*? Or do you expect me to idly and blindly trust all of you at once?"

From the door, Hammer dropped his hand to the heavy iron namesake he always kept on his belt. "I sure as fisk don't."

"Your sister did," the thief-of-priests snidely snapped back.

"Only thing my sister had was her ears stuffed between your legs. If she knew what –"

"*Enough* about that, you two," Aldeina hurriedly interrupted. "The point stands. Not only does the point stand, your dispute of who worships where and how is exactly *why* we *need* a new boss."

Yuchin shook his head again and banged his fist on the desk. "We do not. The Fleetfinger's Guild has existed just fine for centuries in situations like this where the ruling council – *us* – divvies up a city and operates it accordingly.

Much like we *already do*. All the Mind was good for was to keep the Guard happy."

"You would suggest then, what?" the woman with the nearly perfectly white hair demanded with a fire blazing in her brilliant blue eyes. "That one of us go and speak to Hannock or Henderschott and tell 'em 'All is well, we'll behave?' Do you think they'd respect that, let alone believe it?"

"Yeah," the tradesman grunted, "I do."

"And what if the 'one' says something else? 'All is well, we'll behave, except for Yuchin?' I don't think you'd like it none that much if I did, would you?"

"You wouldn't," he snapped.

She gave him a venomous little smile. "You wouldn't know. Not 'till you struggled to stand on your tippy-toes with a noose around your fat neck."

"Then we drag the Overseer in here in front of all of us an' tell that fat asshole who *really* makes the rules in 'his' city," Hammer suggested with a hopeful grin of his own.

Bantia gave him a sly little look from the corner of her brown eyes. "I would much rather prefer that neither he or the Lieutenant-Commander have no knowledge of my face," she said, and then as Hammer opened his mouth and showed off rotting teeth all over again, she interrupted him with a firm, "And no, I will not wear a bag over my head."

He grumbled something disparaging about his sister under his breath but otherwise stayed silent, which gave Aldeina another chance to run her mouth. "Then what do we propose to do? Bantia is correct, it will only be a matter of time before someone attempts to undermine our authority. We have grave enough concerns with what's unfolding as it is. The intruders are already past the damn gate, as far as our business is concerned."

"Who dares?" he demanded as he suddenly gripped the handle of his hammer tight.

"You already know him," Cel responded with a disgusted look. The innkeeper rapped her knuckles on the wall behind her three times in a row and a moment later, a wiry-looking thug shoved a hooded, tied up man into the back room. "Ladies, lords. This is Donta, and he's the bodyguard to the woman that keeps involving herself in our business – that so-called 'Lady' Anais."

Bantia looked him up and down and took note of how nondescript the bodyguard was trying to look. There was nothing special about his outfit, no sigils or other markings. He'd have fit in as easily in the merchant's quarters as the priestly one. The only thing that made him stand out was that his arms and hands, what little could be seen of either, were decidedly paler than your average man. "Been doing more than asking questions, has she?"

"Not that I've seen. Just that she asks a lot of questions," Yuchin muttered, "though she tends to spend gold as if she shits it."

"Asks questions. Buys land. Buys favors," Rodric added with an unpleasant sneer. "She's made a name for herself recently in certain circles. She's the hushed talk of the town over in Giffil. Made me a fair amount of coin in West, won't lie, and fairly sure she's lined Aldenia's purse in the East."

Cel scoffed at him and dismissed him out of hand. "Liona didn't trust her, and now she's dead. Makes a bitch wonder."

As she talked, her man ripped the sackcloth hood off of the mercenary's head. He was bald, navy-blue eyed, and furious. "You stupid shits," he snarled with a grave, gravely voice.

"Oh shove it, baldy," the innkeeper snapped. "You don't come walkin' into our city and start undermin' what we're doin' without there being some kind of punishment. Don't care how many crowns you've been makin' some of our less-demandin' members – 'bout time to pay up."

Aldeina gave a grave nod and addressed him directly. "I have spent a great deal of time looking into you and your employer. I am aware that she's traveled wide and far – from Civa to Dawnfire to the Midlands and back – and now she's here. Here, and dipping her toes up to her thigh in all manner of businesses."

"She's worked more of the merchants in Piapat than *I* have," Yuchin agreed. "You think I wouldn't notice? Think that any of us wouldn't notice? Or talk to each other?"

"Worked deals with half of you," he grunted. "You weren't complaining then."

"People weren't being murdered in the street *then*," Bantia stressed. "Now they are. This is a problem for us. All of us."

"They were, just nobody important," Hammer pointed out.

Donta gave her a foul look. "You think she's doing it?"

Raes cleared his throat and slipped a wickedly-serrated blade off of his belt and menacingly laid it on the table. "*I* think that even if she *isn't*, she knows who *is*. It didn't start until she showed up."

"Now that ain't entirely true. The missing people..." Yuchin started before Cel interrupted him.

"You. You and that crippled priest," she grunted. "Bringing that shit up again and again. People *leave* the damn town. It fisking *happens*."

The tradesman from Piapat shook his head and wagged a finger at her. "Cel, I know your father did, but most of the time people *don't*. Move, sure. Get up and vanish in the night an' leave their babies behind? No. There's *fisking off and away* with the town's chief whore and then there's *missing* and it's been going on longer than we wanna admit."

For the first time since the meeting was convened, a voice spoke up from the back. It was rare he attended such events, but their former boss had a soft spot for him – and he knew more about what she did than most. "Yuchin is right," Ronald Telpid, the Sergeant-at-Arms of Medias Manor intoned from back in the shadows. "The Guard's known about it. Hender just hasn't given a shit."

Bantia glanced over at his direction with her turquoise eyes piercing the darkness. "Why are *you* here anyway? You're not part of the council," she told the middle-aged, slightly balding, and slightly out-of-shape for a guard.

"The *saa* is Liona's former right-hand," Cel interjected before Ronald could explain himself, with a distinct pronunciation of the title as 'sahh'.

"The pits," Hammer grunted. "Errand boy, at best."

The sergeant made a rude gesture at the thief from Akkador West. "She meant a great deal to me. It pained me every time she had to pretend she didn't know me."

"She didn't pretend, you ass," the walking pile of muscle grunted. "She just didn't give a shit."

"Oh she gave one," Celestine contested. "How much is the question. I brought him here to get his thoughts on her successor. But first, this fool."

Donta whipped his head around and unsuccessfully (though not entirely seriously) fought against the wiry enforcer holding his arms behind his back. "Fool? Try saying that again."

"Fool," she repeated, "a *damn* fool. You and your boss move in, start getting people in our territories to owe her *favors*, then our boss drops dead? Then a whole bunch of others? A hunter, the Priestess of Stara, and that Granalchi? You two think you can come in and start clearing house like that?"

"Clearing *our* house like that?" Hammer added.

"Yet we don't know if they had any direct involvement in each of those, do we? There's a great number of sinners in this town, and I have yet to see solid evidence that says –" Bantia tried to interject.

"There's reason enough," her counterpart from East Giffil interrupted. "A mage, a hunter, a priestess? And all the while this one and his employer are asking question after question about what's stuffed in that Oo-lo fortress?"

"It is a temple, not a fortress," she corrected. "You and I have discussed this."

The white-haired woman rolled her eyes. "We've discussed how you think that the Goddess of Love tolerates Her followers playing in the underworld."

"Love can be found anywhere and everywhere," the thief-of-priests scolded.

"An' so can this cock," Yuchin said with a foul gesture at the restrained assassin. "Think it's any coincidence that I just got a letter from a guy from *Gonta* that said there's an interest in us by the Guild over there?"

"You got it? Why you?" Hammer demanded.

"Don't know," the tradesman answered honestly. "Pretty smile? But *his* boss? Last place she came from. Gonta. And now we're getting messages from the Guild *from* Gonta. Ain't a coincidence."

Cel felt her lip upturn and gave the gray-bearded thief a nasty look. "Oh we'll be talkin' about that later, Yu," she promised before turning her attention back to Anais's agent. "If you've got any words to speak in your defense baldy, you'd best speak them now."

Donta flexed his shoulders and twisted his arms away from her enforcer. "You get one chance. One," he cautioned.

"Oh? We do?" Bantia retorted with a bemused grin. "From a man tied and bound, that's not much of a threat."

"Guard just arrested someone for killing Lex," the thief-of-mercenaries responded with a grunt. "Blaming him for Liona – or maybe he just knew her as Livstra? Either or. Her *and* the Hunter. He didn't do the mage, but they are hunting for his bitch now."

"His bitch?" the thief-of-priests charged with a disbelieving, insulted look on her face. "That is a cold way to describe the Lady of Shadows."

Raes nodded and stretched in his seat. "Ah, yes. They arrested a battlemage, didn't they? A Specialist-Major? They seem to think that he is working closely with the Mother Eclipsian herself."

"I've *met* the Mother Eclipse," Yuchin added. "Erine is one of the holiest women I've ever known. Sure, she worships the darkness and all that, but even the ones that've crossed her have never come to an end befittin' their sins. She would never seek to draw blade against *anyone*."

"I'll second that," Hammer agreed. "Ain't no chance she had a hand in any of it."

Cel nodded her head and rapped her tankard on the wooden desk again. "Thirded. Council agrees – there's no way that our precious Erine would have *anything* to do with *any* damn murder. Not today, not tomorrow. Since she's taken such a likin' to that Badin fellow, safe to say he didn't do it on her behest, either."

"That battlemage drinks like a fish. That he could drop anyone... I would decline to believe it. A soldier, yes, as I imagine his superiors could force him sober long enough to deal with a threat to the Kingdom from time to time, but to murder of his own accord? Doubtful," Aldeina retorted. "Quite surprised the fumes on his breath don't catch fire when he lights his sparks."

The innkeep leaned in and gave Donta a wicked, toothy smile. "So you bald little shit, if it ain't *them* then it's probably *you*."

"Have we ruled out the midlanders?" Bantia quietly asked. "My understanding was that both the regional Consort-Blade and the Betrothed seemed to believe that it may just be politics as normal?"

"Have you *ever* known a midlander to gut anything bigger than a cockroach and not brag about it?" Cel countered. "If it'd been one of those tall, dark-haired hunks of dickmeat and abs they'd have hung a sign on the city gate proclaiming it."

As Rae laughed from across the room, Aldeina pursed her lips and gave a slow nod of agreement. "Crass as it is, Cel has a point. So, yes, Donta. We do have one chance to make this right. It is fitting that you happen to be her messenger, because it seems you are to be our message *to* her," the thief-of-nobility said as she voiced the implied edict to the rest of the council.

Donta's eyes narrowed and he gave the white-haired woman a murderous glare. "*Last* warning. Let. Me. Go," he demanded.

"Don't think you grasp the situation you're in," Cel retorted. "See, if you hadn't killed Liona, we wouldn't be without a boss. With a boss, we might be talked outta having you hung in the square."

"Yeah," Raes agreed. "Now we've had weeks to fume about it and talk to each other and come to a *group decision* about you."

"Hated every minute of it, too. Just didn't know you were the one to do it," Yuchin added. "Had big plans for the sod that took her, no matter who it was."

Bantia nodded along in agreement. "Truly. It is reason itself, to nominate someone new. Telpid, who would she have suggested?"

The saa of Medias Manor looked at her in surprise and gave a vigorous shake of his head. "You're getting ready to take his face off and you're asking the only person in this room that doesn't own a district his opinion? What if I choose *wrong*?"

"Choose wisely, would be my suggestion," Aldeina answered earnestly.

"I'm not gonna choose at all!" he shouted. "I *like* my head where it is!"

As he exclaimed his objections, Donta just shook his head and muttered something under his breath.

"What was that, cockmunch?" Cel asked with a smirk. "Couldn't make it out."

"Said *too bad*," he snarled. They all heard a sudden wet ripping sound and the thug holding him steady cried out in pain and doubled over. The mercenary flexed his arms hard and ripped free of the ropes that had kept them behind his back. As he whipped them back around to the front, a pair of spikes jutted from his palms and ripped his captor's stomach out in two different directions.

Hammer tried to free his namesake weapon, but Donta spun around and drove his right-handed spike up and through his cheekbone and into his brain. The thief from Akkador East crumbled against the basement wall and died without another sound. As blood pulsed out of the former enforcer's face, his killer jumped up onto the table as the other Fleetfingers tried to scramble away or bring a challenge to his rampage.

Not that it did any good. Yuchin died next; and Donta made sure that he suffered. The spikes went into and through both sides of the tradesman's neck and ripped his throat clean out. A fountain of blood sprayed on Bantia's white robes. Her blood joined his a scant five heartbeats later when Donta ripped his bony blades free and left a gash from her shoulder to her eye.

As she crumpled, the assassin jumped off of the desk and made sure Yuchin was dead with a single thrust into his heart. Telpid, to his credit, attempted to cut the killer down with a swipe of his sword, but his attack was easily dodged. Donta backhanded him with a blow hard enough to knock the saa to the ground and bloody the side of his face. He would've died then and there, had the lady that spoke too much not screamed in terror.

It was the last sound she made.

Donta perforated her throat first, and then took care to stab both of her lungs. As Aldenia died in her chair, he took a moment to drive the sharp tip of his left-handed spike into the center of her forehead. Rodric was quick to join her when he tried to lunge at the inhuman murderer with a pair of curved daggers.

His knives proved to be no match for Donta's blades. He was dead before his body toppled to the floor and the impact sent Aldenia's dying body the ground with him, which left Celestine and Raes as the only two left standing (and Ronald bleeding on the floor with his sword casually knocked under the desk). "Don't. Even. Try," he whispered with a tone to his voice that echoed in the basement and made their souls feel like they were having an audience with the damned.

They didn't know it, but they were.

"You can still breathe," he growled. "We need the underground. *You* will *give it*. Don't give a *damn*. Not about your Guild. Not about your people. Not about this city," he continued as they moved closer to each other and held whatever weapons they managed to pick up as tightly as they could in their hands.

"What... what the pits do you want?" Raes demanded.

Donta wiped a blotch of someone's blood off of his face and flicked it into the saa's general direction. "Want what we want. When we have it? We're gone. Until then? You are *mine*."

"Fisk," Cel muttered under her breath.

"WHAT WAS THAT?"

She huffed and puffed up her boisterous chest and crossed her arms in defiance. "I said '*fisk*,' you bald bastard. Fisk, fisk you, and fisk this," she continued before raising her hands slightly when he took a step closer, "but it ain't like we've got a choice, now do we?"

The assassin smiled coldly at her and the lantern-light in the room made his eyes glow (or at least, that's what she told herself). "You don't."

Cel looked down at the dead councilmen and moved away from a quickly growing pool of blood from Yuchin's still-twitching corpse. "Did you *really* have to kill everyone?"

"You wanted me dead. I did them first," he retorted with a huff.

"Fine, granted, self-defense *here*," she admitted. "But Liona? Did she not want to play with you? You royally fisked with the whole damn city when you did that. And Lexcanna? I wasn't her biggest fan by no means but she was *kind*."

Donta shook his head and his spikes slowly retreated back into his hands. "*We* didn't. That hunter? That was me. The rest? You've got bigger problems," he swore. "They've got fangs."

Outside, a towering man with a hand on his sword and a nasty scowl listened close to the exchange before he crept away quieter than should've been possible. Aside from 'big' and 'tall,' he had few impressive features — except for a scowl. It was the type of scowl that only came from getting bad news when you knew that you had to take it to someone worse. After weeks of traveling from Gonta to suss out the lay of the land, Austilin just *knew* his boss was going to decide to be *worse*.

And he made sure he was long gone before Donta or his surviving victims ever realized he'd even been there.

***

Ronald's day wasn't over — no matter how much he might've wished otherwise. Or rather, while his day was over, his night was just beginning. He saw the soldier coming in the torchlight around the manor, though until she got closer, there wasn't much he could tell about her. It didn't help that his left eye was swollen half-shut, or that his face was still throbbing like mad.

He recognized her a moment later, and immediately wished he hadn't. She'd arrived in town just three nights ago and had quickly made her presence known to an unlucky few — himself included. There wasn't any mistaking who she pretended to be, though he knew damn well that there was more to her than just her old rank-and-title in the Grand Army of the Dawn or the dragon tattoo on her cheek.

Her name was Sherril, and while she claimed to be a Specialist-Major from the 5th Ray of Dawn, the truth was that she hadn't been on the Army's roster for a long time. "Oh. It's you," he grunted by way of non-welcome.

She was, however, in the direct employ — if you could call it that — of Ronald's *third* boss, or at least, his blackmailer. "You expected other?" the smokey-ash-haired woman with a dragon tattoo on her cheek slyly responded.

The Sergeant-at-Arms shook his head and gestured back at the manor. "Other's already been."

"Oh has he? Gone already?"

He looked at her with a bland, bored glare. "Don't you know?"

"Perhaps," the battlemage admitted. "Perhaps I thought I'd come see where he spends all his time."

"Spending his time getting me in trouble," the guard retorted as he gestured at the bruising on his face and a scratch down his neck.

"Having a bad day?" she mocked. "A patient take a dislike to you?"

Saa Telpid took a few steps closer and whispered just loud enough for her to hear. "Someone hunting you and yours did. You-know-who has made enemies."

Sherril pursed her lips and wetted them with the tip of her tongue. "By his nature, all are enemies. Who, pray tell, has he angered now?"

"That killing spree he started on a couple months ago? Just caused the Fleetfinger's to turn upside down. Now they've got a new boss, and most of the council is dead because of it. They're gonna hunt for him next, can all but promise it."

"Bodies dropped a month ago causing upheaval now?" The mage rolled her shoulders and made her chainmail tunic clink as she shifted. "Causing chaos in the shadows, hmm? And you think they are after our Meister?"

"I think there were powerful people that wanted the streets to be unwatched by the Garrison. Now there's eyes all over the place. They ain't happy about it," he retorted before adding: "and he ain't my 'Meister' or whatever else you call him."

"To you, he is whatever he says he is," she snapped. "Do not forget that. For us, you are eyes and a gatekeeper."

Telpid glowered at her and decided to leave out the part where Donta had named the killers for what they were. That, he decided, was information that may save him from a noose if it came down to it. "Whatever," he grunted. "I couldn't care less. Just hurry and get what you want and out of this damn city and get out of my damn life. He already took Liona… Livstra… from me. I don't need him taking anything else. It's not safe for any of us."

"I am not concerned with *safety*," she countered. "I *am* concerned with *names*. Who is it that hunts for us, Sergeant? If we are being stalked, then the favor will be returned."

Ronald grunted and looked away from her. "Who haven't you two pissed off? The Guard, the Guild, the Annex, the Staras? They all want you two dead. The whole damn ruling class is furious over Lexcanna's murder, and whatever happened to Erine has everyone in the alleys ready to riot. *As if they needed the encouragement*," he stressed. "Pits. You've even managed to upset one of the *residents* in this damn place so much that he keeps asking questions. Him, the bastard that messed up my face, and *his* master, some bitch named Anais? They don't have a clue who you two are but they aren't feeling *picky* as long as someone gets blamed and it *stops*."

"That is a list," she agreed after a moment to think about it. "I'm surprised, though. Meister Annix has had free reign over the city near-on half a decade now. Suddenly everyone wants his head?"

"He wasn't dumb enough to assassinate the Fleetfinger's chairwoman back then," the guard argued. "Or one of the Annex's Adepts. I *warned him* that if he just stayed quiet that nobody'd know. He didn't listen. What'd you expect to happen?"

She gave him a wicked, content smile in response. "What happens is whatever Meister wants. He has a plan for this."

Ronald dismissed her with a grunt. "Hope he has a plan to run. You two have stirred a hornet's nest I've never seen in my life."

"He has had a very, very long life. Why would you base your expectations on the scant few years you've had in yours?"

"More than you've had," he retorted. "Be careful of what cart you hitch your horse to."

"May have only had a few years now, but I have centuries to explore the world with his gift. You never know, Ronald, you may yet get to enjoy timelessness as we do," she said with a laugh. While he glared at her, she flicked her fingers and sent a thin arc of lighting up and into the dirt by his feet.

The saa flinched back and stomped at the smoldering ash left behind. "Both of you are fisking mad. Any more of your ilk coming around?"

"Where we go, more of our 'ilk' can always come around, as it were," she said as she opened her mouth wider and showed off a pair of glistening fangs that protruded from her incisors. "Now, perhaps you can tell me the names of those whom have an interest in us? Start with the patient of this hovel."

Ronald Telpid, Sergeant-at-Arms of Medias Manor, former confidant of Liona Reanage and her alter-ego, Livstra Oliana, and current blackmailed-assistant to the Butcher of Basion City, looked back at the manor and sighed. "Well. His name is Akaran, and he's something of a whining asshole. Honestly? I just want to punch him in the face."

II. RETURN TO THE REPOSITORY
Wundis, the 22nd of Riverswell, 513 QR

Two days later, and they let him out of the Manor.

It was a decision that at least one person immediately regretted. "I am not entirely sure I should let you in here," Catherine coldly intoned as she stared at the priest standing across from her desk. She looked... frumpy. It was not a good look for the fifty-two-year-old woman, no matter how motherly she seemed.

It was not a good sign for Akaran, either. "Maiden Prostil, I am so very sorry. I had no idea."

"Nor did my niece," she seethed.

"I am *so* sorry."

The Maiden-Templar of the Repository of Miral, the highest-ranked titleholder of the Order of Love in the entire province, *and* the commanding officer of the largest Order of Love outpost in the province was *not* mollified. "Oh I *don't* doubt that at all and there *will* be time for you to explain how sorry you are. Why are you here? I have a feeling it isn't just to continue your lessons."

He took a deep breath and leaned forward on his cane. "It isn't, I'm afraid."

"Then I really shouldn't let you in here," she said as she crossed her arms. The move made the sleeves on her ruby dress roll up some and exposed a latticework of scars on the underside of her right arm. "What do you need?"

He looked over his shoulder and then used his stick to close the door to her office. "Maiden, I need access to the mission reports for an exorcist named Bistra Enil. Also, if we have any records on a woman named Appaidene, that'd help. No last name, I'm afraid. I know where she came from before she landed in Ridora's care, if that'll help."

Catherine leaned back in her chair and narrowed her eyes. "Not the request I was expecting. For whatever possible reason?"

"Because I have a feeling that Livstra might have been murdered because she was looking into what put one of them in there. From what I learned at the Manor, she had cut her workload down to just the two of them before she was killed," he answered. "I realize I might be grasping at straws in a barn, but..."

"...but in terms of motives, it is the only potential one in front of you, is it? A lack of all other excuses leads to an interest in any excuse."

Akaran sighed under his breath and felt his shoulders slump. "More or less, yes. It's not conclusive of anything, I know. It's the only thing I have to go on so far, and to be fair, you're the one that suggested I tear into this from top to bottom."

That earned a sharp rebuke for his troubles. "I *know* that you've been told to stop looking at those deaths."

"I was."

"And you're promptly ignoring it, I see."

"I am," he admitted with a little shrug.

She sighed and closed her eyes with a slow shake of her head. "Should I even bother to ask why? I *know* that Ridora doesn't want you working on this. I know that the Guard doesn't want you to look into it. I'm fairly sure that the Guild doesn't want you involved in it. After what you did with the wards, I *surely* don't want you doing it. And yet here you are."

All he could do was nod. "And yet here I am."

"You're going to make me ask why, aren't you?" she pushed before she lifted a hand and shut him down. "Don't answer that. Fine. Why are you disregarding the wishes of every superior you have in the province?"

"Because nobody seems to care," he retorted

"That isn't true. You should know that you've stirred up quite the hornet's nest with the Guard. More than you probably know."

Akaran cleared his throat. "Not surprised. The Guild, too. They're *really* not fans and they don't want to be helpful."

"Rarely are they of the Order's work, unless we've placed them on retainer. Should I ask if they have a contract?"

He nodded and slowly sat down across from her with a snort. He started to explain his brief encounter with Elsith the same day he had tripped the wards in the atrium. He finished by saying, "The short form is that they have a lot of money at risk if someone solves Adept Odern's murder before they do. That'd include the Guard, the Granalchi themselves, or *us*."

Catherine sucked on the air for a second and had to admit he was right. "So then you assume that even if they *have* learned something the rest of us have not, that they wouldn't share the knowledge."

"No, they won't, which will cost lives."

"How so?"

"Well. If the same person killed Odern and Livstra both, then they're probably going to do it again. Gut feeling on that. If the same person that killed them is *also* making vagrants disappear, you're looking at even *more* bodies piling up. Even if you ignore *all* of that, whomever killed Liv got into the manor and could have killed anyone else. What's to stop that from happening again?"

"Find the person doing it, I agree. It's the only way to stop any murderer, regardless of other circumstances. I agree with that much but I don't agree that you're the person to do so. I shouldn't have tasked you with the job to begin with, I fear."

"But you did," he pointed out.

She frowned and glared at him through her long eyelashes. "I did. And I'm regretting it still."

"To be fair, I could've banged into the runes at any time. Could've been in prayer or just walking past them or…"

You could hear her getting older in the sigh she responded with. "What do you intend to do about it if you read the reports and find something?"

That wasn't a question he'd prepared himself for. "Whatever I can, I suppose."

"That isn't good enough," she retorted. "Akaran, they told me that you are still obsessed with the idea that you are being controlled by an abyssian spirit. Is that true?"

"Controlled? No." He left out the part where the spirit in question had made it clear she was in control of a much larger entity and the only thing that kept her from manifesting was that she was as trapped in Akaran's mind as his magic was trapped in his aura. While probably pertinent… *She wouldn't believe me if I told her. Fine. Then I won't tell her.*

The smoldering glare didn't let up. "I cannot say that I feel that you're being entirely truthful with that response, exorcist. I *know* you know better than to lie to your superiors."

Akaran took a ragged breath and then squeezed his leg. "Maiden, in truth. With the understanding that the Granalchi have, I am saturated in the aura of another plane of existence that has rendered me incapable of correctly interacting with magic on this one. I don't think that anyone is qualified to tell me what else is inside me right now when nobody can even figure out how to get that garbage *out* of me."

"So you're saying to ask me to trust you when you don't trust us to help you?" she pushed with her eyebrows arched so high they almost touched her scalp.

"More or less."

She let his response hang in the air for several long minutes before uncrossing her arms and leaning forward. "You're aware that gives me even less of a reason to let you have access to those records."

He nodded, then shrugged. "But you're going to anyway."

That earned him a blink and a slightly-stunned look of confusion. "Why, do you think, I would do that? You know that Henderschott has claimed they've found the person responsible, yes?"

He sat straight up in the chair with his eye huge. "They have? No, I hadn't? Who?"

"Some mage," she replied. "I'm afraid I don't know the name."

He frowned and continued to stare down at his knee, confused to say the least. "Have they released anything akin to a motive?"

"No. No name. They claim he was working in conjunction with the Mother Eclipsian."

Akaran's brow furrowed even deeper. "That's... her name is Erine, isn't it? Bit shorter than me, looks surprisingly young for a woman in her position? Dark hair?"

"Looks can be deceiving. That woman is usually the envy of all of the women of the city. Would you believe she's older than I? She's seen more than sixty years pass and she manages to look like she's lived a scant twenty."

"She's... what? That old? But... *how*?"

Catherine huffed and rubbed at a wrinkle in the corner of her eye. "Magic blesses each of us differently. I'd like to take some of it and −" she started to mutter before she caught herself and cleared her throat. "I mean, yes. She's an odd one. Not an enemy of the Order by any means, but not one that was fondly looked down upon by the rank and file of the city. You've met?"

He nodded. "At the Danse Festistanis. She was with a friend of mine."

"I didn't realize you'd made friends here."

"A few, but, no, he's a member of the 13th. Specialist-Major Badin. He's the guy that brought me up here."

"Badin... a Specialist-Major, you said?"

He didn't notice the slight catch in her voice. "Yes? He's a battlema..." he explained before it died in his throat. "Oh. Oh no."

"You don't think...?"

Akaran shook his head 'no' as vigorously as he could. "There's no chance. None. He's a drunk, sure, but he's not a bad guy."

"But he is a mage," she pointed out.

He scoffed at the idea. "So's the entirety of the Granalchi Academy and a sixth of the army. About a third of the Guild, too, if I remember right. And how many priests of the various Orders know how to use spells?"

She nodded, but then pointed out the other obvious point. "I thought you said he was in her company."

"I have a strong feeling she keeps a lot of company," he grunted.

"Don't speak beneath yourself, Akaran."

He pointed a finger at her and glared. "You just told me a man that I nearly sent to his death keeping the Abyss from consuming Toniki, a man who *did* stop an infestation of wraiths from spreading through *the entire Kingdom* when he sunk a warship poisoned with them, and the man who served as my escort from those damn mountains all the way here − you just told me that he's accused of murdering the High Priestess of Stara. You should hear the things that I'm *not* saying."

"A hero one day does not keep you from being a villain the next. Even good intentions can result in unchecked and accidental bloodshed. From what you explained of your own actions back there, I'd assume that you'd have learned that lesson."

If she was trying to piss him off, that worked. He stood up and barely caught himself from leaning forward and cussing her out before he regained his composure. "I don't accept that. Catherine, *Maiden*, you've *got* to let me set this right."

"No, I don't," she retorted. "If he's innocent, then Henderschott will find the truth. The man is not an idiot."

"Be honest: the man's an idiot. Worse, there won't be time. If they think he's done multiple then the Queen's Law in the army dictates that —"

She raised her hands up defensively and waved at him until he sat back down. "No, Akaran. Just no. His trial has been delayed pending the wedding. The city has no need for more drama than what we've already gone through. Plus, without Erine in custody, they are afraid to lose a witness."

That realization set him back a moment. "They don't have her?"

"No," the Maiden admitted. "I'm honestly afraid I don't know much more."

"I need to go find out. I know the man. It's not possible. Besides, the first murder took place before we even arrived, so he couldn't have been involved."

Catherine relaxed a little as soon as he leaned back in his chair a little. "That I one of the reasons they believe he was working with her. That she carried out the first, and maybe the second. Not the others."

"Others?"

Her face went dark as her eyes narrowed. "You really don't know about…? Oh don't tell me – that *woman* decided it would be best if you… of course she did. She'd set you loose and let you find out so she wouldn't… I swear that *woman* makes the hairs on my —"

"Know *what*?" he demanded.

She pursed her lips and stared intently at him, and then his stick, and then back at him. "I don't trust that you'll behave if I explain, but I also don't trust that you won't leave here and go beat up some page or a *locurat* until they tell you, either."

Akaran started to lie and say that he wouldn't when she shut him up with another wave of her hand. In short order, she filled him in on the bodies that had piled up while he was otherwise unconscious. Lexcanna was the first on the list, and while she glossed over the state of her body, she made sure that he understood that either it was related to Odern and Livstra, or someone had decided to copy the style.

Neither option made him feel better, a sentiment she agreed with. She continued on to tell him about a hunter that had been found over the course of two days, and in just as many pieces. "Cassanol, I think his name was, if you ever met the man." His death, she explained, hadn't been *as* violent as the others, but a man without a head is still a dead man. Even if it hadn't been severed from his neck, the hole in the center of his face would've done the trick just fine on its own.

"That brings us to your friend. He was found over Lexcanna. Later, when the Guard went looking Erine, they couldn't find her – or her personal assistant. Then they went to find her sister, and I cannot believe that thundering twat didn't tell you, but…"

His hand flew over his mouth as he slumped back into his seat. "I haven't seen Raechil since…"

"Her sister is Kiasta Lamar. As I said, she's Erine's right hand. When they couldn't find her, they went to the Manor. They didn't find Raechil, but they found blood in her room."

"Shit. Just… shit on me. And there's no doubt that Lexcanna and the others…?"

Catherine shook her head 'no,' again. "She was splayed out and on display just outside the Ellachurstine. To commit such an act is one thing. To do so and desecrate such a holy shrine… it is unconscionable."

He slumped a little and dropped his head into his hands. "I… I had no idea. I don't… I'm so sorry. Nobody…"

"Knowing Ridora, she likely imagined that your mental state wouldn't be up for it," the Maiden grumbled. "Also knowing Ridora, she didn't give a thought to you overhearing someone out in the street."

Akaran shifted in his seat a few times and tried to make sense of it. "I just… I don't know what to think. He'd never. I *know* the man. He fights when told to fight but murder isn't his thing," he said before adding a muttered, "namely because it would take too much effort."

"All it takes for a man to murder is for a cause," she replied, then pointed at the sigil hanging from his neck. "*We* know that more than nearly anyone."

"Okay, that's true, but the timing doesn't work. I know, you said they think that he didn't do the first one but you can't think he actually did the others. Not now."

"I don't know," she answered. "I know that you are the last person that should be allowed near it after what happened in the Manor."

He looked up at her and wiped a sudden cold sweat off of his forehead. "He's my friend. I'm *going* to help him. It's what we do in this Order, isn't it?"

"Our Order exists to not just spread the will of the Goddess but to contain the dark," she pointed out. "Sometimes dark exists in the most well-meaning of men."

"Why do I think you mean me?"

For the first time since he walked in, she gave him a smile. A sad one, but it counted. "Unfortunately, I do. You show every sign of being mentally ill –"

"That's uncalled for," he interrupted as he wrinkled his nose.

"– but you *also* are right that there are more questions than answers," she continued. "I'm in no more of a mood to wait to see if Henderschott is correct than you are. The issue is if *you* are capable of working on it."

After he took a deep breath, he steeled himself in his seat. "I am. Maiden, I promise, I am. If I was a threat to anyone, I'd secure myself away. I promise."

"I believe you feel that way, but you're not entirely being honest with me. You may not be a threat to me, or anyone else in the city – but are you a threat to yourself?"

He blinked and looked at her like she'd just grown a second head. "What in the world does that mean? I'm not about to go out and stab myself. I'm not that far gone."

Catherine cracked her knuckles and pulled out a scroll out of a stack of them on her left. "I re-read what happened to you at Toniki, and I've gone back over your own records from the Manor. I have absolutely no reason to think that you weren't purged of any influence of this Daringol creature when you battled it."

"I don't agree. I can't get it out of my head. I saw it react to the wards on the statues in the atrium. It's there. It may be hiding, but it's there."

The admission came easier than she expected, but it didn't do him any favors. "If you truly believe *that*, then you must realize that you pose a threat to everyone around you. If you are somehow a haven for it, or you have somehow been turned into a vessel for its containment, you are a danger to the people of this city – and this institution."

He sighed and slowly stood back up. "I am. But if I'm a threat, it's to myself. Not anyone else."

"Yet you can't know that," she argued. "You either have to trust that you are not as contaminated as you think that you are, or that you are, and thus, too dangerous to be allowed to roam free unchecked. Which is it, or do you know?"

Akaran glanced down at his knee and shrugged. "I don't know, Maiden. Since nobody believes me anyway, does it matter?"

"You are an exorcist. If you believe you are compromised, then you are," she pointed out. Before he could come up with a response to that, she slipped around the table and opened the door. "I do not see a reason for you not to stay at the Manor to be treated for now. Until you believe that you are no longer somehow possessed or are otherwise carrying the essence of the dead with you, it isn't safe for you to be here."

The refusal wasn't unexpected. Being banned from the Repository, however? "Maiden. Please, let me work. Let me do this."

"I was wrong to give you this job," she quietly lamented. "Go back to the Manor, rest, and pray. It is all you can do for now."

He didn't even bother to argue. It wouldn't have done any good, and might've done worse. Lost in thought, he barely paid attention to where he was going – and almost got run over by a scribe running to her office screaming her name at the top of his lungs.

"Maiden Prostil! Come quickly, you've been summoned to the gate. Something… bad… has happened. We need you right away. We need everyone right away."

Something bad…? he wondered to himself as he quietly ducked into an alcove to get out of the way. Catherine didn't waste any time in rushing out after him, but the only thing that the priest could understand as they walked past was, "...and it flooded and..."

Probably just that stupid lake at the bottom of the Falls. Must've rained while I was unconscious, he grunted. Before he could finish the thought though, a man in an old Hunter's garb interrupted him.

"Oh," the gray-haired man began, "you're the one that had everyone at the Annex buzzing. Akaran, isn't it?"

He looked over and sized the wizard up. Silver and dusky brown hair adorned the top of his head, while his sunken eyes and dull green cloak suggested that he was a man that had done too much to too many. Combined with his withered hands that couldn't do more than hold a quill, he looked less impressive than anything else – but the Guild wasn't known for employing the worthless. "Yes? And you...?"

"Ledger Philanus," the mage replied by way of introduction. "I am Huntsmatron Gorosoch's liaison with the Repository. I have to say, I read your file."

The internal monologue stopped cold. "You did? How?"

"How?" Philanus responded with a bewildered look in his eyes. "It's a matter of record."

"No it's not," he retorted. "That is for Order-eyes only."

The mage straightened up a little and clapped his hands in front of his face. "Oh! No, you misunderstand. With my position, I have access to much of the documentation from field agents in the Order as it comes in. I have... it's hard to explain. I am the liaison between the Lovers and the Guild. My heart to the Goddess, Love be Her name. I was never able to channel divine essence, but I have other skills."

"Oh. So you're not huntsman?"

"Oh, no, no I am. I did not have the... calling... to serve as you do. Early in life, the Guild was a way to... grow, shall we say? But at the same time, I wished to serve the Order. I found myself in a position to do both at a point in my life," he explained. "This arrangement between the two groups has proved to be very beneficial. I assure you; there's nothing that I have relayed to the Guild that would put any part of the Seal of Order on your file to risk."

"Uh... huh," Akaran grunted. "I... see?"

Philanus didn't believe him, but didn't really care if he did or not. "I would love to ask you a few questions," he went on to add with more than a little hopeful smile.

Not that it worked on the exorcist. "I can't discuss it," he replied with a shrug. "I don't even remember everything I wrote down."

"Are you sure?" the hunter pressed. "Having read the report, I just want to make sure I understand the full contents. I'm most curious about how you said you traveled to and from Frosel that –"

"Frosel? I didn't –" he replied before he shut up and entertained a sudden thought. *I didn't go to Frosel... oh this sneaky little shit. He's lying about reading the report.* "I mean, I didn't have time to adequately explain that part," he clarified and then shrugged his shoulders, "and that should tell you why I can't." He paused for effect for a minute and scratched at his goatee. "But let's say I could. What's in it for me?"

Philanus blinked. "For you? Nothing really. This is purely a matter of tracking. The Guild has a vested interest, almost as much as the Lovers, in making sure there is a full *accounting* of what comes from the other realms into this one."

"Oh. Well, in that case, I can't. Sorry," the exorcist returned as he started to turn and walk away.

"Wait," the mercenary-turned-scribe implored after he grabbed Akaran by his arm. "I really do have some questions. It's hard to make sense of everything you put down. Maybe there is something...?"

Akaran flashed him a quick smile. "You said you've got access to the reports as they come in?"

"Well, yes," he admitted. "Maiden Prostil works closely with the Huntsmatron to –"

"Tell you what," the priest interrupted before he placed his arm around the older man's shoulders, "maybe we can work this out. There's something I've had a really hard time finding..."

A few lies and an hour later, and the two of them parted company. The hunter left with a carefully crafted tale about how Akaran had walked back and forth between the shores of Frosel and the Sands – lies built on his nightmares – and how the portals had been charged by massive piles of ice infused with blood and other substances. By the time he finished, he gave himself a smug little pat on the back.

A pat that was made all the easier with a pair of reports that Philanus was only happy to dig out of the bowels of the Repository and give him copies of.

Elsewhere, a new report was about to be filed.

One carried on the backs of a multitude of bedraggled guests.

***

The only thing good that could be said of the scene unfolding before Anais and her bodyguard was the simple fact that it had stopped raining. Maybe the Gods had decided that the line of refugees had already seen enough grief. Maybe they had decided that the constant pitter-patter of tears dripping off of their cheeks was precipitation enough.

Or maybe, just maybe, the Gods decided that there was no sense in making them even wetter. "Second group," Donta grunted.

Anais shook her ruddy-brown hair and crossed her arms slowly as she looked down at the downtrodden souls marching through the city gate. The two of them had found a vantage point on the balcony of a tavern only a couple of blocks away, and they were gawking as the line of the Queen's citizens marched down the streets. They, and everyone else in the city who could find a perch, a window, or even just a spot on the street.

As people peered on in stark, somber horror, Anais cleared her throat and replied slowly. "This is unlike him. Normally he is very careful. Quiet. And... on time. That irritating little pissant Rishnobia implied that whatever he was going to do it would've been done days ago. This is... late, among other concerns."

"He was. There was a delay. This wasn't intentional."

She tilted her head to the side and stretched her neck. "Able to query them so quickly? Well done. What did you find out?"

"Ceremony at Vahail. Hall of Sea's Song. Few days before. Pilgrims should have left. He gave them time," Donta grimly replied. "Wasn't just them."

"Ah, well. Respectful of others as always. I assume whatever he did wasn't bloodless, was it? Surely there weren't this many people at the Hall when he did whatever it was he needed to do? Not if he let the pilgrims walk away first?"

Off in the distance, Maiden-Templar Prostil and the Lieutenant-Commander of the city guard were busy trying to direct hungry peasants to the closest relief station – and they weren't having much luck with it. Nearby, Lady Ridora and several of her assistants were trying to do their best to tend for the wounded being carted in. "No. Most from Mardux. Village near it."

"He attacked at Vahail, yet these are from a village nearby? That is most *definitely* not like our benefactor. He only unsettles the way of things when he must; we've learned that much in our dealings with him."

"Not him," her bodyguard clarified as he adjusted his hat. "Some fool. Wanted to save it. Thought to sink it. Protect the shrine underwater." He scoffed and spat over the edge of the railing. "Idiot. Destroyed a dam. Ruined the shrine. Mardux drowned."

"So... not *his* work?"

"No. Not his fault. Directly."

Anais moistened her pale pink lips and let her gaze travel to a group of paladins marching their way through the throng, Order of Love banners held high. "How large was the shrine?"

"Twenty three. Village had two hundred sixty, more."

"Survivors?"

"Less than that," he grunted.

"Such a shame," the broker replied with a little sigh.

Donta cast a glance at her through cold, dull, tan-colored eyes. "Some swim with Aqualla. Assume they are happy."

"These ones do not look happy," she pointed out.

He stood in silence for a moment before thoughtfully replying, "I assume they can't."

She reached up and started to rub at her eyes, sighing in tired frustration. "Wonderful. This will delay us. You know that, yes?"

"How? Aquallan followers? Shouldn't be a threat."

"It's not that," she argued. "It's witnesses. Depending on how quickly the temple flooded, there may not be survivors. Or there may. Or the ones that survived at first spoke of what he did or what he was after. You know his rule on that."

Donta growled deep in his throat as his shoulders tensed up. "Does what he does. Expects us to fix."

"Yes. He has a penchant for making others clean up behind him. He might even grant us some kindnesses."

"Advocating murder?" he asked as his eyebrow lifted. "A change for you."

"Advocating silence," she pointed out. "Some things are better left as rumors. If we don't silence them, he'll send... him."

"Him? Which?"

Anais shuddered and turned back to the crowd. The second wave of refugees had brought another fifty bodies through the gates, and every single one of them had some kind of story to tell. There just weren't enough guards and unlucky passer-byes able to stop and listen. That was in addition to the first thirty, and there was a rumor of a group twice this size still to come. "The Maelstrom."

"The assassin," Donta grunted. "Deal with the mote. Safer. Easier."

"Yes. It would be much, much better for us to do this than *him*. We do not need the attention he will bring."

"Enough corpses. Agreed."

She nodded in complete agreement. "Yes, and those refugees will no doubt bring trouble of their own. I'm sure we can capitalize at some point; there may be silver linings here. The mote mentioned something about 'pandemics loosening lips,' a few days back, but I thought I understood that it was something that would happen later. Not necessarily related to this, but it is possible I was wrong."

Her bodyguard-and-sometimes-enforcer shook his head. "Maybe. Bodies and more disappearances. Four. Maybe five. Last week alone."

Anais curled her lip. "Has that exorcist been looking into them still?"

"No."

"No? I wonder why."

"Pain," Donta replied. "He's been punished."

She turned and stared into his deathly eyes. "That's a subject the two of us have some measure of familiarity with. However so?"

"The Manor's warding. Disrupted," he grunted back. "It's... unpleasant when near. Burns my skin now. Heard he recovered. Only released early today."

"Quaint," Anais muttered in response. "Personally, I haven't been able to find much to answer the question as to what happened to him to leave him in such a state to start with. He's earned the interest of too many parties that have no desire to share their work with each other. Or to work with me."

"Don't ask now," her companion retorted. "Can't risk it. Danger to expose ourselves. Wait. Press after this." he grumbled as he waved at hand at the crowd below. "Yet..."

"Yet?"

"Don't like him. Illness in his eye."

That earned the first smile she'd worn since the downtrodden masses started to pour into the city. "There is," she agreed, adding, "defeat. Frustration. Anger. Self-loathing. All things that you and I are very adept at exploiting."

Donta chortled for a moment and then looked up at the sky as a stray thought entered his mind. "He recovers? Give him the mote. A gift."

The information broker had to stop herself from unleashing an uncharacteristic peel of laughter. "Oh that's a wonderful thought! Maybe we could also introduce him to the assassin. Solve most of our problems in one swoop."

"Maelphistiphan and an exorcist," he mused. "Interesting. Crowns could be made. If we bet."

Anais flicked her tongue against her lips again. "If we can't get into the Repository soon, I fear that he may be sent to do our job for us. You are aware that's an option that has been discussed, yes?"

"We'd never be free."

"Free or not, we would absolutely be worse off," she admitted. "Worse still if we become the job that follows."

He cast a side-eye glare in her direction and slowly flexed his right hand. A small little bone spike started to emerge from the center of his palm before she quickly closed his fist around it before anyone else could see it. "I don't fear him."

"I know, which is why *I* do," she returned. "Well. Enough chatter. Work to be done now."

"Much."

She squeezed his hand tight a second time. "Donta. *No bloodshed* unless absolutely necessary. Only if nothing else will silence a tongue."

He agreed without comment and made sure *not* to comment about the incident with the Fleetfinger's Guild. And, more importantly, continued to keep silent about his discovery in the caves behind Orshia falls. *Doesn't need to know*, he repeated to himself. *Not about their fangs.*

***

It took a while for Akaran to make it back to the manor, and not only was it dark by the time he got there, someone had gone through his room. In fact, he caught her as she was finishing up, and it was hard to imagine that the ensuing argument hadn't been heard halfway through the asylum. It was just one of the fifteen or sixteen faceless aids that worked for Ridora, and to hear him say it, she'd be best off never to be noticed again.

Though she wasn't *actually* faceless, just not someone he cared enough about to make note of. They barked accusations back and forth, with his suggestions that she dig through her own room being countered with nasty retorts about *her* room actually being clean. When he realized she was taking away one of his prized bags of cocasa, the argument turned even worse.

An argument that he promptly lost. Before she stormed off muttering impolite (although not inaccurate) accusations about his character, she informed him that it was Ridora who had ordered his room cleaned out and that she was gone for the night. The jug of calming, larochi-laced tea she offered him was rudely rejected, and he settled for sitting down and being pissed off about the entire sequence of events.

It didn't stop him from prying up a loose floorboard in his room and storing some of the weed he had on his person safely away, but it still left him pissed off. Pissed or not, once she was gone and his supplies were stored, it was time to turn his attention to the goodies he had obtained at the Repo. Once he had them laid out on his unkept bed, it was time to get to work.

One distinct advantage to having mattanic mages on staff at the Repository was that you didn't have to have a scribe sit down for days with a quill copying text from one scroll to another whenever someone needed a copy of a scroll. That wasn't to say that the old-time methods of ink and paper weren't still used as an educational tool, but when it needed to be done quickly, the option was there. *Finding* one sometimes was a problem but as luck had it, Ledger Philanus was extensively trained.

Interestingly enough, the method of making a copy wasn't just to simply will an exact duplicate in place. A blank journal and ink was still needed, as were several pieces of silver (used as a "conductor of energies" and not, as Akaran had guessed, used as a "conductor of a weighted purse,"). Once placed in the middle of a simple spellcircle, all it took were a few spoken words and Akaran had reports in hand on Bistra and Appaidene both.

Not that there was a lot to have about the latter – a task made decidedly easy because of the unquestionably best feature that the Repository had to offer. While some libraries resorted to legions of scribes and apprentices to dig out musty tomes, the Order did something entirely different at this outpost. If you had been granted permission – as Philanus had – you could simply walk into the Central Indexiary and speak to a spindly golem installed by a handful of Eberenth followers.

Who would have imagined that followers of the Goddess of Knowledge would be eager to earn the favor of the Order's largest library? Or that the Goddess of Love would have access to secrets known only to the hearts of men? Apparently, it worked out better than anyone could've imagined.

The golem in question had one task and carried it out quickly. All you had to do was present a special coin gifted to attendants of higher rank and tell it who or what you were looking for. As long as your coin matched or exceeded the level of secrecy on the scroll or book or *other* you were looking for, the golem would fetch it.

It made the task go faster for the Repository than nearly anywhere else in the Order, to say the least. It was one of the first things he had discovered in the outpost and the one that had made him the happiest. His initial thought was that his first mentor at the Grand Academy of Love couldn't have *possibly* known or else he'd not have made him spend years copying scroll after scroll in-between his other studies.

All of that said though, finding note of her had taken significant effort. The wax-and-clay automaton took half a candlemark to process her name against its own internal inventory enough to figure out where to look for her. Her name finally turned up in a list of *"Residents of Unknown and Questionable Origin,"* filed by the Basion City Guard. Other than a brief description of her build, what little it contained repeated what Seline had offered.

Appaidene had wandered into an encampment of the 7th Garrison with her stomach cut open in a crude spiral slice and in complete shock. Scouts at the garrison traced her steps and determined she had been assaulted in a grain silo several hours away. How she had managed to survive and make it as far as she had was a mystery.

The mystery itself only deepened when they realized someone had carved the first five Testaments of Geshalda across her back. The working assumption was that she had been pregnant and someone wanted the child. Who, why, who the father had been, if it was one child or if she was carrying twins (or more)? Nobody ever figured out the rest of it.

The only clue that they had was from the Testaments. Either someone was a devoted follower of the Goddess of Envy and Jealousy, or, they had made a deal with The Unfulfilled. The cult of the Covetous One could always be counted on to carry out an act of greed, if you could find them.

After a year in the (allegedly abusive) care of the 7th, her story reached Ridora's ears. The Lady herself had made the special effort to travel all the way to Ummasil Province to collect her in 510 Q.R. She had been a resident of the Manor ever since.

It tracks, if that's really the case, he mused inwardly. *The third Testament is to, "Take what you can," with an addendum of, "If it can make more, keep it intact if you can't take it with you." They're pragmatic, even if demented.*

A sad story, but not one that offered any fisking help.

The story behind the Auramancer Exorcist, on the other hand, was full of interesting tidbits. Bistra had a long record of successful banishments, exterminations, and a habit for rooting out heretics across the Kingdom. Any other time, and Akaran wagered he'd read everything she ever filed just as a lesson on 'how to expel the damned and survive.'

Unfortunately, the last report filed under her name wasn't written by her; it was written *about* her. That, he decided, was absolutely *not* a good sign. Going through it only reinforced his assumption. It also had an odd wax seal that the golem had copied – a red wax blob with two moons and two mountain peaks.

That mark. That's... nagging. Where've I seen that before? Training? Fisk. If my knee would stop throbbing maybe I could...

The beginning of the report looked about as interesting as the start of any other. It named the assets involved, the dates the mission carried through, and a reference to the missions prior – just in case. *Okay, Lastgrow in 508. End of summer... not a bad time to be on the border, really. She'd spent most of her time around there, up in Lowmarsh. Smaller villages mostly... let's see. Kellspout, Swampnest, Squistal, Grimedeep... yegh. What is* with *those bordertown names?*

Oh, odd. After Squistal, she stayed in that area for another six months. Trying to find someone that went missing from the 5th. A specialist major? Battlemages don't wander off of their duty as a general rule, Badin excluded. Hmm... and then she went right back to the Grand Temple. Took a three-month 'Request of Spiritual Remittance' before going back into the field. Or... well. The swamps, at least.

Wonder what that was about? Injury or exhaustion?

Her final mission had sent her to the small-ish city of Stovannahsburg near the contested border of the Missian League. The League itself ever being referenced was generally considered a foul omen. Luminary Cobliver, who was the de-facto ruler of the League, was a devout follower of both Neph'kor *and* the Lord of Hate. It was a troubling situation that was all-but promised to lead to an eventual "corrective diplomatic action," in the words of people who were paid to come up words to justify such endeavors.

Current affairs aside, she had been sent to hunt a demon named Solg that had been doing obscene things to and with both local livestock and farmers alike... and in the same way. *Those* details he glossed over as quickly as possible for the sake of both his eye and his stomach.

Oh. No, not a demon named Solg. An actual solg. What kind of sick fisk decided to pull one of those out of thin air...? Given that solgs were known for having *appetites* that defied imagination, the report had *vastly* more information than he wanted.

Ever.

I wonder what the presenting evidence was to warrant an action on the border? That question was quickly answered, but without much merit. *Mutilated locals, mutilated animals, check. Agriculture irregularities? What could... let's see. 'A report of local crops found exsanguinated of life; otherwise healthy harvests turned to limp ashen lumps. Notable damage included an apple orchard, thorn-bearing flowers, and undja.* Akaran pursed his lips and shrugged it off. *The solg shit in a field and ruined the harvest. Nothing special there.*

But that's where the report seemingly went two ways at once. She had been accompanied on her jaunt by members of the 5th Ray of Dawn, which wasn't too uncommon, but a Hunter by the name of Levandarious had been assigned to report in on her efforts separately. Solgs were dangerous, but as demons went, they weren't bad enough to warrant both a secondary tracker and an armed support team. Normally one halfway competent exorcist and a healer was enough to do the trick, though numbers never hurt.

Maybe... well. That close to the League? Wanted to catch it before it crossed over, possibly. Save the trouble of a diplomatic incident. Once he rationalized that concern, he kept reading. The report went on to state that she never actually set foot inside Stovannahsburg, although the solg was never seen again.

That's good, he mused, *just means she caught it and never had to go into the village. Strange though, because she should have. Solgs don't just manifest out of thin air. The fact that someone even knew what it was to specifically list it as the reason she was sent is another. Sure, the Sisters could have picked it up but it's unlikely that they were able to identify it from so far away – they're just not that strong. Solgs OR the Sisters.*

What made it even more unusual (at the very least) was that there weren't any notations in the mission report that listed the details of the exorcism. There were no notes on where the demon had been found, what it had been doing, what methods were used to dispose of it. Or even if any evidence was discovered as to where it originated from on this plane. Every single one of those questions was a hard requirement to add to *any* report filed just in case it became necessary to establish a history of paranormal events in a given area.

Okay, that's beyond incomprehensible. The moment she put that thing down, she should have made a note of it. Before she laid her head down to sleep, an accounting would be required. The only way not? That's if she had suffered an injury in the fight, but the rest of this doesn't mix with that. This woman is supposed to be one of the best exorcists that the Order ever fielded. Or if her journal had been destroyed, maybe? But after the fact?

In fact, who even filed this?

That particular honor, he discovered, went to the Huntsman. And *that* made the unanswered questions even more concerning. Of all the things the Guild did well, it was their reputation for record-keeping that was the envy of librarians everywhere. Feeling utterly convinced that by this point the Ledger hadn't copied a report but instead a rather thin and sweet pile of scribbled bullshit, Akaran realized that the worst of it was towards the end.

Levandarious had lost track of all five members of Bistra's party at the beginning of a two-week-long endeavor to hunt the solg down. *Another red flag – solgs don't bother to hide. They get loose from perdition and treat the mortal world like a sailor treats an all-you-can-bed-whorehouse. If it took them two weeks to find it, someone was blind and deaf. And how does a Hunter lose FIVE people? Hope he had his pay docked.*

After flipping back and forth through the packet, the next realization was that there wasn't a single line about what happened to the soldiers after they vanished with the Auramancer. They were there, then they weren't. And, as best as he could tell, absolutely nobody cared.

She, on the other hand, was found two day's worth of travel past the borders of Dawnfire. *How* she ended up that far away was a good question. *How* and *who* found her in a wine cellar under an abandoned Leaguesman's Hall wasn't explained either.

She presented with signs of starvation, torture, and they discovered her eating rotten food. If the Hunter had attempted to identify the bodies, they weren't listed individually. Nor was she found alone.

There wasn't a lot to be said about the other victims, only that there was more than one — and that the one they noted had been carrying a symbol of Neph'kor's cultists, the Circle. Aside from that? Nothing.

The report happily skipped over what was done about the bodies, what was done to the Hall she was found in what the Circle had been up to, and every other question anyone could have reasonably had about the disaster. It jumped from there to the brief passage of how the solg was banished and then to how the Huntsman had half-pulled-half-carried Bistra to another city (again, not Stovannahsburg) for help.

It did point out that she kept claiming she hadn't done it, it wasn't her fault, and that it was all because of her shadow. For months, she had to be kept in a room that had lit candles on all sides to try to keep her from screaming in terror. When that didn't help, it was determined that the best course of action was to simply leave her blindfolded (assuming that if she couldn't *see* shadows, they'd not scare her) and left to her own in a small convent where she deteriorated further. Eventually, someone that wasn't a sadistic asshole took notice of her plight and sent her off to Basion.

She joined Appaidene in being admitted to the Manor in 510. From that point on there were only a few brief pages almost every six months, filed in reports with cheerful names such as '*Updates on Disabled Assets*' and '*Interest in Exposed Auras*'. The only things to be gleamed from them were a worsening of her fear of her own shadow and a deterioration of her mental condition.

There no excuses as to what happened in the League, or how she got there. There was no suggestion as to if she had gone willingly or had been kidnapped. There was nothing more than a signed statement of mental defect that would keep her locked away until the healers assigned to her determined she was sane.

Or dead.

Either would work as far as the Order and the Army was concerned from that point on. As he sat there staring at his knee, it didn't give him much hope for his own future. *Immediate or otherwise*, he sighed.

When Seline burst through his door two hours later, the *immediate* future took a whole new meaning. "Can you walk?"

"Not at this time of night," he grumbled while he pulled a pillow over his face.

"Learn. We need help. The Guard is tied up, the Guild is tied up, the Order is tied up. Anyone with the ability to issue orders is being pulled out of whatever hole they've crawled into."

He sat up and looked at her, blinking a very tired and bloodshot eye. "I didn't think I was allowed to issue orders anymore."

"Do you want to?"

"Yes."

"Then you're allowed," she retorted as she flung his signet across the room and into his lap, "so hurry and get dressed."

III. REFUGEE OF INSANITY
Madis the 24ᵗʰ of Riverswell, 513 QR

The refugees had shown up two nights ago.

Two long, exhausting, irritating nights ago.

When Sel had offered him the chance to give orders again, he had expected a chance to direct other priests in dealing with some kind of freak magical threat. Or to order the guard around to quell a riot. Or to push back against some kind of unexpected an insurgency. *Something* that would play to his strengths. Any strength. Any strength at all.

Not, he groused for the fifth time in the last hour, *these fisking stupid HOUSING INSPECTIONS. I'm a Goddess-damned EXORCIST and they have me doing HOUSING INSPECTIONS.*

"For the tenth time, *Sire* Alverach –"

"My name is *Elverich*, you disrespectful goatsuck," the other man seethed.

Akaran just sighed, looked down at his feet, and let the papers he carried droop to his side. "Right, Alverach. Look. There's only so much space in the city. We can't move all of you into the Orshia Falls."

Sire Alverach, or Elverich, or '*profoundly irritating prick number seven tonight*,' depending on how you wanted to approach him, puffed up like a gaseous toddler and shouted at him like a banshee with gravel stuck in her throat. "You can surely make room for us! My family has been one with the water for generations!"

Everyone from Mardux has been 'one with the water' for generations, he grumbled to himself, *bloody surprised the fools don't walk around looking like old prunes. Or have gills. Do they have gills?* "No, we really can't. The caves behind the falls weren't in great shape to begin with. It's going to take the Granalchi another week to reinforce them so that they're livable." *And boy did that piss off the local Oldstone. Altund something? Kept ranting about exchanging a blessing for the rights to it for himself...?*

46

"You rely on wizards to do the work of the city?" the paunchy, short, and balding man snapped at him. "There are so many of us that need jobs, men that know how to work tools! Put us to work and we will carve our own path!"

"Which would take a lot longer to do right if you did," Akaran argued. "The Headmaster-Adept is graciously donating the time of his geomancers and elementalists to take care of the caves. They'll get it done with magic and manipulation faster than tradesmen – and in the meantime, there's only so many places we can stick people."

The refugee crossed his arms and tried to intimidate the (much) younger priest. "Then move another family out. I have five children. They need to be somewhere better than this... slum. There's not even a shrine to Aqualla here!"

"That's being worked on, too," he pointed out. "My understanding is that you have... let's see. Tidesinger Quinchero. He's dealing with it. No idea what or how, but he's dealing with it."

"You don't know how?!" he insultingly demanded. "How can you claim to know what work is being done if you don't even know the right titles to grant a person of their stature?! So yes, it had best be! Such a grand river and falls, and there's no place for us to live beside it? No place for us to worship?!"

"Alverach –"

"ELVERICH!"

That was almost more than the priest could stand to listen to. "*Whomever,*" he growled back. "Nobody is stopping you from going and praying at the riverbanks or at the lip of the falls or even at the bottom, if you really want. I'll find you a large rock to hold so you can get down there easier." Before the jackass could respond, Akaran continued on to explain the reality he was going to have to face, like it or not. "There's just not room to move you in. The Overflow is the best place the city can offer."

Elverich huffed and tilted his head up to literally look down his nose at the exorcist. "I doubt you even have the authority to speak for the city. I've seen your kind before, Oo-lo. You only speak for yourselves."

"Right now I'm speaking for my headache and you're testing my patience with it," he pointed out as he tried to adjust the fit of his vestments. "If you don't like the accommodations we've provided, you can leave."

The older man's jaw dropped, which did nothing for his jowls. "Are you threatening me?"

"Giving you your options," the priest retorted. "You can stay here in the tents until the caves are cleaned up or you can buy your way into one of the last few beds available at any of the inns, or you can leave. Nobody is happy with this situation."

"Not happy? Not *happy*?! I lost my home! I lost my brother! I lost my livelihood! What do *you* know about loss?"

Akaran clenched his fist around the head of his cane and gave the problematic pain in the ass a smoldering glare. "I know quite a lot, thank you."

"Oh, how I doubt that."

"Doubt what you will. So do I mark you as staying or going? Because if you're leaving, I'm sure I can find someone else that would love to have your spot."

The refugee grit his teeth and looked just past Akaran's shoulder to a group of children playing on the banks of the Orshia Overflow. "I have no money to get an inn or buy travel away from here."

"Then you're staying."

"As I must," he finally sighed. "Has anyone bothered to say where work can be found?"

"What do you do?"

Elverich drew himself up to his full, yet unimpressive, height. "What do I do? Isn't it obvious?"

Aqueduct dredger? Akaran just barely stopped himself from saying out loud. "No."

"I am a *watersculpt*," he replied matter-of-factually as he stomped his foot down and thrust his head up like a preening peacock, as if that suddenly explained everything.

Everything except to the priest, who stood there with the dumbest look on his face someone could possibly have. "A what?"

"A watersculpt," he repeated.

The priest nodded slowly at him before he sketched a note with a piece of charcoal the small journal he had carried along with him. "Watersculpt. Right. I'll pass it on to the garrison."

Elverich huffed at him and pointed a slightly crooked finger at Akaran's nose. "You had best do so. My family has needs."

"We all do."

"Some of us have more needs than others. I will expect to hear back from you tomorrow."

He looked up from the journal and arched his eyebrow. "I wouldn't."

"You wouldn't?" the watersculpt repeated. "Wouldn't what?"

"Expect to hear back from me tomorrow."

It was hard to imagine the irritating refugee looking any more indignant. Yet, he succeeded with gusto. "*What*? How dare you. I just told you I have no money and my family has needs. You *will* return tomorrow with news for where I can find work for someone of my stature."

The urge to (re)explain the situation in blunt(er) terms was only conquered by the knowledge he might end up punching the bald-headed irritation, and while that sounded fun, getting in trouble for it didn't. "Elverich, understand: you and your children are six people out of a group of one-hundred and sixty-four refugees that just showed up. Without warning. The Overseer and the Guard are absolutely buried in people trying to find work, beds, and food. I don't know when I'll get to you. I will get to you, but I wouldn't expect it before Zundis."

He didn't get the credit he deserved for finally getting the name right.

"*Zundis*?! That's four days from now! It's Madis!"

Akaran shrugged and started to put another mark in the journal. A *special* mark that only he knew what it meant. "Or it might be Wundis," he replied as he added an extra day to the paperwork. "Possibly sometime after Lundis next week."

"We can't wait that long! We'll starve!"

"Rations are being passed out at the Ellachurstine Chapel," he replied with a smile that attempted to be reassuring, but came off like he was mocking the poor man where he stood. "They'll be available until the crisis ends and everyone finds either employment or a caravan leading elsewhere."

"I won't stand for that. I demand to speak to your superior."

The priest couldn't stop himself. He wouldn't've even if he could've. "Then I'd drop to your knees and start praying."

You could almost watch the steam start to boil out of Elverich's ears. For a brief moment, Akaran hoped he'd actually see it. He could barely contain the smirk as the watersculpt blew his top. "EXCUSE ME?"

After a cough to clear his throat, the priest said exactly what he felt, how he felt, and made it clear exactly how he meant it. "I said that if you want to speak to my *superior*, you'd best land on your knees and pucker your lips to place on Her divine ass. Should you not, I can always be sure to come back around *next* Madis."

The shaking, pointing finger returned as the kids at the waterfront finally turned to see what all the commotion was about. "You should watch your tongue boy. I've already lost everything in my life. There's nothing stopping me from putting you on the ground and going over your head."

Slowly, the priest braced his weight on his left leg and lifted his cane up for the older man to see. "There's at least one thing."

And that's when the fun ended. Or started, depending on how you wanted to look at it. Either way, the change came as a result of one screaming little blonde woman, and she was not at all impressed with her charge. "Akaran! That's enough!"

"Hey! He started it!" Akaran shouted back at Seline. "I'm just defending myself."

Her fury descended on him like a plague of locusts. "You're being rude and obnoxious. I've had nothing but complaints about you all blessed day," she spat before she looked over at Elverich. "I am so sorry if he has done anything to bother you."

"He has been nothing but the avatar of ill-manners. Covorn would be proud."

Akaran spit something profane onto the street, much to the healer's absolute disgust. "Oh trust me," the priest seethed, "if the God of Hatred has an interest in *either* of us it is *not* my one-eyed ass. You've been the one doing nothing but demanding everything to happen right away."

"Of course he has – and you need to show some empathy," Ridora's aid snapped back as she glared daggers at the exorcist. "If you can."

The priest tried to cross his arms, but holding the cane, the charcoal, and the journal all at once made the act of defiance harder than it should've been. "I am more than capable of being empathetic."

"You are more than capable of being an ass," she shot back as she swiped his journal and stuffed it into the leather satchel tied to the braided leather belt along her waist. "Go home, Akaran. I will see to it someone else is assigned to you, Sire Elverich."

He tried to reach for the journal and she slapped his hand away. "I'm perfectly capable of handling this."

Seline gave him another withering glare from her otherwise kind, sweet brown eyes. "No, you're not. Go home."

"But –"

"NOW, Akaran," she growled. "This *isn't* a request."

After he made a barely-hid rude gesture in her general direction, Akaran turned and stormed off – as much as his burning leg would let him. He managed to make it off of the main street and behind a shop before the shooting pain from his knee coupled with a familiar one that squeezed his stomach like it was caught between two castle-sized bricks. When he finished trying to vomit up something that wasn't there, he thought he heard a woman laugh in the distance. "*Oh I can't wait for this*," he swore he heard her say.

Then she was gone, replaced by the voice that had just chewed him out. "What is *wrong* with you?" Seline demanded through clenched teeth. "You've been avoiding me for days. Then it's nothing but you accosting the refugees. And now you're… having dry heaves in an alley?"

He didn't answer the question directly. After he wiped drool off of his unkempt goatee, he met her with a hushed demand of his own. "When were you planning on telling me about Badin?"

The question – and the name – brought her up short. As her eyes went wide, he knew he'd struck a nerve right away. "What are you talking about?"

"Come on, Sel. You know he's my friend. Why didn't you say something?"

She took a step back and brushed her adorable pink dress against the wall behind her and it took *everything* he had in his willpower to keep from going over and brushing it off. Thankfully, the feeling didn't last any longer than it took for her to answer. "Well… because… Ridora didn't think it would be helpful."

"Thought it'd be better for me to hear it on the street? I found out about it two days ago and you *still* haven't bothered to be honest with me?"

"There's nothing you can do about it. We told you that –"

Akaran raised a finger and pointed right at her pert little nose. "You told me he had left the city. Not that he'd been locked up *under* it."

It was finally her turn to swear under her breath, and she did it with just enough gusto that it would've left him impressed under just about any other circumstances. "Because we know if we did that you'd go off and try to see him. It wouldn't have gone over well with Hender and Ridora felt that you were under enough stress as it is."

"You mean like how that asshole L-Comm forbid me from seeing him?" he charged, making sure to stress the 'l' to sound like he said, '*elle-comm,*' rather than bothering with the full title. "You know the only reason I haven't sent a missive to Brother Steelhom to have him come here and get Badin out is that I know you read my letters, right? I assumed if I even tried you'd lock me up beside him."

Seline paused and blinked in slight surprise. "Read your...? We don't read your letters."

"Oh bull, you read everyone's."

"Akaran, no, I promise we don't," she promised before adding, "Come to think of it, you're the only person in the Manor that could even be able to send one if you wanted."

It was a choice of believing her denial or accepting that they were dumber than he had given them credit for. He opted for both at once. "Then you aren't taking good care of your charges if you think they're safe to write to Gods-know-who without seeing what they do."

"I just said that nobody there has the mind to —" the healer retorted before it hit her. "You're saying we're bad if we do and bad if we don't?"

"It's just... whatever," he sighed. "The point is that you don't trust me."

Seline stepped over and tried to grab him by his shoulders. She missed as he lurched backwards like she was some kind of toxic pitbeast trying to hug him. "What? Yes I do!"

"No. You don't," Akaran retorted firmly — and so pointedly that he cracked his stick on the loose cobblestones for emphasis. "You *don't* believe me about Rmaci. Or my dreams in general. You *don't* believe me that there's more going on in this city with the murders and the kidnappings, and you *don't* trust me."

She shook her head and her blonde hair fluttered loose from the bun she had tied it in. "Akaran, no. It's not that I don't trust you. It's that you don't show signs —"

The exorcist interrupted her with a barely contained snarl in his voice. "You can't *prove* I'm right so you don't believe *I'm* right when it's *my* body and I know *damn well* that *I'm right.*"

"You have to understand," she tried to argue, "your aura is compromised by the magic in your system. Lady Medias and I believe that once it's gone you'll be so much better. The cocasa isn't helping either."

He pulled the pouch out of his coat and flung it to the ground at her feet. "Right. The painkiller. Let's blame me *for being right* because of the painkillers."

She wrinkled her nose and gave him a foul look. "Okay now you're just being paranoid. Which, if you remember, is a result of *taking* that damn —"

"— the damn medicine that you two decided I don't need anymore when I can barely stand to *walk* so you decided to take it away from me without asking if that's what I wanted?" he finished for her. "Yeah, thank you for that."

"Would you quit interrupting me? Dammit Akaran, we're *trying* to help you but you have to *let* us."

"Help me by *listening.* Not by *judging,*" he demanded. "There's more going on here than just a couple of people getting killed!"

"One of those people was my mentor, in case you haven't forgotten! Don't think that we're not taking it seriously!"

"If you were taking it seriously, you wouldn't let Badin stay in prison. What about Raechil? She's important too. I could be going out looking for them *right now* but you've got me dealing with *housing inspections*!"

"The Guard is looking into it. I've told you that repeatedly. The Guild, too. There's not much more that we can do. We even received permission to request a writ from Elsith and –"

"– and if Henderschott could find his ass with both hands and a sextant I'd actually feel confident with that! Or how about what's coming, huh? Are you just going to patently *ignore* the warning I got?"

She couldn't stop herself from rolling her eyes. "Yes. The warning. From a dead woman supposedly haunting your dreams. A threat that a ship that sank is going deliver a cadre of damned souls to the city. A *landlocked* city. You can't get a boat up Yittl even in the flood seasons! You understand how crazy that is, don't you?"

"Supposedly? Seline, she's trying to get out of the Abyss. She's... she might already be here."

Seline stepped forward again and caught his cheek with her hand before he could move away. To his surprise, she didn't slap it; she cupped it. "Akaran, listen to yourself. Just *listen* to yourself. If you were *us,* how would you feel? How would you react?"

"What is that supposed to mean?" he demanded as he started to reach for her wrist but stopped himself after a moment of hesitation. "You don't think that I take *you* seriously? Are you trying to turn this back on *me*?"

"No! I mean, no," she clarified before she confused him again. "Actually, yes, I am. You are a neophyte exorcist with a broken leg that won't heal and a drug addiction. You can't do anything about your situation so you're sticking your nose where it doesn't belong and acting like you've got all the power in the world. You're claiming that you're being stalked by a dead woman who is trying to... I'm not even sure what it is you think she's trying to do!"

"Get out of the Abyss. Spread. Hunt like a... a *snake* and spread like a *plague.* She's part of the arin-goliath I destroyed."

She shook her head but didn't step away. "Maybe you shouldn't be congratulating yourself so much if you think the arin is still around. Are you admitting that you failed to banish the only creature you were sent to excise? Are you admitting you're just a failure trying to fix his mistakes?"

"I did the best I could!"

"And that's part of the problem!" she snapped back as she pulled away and turned her back to him in complete frustration. "You *weren't* suitable for the task you were given, you came back from it with your mind as wrecked as your leg, and you're seeing shadows where there aren't any. You expect us to believe all of this without *any* proof, and no matter how many times you seek counsel with the Maiden-Templar, she can't find *anything* wrong with you."

"Except for the fact that I can't channel magic," Akaran spat.

"Except for that," the healer agreed. "Don't you think that maybe, just maybe, the fact that you're cut off from the ether is making you hear and see things that aren't there? I can't imagine what it must be like for you, someone that's attuned to the other world but you suddenly can't hear or see it anymore. It must be like... like going blind in one eye!"

He clenched his teeth so hard he swore he felt one start to crunch in the back of his jaw. "I promise you, it's a fisk lot worse than that."

Seline realized what she said a moment too late and turned back around to apologize. "Shit. No, listen, that's not what I meant."

"It's *exactly* what you meant," he grunted. "You don't think that I'm qualified to figure out what's going on because I can't *see* what's going on."

She did her best to soften her tone and sound less condescending and more caring. It didn't really work, but at least she tried. "I think your vision is clouded and your mind is playing tricks on you. That's why you're here. To help us help you find peace but you *have* to quit poking at every bush you see trying to prove that you're right when there *isn't* anything there!"

"You keep telling yourself that," he retorted with a nasty little curve to his upper lip decorating his face. "When you find out I'm *right*, I expect your lips *firmly* on my ass when you have to apologize."

"Akaran, stop. Just... stop," she pleaded. "*We* want to help you. *I* want to help you. We *can* help you if you just let us. Just go home, go lay down, and get some sleep. Tomorrow will be a better day."

"No. No I don't think I will. Until you believe me, you won't be *any* fisking help *at all*. Not that you've been any help yet as it is," he shot back as he pulled away from her and started to storm off. Seline grabbed at his arm and he moved without thinking – and lightly smacked her across the jaw with his cane. "Oh, Sel, I –"

The look on her face was more emotional hurt than it was anything else. She managed to close her mouth but couldn't do anything for the shock in her eyes as she took a few steps back and away. "On second thought, don't go home. Go somewhere else. Anywhere else. When you get done being a petulant *asshole* then you can come back to the Manor."

For a change, he finally did the right thing. He shut up, agreed with her, and walked away in silence. He made it another block before he hobbled back and grabbed the pouch of cocasa he had thrown at the healer, and cursed himself repeatedly for getting it wet. He didn't even get a chance to take a bite before another wave of pain and need rushed through his body so violently that he spent a few moments trying to throw up in the gutter.

That was when his night got worse, and worse in arguably the worst possible way. *"With all this going on, I can see why you haven't been sleeping with me recently,"* the voice crooned from behind him.

Akaran whipped around and nearly twisted his leg out from under himself in a complete panic. "YOU! HOW?!" This had the added effect of causing him to stumble out into a busy thoroughfare – and as much as he tried to keep his composure, his foul breath, vomit-stained tunic, and his unsteady feet gave off one (and only one) impression on the people that saw him lose control.

"Calm yourself, little priest. I'm not here to hurt you," she called out again. Again, it sounded like she was behind him. Again, she wasn't there when he twisted around to see her.

"Every nightmare I've had in the last three months would disagree!" he shouted out.

That didn't endear himself to any of the passers-by, but it did earn a response from her. The speaker allowed a chuckle that sounded a lot like glass being ground under a millstone to grate his ears. *"Every nightmare you've had has been earned and deserved. The least I can do is share,"* she added as he felt a hand on his shoulder.

When he twisted back around, there she was, in all of her glory: Rmaci, free from the confines of his mind. She was naked and bloody, blistered and burnt, a horrific obscenity of the sanctity of life, with every inch of her ruined body on display for the throng of Basion's otherwise oblivious citizenry. When nobody reacted to her presence or paid a lick of attention as she walked from the middle of the street to lean against a nearby building – and left bloody footsteps in her passing – he came to the first realization that helped calm his nerves. "You're not actually here, are you."

Not that it mattered much. *"I'm here enough,"* she crooned as she tried to kick a loose stone into the street with no luck. *"Not 'enough' enough, but here enough."*

"Goddess. No," he groaned.

She flashed him a mirthful smile around melted lips. *"Not a Goddess; you know better. Not yet, at least. Never know, really."*

Akaran stepped out of the thoroughfare and tried to resist the urge to bang his head on a wall. "I wasn't talking to you."

"Well that's just rude."

He didn't rise to the bait, but he did directly his annoyance to the world. "Oh God. Why?"

"–dess, Akaran," she scolded. *"Don't forget that last part. You have enough trouble without Her getting cranky with you."*

"What fresh torture is this? What's your plan, you damned thing?"

She lifted her hand up and focused on her fingers as she flicked them back and forth. Little droplets of phantom blood arced into the air before disappearing into nothingness. *"Well. You're barely sleeping. That's taken half the fun out of bothering you. Why not see the world through your eyes for a while?"*

Watching her absentmindedly play with a loosely-hanging fingernail made him gag as he desperately tried to find his pouch of cocasa for a second dose. "That's it, I've spent so much time in that madhouse I'm losing my mind."

"*I wouldn't bother. That stuff just soaked in the gutter, and it's going to taste more like piss than normal. She's cuter in person, I admit. You* do *plan on defiling that dress of hers at some point, yes?*"

It was impossible to even give a profane retort to the thought. "Please go away."

"*No, no I don't think I will,*" the wraith retorted with a smirk. "*What exactly have you gotten yourself into the last few days?*"

The priest sighed and slumped against the same wall she mocked him from after he realized that yes, she was right, he was out. "A stress-induced breakdown?"

"*Not that,*" Rmaci replied. A moment later, she clarified herself and retracted the answer. "*Well, yes, that. You know that I hear you, yes? That when you talk to people, that when you're awake — I'm there. I'm with you. Always part of you, listening to whatever comes around your desperate sad little mind.*"

He felt his face fall as the implications hit him. "No. No I didn't know that."

"*Everyone you talk to. Everything you do,*" she taunted. "*Every time you go pray, or go eat, or play with your little dick when you don't think anyone is paying attention, I'm watching you.*"

Akaran bit back his first response about the size of that specific appendage, and instead just swore with profoundly unhappy, "Shit."

"*That too,*" she pointed out. "*I know that you've been trying to get rid of me. I know that you are terrified that if you tell that sweet Catherine woman everything we've done in your dreams that she'll personally throw you out of the Order.*"

"Catherine doesn't believe you exist," he argued.

"*But you do.*"

"A fact that I can see clearly."

She put on a profane imitation of a stretch and a rib poked out through blackened muscle. "*Are you? Are you sure you're seeing me?*"

That thought was the exact opposite of helpful but he refused to give her the satisfaction of hearing him dispute it. "I'm sure that I'm fisked either way. Trying to decide if you being a vision is worse than you being a wraith."

"*Why not both?*" she coyly asked.

"Because both would be bad."

She flicked what appeared to be a slightly forked tongue out at him. "*Either would be bad,*" Rmaci replied, "*both would be delightful.*"

"From your standpoint," he huffed.

The former spy and current not-quite-living nightmare pouted. "*If I have a standpoint, then I am more than just your mind playing tricks on you, aren't I?*"

Akaran shook his head. "That assumes I believe you and... fisk. We're having this argument, aren't we? I'm arguing with you over if you're real or not."

"*I'm enjoying it, myself,*" she replied with a mockery of a loving smile. "*Of course, I'm the only one. What do you think if they saw me as well as you did? Not the stuffy sods in the Order, of course. But them,*" she replied as she gestured at the people walking around them in the street. "*Those people. The ones that see a gimp limping down the street and think, 'What type of fool was he,' or 'How pathetic, I hope he doesn't want to ask me for crowns.' How do you think that they would react if they saw me? If they knew what was coming?*"

As she spoke, she calmly walked out into the middle of the road and began to spin around and dance in all of her naked and grotesque glory. The only thing that kept him from throwing up at the sight was the fact that his earlier fit had already worn his stomach out. "Who knows," he sighed after a few heartbeats. "Some would be terrified. Some would spend the rest of their lives terrified. A few would fight."

"*Only a few, you think? You think them helpless and panicked, like mewling children?*"

"A lot of them are mewling children," he retorted.

"*A fair point, I suppose,*" she conceded. "*I imagine they'd more likely riot. Trapped in this pit, with the only way out up the walls? Can you imagine how they'll act once I'm reunited with the rest of my essence?*"

He looked up at her with a cold disgust in his eye. "You mean when you try to kill them all."

"*Only as many as it takes to kill* you," Rmaci growled with a sudden snarl. "*Once you're dead I really have no interest in these... people. Maybe I'll go back and pay that Evalia woman a visit. I think that's for the best.*"

The exorcist shook his head again and sighed like he was having to explain something to a child. "It won't work, Rmaci. Worst case scenario is that you murder a handful of people, and maybe you get me. You're assuming that the Order won't just burn the city down to root you out for good."

"*The Order will try,*" she argued. "*Daringol was single-minded. That made it weak. I am unfettered by such... restraints. You did that much for me, I admit. Destroying the former essence of this* thing *made my... not quite life, is it? Existence, maybe? Whichever – it made it* easier *on me.*"

"Focusing on murdering me isn't?" he quipped back at her. "Sounds like you're trading one bloody desire for another."

She scoffed at him and went back to dancing between the harried locals who were trying to get home, or get to a tavern, or get anywhere other than between what was apparently a one-sided conversation from the priest and the wall. "*Having a goal doesn't mean that you can't take the time to stop and smell the roses,*" Rmaci replied with a smirk. "*Or I suppose I could if you hadn't let that fisking cunt burn my nose off,*" she snarled hatefully.

Akaran rolled his eye and let his cane lean against the alleyway entrance before he hid his face in his hands. "That's it. I have lost my mind," he sighed.

"*No, you haven't,*" she countered, "*but you really are in a mess, aren't you?*

People going missing, mages getting murdered, a physician getting slaughtered in her office right above your room... and your best friend is locked up? There's so much going on in your life I'm surprised you have time for me. I'm honored, truly, that you dedicate so many of your thoughts in my direction."

"I don't," he snapped. "I don't have time to stand around and listen to you make idle threats either."

She vanished from the crowd in a bloody mist and reappeared right next to him with her mouth almost on his ear. He lurched back and nearly fell over. *"They're not idle, though no, you don't. However, I think I like it here. It might just be a nice little place to put down roots."*

He managed to grab his cane in time to avoid falling face-first into the trash and other gunk along the side of the street. "Please. Go away. If you're a hallucination, you've had your fun. If you're *really* Rmaci, there is *nothing* going on right now that would be of interest to you."

"Oh! Now that's where you're entirely wrong."

"If I have learned one thing, it's that I am *rarely* entirely wrong," he whined.

"You are entirely cocky," she shot back. *"You forgot what it was I did before you oversaw my execution, didn't you?"*

He gave her a foul look. Not a long one; even glancing at her made the skin on his arm stand up in disgust. But, still a look. "Murder people?"

Rmaci flung her arms out dramatically, but it lost some of the intended effect when they passed through the stone wall behind her without a sound. After she realized it, she let them drop and just sighed in vague annoyance. *"I was a* spy, *you daft man-child. My life was spent untangling plots and finding things people wanted to keep hidden. To hear you grumble about it this is the greatest mystery to fall on the Kingdom in a decade!"*

That was almost all he could take. "Are you... serious?" he demanded as her intentions dawned on him. The thought of trying to throw up again quickly jumped back up into the forefront of his mind.

"Completely," she replied with a horrific grin that was wider than it should've been physically possible to be. *"I am* utterly *intrigued. Of course, there's another reason."*

His eye went wide and he gave up *any* attempt at keeping his composure. "What possible reason could the *dead woman haunting my dreams and terrorizing me with threats that she's going to meld with a group of damned souls I've already banished* have for being interested in this *mess* I'm not even supposed to be involved with anymore?!" he shouted so loudly that all eyes turned to him and everyone walking down the street suddenly started walking a bit faster.

"To get you to do that," she replied with a cruel snicker, *"and simply because if you poke your nose around places where it doesn't belong and get killed, I won't get to have fun with you anymore."*

His jaw dropped as she explained herself and the real reason popped into his mind. "No. It's not that," he countered. "It's not that you won't get to have fun. You want to help because if I get killed before you meld with the rest of the arin-goliath again, you go back to the pit. I die and you're *fisked*."

"*That would decrease my fun,*" she reluctantly admitted.

Akaran couldn't stop himself from staring. For the longest time, that was all he could do – just stand there, look at her with his jaw hanging open, and his eye dead focused on her rotting face. The only sign of life he gave was just the way his hand kept clenching on the head of his cane. "This is officially Pi's work. I'm going mad. I am losing my damn mind," he finally replied.

"*Not yet,*" she argued, "*but soon. I've seen glimpses of your future, my boy. A joy of being trapped between worlds… time doesn't always… work… the way you'd hope.*"

"The pits does *that* mean?"

Rmaci rolled her shoulders and stretched as she peered over his shoulder at something in the distance. "*It means that if I don't get to kill you? Then I am only slightly sad to say you've got a long trip into the desert ahead of you and sanity will be the least of your concerns. If I were you, I'd help me get to the Hullbreaker – and then die quickly. You'll be happier that way. Take that for what it is from one tortured soul to another.*"

Almost none of that made sense, though that kind of statement rarely did if you took it for the bald-faced meaning. "Am I getting a prophecy from a dead woman? Is that's what's happening?"

"*You had a prophecy from a frozen one, didn't you?*" the former spy pointed out. "*I heard that one, too.* 'When you return to Toniki, you will be a dead man,' *or maybe I should talk about the* 'girl with golden hair,' *or the* 'woman with hands of razors,' *that are to* 'bring you joy and peace?' *That's what she said, wasn't it?*"

"She wasn't of this world," he argued. "Who knows what she meant."

"*I'm not of this world – now, anyways. Does that make me any less valid?*" she asked. Before he could respond, she stood up on her skinless tiptoes and pointed behind him. "*By the way – remember how we just spoke of riots?*"

"Riots… what?"

"*Don't you think you should be doing something about that one?*"

He blinked in confusion before he started trying to massage away a splitting headache. "What one?" he demanded as all of this suddenly made his head just absolutely throb in distress.

Rmaci slipped close to him again and placed her hand on his shoulder and pointed with the other. "*That one,*" she replied with a soft voice and slow smirk.

He turned and followed her direction and watched a mob of people chase another group down another alley – members of the Odinal delegation, he guessed, being hounded by some of the local citizenry. "Oh, shit."

"*I remember you swinging your cock around like it was the embodiment of the Queen's law – so shouldn't you try to make the peace, oh peacemaker? Since you're not getting rid of me anytime soon, at least.*"

IV. A SECRET RAGE
Madis the 24ᵗʰ of Riverswell, 513 QR

While Akaran dealt with the voices in his head and what promised to be a brawl in the streets, a different kind of power play took hold in the *Uncrested Wave*, a taberna located not that far from the Repository itself. The Chiadon district was known for being a haven for all manner of priestly folk, and normally, Lady Anais gave it as wide of a breadth as possible.

That said, Donta had made good with delivering the blessing from Altund Obermesc around a week ago. She had told him she needed it for safe passage through the cave systems and the underground – though in this case, dealing with the underside of the holier-than-thou's in Basion made it just as imperative to her interests. She idly plucked at the thin sliver of a dark tan, almost muddy, stalactite that dangled loosely from her neck while she talked with her inebriated companion. "Well, of course. I mean there are those that think that they have all the right in the world to walk all over us just because we're *women.*" She flicked at the piece of stone again and smiled. It may not look like much, but it had enough magic into it to ward off creatures of the Undertunnels – and to make any creations of stone, mineral, or other gifts of the ground crafted in its presence all the more potent.

Which was being ever so subtly experienced by her guest.

The other woman in question had far more in common with Altund or Akaran than Anais ever could – and even though she was wearing clothes that were more peasantry than priestly, you wouldn't mistake Faldine for anything other than a knight. Even on their worse days, they just had a look about them; if nothing else, her half-bare and powerful arms suggested she was more than just some midwife. Truthfully? She could probably pick up any of the men in the taberna and throw them out the door if she so wished.

While the handful of drunken sods off in the corner knew it (and had been making remarks discussing what they'd let her do to them), they wisely kept quiet. However, even though the dregs of the district knew better than to underestimate her, apparently her superiors did not. "Men. All they do is look at us like cock warmers and baby carriers."

A simple fact that Anais, in all of her long-haired and regal glory, was all-too-happy to take advantage of. "Oh, I know. My own father tried to marry me off when I was no more than twelve winters old."

"Did he?" Faldine asked with a snort as she took another long drink from a polished stoneware cup. "Well, not uncommon. Did it work out for you?"

The self-professed 'Merchant of Secrets' extended a dainty hand and wiggled her naked fingers. "You don't see a ring on my hand, do you?"

"No, I don't. I wouldn't have known if you hadn't said," Faldine said with a giggle and then she flashed her own bare hand at Anais. The contrast between them was striking; the paladin's hands were strong, scarred, and a little swollen around the knuckles. The older woman sitting across from her wasn't dainty, but she was pale, her nails expertly trimmed, and her aura was simply elegant.

The difference was night and day, which was true in more than one way. "Then it worked out just fine. Husbands are fickle creatures and prone to flights of fancy. I've better things to do with my time in this world than put up with them."

"You speak truth," the soldier with wheat-tinted hair agreed. "You know what? I am a *paladin*. I have served the Goddess of Love through blood and suffering and glory. I lead great men into battle. I've held stronger men in my arms as they have died. And just because I wouldn't... *tolerate* some disgusting *wannabe latrine-digger* trying to take liberties... the Holy General banishes me to this... this... quiet little puddle?"

"A true paladin?" Anais asked. "No doubt you've fought all manner of beast to carry that title."

Faldine's dark brown eyes turned even darker as she glanced down into her cup. "You have no idea what lurks in this world. Pray you never do."

The older woman turned her head to hide a haunted look of her own – and bit back a sharp intake of breath as she caught something flickering in the rafters over her newly-made friend's head. "I'm sure what exists defies imagination," she sighed before she took one final drink out of her own goblet. "Honorable paladin, I do hate to go but I have an appointment to see to and sadly, he does hate to wait. I am so glad we could finally have a chance to talk."

"Another needy manchild, huh?"

"One of the most irritating beings I have ever come across in all my days, I will say that," she replied with another glance at the rafters. The little shape bounced a little, like it was mocking her. "We must do this again, soon."

In return, she clutched at the stone on her neck while the paladin tried to offer some words of encouragement. "Don't let him get to you. You're a bright one, Anais. Use that to your advantage, and no man will ever be able to lord over you."

"I do my best, with every waking day," her dinner partner agreed. She stood up, bowed slightly, and walked out of the taberna like she didn't have a fear in the world, which was the biggest lie she'd told all day. She made sure that Faldine hadn't wandered outside to follow her before she ducked down an alleyway. Then, without warning, she bent down and scooped up a piece of loose cobblestone – and chucked it into the air at the shadow following her with far more force than her dainty, refined form should have been able to muster.

The shade flinched. And chortled. That damnable chortle.

Its laugh sounded like a wounded boar desperately clinging to life, and only served to piss Anais off even more. "*Rishnobia*! *Do you have any idea what you just risked*?!" she hissed as her fingers dug so hard into her palms that if she could have bled, she would've. "That could have been disastrous for *everyone*!"

Rishnobia. If there were fouler denizens of the Abyss this side of the Veil, the merchant had never met one, and never wanted to. It wasn't that he was gross or disgusting; he was just a mote, a head-sized monster with more hands and feet than it knew what to do with. It wasn't particularly ugly; it had a body of silver and black fur and a pair of ruby-red eyes that might, *might* have been pretty had it been a wolf.

The truth of it? It was so vile because it was rude, it was nasty, and it was – unfortunately – the preferred messenger employed by Anais' benefactor. Or, as it liked to brag, his master's 'favored acolyte.'

A fact that it liked to rub into her face at every opportunity it had.

"[No cause/No worry! But question for you?/Speaking with a lover?]" the damnable little beast retorted. "[Risk you claim I cause/Risk between your wet thighs.]"

"I take *precautions,* you irritating mote! Which seems like a great deal more than you do!"

It started to come into better focus as the bars began to empty out on the streets nearby. "[Precautions you say?/Precautions worry you?]"

"They *keep* me from being worried you blasted thing," she argued back with her eyes dark and burning with fury. "What is it you want? I reported in three days ago!"

Rishnobia vanished from sight and quickly reappeared back of her shoulder. "[Master once again sends word/Master urges efforts to slow. Vahail did not go as wanted/this is not the chaos intended.]"

"Stop? He wants me to stop? We're so close to confirming that the Urn is –"

The beast bristled slightly and she saw him clutch his twisted little claws tight to his chest. "[Grand army of Dawn/soon sets on flood. Shit navy of Dawn/ sent to aid drowned. Fewer the guards/easier the access. But if Aquallans are heard/his goals will be clear.]"

"His goals aren't even clear to his employees," Anais quipped in irritation. "Are you saying he's afraid that the Lovers will show concern about his efforts on the coast?"

"[Master does not fear/Master wants the Urn. Things he needs may be easier/if found without eagerly whispering lips.]"

"There are fewer lips moving now than there were," she charged. "You may tell him that Donta and I have gone to great lengths to quiet those speaking ill of his crimson robe."

The mote's hair stood up on end as it blinked in surprise. "[Truly now?/Without ask? Attempting to supplant Rishnobia/become master's new favored?]"

The term rankled her whenever she heard it, and right now as absolutely not an exception to the rule. "I am not one of his acolytes. He is my benefactor," she retorted as she moved away from him. "I am his employee."

"[As such lower than I/Remember that when you speak.]"

Anais glowered at him for daring to chastise her. "Don't push it, Rishnobia. You may be his so-called 'favored' one, but I have brought bigger demons than you low in my time."

The beast cut loose with another mocking, tortured-boar attempt at a laugh. "[With the years spent in Avaritisha's Palace?/Brought them low while on your knees.]"

She went ash-white and then turned red-hot with fury at the mere mention of her time *there*, let alone the way he so casually said it out loud and near *people*. "What do you want, you piece of shit?"

Rishnobia's crimson eyes glowed with delight at her anger. "[As stated/As said. The move for all his benefit/will be made within days fourteen. There will be etheric consequences/All of us must hide.]"

"Dammit! Rishnobia, I can do a great deal in two weeks time. Maybe not as much as I would like, I agree but I may not even need his help! Does it have to be now? Can you ask him to wait? We are so close, I can feel it."

"[It is not mine to say/Only it is mine to relay. His actions are not just for you/Men make follies that must be corrected. What he sends men made/Men must balance their fate.]"

Lady Lovic balled her fists again and quickly glanced out of the mouth of the alleyway to make sure they weren't being overheard. "Relay back to him that this isn't a good time. I am *busy*. Slowing down or stopping now would put everything at risk."

The mote dove back into her field of view, and utterly ignored the risk it was putting them in. "[At risk/Everything is. Master felt a strong disturbance here/The ether rippled with Love's anger. His concern is increased/Feels move is imperative. Is this your doing/Is it your actions?]"

"Mine?" she repeated quizzically. "No. I've done nothing to antagonize the Lovers." After a moment she quantified that with a shrug and a simple, "Yet."

"[Except a dalliance/with a paladin,]" the disgusting little creature pointed out.

Anais flipped her hand dismissively. "She knows nothing. She's how I am going to deliver the Urn to him. You can tell him as much. She serves him as unwitting eyes."

The mote silently twitched a few times as it studied her for truthfulness.

"[In your efforts to find/have you seen anyone odd?]"

"Odd? For the Oo-lo? When are those misguided fools not?"

"[An honest answer/one quite true,]" he admitted. "[Still I must ask/Have any been odd?]"

It didn't take her long to answer – and the demonkin *immediately* wished she hadn't. "The madhouse has had a new resident from their Order as of a few weeks ago. Some young one-eyed fool that can't use magic anymore."

Rishnobia tensed up and shrunk in on himself with a nervous little quiver. At the same time, his eyes went from rose-crimson to leaf-green. "[An isolated eye?/Two orbs one? Describe this cyclops/I must know.]"

"What's there to say of him?" she asked flippantly. "Barely a man, has a broken leg, a dreadful goatee, hair the color of amber-stained sand. Supposedly an exorcist. I'd say he's, oh –"

"[Name you deceitful wench!/A name is needed!]"

Anais took the insult with a smirk. "Then you should've asked. He calls himself Akaran… DeHawk, if I recall correctly." As the demon's claws gripped a nearby wall so hard that the stones cracked, she went on. "I've had a pair of opportunities to interact with him. I assure you he's nothing spec–"

For the first time in the years she'd had to get used to his repulsive presence, she got to watch the little beast *pace* back and forth in what she could only presume was some kind of nervous breakdown. "[Oh no/no no. Knew he was near/but now interred there? Assumed remitted for training/not trained to heal. Ripple explained/anger understood. But lame he now is?/Gimped of magic and body?]"

"Yes, quite pathetic," she remarked. "Why? Should I have concerns about him?"

"[Yes/Should,]" he grunted as he continued to pace back and forth. His eyes kept shifting between red and green with no shades in-between. "[Not the news I wished to bring/Master will not be happy to hear. Agitated angry frustrated himself/Ether will boil now. Will not be pleased/not to have known.]"

She crossed her arms and replied with a pained sigh of annoyance. "I have a deep dislike of you, mote, and moments like these make it worse. What about this child has you upset? IF you wanted him tracked you should have asked."

"[Many things/all things,]" the demon groused back. "[Master want to know/Oh will he want. Orders now/Orders important.]"

"I don't believe we are at a point in this relationship where you can give me orders, acolyte," Anais hissed as a sudden bulge on the side of her neck began to twitch and a shape started to amass under the skin.

Rishnobia actually flinched back; the first *wise* thing it had done since appearing. "[Consider less than order then/This will earn his favor. Discover the cause/all you can. Master will want to know/what made him this way. It is most important/More than much else.]"

The request, if you could call it that, left her confounded. "What in the…

why would *he*, of *all* people, have an interest in a broken little priest? I'd sooner understand your skittishness than I would *his*."

"[The why is not the wonder/The wonder is why he's neutered,]" the mote muttered back as it paced back and forth along the outside wall of the shop. "[AVOID HIM/RISHNOBIA STRESSES.]"

"I've met the man," she said dismissively. "There's nothing to fear of him. Plenty of ways to use him as a tool. I have plans with him that are critical to securing the Urn of Xabraxis. Tell your Master that and then I'll consider leaving him alone if he —"

"[If him you do not fear/Fear his past and his blood,]" the beast warned. "[Complication none of us needed/Not with Master engaging questions.]"

Anais took a moment to study the little cretin with more interest than she normally bothered to give, and after a moment, actually softened up a little. "You are truly worried about this, aren't you? Oh, I like that look on your ugly little face. Whatever makes you miserable makes me happy," she said with a sigh and a shake of her head. "If it's important enough to make you panic I suppose it's important enough to pay attention to. Tell him I'll suss out what I can. When I'm allowed, apparently, since I can't do it now."

Rishnobia gave her a quick pulse of his tiny body in return. "[For now show care/continue a slow search. Both the Urn/and his fate.]"

"When will I know it's safe to get back to work?"

"[There will be no subtlety/Word will spread most quick,]" he warned. "[He will not act here/though it is somewhat near. His movement comes by sea/A spiritual sickness to spread. Sickness to be delivered here/to aid your questions elsewhere.]"

As vague as that was, it was utterly unimpressive. "Spiritual sickness and questions? My dear mote, have you not met the people of this town? Drug addicts, whoremongers, politicians, drunkards, gamblers. This town is so sinfully *ill* that the only reason that people assume it is *safe* is because they're all too busy dunking their dicks in wine-soaked sluts to dip their knives into each other."

If it could've shrugged, it would've. "[Corruption of ethics/easy to manipulate. Corruption of souls?/Easy to spread. Corrupted souls are different/Rotting frozen souls worse. Master sends a distraction/the Order will respond. When they respond violently as they will/then you may act against them all.]"

The lack of an answer in his answer made her as much frustrated as it did disgusted. Neither of which mattered — if her benefactor, the man that titled himself the 'Man of the Red Death,' so desired, so it had to be. "Fine," she eventually replied. "I'll reign in Donta. We'll wait before doing anything else," she agreed — the lie rolling off of her tongue as easily as water off of a duck's back.

Rishnobia visibly relaxed and his eyes went back to their natural bloody red tint. "[As is wise/Will report now. If there are orders new/I will return very soon.]"

"Oh, be still my beating heart."
"[Beats now does it?/News to this mote,]" it mocked as it faded away.

***

The exorcist could hear the shouts before he found the mob – though you'd have to be completely deaf not to. Chants of, "You aren't welcome here!" and, "Hylene is too good for you!" were mixed with a strong helping of, "You've no right to take her from us!" The only reason the Guard wasn't already on hand, he finally had to admit, was that some of the rioters probably *were* guardsmen themselves.

The thought was confirmed in a hurry when he recognized at least two familiar faces that *should* have been wearing the red and gold of the 4th. It never ceased to amaze him how people thought that a little bit of authority excused themselves from following the law they were supposed to enforce. Of course, they weren't alone – which made this all the worse. It was one big ragtag group of civilians, merchants, laborers and more all mixed in.

Another cry echoed out. "We're not here for trouble! Just let us go and we'll forget this!" That shout belonged to someone in a group of four that had the misfortune of being pinned at the wrong end of a long alley. It wasn't a shock – the smaller group were members of the Odinal delegation. With everything else going on, the contested wedding had been the last thing on his mind.

Apparently, it was still fresh for everybody else.

But if he was right about the two women from Odinal – meekly hiding behind the men – then getting involved in this mess would be the only way to stop the streets from running red. *"You mean running 'redder,' don't you?"* Rmaci purred behind him.

Before could argue the point, someone in the mob threw a rock at the smaller group. "Let you go? HEAR THAT? They want us to let them go!" Of course, the challenge only elicited more chants and shouts of hatred from the others. "FISKING MIDLANDERS! Barbarian fools!"

That, in turn, lead to a response from a man that had to be at least twenty years Akaran's senior. He was athletic, gray hair, and wore a dark brown vest with matching leather leggings. "We are no barbarians! We are here to celebrate the love between two wonderful people."

You could predict the reaction he earned. "He doesn't love her!" "He wants to bed a real woman, not one of your filthy whores!" "Whatever you threatened her with isn't going to work!! We won't let it!" and more all echoed down the street.

The writing was on the wall for what was about to happen next. The pair of brown-haired, black-robe-garbed women made a show of cowering in front of the mob while the other midlander extended his palms and called for peace. The only thing that stopped the riot from falling apart was one loud, demanding, booming voice that silenced everyone in one shout.

It even made him feel good to get to use that tone of voice for a change. "WHAT IN THE NAME OF THE GODDESS IS GOING ON HERE?!" Akaran demanded as he stormed his way through the gaggle of idiots with sharp raps of his cane punctuating every word out of his throat.

While that made some of them cringe away, it didn't impact many. The midlanders took one look at him and retreated to the back wall of the alley just enough to make it clear that they were only putting on a show of deference. One of their speaker's bodyguards gave him a withering look through a loose lock of her walnut-tinged hair. *"She's scary,"* the wraith whispered, *"I think I like her."*

"Don't get attached," he muttered as a hulking man stormed out of the mob and crossed his arms, "and go away. I *don't* need to deal with my imagination breaking into bits and pieces right now."

"How cute you think I'm imaginary," she taunted.

The lead speaker for the mob flexed his arms again for show. Arms, the exorcist noted, that were far larger than they had *any* right to be. Even without his stick, the idea of getting punched by someone using them did not settle well. "Ain't none of your business!" the riot's leader shouted at the top of *his* lungs, like he was trying to assert dominance over Akaran's.

Neither that attempt – nor the matching cry elsewhere on the street of, "Oo-lo'er! You stay outta it!" made the priest flinch back in any shape or form.

"Not happening," he snapped back at the bigger, bulkier, and admittedly more intimidating local. "I'm an Officer of the Crown, and whatever you're thinking of doing – or *not thinking* – looks illegal as all and you're going to stop doing it. Right now."

The big man flexed again and dropped his hand to a hatchet hanging loosely in his hemp rope belt. "We don't answer to you, boy."

A woodcutter, he groaned, *I had to pick a fight with a man with an axe.* "Yes, you do. I don't care if you like it or not, but yes, you do."

From behind him, the Odinal speaker decided now was a brilliant time to interject himself back into the dispute. "Sir priest, please. Your assistance would be welcomed. All we want to do is get back to Avager Hall."

"Is that where you're staying or elsewhere?"

"They bullied Lord Avager to make him give 'em beds to stay in!" the big man shouted with a chorus of agreements echoing up from behind him.

The speaker lifted both of his hands in penitence. "We did no such thing! He offered us a place to stay out of the goodness and kindness of his heart."

Once again, the woodcutter spoke up. Every time he did, Akaran thought his eye was going to roll so far up into the back of his head that he'd be blind for life. "Threatened his wife and children I'm sure!"

"Or threatened to burn it down if he didn't!" someone else charged. "That's how you people act!"

Akaran gave the second speaker – a dirty, wrinkled, gaunt, unwashed woman – the foulest look he could muster. "The only people I see threatening anyone is you lot of fools. What are you idiots doing?"

The presumed woodcutter got up right in the priest's face and stared down at him. Up close, his breath reeked. "Whatever we do is our business and ain't any of yours. You get out of here before we make you get out of here."

Up close, it was also hard for Akaran to tilt his head up far enough to see the angry laborer's face past his excessive – and prominently exposed – mounds of chest hair. "I'm gonna be nice and pretend you didn't threaten me. Wouldn't do it again."

"Oh? And who's gonna stop me?"

The priest smirked gestured over his shoulder. "Well, if *I* don't, then that means you'll have knocked me out or killed me," he started. "If you *don't* kill me, I'm gonna have you all thrown into a dank hole so deep underground you'll forget what light even looks like. And if you do kill me, there's witnesses. There'll be an investigation. *And* anyone that had a hand in it will end up with their head on a pike as a warning not to do it again. You'll go rot in the pit and I'll be relaxing in the arms of the Goddess. Far as I'm concerned, that's a win either way," he finished, a cold smile growing on his lips with every single word he uttered.

"*Didn't we just have a discussion on how you dying wouldn't be fun for me?*" Rmaci growled from somewhere just behind his left ear.

"It's my silver lining," he hissed at her out of the corner of his mouth. "Now do you idiots want to see how this goes or can we just agree that *home* is a better place for all of us?" Then, back at the spy, he added just loud enough for her to hear: "*You included, you toasted twat?*"

As the gruesome vision huffed back with an indignant retort, the mob started to make noises like they understood how deep of a pile of horse dung they were in. Sadly, while the mob started to show some sense, their leaders weren't. "Our home has been infested with these... disgusting BARBARIANS!"

"Good man, you have no idea what an *infestation* of outsiders looks like, and you can take it from someone that's had an up-close and personal experience with just that," he snapped as he rapped the tip of his cane on the cobblestone street. "Now, let's talk this out. What do you want?"

The Odinal speaker again decided that the situation could be made worse – though he probably hoped to make it better – by opening his mouth again. "They're trying to get us to cancel the wedding. We couldn't even if we wanted! We don't speak for the clan!"

Akaran sighed and rubbed his throbbing temples tiredly. "This true?"

"We ain't about to let the Baronessa of Basion get degraded and used by those filthy scragcunts!" the presumed woodcutter's equally-presumed wife shouted back. "An' if we have to give a beatin' to every single one of them that've invaded our city, we damn well will!"

As often does, profanity and insults won the mob over. "Yeah!" "Scragcunters!"

"You touch them, and you're going to find out what's meant by the phrase 'divine retribution' in all the ways you *don't* want to," Akaran cautioned. "That I can promise."

"You ain't in any kind of position to offer a threat, cripple."

"I wouldn't be so damn sure of that," the priest shot back. "So far you've threatened an Officer of the Crown, threatened dignitaries from outside our borders under diplomatic protection, and you've organized a riot. I can *personally* have you set in a pillory before the sun rises if I want. That's gonna make a few of you have to come up with a lot of *extra* excuses to give to Henderschott, for the record," he growled as a few off-duty guardsmen started to back away from the center of the mob. "How bad do all you want to have your week go, exactly?"

The woodsman laughed the promise-not-a-threat off with a hearty chortle. "I don't take orders from you, heretic. Get gone or we *will* do something about it."

With anger overriding the pain in his leg (and ache in his stomach), the exorcist moved back so that he was directly between the woodsman's line of sight and the midlanders. Not that it helped that the towering monster of a man could just look over his head, but at least the intention was there. "I don't think you understand the gravity of your situation. I follow the Goddess Niasmis, and you're threatening people that are IN LOVE. *This is exactly what I am sworn to protect.*"

"They ain't in love. She's being treated like cattle!"

"I've MET the two of them," Akaran argued with his voice trembling with rage. "He loves her. Plain as day. Don't think you could get that much more in love if you tried. Far as I can tell she loves him too," he added while a little voice in the back of his head added a silent, *I hope.*

The woodsman made a move for his hatchet and the priest slammed the point of his cane on the ground right next to the rioter's foot. "Fisking LIAR!" he thundered. "That's what the Overseer wants us to believe! We ALL know it's just politics! We won't stand for it!"

Akaran brought himself up to his full height and called on every ounce of gravitas he could muster to shut him down. "*I SPEAK WITH THE VOICE OF THE GODDESS OF LOVE. My LIFE is devoted to the concept and execution of Love. I HAVE PERSONALLY SENT SOULS TO BE DAMNED FOR ETERNITY IN HER NAME.*"

Rmaci popped up behind the mob's leader and frowned, which had the unfortunate side-effect of causing a chunk of her cheek to slough off and dissipate before it hit the ground. "*Well that feels personal.*"

"Shut up," he snapped back at her, though it had an added bonus of killing the woodsman's complaint before he started to utter it. "Understand me: my every breath hangs on Her word. I am sworn to defend it and defend those that embrace it. So that means, once more since you're deaf, *I STAND HERE.*"

His wife wasn't quite as smart. "Then you can defend —"

"I WASN'T FISKING FINISHED," the exorcist thundered. "Get this through your damn head: If this was just *politics* then they would have saved themselves the grief and the threats and would have had her thrown into a barrel and hauled up the mountains to lay her down in Malik's bed without putting up with all the bullshit you fiskers are putting on here."

"Over our dead bodies they will!"

Akaran rapped his cane against the cobblestones again. "Did you *forget* who you're talking about? Are you seriously saying that a bunch of ragtag piss poor peasants have a chance to stand up and fight off the Berserkers of Odinal? You realize that even if you roll over me these four are going to hand you back your asses in the tankards you found your courage in?"

Finally, the mob's mouthpiece started to back down. "We outnumber them almost four-to-one! They ain't gonna do a damn thing to us!" he challenged – though there was a little glimmer in his eye that implied that he didn't quite believe everything he was preaching.

"Except beat the ever living shit out you?" the exorcist countered. "Understand me, you ignorant halfwits. There is *no* way this ends well for you. You end up in jail, in a medic's care, or in the ground. Possibly all three and in no particular order. And you do it because you're too blind to realize that the two of them give an *actual damn* about each other which is a thing that just doesn't happen all too often these days and you fisking well know it."

"She's the Baronessa! She's OUR Baronessa!" his wife pleaded with a nasal voice.

Akaran pointed his cane in her general direction and curled his lip. "Do you own her? Are you a slaver? Do you keep her in a gilded cage? Is there a *leash* in your hand I'm not seeing?"

"Well, no, but she's OURS! She's OUR Baronessa!"

"She's a grown woman that's made a fisking choice," he spat. "If she's the Lady of the City as you've said, then what makes you possibly think that anyone forced her to do anything she didn't want to do?"

"*Aside from her brother? That pompous ass got on my nerves and I couldn't even –*"

The growl from his throat would've made a rabid wolf pause. "Enough. Both of you. *All* of you."

Their leader shook his head and sent droplets of sweat splashing on the priest's face. "But it ain't right. She's got no business leaving us! We need her!"

"What you NEED is to understand that when Love is the question people will do anything they can for the answer. It ain't up to me, it ain't up to them," he said as he gestured at the midlanders, "and it damn right fisking sure it AIN'T up to you."

The woodsman continued to falter under the raw fury brimming in Akaran's lone eye. "We love that woman too! She's OUR Baroness! We need her here! Nobody else has ever spoken up for us!"

"So you thank her for that by doing this?" he spat back with a snarl. "You say that you love her and appreciate what she's done and you're out here going, '*Gee we really appreciate you, so here, let's try to murder your fiance's friends and family*?' That doesn't sound like much of a '*thank you*' to me, you whining prat."

The words hit home with his wife, at least, and she cringed away from the Order's soldier as she tried to salvage their argument. "Well no, we're just trying to keep her from going so she'll stay here. Stay with us and help us!"

He took a deep breath and took a step back away from the mob. "Okay. Say you do it. Say I step aside right now..." he began as he moved away from both groups. The women behind him, in turn, very slowly opened up their cloaks and put the long, serrated, and wickedly curved blades hanging from their waists on full display. "...and watch you pick a fight with them. What happens if I do this, exactly?"

Their speaker cleared his throat as the warmaidens stepped up to the challenge. "Priest, this is not an advisable thing for you to do. One could think that if you are granting them permission, you agree with their opinions. That would be unwise," he cautioned.

"Now. Say you fight them," Akaran continued.

"Priest, I will not warn you again," the older traveler repeated.

"Say you fight them and maybe, maybe, at the end, the one or two of you left standing will be able to say you defended her honor," he added as he slowly looked at each person in the mob. "Ignoring the question of which two or three of you don't bleed out into the gutter, what happens after?"

The woodsman tried to answer that as a couple of people in the crowd threw their hands up and abandoned their friends. "Then she breaks off the engagement."

He nursed on his lip for a moment and nodded ever so slightly. "Say she does. She'll stay. Most of you won't live to see it, but she'll stay. Then what? What makes you think she'll do anything for you ever again? You murder people to keep her away from the man she loves? What *possible* result do you think that will get you? A parade and fewer taxes?"

"Well she's always..."

"Don't think that might change if you break her heart? I'd change my attitude towards you if it were *me*."

More of the mob broke away and went off to go do whatever they should've been doing instead as his words hit home again and again. "But she... but... she's gotta stay and..."

"Then ask her to name a successor," Akaran suggested. "Find someone in your group that's *decent* and has had a *bath* recently. There's a damned *river* twenty minutes hobbling walk from here. Go stand it in first. Then approach her and tell her you're scared. Tell her you don't know who else will support you like she did. *Talk to her.* I've heard that she *routinely* holds public audiences to listen to the grievances people have to work them out with the Overseer. Let her pick someone to represent *you* and go about it that way."

"What if they don't? We've never had someone like the Baronessa!" the woodsman asked with a bit of... not quite fear, not quite sadness, but a bit of miserable melancholy finally showing through past his anger and misplaced rage.

"You said that already," the priest replied with a shrug. "If you trust her this much this long, then trust her to name a successor. This though? Doing *this*? This won't end well. And hey. It may *not* end well when she's gone. Short of an armed rebellion against the Queen – which would be a *bad* idea in case anyone gets the idea that I'm suggesting one – that's just the lot in life we *all* have to deal with."

"Not for the ones who fall," the midlander's speaker pointed out. "Less for the survivors. People will fall if you continue this course."

"Survivors are always the ones that get the short end of the stick," he grunted before looking up and staring the woodsman right in his eyes. "Nothing new there. Just keep in mind, big man, the dead fall a *lot* farther."

"*That* was *personal*," Rmaci grumbled as she stuck her tongue out through her cheek at him.

"It's up to you. Go home, I forget I ever saw any of you, and we all go back to our miserable lives in the morning."

The crowd murmured, and about half of them agreed and broke away from the pack. That left the woodsman, his wife, and a couple of diehards that were going to die painfully if they pushed their plot forward. "This ain't over, you understand –"

"It's over," Akaran forcibly interrupted. "*Period*. You don't do this again, I don't see you give these people – *any* of these people – a dirty glance for the rest of their stay. You spread word to the other morons thinking of trying something and make it *damn clear* that the Order of Love *will not tolerate* an interruption of the wedding celebrations."

"We're acting out of love, too!" the bigger man protested.

"You're acting out of *petulance*."

He violently shook his head again and the priest couldn't hide his gag as a bit of sweat flew onto his face. "You're not from here. You don't understand!"

"No. I'm not," the Lover admitted, "but I have more concerns on my hands right now than to want to put up with a bunch of chest-thumping *shits* that are feeling *pissy* because they can't keep a woman that I doubt *any* of you have met in person to stay in town. *Do not* give me reason to turn my attention to *you*."

His scraggly wife huffed up and pointed a shaking finger at the priest. "Threatening us ain't gonna change anything, boy. It ain't gonna make this better."

Akaran glowered her into submission all over again. "I don't give a shit how it makes you *feel*," he snarled. "Nobility is going to do whatever the fisk nobility wants to do, and it fisking sucks for every single one of us – my broken ass included – but nobody *gives a shit* about your *feelings*. They *will* give a shit about diplomats getting mugged or dead. And if *they*, those kind people right over there? If *they* don't kill you, I *can fisking promise you* that Paverilak will put the full force of Maiden Esterveen's consort so far *up your asses* that the Queen's Flag will dangle off of the end of your tongue by the time they're done. *Am I fisking clear?*"

She started to unleash a series of profanities that made Rmaci clap her rotting hands in glee, but her husband wrapped his arm around her shoulders and quieted her down. "You're not much of a priest."

"I'm the hurt-people kind. You want forgiveness? Go to the Ellachurstine."

The riot's leader growled down at him but began backing away. "You've only made this worse. You know that? You've made this worse."

Akaran wiped the sweat and the bigger man's spittle off of his cheek with a disgusted shudder. "Fine. Be angry. Be angry *at me*. I'm a big boy. I can take it. Leave these four idiots out of your warpath, that's all I'm asking. *You* don't want blood on your hands and *you* don't want to deal with the consequences of your actions if it gets there."

"Killing is a part of —" he started.

He didn't get to finish. The exorcist quickly stormed back up to him and roughly grabbed him by the front of his tunic. "A few months ago, I cut someone's head off and saw someone burnt alive because of their sins."

"*Still looking at her too, don't forget!*" his personal wraith chimed in.

He ignored her to the best he could, despite her dancing down the side of the street with a small cloud of snapping embers following her every mad step. "I *know* where their souls went for their crimes and I *know that* because I personally *sent them there* kicking and screaming. I even watched a soul get sucked into that living nightmare through a crack in the air where I saw *exactly* what awaits on the other side."

Rmaci stopped her macabre movements and tilted her head at him. "*Oh. So the glimpses of the pit I've shown you aren't your first? I'm not your first...? Well. Here I thought what we had was special.*"

"You want blood on your hands? I hope you're ready for someone like me to cut them off after because *we will* and your little *temper-tantrum* will earn you burning agony for *eternity*," he spat.

The cutter's wife clasped her hands over her mouth and swore. "Oh *fisk*. Darvol — that one ain't just Oo-lo. He's an *exorcist*. He... he ain't kiddin' about what he can do."

"Damn right I am," he confirmed, "and *damn* right I'm not joking."

"Cane or not, we don't... we don't want trouble with one of *them*," she groaned with another muttered curse under her breath.

Akaran gave her a short nod. "No. You don't. I get it. You're upset, you're scared, you love the Baronessa, and you want to keep her. The idea of some thick-skulled savage breaking her in as his own private breeding mare is driving you nuts, isn't it?"

The woodsman — Darvol, apparently — started to seethe with anger all over again. "Breeding mare!?"

"*Oh, that may have been a poor choice of words,*" the burnt-up wraith called out with a slight cringe. *"Accurate, but poor."*

"Think of all the good she's done for you. Think of all the amazing things that she's helped you with. I've heard the stories. Established orphanages and schools in every district, makes sure that your children are taught? Helps to make sure that winter is that much easier on you? All that and the city-wide parties she throws?"

"Not sure that reminding them is going to ease things over..."

The priest took a deep breath to calm himself and stepped back a little. "Now stop. Think. She's not going to be *gone* and she won't *forget* about you. I don't know a lot about midlander culture. I really don't. I don't know *how* those people live *but* imagine how much good she'll do taking the Queen's Rule out into the wastelands."

"We have our *own* rule, priest," the well-meaning idiot behind him interrupted. "We don't –"

"Shut up," Akaran hissed at him before he returned his attention back to Darvol and his wife. "While she does *that*, ask yourselves: how are you going to honor her?"

"What's that supposed to mean?" the burly troublemaker demanded.

"She's leaving. There's dick you can do about it," he replied. "Question is, does she leave *scared* or does she leave knowing that someone's gonna take up the cause in her stead? Say she doesn't get to appoint some kind of successor. What are *you* going to do about it? Storm down the street and threaten people? Beat each other up? Act like a pack of dogs? Or are you going to honor her and build this city into something greater?"

Darvol grunted and gestured at his wife and the couple of fools still standing by him. "We ain't *nobility*. We can't do anything like that!"

That was when the exorcist shook his head for a change and gestured widely with his arms. "You can do more than you think. The community *thrives* on local leadership as much as it does the snot-nosed silk-swathed shitheads in the Overseer's Manor and you know it."

The remaining mob, Darvol's wife included, murmured in reluctant agreement with him. Even the wraith gave him a moderately-respectful nod for his effort. The woodcutter tried to speak up again, but the priest quieted him down with a quick strike of his cane on the stones at their feet.

"So. You can act like pissy little twats and get yourselves thrown into the dungeon, *at best*," he warned, "or you can keep throwing fits like this and she gives up on all of you and goes and does whatever she wants *like she's going to do anyway*. Or! Or, you can start working with each other to make some kind of difference to make up for what she can't do anymore. *Those* are your choices."

"What makes you think anyone would listen or let us?" Darvol asked after thinking about it for another few moments.

"You managed to get more than a dozen people to follow you with the intention of killing these twits," he replied with a frustrated wave of his hand behind him (much to the bemusement of the two warmaidens, and the dirty looks from their charges), "so surely that means you can get a few dozen more to organize a party in the market square twice a month. Promise you, people like beer and bread more than they do bones and blood."

"Or as many consequences," the Odinal's speaker remarked.

Rmaci cleared her blistered throat as much as she could. "*That isn't necessarily true. Have you ever –*"

"And that," Akaran agreed as he slipped into a more relaxed posture that he didn't really feel, but felt the need to show anyways. "Now I really need to go take a piss and I don't have any more time for this so, *are we good* or do I need to start planning for a few funerals?"

Darvol started to argue, but his wife interjected herself ahead of him. "You've made your point, priest. This is done. Can't promise that it won't happen again."

"Try *very, very hard* for it to not happen again," he cautioned. "That outpost on the hill means that the Order has a *deep* interest in the peace being kept, and we are not opposed to *keeping the peace* if we must. Is that understood? Especially when it comes to fighting for Love and all that."

"It is," she sighed. "This ain't gonna win you friends here, boy. You'd best be careful what streets you walk down in the future."

Akaran snorted and flicked the tip of his cane at them. "If you value *his* head, then I'd make sure that word gets out that the streets are *incredibly* safe for me, for them, and for anyone else with Love on their lips. *Is that clear?*"

"Sack of balls on you bigger than your brain, will say that much," Darvol grumbled.

"Wanna find out if they're bigger than your mouth?" the exorcist shot back. But, before the insult could earn him the fist in his face he probably deserved for it, Darvol's wife grabbed him by his wrist and pulled him away. He waited until they – and the remaining stragglers – dispersed and went out of sight before he sagged down into a barely-standing heap. "That could've gone better."

"*I don't know,*" Rmaci quipped. "*I think that went surprisingly well. Of course you didn't have to drag me into it. Some of those comments were totally unnecessary.*"

"We don't always hear what we want," he grunted under his breath. "Do you think you could get dressed? Or... wear bandages? Something?"

The wraith flickered in and out of sight for a moment. When she returned, she was wearing a threadbare imitation of Seline's pink dress, complete with a ratty bow on the top of her head. "*Better?*"

"Goddess. I hate you."

"*Not a good attitude for a man of Love,*" she quipped.

Before he could comment further, the Odinal's speaker interrupted what they thought was a one-sided conversation. "Priest. Are you well?"

Akaran gave the wraith a dirty look before swinging back around to face the midlanders. "Fine. I'm fine."

"You are not," the older man pointed out as he gently grabbed the exorcist's arm to help steady him. "Yet you are brave, and your bravado is not false. That could have been far worse than it was."

"What I am was lucky," he pointed out. "If your warmaidens hadn't been armed I don't think I could have kept them back."

"Yet they were. Did you know?"

"I guessed," he replied as the blonde smirked. "You're *midlanders*. It goes with the territory, doesn't it?"

The older man chuckled as the two women sashayed past them and made a show of gawking mockingly at the priest as they went past. "Oh, it does," he admitted as he gave Akaran time to stand up straight again on his own. "You saved many lives tonight – ours and theirs both. May we be so lucky that your sermon will reach the ears of others that share similar thoughts. "

"I have a bad feeling it'll only be worse," Akaran admitted. "Start traveling in larger groups."

"As do I. Yet..."

"Yet?"

Their leader clasped his hands and bowed his head slightly. "Yet your words and works will not be forgotten by us. You had no reason to stand for us, though one would have been happier to not have been referred to as, 'these twits,' and other such comments. Aside from that, you've made no shortage of friends this day."

"Or enemies."

"Making enemies is how those like us make friends," the traveler pointed out.

Akaran thought on that for a minute and slowly smiled with a little chuckle. "Huh. I like that. Thank you, midlander."

"And you, exorcist," the other man returned. "I am Parl, Enth-Blade of Odinal. My voice may not have the command of yours in these streets, yet within our clan, our words of your voice will be heard in the mountains. You have our thanks."

The younger man bowed his own head in return and tried to keep his balance. His knee was not accustomed to him standing straight for an extended period and it was letting him know *all* about it. "It is taken and appreciated. If I can suggest it, Enth-Blade, please hurry back to Avager Hall?"

The Enth-Blade – whatever that was – nodded in reluctant agreement. "I feel that you are wise in that to request so. It will be done. May I make a request of my own?"

"No promises I can do it," Akaran replied. "I need to rest more than anything."

"That is the nature of my request," Parl replied as he reached into his robe and pulled out a small satchel of jingling with coins. "If your home is not near, find a place to stay the night. It is the least of what we can do. If it is near, take wine home with you. Find peace, either way."

The priest thought hard about refusing it but between realizing that there was probably enough to both get lodging *and* a fresh dose of cocasa? He caved and shamelessly took it. "Thank you, Enth-Blade. I will."

Parl expressed his thanks again with a smile and gathered his people. They were out of the alley before Akaran could say or do anything else – which was perfectly fine as far as he was concerned. Once the last of them were gone, he turned around and promptly tried to throw up into the gutter all over again.

Rmaci popped back into view again with a shudder, and the dress she had mockingly covered with herself dissolved into a cloud of fresh embers. She frowned and gently, almost comfortingly, put her hand on his shoulder. He couldn't even bring himself to care as another wave of nausea wracked his body. *"May I suggest finding a vendor for that dreadful root you've been chewing on? I daresay you need it."*

* * *

About three blocks away, Lady Anais was having a similar experience.

As she stepped out of *Heaven's Wing*, she let the door to the tavern close gently. The second she was out of sight of its clients, she balled her fists up and tugged at her dress so sharply she almost tore the faded pink velvet fabric. "Donta may well have been right," she groused quietly to herself, "these fools would have been better off had they learned to swim. How can you possibly claim to follow the God of the Waves if you do not plan or expect that the water will swallow what you hold dear?"

She continued to fume with every step she took away from the inn and into the first alley she could find to try to find some sense of composure. She kept the rest of it to herself, just in case someone might overhear her. *If my benefactor knew what I just had to give away to cover his tracks, he probably would've sunk them himself. Having to promise to find a way to get that one into a judiciary appointment or else he'll remember seeing a man in a striking red robe storm the Hall of Sea's Song?*

Utter lunacy. I hope whatever he was after was worth risking our efforts here in danger of failing. And what could he possibly mean by a 'plague of souls'? If the Order is unsettled, then it will make it all the harder to get assurances that the Urn is even in the Repository, let alone recover it.

Anais paused and twitched the end of her nose at that thought. *Unless he plans on recovering it personally and needs to distract the Lover's garrison. Drag them elsewhere so he can walk in and collect it himself?*

I don't like that thought. If he does, our agreement will be voided. Anais shuddered in dread at what that thought might mean. Then, with a frustrated sigh that you could almost hear at the end of the street, she started to rattle off the names of the various dopes that she was going to have to talk to and...

...and realized that she wasn't alone.

"Hmm. Hello?"

The question was greeted with silence. She pursed her lips and ducked down an alleyway to ensure some privacy with her stalker, should it be needed. There were far too many people on the streets tonight as it was, and she'd already heard what sounded like a screaming argument a few blocks away once already this evening.

"You may as well come out. I feel you."

Finally, a rough and raspy voice slithered out of the darkness over her head. "Granalchi. Sense much. Think little."

"Granalchi? Is that what you think I am?" she called out.

The raspy voice spoke up again. It was around her, behind her, but she refused to turn to look for it. "You reek of magic. It swarms about you."

Anais gingerly straightened up the collar of her dress and brushed a flake of dust off of her shoulder. "Well yes, I imagine it does. It's been a while since anyone noticed; I must say that I'm most impressed." *And annoyed*, she sighed to herself as her fingers wrapped themselves around a charm that dangled loosely from her belt. *Must this fail me, too?*

"Should be," the darkness replied slowly. "You hide well. Not perfect. No human ever is."

"No, humans most assuredly are not," she agreed with a slight nod of her head as she focused on where she thought the talkative shadow was. "Should I assume that you are as imperfect as I?"

"You think I'm human?"

"Who said that I did? Though I feel I'd much prefer it if you were." she quietly challenged as she began to weave a spell in the air. Little rivulets of mauve light spun around her extended fingers as she taunted the creature and worked her magic.

"Your type senses much," it threw back at her, before it added, "and thinks little."

The lady scoffed as little glowing streamers curled away from her fingernails and wormed their way into the shadows at her feet. "Please don't repeat yourself, my otherworldly friend. I am a busy woman and early repetition is not the sign of a mind worth knowing."

"I'm not otherworldly."

"Nor are you human, you say? That limits things, now doesn't it?"

It chuckled at her and she felt it shift in the shadows behind her head. It had thick, heavy aura to it. It wasn't like anything else she'd felt before – but it was starting to answer the questions she'd had about the recent murders. "Sense much."

"Think little, so I've heard," Anais sighed. The ruddy-haired woman flicked her fingers and watched as a thin strand of magic sprung from her fingertip and dove down into the shadows at her feet. It flickered, once, and the moment that it did, all of the shadows around her flashed the same pale purple color. All of them, except for one. The shadow that didn't change *did* flinch and move back behind a pillar holding up an awning. "Though now I see you."

It made a nasty little growl and slid back and forth behind the pillar like it was trying to stay hidden. Trying, maybe. Failing, absolutely. It would've worked on just about anybody else in the city – but not her. "I have seen you for longer," it taunted.

"Ah, men," she said with a bored shake of her head. "Always concerned with how long it takes them as opposed to their fairer companions. A curse of your gender."

The mocking cretin jumped from one pillar to another, a shadow still cloaking it. She still couldn't get a feel for what it was or why it was still trying to stay hidden even when it wasn't succeeding. "It will be quick... it will *feel* long."

"I can't say that's much of an argument in your favor," she chided. "Why don't you step away from the dark and let me have a good look at you."

The shape in the dark bounced from one pillar to another, and then it jumped up on top of a nearby building as if it was trying to show off its abilities. When she didn't react, it landed in front of her on all fours just long enough for her to see it's porcelain face and glassy eyes.

But most importantly, it took that moment to show off his long, silvery, dripping fangs. "Enjoy me while you have eyes!"

Both her jaw and her guard dropped as she realized what she was staring at. For every question it answered, three new ones took their place, and she didn't have time to deal with any of them. All she really had time to do was just scream out at the vile thing before it jumped at her. "Are you SERIOUS!? A –!"

Her assailant landed on her with his hands on her wrists to pin them down at her sides. Shocked into near-paralysis, she couldn't think fast enough to stop it. When it bit down on her neck, his joy lasted for all of a heartbeat. Or, it should've been a heartbeat.

Anais briefly heard Rishnobia's cackling accusation in the back of her mind as the damned creature looked at her with bewilderment on his face. *[Beats now does it?/News to this mote,]* she heard his voice mock even as her attacker had an entirely different response.

Her attacker scrambled away and spat clouds of reddish-gray sand out of his mouth as more of it poured down her neck. "YOU AREN'T –!"

Nor did he get to finish his thought.

A rough hand grabbed the back of his head and twisted him around. That, in turn, presented him face-to-face with one very pissed, very tired, very frustrated, and very *eager* man with a wicked right hook. Akaran's fist slammed into the murderer's jaw hard enough to split open his lip and send blackened blood flying across the alley. The impact knocked Anais's attacker away from his intended victim and sent him sprawling on the ground.

He didn't get much of a chance to retaliate, either. Each time her assailant so much as twitched Akaran planted the end of his cane between aggressor's eyes. The billowing blue fog around her attacker faded into a thin fog that gave away more of its body – but not enough for the exorcist make sense of it.

Not until Anais flung a ball of light into the air above their heads, at least. The flash made stars appear in Akaran's eyes and when he jerked in surprise, he missed an otherwise perfectly aimed blow that might've knocked his opponent out, if he'd been human. Instead, it gave the murderer a chance to recover.

A chance that didn't come without a little clarity. For the first time, the exorcist got a good look at the person – or thing? – that had he just *knew* had been making people vanish across the city for years. *This* was the murderer that had claimed the life of Odern, the monster responsible for Livstra, that had probably taken Lexcanna, and the sociopath responsible for untold levels of grief. He was right. He was wrong in some ways, but by and large, he was right.

Flawless ivory skin glinted in the light from Anais's spell, and his acorn-brown right eye blazed with fury. But his left eye was dead and speckled with gray flakes – almost like it had been carved fresh from a slab of marble. It was his outfit that explained a lot; not who he was, but how he'd been hiding.

You could mistake him for a huntsman, provided the shadows obscured his features – and that, the priest realized, was the point. The weathered brown leather cloak, belted to his lanky frame, swept over the ground as he stood up faster than he had any right to. His movements were nearly silent, partly muffled by the soft, supple leather encasing his feet and wrapping halfway to the knee and laced tightly with sinew and partly due to whatever magic the bastard was using.

Akaran didn't have time to dodge out of the way as the madman bolted forward and tackled him. He hit hard enough that the priest felt like a herd of cattle just plowed through his stomach. His knee twisted and buckled, which elicited a scream from his throat that you could hear for ten blocks in every direction. "YOU DARE LAY HANDS ON ME? YOU DARE FIGHT ANNIX?!"

After the brief heartbeat Akaran had to register the name, the murderer retaliated with a punch of his own that slammed into the priest's patch-covered orbital bone and it hit so hard that it rocked his head against the cobblestone passageway. The covering ripped away and exposed the brilliant blue rock he had nestled into the scar tissue where his eye had once been. A second punch split the exorcist's lip open and caused stars to erupt in his vision. When Annix's bloody fist hit his ruined eye a second time, there was an explosion of pain in the priest's face.

And an explosion of ice that lacerated the vampire's.

The coldstone flared a brilliant blue that completely lit up the alleyway and blew a torrent of tiny icy razors out from the socket that peppered Annix from forehead to throat. It wasn't enough to make him retreat, but it did cause him to grab at his bloodied face and howl in pain. It also gave the priest a moment to recover... and a moment to take another swing.

The impact of his punch sent the pale murderer sprawling onto the muddy ground and turned his cheek into a bloody pulp. It was more than either of them expected, and it even earned a gasp from Anais when she saw how much

damage he'd done. All he could do was stand there and stare down at Annix –
and look at his own fist in wonder.

He didn't mean to do it.

He didn't know he could do it.

He didn't know how he did it.

But when his fist landed across the sociopath's chin, it was covered in a
rough gauntlet of ice covered by jagged spikes. Blood, bone, and skin shattered
and ripped away from the murderer's face and left him in a heap on the
ground. Before the priest could capitalize, Annix rolled away and jumped onto a
nearby brick wall before he scaled it to the rooftops with a howl of rage.

The monster gone, Akaran took one look after it and finally relaxed down
onto the street. "Goddess, that wasn't… that couldn't… not human. What the
fisk was…"

Anais looked down at him and carefully offered him her hand. When he
refused it and settled for laying on the street instead, she marveled down at
him. "You. You saved my life. I am most surprised to see you again, but I cannot
express how grateful I am for your arrival. *Thank you*, exorcist."

"Goddess, my leg," he groaned before he caught sight of the ice still stuck
to his fingers. It melted away as he stared at it. "My *hand*. What was that?"

The realization that he didn't know what it was granted her a huge relief for
a number of reasons, not the least of which being that he probably hadn't
realized anything about *her* either. Instead, she pointed at the puddle of bloody
water under his fist. "That… that was an interesting trick. I didn't know the
Order trained elementalists."

"We don't!" he half-shouted as he tried to get comfortable. "I don't know
how I… Goddess. Ice. It had to be ice, didn't it?"

"Not a fan of the cold?"

"I hate ice," he grunted. "With all the fire in the heavens, I hate ice."

She made a mental note of that and pointed out the obvious. "Except for
right now, I assume."

Akaran ignored that particular thought and looked at her. It wasn't easy to
make out a lot of detail in the dark, but he was shocked that there wasn't any
blood seeping away under her palm. "Are you okay?"

The lady smiled and pulled her hand away. A faint trail of plum-colored
ether wafted up from her palm and the side of her throat. "I am fine, nothing
that can't be overcome with ease," she replied before she bent down and
helped him up. "I don't think the same can be said about you," Anais pointed
out as his leg started to twist under his own weight." A trickle of sand fell off of
her shoulder, but in his battered and muddled state, he barely took any notice
of it.

Rmaci did, and her eyes (and only her eyes) appeared in the shadows. They
narrowed at the woman and for a brief moment, she debated speaking up.
That moment faded when the priest's leg buckled completely and he fell back
down.

The buckling came with swearing. "Goddess. Not again."

After she took one good look at the bloody stain growing on the side of his thin wool leggings she bit back a curse of her own. "You need a healer. I daresay right now."

"Not. Again," he grunted as he tried to put weight on it a second time. When it failed, he painfully slumped back against the alley wall. "Goddess..."

"You're shaking, too," she pointed out. "It's not just from the pain, is it?"

"I'm fine, I'm fine."

Anais leaned in and used her fingertips to tilt his head up in the direction of the moonlight. "Ah, no. You most absolutely are not. You have the shakes, your eye is bloodshot, you have vomit on your breath. These are all things that mean you are *not* fine, young man."

He shook her hand away and sighed in not-so-idle frustration. "Do you... *fisk*... mind? You don't hear me judging your life choices."

"You're not drunk," she went on. "You're... oh. You're in withdrawal. What is it? Alcohol? Gaundant? It isn't tev'alin, is it? I know there's a dealer a few streets down that can help if it is..."

Akaran finally relented to the questions and ducked his head in shame. "Cocasa. I need it. I need it so bad."

That was a word she just didn't see coming. "Is that all? Only just cocasa?"

"It's... enough."

"It seems as that it is," she marveled. "Aren't they supplying you at the Manor?"

"They were. They quit. Said it was bad for me."

She made a disapproving 'tsk' sound and shook her head vehemently. "No such thing as bad when it mitigates pain. I will trust you to understand I do speak from experience," she replied as she pulled out a small clay coin from a pouch on her waist and placed it in his hand. "Come see me as soon as you can at Thesd Villa. I'll make sure you are taken care of."

It wasn't one of the Queen's crowns, that was for sure. "What's... what's the coin for?"

"That will get you past the gatekeeper. He's a bit of a curmudgeon, but he'll recognize it and let you through. It is the absolute *least* I can do."

Before he could ask, they were interrupted by a different — and extremely gruff — voice calling out to them. "HEY! What's with the screaming?"

The gruffness belonged to a guard that looked like he hadn't seen a bath in a month and smelled just about as bad. "Soldier! It's a relief you're here. We were attacked," Anais answered back with a sigh of relief so utterly *fake* that even the exorcist had trouble believing it.

The guard took one glance at them and put his hands on his hips. "Attacked. Right. Someone just ran down the street complaining about some fool yelling his lungs out. Go find an inn before I drag you both into the dungeon for disturbing the peace."

His smarmy attitude went away as Akaran turned slightly and showed off his ruined leg. "Shove it. I'm with the Order. We were just attacked. I need to speak with Henderschott. He knows me."

"You're... oh," he muttered as he caught sight of the cane laying nearby and eyepatch on his face. "You're *that* exorcist. Fisk."

"I need Cath... Maiden-Templar Prostil. And Henderschott. And you need to start searching the area. I just fought... it wasn't human. I don't know what it was but it wasn't human."

Before the guard could respond, Anais countered his request. "No. He needs to be taken to the Manor right away, and he needs help getting there. Get assistance right now."

In his defense, the priest tried to argue the point but he gave up when his leg buckled under him again. "What she said," he reluctantly agreed. "Please. AND Catherine."

"He's right. Go, and hurry."

The guard thought to fight them about it, but after one more look at the priest and his bloody leg, he gave a reluctant nod – and a surprising salute – and went off to find someone. *Must be a Lover*, Akaran muttered to himself. Then, to Anais, he asked, "Could... I hate to be a bother but... could you wait until after he comes back before...?"

"The man who saved my life is concerned that I may somehow find him to be a bother? You are no such thing," she chided. "The more important question is are you going to be okay? Can you walk? Do I need to find someone to bring you a crate or a stool of some kind?"

"Walk?" he questioned as he thought about how painful *that* was going to be. "Eventually? Fisk. What *was* that?"

"I don't know. It... it appeared to be a hunter? But why would a huntsman attempt to attack me?"

"Dressed like one," he countered, "but wasn't one."

"How can you be so sure?"

"Guild may be a bunch of assholes, but they don't hire subhumans," he deftly pointed out. As she pondered that, he pulled his legging up and realized he'd pulled open the gash on his knee again. "Son of a bitch. I'm so screwed."

Anais got a good look at it too, and she liked what she saw even less than he did. "That looks terrible!" she exclaimed as her mind started to churn through the possibilities – mixed with a mild hint of empathy. *He isn't rumored to be broken. He IS. What a poor man!* "Please, what can I do to help?"

His first answer was just to swear vehemently under his breath as he tore a strip of fabric off of his tunic. When she tried to help him turn it into a tourniquet, he pulled away and made an effort to get it done himself. "Tell me who in the pits that was. Why was he after you? I heard a name. Annix?"

"I will tell you truly, I don't know," she replied. To herself, the thought was a little darker: *But I promise I will find out – and find him myself.*

"What were you doing out? Maybe it was related."

An idle thought about answering honestly popped into her mind, followed by the realization she'd have to kill him if she did. *Save that for Donta, should it come to it,* she mused. "Oh. I was seeing what I could do to help the refugees. I have contacts all along the southern shores and I hate to see coastliners in distress."

He nodded slowly once the dirty, makeshift bandage was firmly in place. "That's... that's kind of you."

"No kinder than what you're doing. Thank you, again, for saving me."

"Consider it..." he began as a wave of vertigo snuck up on him, "...just me doing... my..." he tried to say as he sagged against her arms and crumbled down to the ground, "...job..."

When a detachment of guards arrived a few moments later, they found the lady holding his unconscious body in her lap. She looked distraught, scared, and a lot like she had been crying. It was an act, of course. If they could have read her thoughts, they'd have realized she was anything but a timid, scared woman afraid for her life.

If they could have read her thoughts, they would have turned around.

They would have turned around and never stopped running.

***

Hours later, Anais was safely back in her room in East Giffil at Thesd Estate. When Donta made the mistake of walking in unannounced, she nearly scratched his face off with a swipe of her hand and the etheric dagger that just as suddenly manifested in it. "Damnable woman! Be careful!"

She shoved past him and pulled every part of mossy-green curtains shut that decorated her room before she took the time to answer him. "Careful? You want me to be careful with the night I've had?"

"Can't be worse than mine," he grunted as he held up a pair of bloody hands. "Loose lips. Tongues wouldn't stay still. Removed those not needed."

She glowered at him with her hands on her hips. "I hope that their tongues were all you removed."

"Hope is a precious thing," he countered.

"How many?"

"Two," he admitted with a smug glint to his otherwise dark, navy-blue eyes.

It could've been worse, she admitted inwardly, but two was still too many. "*Dammit.* You had to do that *tonight* of all nights."

Donta didn't so much as flinch. The cocky son of a bitch almost never did. "Dead is silent. We needed silent."

"I told you no killing!"

He smirked as she went to work digging supplies out of a locked chest she kept hidden under her bed. Intentionally or not, she kept her back to him so he couldn't quite tell what she was getting out. "Only if we needed. I needed."

Anais looked up from her box of letters and parchments to reprimand him. "We do not need to draw attention to ourselves! People notice murder!"

"They don't solve it," he grunted. "Not here."

She finally found what she was looking for with a sigh of relief. "Our benefactor *did not* resurrect us from the Abyss just to swim in a bloodbath."

"They're dead," he pointed out. "Bodies buried. No risk. No matter."

"It matters a *great deal*, Donta!" the dark woman pointed out with an angry fire burning in her eyes. "New scrutiny on our heads is *not* what we need. Not tonight, of all nights!" she added as she pointed a twisted metal dagger at him – her prize from the chest.

The mercenary took one look at the Abyssian-steel dagger and realized (far later than he should've) that she wasn't just upset over his kills. "Calm down. Why are you angry? Less luck ensuring silence?"

"The ones that had to be bribed were bribed," she retorted. She took a deep breath out of (very) old habit and glanced down at a smear of oily sand that her hand had left behind on the dagger's flesh-colored leather hilt. "If you're so eager to kill people, then I have a mark for you."

"Hypocritical," Donta snapped. "Lecture me for killing. Then ask me to do it?"

"If not you, I'll have to send for the assassin."

"He would not help. Thought we agreed?"

Anais shook her head and started to weave a simple spell with her fingertips. Thin strands of pale brown light crackled in the air with her every gesture. "We do not need to add an additional player underfoot, but he is a piece I will bring to this game if I must."

He recognized the effect she was aiming for and stepped away before the spell could kick in. "You're serious. Why?"

"I wouldn't expect a vampire in the city, but here one is," the lady sighed as a cool gray light began to throb in the middle of the room. The runes she wrote in the air hung there for a few long moments before they faded away. "I'm willing to adapt when the time does call for it."

Donta's eyes went wide. She assumed it was shock from her claim – and it was. Just not the way she assumed. "Tried your own alchemy?" he accused with a hopefully-dismissive grunt.

She tilted her head as the last rune vanished and the color in her arms began to fade away as well. When the lack of color reached her neck, the magic she used to hide the gaping hole in her throat vanished along with it. "That priest you've taken a dislike to? The one with the gimped leg? He just saved me from having my head torn off by a Nithian," she snarled. "A NITHIAN!"

The sight of the wound caught him entirely off-guard. If she'd been human, shed be dead; if she'd been human, she'd have been dead with a hole a quarter of that size. She hissed through clenched teeth as she placed the edge of the *esth-atatic* blade against the hole and he could see strands of gray flesh start to stitch themselves back together as her prized weapon fulfilled one of its two purposes. "No. Not a Nithian," he argued before he realized what he was doing. "Doesn't bear their mark."

"I'd much rather it be one of the Council than a vampire loose on it's own without guid –," she started before she pulled the knife away and stared at him on surprise. "Ah, a moment, please? How is it you know what marks it does or does not have?"

"I... assume," he hastily replied.

"No, Donta, of all things you do, randomly assume is not one of them," she replied slowly as she sized him up. He still didn't flinch, but his otherwise stoic stance started to falter. Not a lot, but it was enough. "You *know*."

The debate to lie or not waged a short but heated war. He almost did, and then he saw a bulge on the other side of her neck begin to swell up. The spikes in his arms twitched in response, as if they recognized that a lie would start a fight he didn't want to have. "I know."

Anais nearly dropped the blade as her arms fell loosely to her hips. "You... you knew... that there is one of those *things* loose in this city? You kept it from me? What form of idiocy could you be playing at?"

"The dead hunter," her bodyguard tried to explain. "Him. He knew."

"Dead hunter...?" she asked before it hit her. "The one they found in the lake? There wasn't a bite mark on him. Granted yes, his face was destroyed but..." the lady mused out-loud before she reared back. "*You* killed him."

He flexed one of the spikes in and out of his palm. "He knew. Then I knew. Wouldn't help if he had told."

With the illusion gone, her otherwise shining silvery-tinted gray eyes had dulled to a cold clay color that matched the deathly pallor of the rest of her flesh. Even her hair had lost much of its vibrant sheen. "You..."

"Only choice," he quickly retorted. "Guild discovers? Oo-lo will. Army will. The city? Will be ripped apart. *We'll* be ripped apart," he stressed.

"You assassinated a huntsman to protect a vampire," she replied incredulously. "The same monster that just tried to rip out my throat."

There wasn't any sense in trying to deny it, but at least the other half of her accusation wasn't his fault at all. "Don't know why."

"You don't know why, but you know it existed," she countered. "A fact, I must add, that you kept from me. How long have you known?"

Donta looked away from her furious stare and debated lying again. "A week."

The bulge on the uninjured side of her neck swelled up obscenely and started to throb with a life of its own. "That long?!" Anais screeched. "We agreed – no secrets! Let alone one of this magnitude!"

"Your history. Your interests. Your past," he countered with a violent point of his index finger at her with each remark. "If you knew? You would make mistakes. You prepare to now."

She didn't even bother to try to hide how her hands were shaking from rage. "The only mistake I have made has been having my trust in you, it would so seem."

Donta shook his head again and stepped up to her. "Can't risk a war. You would launch one. Need your mind clear. You'd be distracted. You are distracted now."

"Of course I'm distracted – can you tell me you wouldn't be if it came after you?" she countered. "As far as a war? We're already in one. One vampire begets another. They *spread*, you daft goon. That's what they *do*. They *infest* and they spread. The fact that it hasn't been noticed by now only implies that it wants to hide more than it wants to breed. How are we to know when that will change?"

He – begrudgingly – had to admit she was right. "Sorry. But. Need your head clear. Can't risk your focus."

The lump on her throat settled down but her hands didn't stop trembling even as she lowered her voice. "While I do *appreciate* your concerns over my well-being, you *have* to know how this changes things for us."

"If it breeds? It will be discovered." her bodyguard pointed out. "If it's discovered? It will be hunted."

"Quickly, I would hope, though I don't give these idiots much faith in doing it," she snapped.

"*If* hunted? We are in danger," Donta went on without paying attention to her interruption. "If it's *not* hunted? We have time. If we hunt it? We will be distracted. Have the Urn soon. Then it won't matter."

"No, damnation to all, we won't," she sighed as she slowly put the gnarled end of her weapon against her throat. "Our instructions have changed once again."

His eyes narrowed and the air around him took on a decidedly acrid odor. "What do you mean?"

"Rishnobia has ordered us to do as little as we can," Anais answered as she pushed the metal deeper into her wound with a painful hiss. "We are to do the least necessary, speak to few, and wait. Our benefactor has some sort of *'plague of spirits'* in mind."

"The vampire?"

She gave that a short thought, and was able to dismiss it almost entirely out-of-hand. "No. No, I don't think so. The damn mote made it sound like it was something to come, not something already here. *Dammit*. Of all things, why a *vampire*?"

"Maybe it only arrived."

Anais was able to dismiss that just as quickly, too. "No. No I don't think so. An attack in the middle of the night? It was *stalking me*, Donta, *hunting me*. It's been here for quite some time. Likely longer than you've known of it."

He growled in disgust and made a show of sitting down across from her. "Cockroach with fangs. Let it be. We focus."

"Let it be?" she incredulously shot back. "After it attacked me? No, absolutely not. If it seeks my blood once, it will come for it again. Possibly now even more intently, given that I know what it is and that it knows what I am."

"It does? How?"

The lady – or whatever she was – wiggled the blade in her throat even as new skin continued to grow around it. "How do you think? It managed to draw blood."

"Sand," he pointed out.

"Blood is what we make of it," she contested, "and it pulses in my veins as much as it beats in yours."

Donta let the comment pass without giving it much attention. "You said the priest –"

"He saw nothing," Anais vehemently interrupted as the last of the gash healed up and skin began to crawl up the length of the knife. "Speaking of, we've been warned away from *him* and yet we are to gather as much on the sad excuse of a man as we possibly can. Rishnobia was very insistent about that."

Her bodyguard rolled his head back so fast that his hat nearly fell onto the floor. "Do nothing. Do everything. Could he speak clearly for once?"

"That would be a relief if it could be bothered to do so, but no, I don't feel as that we will ever be that lucky," his partner lamented. "However, *he* can wait. The vampire. That... that must be destroyed. Immediately."

"We can claim it. Train it," he mused.

She gave him another disgusted look. "It's not feral. It has a mind."

That remark didn't have the result she was hoping for. "You let it expose you. If it gets caught..." he started to muse before he realized how bad this might just turn out for both of them. "It could implicate me."

If she hadn't started working her illusory spell back into place, she would've thrown something at the fool. "Exactly," Anais snapped. "Any other task you've had, any other lead you are investigating, stop it. *Find it* and *kill it*. How certain are you of it's markings?"

"What?"

"You said it did not bear the mark of the Council of Nith. As foul as they are, if it is one of their representatives, maybe a bargain can be struck. They rarely have interests this far north but maybe they have a stake in what's buried in the Repository?" she pondered. "I can't think of any other reason that they'd be here otherwise. They learned their lesson centuries ago."

Donta frowned. "Not a great look. Briefly saw through thoughts. The Hunter's. Didn't see any. Think it's alone," he replied – without adding that he'd seen at least one more vampire with the one he'd encountered. It wouldn't do any good to further from their goal than she already was.

The broker sighed in frustration. "I hope you're wrong. That would make this worse by far. Just... find it and kill it," she ordered. "That's going to be paramount to accomplish if we wish to have our goals completed unmolested further."

"It will be done," he finally, after far too long for her comfort, agreed.

"It had best," she sighed. "Assume that we are not working with the safety of time at our hands. If that foolish boy realizes what he battled, the Oo-lo will burn everything down to find it themselves if they have to. The damn thing was idiotic enough to give a name. The only hope that I have now is that nobody believes the one-eyed idiot. If they do..."

Donta nodded slowly. "If he suspects? Will not end well."

Words that couldn't have been more of an understatement.

V. RIME AND PUNISHMENT
Lithdis the 25nd of Riverswell, 513 QR

It was Akaran's second trip to the Granalchi Annex, and three days into withdraw, it looked even gaudier than the first time. The cocasa he'd managed to buy with the Enth-Blade's coin had helped take the edge off enough that he wasn't trying to throw up all over Headmaster-Adept Telburn Gorosoch's desk. Sadly, it wasn't enough to dull the *pounding* headache that he developed the moment he crossed under the giant copper-gilded gateway leading into the campus proper.

The headache, of course, was made worse by actually having to deal with Telburn – but that was a problem that had a solution. The moment that the Headmaster walked into the small classroom-turned-meeting hall, he went straight to the point. "Alright. Let's make a deal."

Gorosoch didn't even bother to hide his surprise. The apparent (but not really) forty-something-year-old man took one look at the disheveled young priest and tried to imagine what could've possibly left him with a black eye and a split lip. "You're back. That's unexpected."

"That's going around."

"Oh? How so?" the older man asked as he made a show (though it wasn't intentional; just something he did as a matter of habit) of sitting down beside him. His tan robe with gold trim fluttered like it had a mind of its own as he got comfortable.

The flamboyant display didn't phase Akaran in the least. The throbbing pains in his face, hands, and knee, on the other hand, pulsed their irritation as the table he was leaning against bounced and shifted. "I got into a fight yesterday."

To the mage, it was the understatement of the year. "I can see that. Those scratches look absolutely painful."

"Can't feel them," he admitted. "Cocasa is underrated, honestly. I'm going to talk to my old instructors about adding it to our exorcism kits."

"I had heard it worked better than the Overseer wants to give it for credit for. The question is more about you got into a fight with. While you are someone that looks for violence – don't deny it, I can tell – you wouldn't get into a battle you couldn't win if you didn't have a choice. Since your mood is darker than your eye, I will assume you had no choice or no victory. Am I right?"

He was, but Akaran wasn't going to admit *how* right. "Don't know what the damn thing was. It wasn't human."

Of all of the things he figured the priest would've admitted to, that was almost on the bottom of the list. "An inhuman? In Basion City? That seems unlikely."

The dismissal, on the other hand, wasn't. "It was humanoid, moved faster than any man I've ever seen, and managed to jump onto a building from the street. Either it wasn't human or it was magically-enhanced in a way that I've never heard of."

"Well, magic can help a man do wondrous things," Gorosoch pointed out after a moment. "Surely it's more that than the former; Basion City is the safest place in the Kingdom."

"So I've heard," the younger man retorted with a disgusted snort. "It also did something you should know about – but I'll get to that in a minute. We need to make a deal."

"So you said. What do you want of me? I seemed to believe that you weren't interested in haggling with the Granalchi."

"That was before last night," Akaran replied with a pained sigh of frustration. Before the Headmaster could ask what he meant, he flipped his eyepatch up and drew out the bright-blue shard of the coldstone. "While I fought that damn whatever-it-was, *this* damn whatever-it-is activated."

The mere sight of it got the mage to sit up and pay close attention. "Activated?"

"Activated," he repeated. "I felt it just before it... turned on. Felt it pulse, felt... felt it in the ether. It pulsed, it turned my hand into a block of ice, and I broke that thing's jaw. It ran, ice vanished, stone stopped."

"Well then, *that's* intriguing."

The priest shook his head and paid for it with a fresh burst of pain in his face. "That's infuriating."

Gorosoch arched his eyebrow. "Infuriating? Sounds like it ended the fight. Might have even saved your life."

"You don't understand," Akaran almost-whined. "It was ice."

"Yes, and?"

"It was *ice*," the priest stressed. "Chunks of ice hard enough to break bone. I'd sooner slit my wrists so deep the blade would go out the other side and dance naked in the Grand Temple Promenade while I bled out than I'd ever want to see a single *snowflake* ever again," he grumbled as he prodded at the accursed chunk of otherworldly stone. "Pretty damn sure that the ice feels the same way about me."

With a bemused smirk, the Headmaster dismissed his complaints with a wave of his hand. "Come now; ice doesn't have feelings."

"Yes it does," Akaran retorted. "I've met it."

Gorosoch pursed his lips and sized up the younger man a second time. On one hand, it was hard to argue with him. On the other hand, it was hard to believe him. "I see why Ridora is forcing you to stay in the Manor. I assure you, the elements don't care for feelings one whit either way. They aren't sentient beings capable of expressing them, let alone understanding them."

"You're talking about the elements themselves," the exorcist respectfully countered. "I'm talking about their existence as sentient beings in their home territory," he clarified as the memories of his trip into Tundrala – and the impossibilities within – raced through his mind's eye. "Either way – it was *magic*. I used *magic*. And I didn't use *Her* magic. What in the pits is happening to me?"

"Ahhh," the Adept replied as the core of Akaran's concerns was suddenly laid bare. "I see your distress. Reasonable enough, all things considered. So what do you want from me?"

For a heartbeat, he had second thoughts. Just as quickly, he swallowed them and committed to the only solution that had come to him after a long night's worth of prayer. "Take this. Study it. Find out what it is, what it actually does. I'm sure that the Adepts studying the larger one back at Toniki already have some ideas. I don't know them, I've learned a bit about you, and you can probably confer with them."

"There's no 'probably' or 'sure' about it," the mage replied. "Three different research stations have already been setup to test how it was made and what the properties of the stone are." The revelation made Akaran's jaw drop and he started to voice his complaints before Gorosoch interrupted him. "*With* full knowledge of the Crown and your Order. I promise. You were far more blunt about the nature of its creation than what we had garnered from the actual site. Would seem that a paladin made sure that every portal you claim existed ended up shut, and more than half of Usaic's research incinerated."

"Thank the Gods," he sighed. "Steelhom always did think ahead."

"I'm not sure how much thinking was involved."

"More than the Academy did to keep tabs on that ice-mage," he huffed.

The remark stung the Headmaster and he stopped thinking of all the methods he could use to work the stone over. "I'm sorry; did you want my help or did you want to insult me?"

Chided, Akaran's shoulders drooped. "Look. I know you want to play with it. So, play with it. Test it, study it, get all the notes you want from it, get some first-hand experimentation. I get it back when you're done."

Gorosoch nodded in slow understanding, but when the other shoe didn't drop, he prodded the younger man for the rest of the story. "What, exactly, is it you get out of letting me entertain myself with it for a while?"

"That... rock... was given to me. Came with a prophecy. If it's going to start turning me into some kind of... of... frost golem or... cryomancer or... *something*? I want to know. And I want to know how to control it," he sighed as he picked up the little rock and stared at it for the thousandth time since he had been cursed to carry the blasted thing. "If it's..."

"...if it's going to let you do magic again, you want to know how to use it?" the mage finished.

"Wouldn't you?"

He had to nod in reluctant agreement. "Again, touche. Does this offer come with a time limit?"

"Just don't lose it," Akaran insisted. "I don't know when I'll need it again. "

"I assume you want it left in the city?"

The priest nodded and leaned back in his ornately crafted oak chair. "Do you know what that damned episturine called me before it ripped Her touch away from me?"

Gorosoch shook his head as he began to draw a rune on the desk around the piece of rock. "Hmm?"

"The 'Guardian of Winters,' of all pretentious things," Akaran replied. "The elemental-kin that uttered that prophecy I mentioned kept calling me that too. Pretty sure that I'm not supposed to let go of it for long."

The Headmaster nodded his head after digesting that and decided to play along with him – potential delusions or otherwise. "Fair enough. I want to interrogate you; everything you know about the stone and Usaic's work. I'll clear my schedule and –"

"Can't," he interrupted. "Not today. I've got to report the attack to Henderschott. And... someone else. You might be willing to handle the message. In fact, I'd appreciate it."

"I haven't been a messenger boy since I graduated from the third tier in the Academy. I think you'd be better finding a less-experienced courier to use," Gorosoch replied with a little bemused smirk.

Akaran bit his lip and set his personal dislike of the woman aside. "Yeah but I'm gonna assume you'll see her sooner than later. It's Elsith."

The mention of his wife's name drew him to a sudden stop. "Go on."

"The thing that attacked me? It was going after a woman. Anais Lovic. I don't know why, but I think I figured out why it's been so hard to catch."

"Hard to find? You assume then that whatever you got into a fight with is the same thing that my lovely bride has been hunting?"

"I do," Akaran replied.

"And you think it's some type of inhuman," the Headmaster mused slowly as he rolled the thought around his tongue. "She hasn't said anything that would lead me to believe that it was."

"With reason," the exorcist pointed out. "That's more or less what people like me deal with."

"I'll assume you have more reason than just training with the Lovers?"

Gorosoch pressed.

Akaran nodded and gingerly rubbed at the bruising on his face. "I do. It was late, and dark, but that thing? Whomever or whatever it was? It was dressed like a huntsman."

That got the Headmaster's attention almost better than anyone else the priest had said so far. "You don't mean to accuse the Guild...?"

"It's either in her house or it's pretending it is," he replied. "Ask yourself: if you wanted to be able to move through the city unmolested, and if you were actively stalking people at night, *and* you wanted to be able to blend in, who would you dress like? The Guard, the Order, or the Guild – pick one. Everyone else would run the risk of being stopped, challenged, or otherwise noticed. Unless she's got a roster of subhumans on her books, I doubt it's working *for* her."

"Distinction noted," the Adept said after a moment. "I'll make sure she knows right away though I don't know how much credit she'll give your accusation. I admit that I don't always keep track of her employees and the Guild has, on occasion, hired the occasional *adequately-civilized...* shall we say... abnormal outsiders?"

Akaran snorted. "If you mean the occasional troll or dwarf, that's true. Whatever the fisk did this?" he asked as he gestured at his newest injuries.

Gorosoch had to agree. "I grant, if it jumped on a building that does seem rule out the bulk of the other-than-locals she might or might not have recently welcomed into her ranks."

"If it helps her claim any of the writs that have been put out on the murders..." he replied with a slow shrug, "...then I don't care who she hires."

"Those writs have been suspended, didn't you know? Pending the arrest of the Eclipsian woman. Once that's done, the Overseer seems to think that'll solve all of our problems. There's little more the Guild can do in this case if I understood the fit she threw the other night correctly."

"I know the difference between 'suspended' and 'completed,' and how new evidence could make them active again."

His magic-using associate had to agree with that observation, too. "Not an inaccurate point, I'll agree. Fair and well, I'll make sure she hears it soon. I can't say she won't have questions for you."

"I can hope she won't."

The reply earned a throaty chuckle from the Adept. "An equally understandable position. It will be done – the stone and the message. Once I'm able to make sense of it, I will let you know. I've yet to see anything cross my desk that may help explain the rest of your situation, but I am still intrigued by your state."

"Thank you," Akaran sighed, "and... thank you."

"You're welcome. Tell me – before I go tug on my wife's ear, what does Catherine think of this new development?"

The mention of her name made the priest cringe, all to the Headmaster's interest. "Not much," he answered as he flashed back to earlier in the day. "She's agreed to look into it," he answered aloud before he indulged himself with an internal whine.

Had to blessedly beg her. She's of the same mindset of everybody else – there are no inhumans in the city and my senses are foggy from the cocasa. I think the only reason she even listened to me at all was because she'd heard the name 'Lovic' before, and she was willing to send someone to talk to her for a separate accounting. Paladin Faldine? I think?

The mage didn't push past his sudden silence and went back to work designing a protection rune on the desk. "Well. I suppose that I'm not too surprised. She thinks much of how the Order protects this town, but we've both seen how little that's done as of late no matter what extent you may think that people are or are not dying or going missing."

"Kinda hard to argue the dead people," Akaran quipped.

"It is a numbers game, alas," he agreed. "Though I do think you're right to be concerned by all of the above. I will be honest; I do not dabble in prophecies or the Divine or any other such trifling thing. I respect such matters for what they are when they are encountered, but my interest is not of them. Prophecies themselves are tricky beasts, and involve discussions of chronomancy I am not comfortable having."

The priest couldn't find any fault in that particular argument at all. He wouldn't admit it, but he didn't feel all that different about it himself. "That's fine. I just want to know what it is, and how I can use it. Soon, please. I can't... I cant keep... and now this...?"

"I understand," Gorosoch replied with a kindly, warm, and for a change, a not-at-all-condescending smile. "It would drive me to madness, as well."

***

In the middle of the city, the air had a tendency to actively reek of barely-washed laborers and the omnipresent rank odor of stale piss. It wasn't much of an improvement over the stench of dead bodies and fear he'd enjoyed in the mountains to the east, but it still did nothing for his stomach. Neither did his next conversation, and the person he needed to talk to didn't smell much better. "Don't even start with me," Henderschott warned. "I talked with your friend again. I don't think he did it. I don't think Erine did it. I can't do anything about it."

Grateful that smalltalk wasn't going to be needed, he went straight to the point. "Then why is he still locked up?"

The Lieutenant-Commander peered down at Akaran from his position on top of the garrison's ramparts. The two guards that had been engaged in a conversation with him prior to the exorcist's arrival made haste in finding something – anything – else to go do. "Because I can't let him out. I'm under orders."

"From who?"

"Paver," he spat. "That stuffy drunk is too concerned how it would look to give a damn about us not having someone in custody that I can't *do* a damn thing."

If anyone was surprised to hear him rant like that in public, they didn't show it. "Hold on. Badin is locked in a cage, you've got the 4th hunting for the Mother Eclipsian, and you're not looking for the *actual* killers because...?"

The accusation rankled the career soldier — but mostly because the priest was *right*. "We are. Just not in a way I'd like."

"What way is that?" the priest asked with a confused scowl.

"A way you won't like," Hender sighed loud enough for him to hear a full story below. "Everyone that gets close to anyone involved in this... *this*," replied with a wide gesture of his arms, "keeps ending up missing or dead. Just hope that when we find her body that it gives us a clue to go on."

The idea that the missing priestess of Lethandria had been murdered wasn't one that really surprised him, but the admission that the guard was leaning towards that idea did. "That's morbid even by my standards. What about the Overseer?"

"Paver has his hands tied, too. He's made it clear that if I 'waste' any effort or manpower into it from this point on, the only celebrations I'll have to worry about will be a farewell for when I'm reassigned to an outpost somewhere in the Alenic."

"At least there's fishing."

"And pirates."

"Pirates have wenches," Akaran pointed out with a little shrug of his own. "I mean... it could be worse. An ocean view, plenty of fresh fish, plenty of..."

Henderschott barked out a short laugh. "Wenches? We have those in Naradol. Speaking of which, why is it whenever there's word about a priest stirring trouble in that district, one matching *your* description pops up?"

The priest looked over at a small group of helmet-less soldiers leaving on patrol. "Your men have something against holy men with eyepatches?"

They didn't respond to the bait, but the Lieutenant-Commander did. "*I'm* developing something against holy men with eyepatches. I'm currently looking at *three* different reports from last night and I am not particularly fond of any of them. What do you think I should say about that?"

He thought about it for a moment and shrugged. "You're welcome might be a good start."

Henderschott gripped the edge of the parapet with both hands and glowered at the priest. "How about, 'How dare you threaten the head of the Woodmason's Guild with the gallows?' Does that work for you, maybe, possibly?"

"Sweaty guy? Looks like a mountain with fur? That him?"

"That's him. He said he was minding his own business when —"

"He say that his own business included leading a pack of drunken slobs that were picking a fight with some sods from the Odinal delegation?" Akaran asked before the guardsman could finish his thought.

Henderschott started to rub his eyes in tired frustration. "No, but those 'sods' put their names on a *second* report that doesn't exactly match the first one. You're in something of a much friendlier light. Which of the two should I believe?"

The priest pursed his lips and gave the one answer that he thought might keep him out of trouble. Or at least, the trouble to a minimum. "Believe that nobody died. Start with that, and work your way down."

"I don't know if I should thank you or yell at you," the 4th's Lieutenant-Commander finally sighed. "It would've solved some problems."

"Apparently it would've stopped any construction projects the Woodmasons had planned," Akaran pointed out. "I mean I can still order charges brought against him if you have something against bridges? Really, wouldn't mind."

"Only when I can't burn them. Moving on to this third complaint..."

As happy as he was that they were finally getting to the point of his visit, the priest had to steel himself for the rank he was *sure* was about to follow. "I asked for that one to be filed."

If looks could kill, the beady stare from Henderschott's pale-brown eyes would've been enough to do it. "If Lady Lovic hadn't confirmed your story..."

"Except she did," Akaran deftly pointed out.

"Except she did, and now she's connected to all this... *this...* too," he groused. "You are greatly enjoying making my life a living headache, aren't you?"

In response, the priest turned so that he could put the side of his knee on display. The wound had already seemed through its bandages and had begun to stain the outside of his clothes. "No."

The guard grunted but slightly. "You put it that way, maybe I can believe you. Anything you want to add?"

"I don't think it's human. Or if it is human, it's using magic I've never heard of. Dresses like a Huntsman, moves like a cat. I don't like it and would like very much for you to kill it."

"You would, would you?"

"Yes."

He drummed his fingers on the parapet and shrugged after considering his options for a few moments. "Well. I suppose I can give you some good news then."

Akaran leaned on his cane as he tried to imagine what in the world the insufferable soldier could possibly think might qualify as 'good' news. "That would be a first."

"As far as I'm concerned," Henderschott began, "I have no idea if what you got into a fight with is related to the recent deaths or not. As such, Paverilak can't tell me that I can't investigate it. I'd like to not believe you but *despite* your other issues you aren't some slack-jawed local that would confuse a bear with an evil spirit or something. If you say what attacked you isn't human, then I'm not going to argue with you. I'm going to be *pissed* about it but I'm not going to *argue* about it."

The admission actually made the priest smile and he enjoyed a brief moment as the helpful response actually helped him relax for a moment. "That is some good news. I'm going to guess it's less my involvement and more Anais being targeted?"

"You're smarter than you look," the guard replied. "Look. I don't like you."

"Same."

"But I don't think you're stupid," Henderschott added. "Hurt, pissed, a drug addict, prone to sticking your nose in places where it doesn't belong, and probably well suited to have to live in Ridora's little house of horrors? Yes. Stupid? No. You think that whatever attacked last night is more than some *other* weed-chewing shithead? Then it was probably more. I don't like it but nobody cares if I do or not."

Akaran pursed his lips and looked around to see if any of the soldiers listening were going to offer their own commentary or not. "I'm not sure if I should be insulted."

"Don't care if you are," the Lieutenant-Commander retorted. "So. I'll look into it. I'll get your friend out of the dungeon as soon as I can. Is it too much to ask that you're going to let me do my job and not interfere?"

"Yeap," Lover responded quickly. Then before the guard could respond, he went on to ask a question. "You said that anyone that gets close to 'this' ends up missing or dead and said that Anais is 'connected.' You've found something that links them all together, haven't you?"

"Links them together? I wouldn't say that I mean... well..."

"You mean what, exactly? "

Henderschott started to backtrack a little as he cast nervous glances left and right. "I mean that..."

When he let the thought trail off without clarifying anything, the priest narrowed his eye and tried to guess at what he meant. "Hender. Out with it."

The non-answer he got was just as important as the answer he was looking for. "Can I at least get you to go talk to your friend and see if you can't get him to calm down?"

Important or not, the brief feeling of hope he had died on the spot. "Why, what's he doing?"

As Henderschott started to explain, the answer was simple:

He wasn't taking any of this well.

***

Speaking of the scent of stale piss, the garrison's lower levels – specifically the underground dungeon – was full of it. That, the priest decided, was probably the least offensive odor; and given the run-down state of the dank hole masquerading as a prison, likely the least offensive of the offensive things to be found. That was starting with, though by no means ignoring, the state of his friend. "Oh now you're finally bothering to come see me," Badin growled at him.

The battlemage had seen better days by far. His typically scraggly beard had taken on a life of its own and they'd stripped him of his uniform. Instead, he had been given a wool tunic and matching pantaloons – though the phrase 'threadbare' should've been included in there somewhere. "They wouldn't let me earlier," his friend replied with a frustrated little sigh. "Didn't you get my letter?"

"I barely have enough light down here to see where I'm shitting," he complained. "You think I'm able to read what passes for your handwriting?"

"So you at least got it."

Badin huffed and crossed his arms. "Not a bloody lot of good it did."

"It was a letter, not a lockpick."

The mage huffed again and leaned back against the dungeon wall. Attitude and clothes aside, it looked he was still being fed and taken care of. "I could use one."

"I think I got you one," Akaran replied before he started to explain both the attack the night before and how Henderschott doesn't think he's involved in anything overly nefarious.

"Well if that son of a bitch doesn't think I'm did anything, how about at least sending down something decent to eat?"

"Will that help you calm down?"

The mage stormed over and rattled the bars of his cage with a snarl. "I'm rotting in the dungeon! How calm do you think I should be?"

Akaran flinched and gestured in frustration. "I... I don't know. Maybe I can try to get you transferred over to one of the Order outposts. The cells are better."

His friend paused mid-rattle and titled his head. "Why do priests have dungeons?"

"If you love someone, keep them close. If you don't, keep them in chains," he replied with a little shrug. "And if you really love them, do both."

"That doesn't make me feel any better," Badin replied, and after a moment's pause, added, "Also, that's a little creepy."

"An old quote from one of the Sisters," his friend explained. "She liked to spend time with new trainees whenever they volunteered to follow the exorcist's path."

The mage bit his upper lip and gave him a slightly-concerned look out of the corner of his eye. "That's a lot creepy."

"Either way," Akaran deflected, "Hender said he's doing everything he can to get you out."

"He put me in here. Why can't he let me out?"

"The Maiden's Betrothed is forbidding him. "

Badin grimaced and let go of the bars with a defeated shrug. "Oh, son of a bitch."

"About how I feel about it," Akaran agreed with a shake of his head. He looked over his shoulder to make sure nobody else was heading down into the cells and quietly slipped a piece of smuggled sweetloaf between the bars. "No matter how many times I heard that you were arrested, nobody has explained to me *why*. What were you doing that made them think that you were involved?"

"Helping."

"With what?"

The mage took the treat with a thankful sigh. "Erine. Gods above know it, and *your* Goddess is probably at fault for it, but I love 'er. Anything she's wanted, I've done. Just happened... well."

"Well what?" Akaran pressed.

Badin took a bite of the spiced bread and noticeably sagged with relief. "Erine had gotten the idea in her head that whatever killed Odern – and probably that Liv woman – wasn't local. Not just not local, but not..."

"Human?"

"Yeah," he explained. "No offense to your chosen profession but I've had just about enough of *that* type of shit for the rest of my damn life."

"It was a calling more than a choice, but none taken," he said as he pointed at his black eye and the scrapes on his knuckles. "She doesn't think it's human either?"

"Aren't you supposed to be, I don't know, *healing*?"

Akaran just smirked at his friend. "To be fair, *it* found *me*."

The battlemage let that go without complaint. "Well. I don't know what she thought it was. She never told me. She just had me looking for it. Said that she was confident I could protect myself."

"You are damn good at what you do," the exorcist agreed.

"Boy, you don't know how close I've come to testing the limits of these runecuffs," Badin replied as he held up both of his wrists and showed off the heavy iron cuffs fastened around them. They were so large they almost looked like (poorly fitting) bracers an Order paladin would wear. "If I thought I could get out of them, I'd have blown a hole in the roof and been out trying to find her by now."

"I'm surprised you haven't tried," he admitted.

The mage gestured over to the corner where a head-sized chunk of bricks were missing and the earthen floor had been blackened with what appeared to be an energy discharge. "Who said I didn't? I just couldn't hold my dick to take a piss for a day after. Just haven't seen the *limits* of these damn things yet and I'm about damn well ready to test them again."

Akaran made a point to note *that* and immediately felt worse for some of the still-magically-inclined residents in the Manor. "Ouch. Well – what was she having you look for?"

"Shit I wanted to talk to you about," he replied. "Weird shit. Dead plants. Dead fish. 'Things dying in places things should not die,' I think is how she said it. Also had me looking for people with 'bites of no natural animal.' Oh – and destroyed crops."

Every word he said made whatever Erine's idea had been sound worse by the syllable. "Destroyed crops? She say what kind?"

"She said depending on what was destroyed, she'd know what to do," he replied with a frustrated little sigh. "I didn't find anything, but I think she did. She was supposed to meet with Lexcanna... told me that she wanted the Order of Stara on her side before bringing in your people."

"Guess I can understand that," Akaran reluctantly admitted. "I don't know what kind of relationship she and Catherine have though I know that the Order of Love and the Order of the Cloaked have had skirmishes in the past. How certain do you think she was that it isn't a human using some kind of new magic?"

"Any of those things sound like a flesh and blood asshole's been causing all the drama?"

"Alright, that's a good point. But how did that entangle you?"

"That's the shitty thing of it," the battlemage complained. "Erine thought that one of those people at the Manor might have had a hand in it, or at least, knows someone that does. Had me out looking for her."

Coupled with the rest, that revelation did absolutely nothing good for the priest's mood. "A patient? Who?"

Badin shook his head. "Not a patient. Some woman – name of Raechil. Her sister is –"

"Kiasta; Erine's bodyguard," Akaran interrupted. "We've met. As far as Raechil goes, she's one of the assistants to Ridora... or was, I guess."

"Was? What do you mean was?"

"She's missing. Nobody's seen her since you got arrested."

The mage's face fell and he started to nervously tug at his beard. "Well. Dammit. We couldn't find Kiasta either. I was hoping that maybe Lexcanna would have heard something about either of them."

That made the priest frown all over again. "Why? I can't imagine that they would have anything in common?"

"Ah, you'd be wrong," his friend replied. "See, Lexcanna helped raise the girls after their momma passed years ago. They kept in touch, even after they moved on to different things."

"And different Goddesses. That's sweet."

"More than sweet," Badin corrected. "It's one of the reasons that Erine and Lex got along so well. Kiasta and her sister helped bridge that divide. They did more for the city than most of the nobility, best I can tell, and damn next to nobody knows about it."

"Except now, Erine is missing, Lexcanna is dead, and the sisters are in the wind," Akaran pointed out.

The mage nodded along. "Except for all that. And I'm stuck in this damn cage without being able to help. I'm really, really worried about Erine. If she's right, pits, if *you're* right, then it's hard not to assume…"

His friend reached through the rusting iron bars and squeezed Badin's shaking hands. "Hender is looking for the thing that attacked me last night. It was dressed like a hunter, so I've made sure that the Guild knows what to look for, too. They won't keep you locked up for much longer, I'm sure. Soon as you're out, we can get to work."

"They better not," he grumbled. "I'm getting damn tired of this. I want to be out there looking for her."

"I'll do everything I can. I promise. I *absolutely* promise."

The battlemage gave him a tired, pleading look, and for the first time in his life, outright begged for help. "Please, man. Please. Erine? She… she's worth the world to me. I need her. I need to be out looking for her. If nothing else, you need all the friends you can get."

***

They were right. They needed a friend.

On the other side of the Kingdom, on the top floor of an inn that charged more per day than most men would earn in a year, news about the vacant leadership positions in the Fleetfinger's Guild in Basion City finally reached a pair of ears that weren't at all happy to hear about *any* of it. He was a short, pudgy man in the ugliest dark orange jacket quite possibly known to humanity. He was also in pain, and he doubled over the balcony rail he was standing beside after the messenger retreated to somewhere safer a few moments later.

He didn't scream, but he clutched a shadowy spot on his face with bloody fingers and growled under his breath. That splotch just trembled and a little tendril flicked off of his skin. Then it doubled briefly in size in the heartbeats before it disappeared back from view. That alone was a brief favor.

And favors were important to him.

A man couldn't lose track of his favors that were owed; it would simply couldn't be done. Not losing track of the favors meant you couldn't lose track of the people that owed them. Not forgetting who owed you favors meant you never forgot your friends.

And he had no intention of forgetting his friends.

No matter how badly Akaran – *and* Badin – may have wished otherwise.

VI. HUNTING TRUTHS
Zundis, the 28ᵗʰ of Riverswell, 513 QR

There was a running joke in the Academy that an exorcist should always get the true name of anyone who is mean to you in your life, for the simple reason that after they die, you may encounter them again.

Lady Lovic's remark that Jeitee Ovokon was a 'bit of a curmudgeon' was something of an understatement. Whenever the seventy-some-odd-year-old dropped dead (*if he ever drops dead*, Akaran idly wondered, as a different old adage about 'taking over' popped into his mind) would be the day that the Abyss would either rejoice in victory or quake in fear. As it was, the gatekeeper could simply be said to be, 'too mean to die,' and 'too cranky to care.'

Anais had no idea what to make of it when she saw the priest write his name down in his journal before he entered Thesd Estate. "Lady Lovic," Akaran began with a bow of his head as he fumbled to put the notebook away, "thank you for agreeing to see me without any notice."

"Anais, please," she replied. Even at this ungodly morning hour, she looked so purely *regal* that she could've given the Queen a run for her money. "Lady is only for those stuffy prats that wander the halls of power. Have no worries about the visit – it is the least that I can do. You did save my life, after all."

"About that – that's more or less why I'm here," he said with another short nod. "Though, I gotta say you were fairly spot on about the gatesman."

"Yes well. We all have our duties, and he does his well enough. He would not be employed if he was nothing more than sunshine and sparkling dew. Nor, I would say, would you," she pointed out as she held open the door to the interior manor.

Once inside, the self-ordained information broker helped him find a chair and offered him a much-needed drink that would've gotten him scolded for back at the Manor. Needless to say, the goblet's wine vanished before his host could take a seat herself. "They never put 'be polite' on the job description," he agreed.

"Simply, 'be effective,' if what I hear about you is accurate."

Akaran smiled at her, though it wasn't a warm one. "You have a reputation for hearing a lot of things."

Anais arched her eyebrow and rested her face into her right hand. "Is that why you're here?"

"Actually, yes."

She tapped at the side of her nose with one of her long, pale fingers. "I daresay I suspected as much. Your name has been making the rounds – though after the other night, I can understand why. What can I do for you?"

"I don't think that there's any simple way to put this," he began as he made his case. "I'm going to assume you know that I've been looking into the matter of Odern Merrington's death, yes?"

"As well as the untimely demise of Livstra Oliana and a few others, yes. Should one assume that you're also now intrigued by the untimely passing of the High Priestess of Stara, as well?"

He answered with a short nod (and a pained wince – the swelling from the fight three days ago hadn't gotten much better). "And the disappearances of both Kiasta and Raechil Lamar."

She made a quiet little, 'hmm' noise as she pondered Akaran's task. "If you're looking for them, one would also assume that you would love to find the Mother Eclipsian? I also have come to understand that you are friends with the poor man currently enjoying a stint in the dungeons?"

The priest leaned back in his chair and studied her face carefully. "You know what I mean? I guess what I heard about you was right."

"Maybe," she replied with a faint shrug. "I can't judge everything you've heard without knowing what that is."

"What I've heard is that there's nobody in the city worth a damn that you haven't either *had* dealings with or haven't been trying to *get* dealings with," he replied as he leaned in slightly and habitually rapped the end of his cane on the wood floor. "You're someone that likes to make everyone's business her own business, and someone that likes to know whatever there is to know."

Anais considered looking insulted, but let the indignation move to a sweet, almost predatory, smile. "I would say more that I make my living trafficking in truths. Knowing something is the only way to make a profit from something else."

"What do you know about their deaths?"

"More than what I know about you," she replied as that smile grew – both in size and in guarded hostility. "Maybe we could find a way to even that out?"

The priest sighed and looked down at the floor for a brief moment. "I had a feeling that you'd want to go in that direction. If you know me, then you know why the Granalchi have been trying to pry as much out of the Order as they can since the... incident... in Toniki."

"Yes, though I'm wise enough to understand that if you aren't telling *them* you wouldn't tell a lady such as *myself*. However, my interest is more in how *you* have been stripped of magic – a rarity upon rarities," she added as she poured herself another cup of wine from a nearby decanter. "Though it is less that the rarity is the question, but the *how*. I know quite a few people that would *truly* love to know how to do such a thing."

A painfully brutal headache took hold behind his eye as Rmaci walked through a nearby wall and glowered at the purveyor of secrets. The wraith left a bloody smear behind as she moved through the wall like it wasn't even there, though it dissipated from view just as suddenly as she arrived. "*I don't like this woman, Akaran. Be wary of her.*"

Great, you're back, he snarled to himself.

"*I never left. You talk to yourself far too much, at that.*"

He looked up and over Anais's shoulder with alarm. *You can hear my thoughts?*

She tasked her split tongue and then stuck it out of a hole in her cheek to wiggle it at him. "*Of course I can. I am quite literally in your mind – did you forget?*"

"Fisk."

The gossip arched her eyebrows and stopped, mid-drink, to reply to him. "Pardon?"

Rmaci chuckled while he tried to make up for the little slip. "Sorry. I... I twisted my leg wrong," he lied (pitifully, at that).

Lie or not, she seemed to accept it. "Ah, yes, a cause for swearing if there ever was one."

"You have no idea," he grunted as he reached down and squeezed his knee. It didn't do much for the pain, but every time he did it, the pressure under his skin stopped *throbbing* and turned into more of a *cutting* pinch.

As he debated – and not for the first time – if that was a good thing or not, he missed the lines around her mouth tighten. "Oh. One would be surprised at what I know of pain." The way she said it got his attention, but she composed herself before he could find a way to press. "Such unpleasantness aside, should I assume that you know how this works?"

"How what works?"

"You ask me for information and I do the same. Either information or service offered for information or service."

Akaran started rubbing his eye to see if that would help make that pain go away, or at least temporarily hide the burnt, dripping wraith from view. "If you're planning on asking me to tell you how to neuter people with magic, I can't."

"I know plenty of ways to neuter men *without* magic, good priest," she replied in equal parts statement and warning, "though the question is, *can* you not tell me because you don't know, or *will* you not tell me because it is a secret of your Order?"

The priest grudgingly shrugged as Rmaci cackled to herself in the corner. "Mostly the latter, but truthfully, I don't know. It didn't happen... locally. Let's say that."

Her gray eyes lit up and she set her silver goblet down with a clink "The cloud of emotions on your face does not imply that your 'local' means Basion, or possibly even Toniki, does it? I do know what type of priest you are — I assumed it was Abyssian by some nature."

For whatever reason, getting her interest in the subject was more uncomfortable to deal with than anything that Gorosoch had put him through. "It was... hard to explain. It wasn't local. That's the only way I can describe it for you."

"So not Abyssian," Anais quietly mused. "If it was you'd warn me against it for fear of eternal damnation, I assume. Interesting."

The wraith made a slicing gesture across her throat with the flat of her hand, and much to his stomach's disgust, the gesture opened her throat all the way to her cervical spine. He tried to desperately focus on the gossip rather than the grotesque show hovering in the air behind her. "Now you've hit the realm of, 'under seal of Order,' and I can't comment further. I can offer coin, if that would help convince you that my cause is just."

"Few people ever must offer coin to do the right thing in life," she deftly pointed out. "Or haven't you yet learned?"

He bit his lip ever so slightly and debated walking away then and there. "As much as I would love to hope that your interest in helping me would be out of the goodness of your heart, you don't ask a blacksmith to make a sword without iron and you don't ask a mason to lay bricks without offering water."

"Nor do you ask a lady that trades in information to do so without being willing to offer something in exchange."

"More or less," he agreed.

She flicked her tongue against the inside of her cheek In a short, steady rhythm. "You are a wiser man than the rumors give you credit for. Well, I'd be lying if I said that your Order isn't absolutely *full* of secrets I'd love to have but I am not so foolish to think that you'd be willing to part with them."

That earned her another shake of his head (and earned him another stabbing protest around his eye). "Secrets can be weapons. I'd like to not arm people that may use them to hurt us."

Anais almost – almost – looked indignant at the comment. "You think that I would?"

"If I did, I wouldn't be here," he retorted. "But who's to say the person you trade to wouldn't?"

Her eyes lit up again and she took another long draw from her goblet before responding to his remark. "*Much* wiser than the rumors suggest. So if you're unwilling to trade secrets, and I have no desire for coin — what do you offer?"

That, he had an answer for. "Vengeance and protection."

Once again, he found a way to surprise her, even if slightly. "Ohhhh. Now I like the sound of that, though I already have one bodyguard. I'm not in the market for another at this time, and... please, find no offense in my words, but I prefer one that can run to my side when the time calls for it."

I miss running, he whined to himself.

Happy to finally have another moment to steal, the wraith flopped onto the floor and kicked her bloody, skinless legs lazily in the air. "*Time for that once you're dead. The Abyss will teach you the value of a good sprint.*"

It took every ounce of willpower in his body not to fire something at her in retort. "No, no offense," he replied to Anais, "but your bodyguard isn't *here*, and the thing that attacked us is still out there."

She gave him a slight nod with the barest hint of a tilt of her head. "Both a valid point. I suppose it should go without saying that I am searching for it?"

"I assumed."

"Then your offer...?"

"I'm hunting for it too," Akaran pointed out. "So I would assume that you would like me to share anything with you that I might know so we can find it."

She pursed her lips and he knew he had her support before she gave it. "Do you plan on killing it?"

"Depends on what it is. Do you?"

The gossip demurely coughed and took another small sip from her goblet. "It would be unwise for me to plan for circumstances that may come to pass without full knowledge of what it is I seek. Though if what attacked us is the same thing that has been preying on the city at large..."

"...then it's less of a question of 'if' I plan to kill it as much as it is 'how,' isn't it? If it's inhuman, it's fair game, but if it's not..."

Inwardly, she blanched, but outwardly, she kept her face even and her demeanor calm. "Fair game? That is a way to say it. Well, while I agree to these terms, there is more that I can offer that you may find worthwhile – and I could use a man with your propensity towards violence to carry it out."

He raised his eyebrow and started to study her carefully. "Violence is a necessity but not one I bargain with. If you're looking for a thug, look elsewhere."

She lifted her finger away from her mug and made a slight gesture in the air. "All actions can be given a veneer of need should one seek to justify it enough. I promise though – what I offer, and the violence that would be inherent to it – are not unjustifiable. You, of all people, would agree – I think."

"Lady Anais, truly? I'm not interested in being someone's instrument of suffering."

"You are, by nature of your calling," she deftly countered. "You are simply picky of who you serve and why – both things are admirable, of course. Hear me out?"

After one very long heartbeat (and a sinking feeling in his stomach developed) he caved – a little. "I'll listen. Won't promise I'll act."

The information broker smiled and jumped into her offer before he could rethink it. "First, I know you'd see through any attempts I make to obfuscate my interest with my offer. So: if you give your word that you will look into this matter for me, then I will gladly direct my own efforts into tracking down the Mother Eclipsian. She is not someone that I have ever had dealings with, and does not represent a group that I have any great desire to entertain."

"That surprises me," he marveled, though he tempered his shock just enough to stay neutral. "As among other things, the Goddess of Night is known as the Keeper of Secrets."

Anais nodded and set her goblet down. "Yes, She is. She keeps them. Not Someone inclined to share them. Thus, not Someone I interact with," she pointed out. "However, a great many people that I cater to *do*, and if Erine or her minions have reached out to any of them to find a place to hide, then I might be able to help her turn up."

Behind her, Rmaci piped up again and actually showed a little interest in it herself. *"That might get your friend out of the dungeon sooner than later. I don't like her – there is something about her that's rubbing me the wrong way. Yet, it may be worth it if you take the time to entertain her, Akaran."*

As he pointedly ignored the dead woman, he had to admit she might be right. "What is it you want in exchange?"

"Do you know of a man named Se'daulif Ocsimmer, by any chance?"

"No? I've never heard of him."

"Then you are a luckier man than I am a woman, I won't deny," she replied with a disgusted little curl of her lip. "This particular man is a shiverdine, of all things. Imagine – one such as he in a city such as this."

The priest frowned and scratched at the messy mass of hair on his chin as he tried to remember what that word meant. It sounded familiar, but it just... "You'll have to clarify. I'm not as traveled as you."

She swelled up a little and gave him a smug, 'I know more than you,' smile that just didn't set well. "Ah, well, yes. Of course not. I shall assume, at least, you know of the Sycian peoples?"

Akaran nodded but his face gave away his disgust. "The whole Order does. Desert-dwellers, for the most part. Utter savages."

She pursed her lips and tilted her head as she tried to think about what could've earned his derision. "The 'savages' part is not as accurate as one may have been told. Their culture and their peoples are in many ways far more advanced than what you would find even in more rural areas of this Kingdom. Surely more grand than what the Midlanders espouse. An argument could even be made that their riches and grandeur is greater than anything that the people of the mainland could ever aspire to."

He shook his head and very firmly cracked his knuckles like he was getting ready for a fight. "Their *culture* is built on the back of slaves and demon-worship. I don't *care* how *grand* they are. They are red-eyed, dusky-skinned freakish Fallen-worshipers that have banished the entirety of both the collective Orders of Light *and* the Guild from operating in their territories."

"Ah, but only because your Orders would sooner see their kingdoms turned to ash," she returned politely, though the ferocity and open disgust in his tone actually set her back. "Though I must admit – I am surprised to hear such racial drivel from you. Bigotry is not a banner that looks good hanging on your neck."

The priest frowned and tried to tone down his open revulsion. Anais wasn't wrong about the Order – any of the Orders. If an excuse ever came around to declare open war on the Jewels of Sycio, as their seven grandest city-states were known as, it would be taken in a heartbeat. They weren't alone, either. More than a few powerful guilds, politicians, nobles, and *others* felt like the desert kingdoms were one bad idea away from triggering another event like the Fall of Agromah.

Absolutely nobody, of any stripe, wanted to risk another near-apocalypse again. Least of all the Order of Love – though with luck they wouldn't get blamed for it (again). "If you're implying that I hate them because of where they're from or what they look like, you're wrong. It's what they do that pisses me off."

"There is a fine line between the two," she countered. "Consider how you speak and you won't be accused of crossing it. You did just decry them as freaks and you offered no difference between, say, the necromongers that cavort with the fallen or the fishermen that simply, well, fish."

"I call them *freaks* because they employ the dead as labor. Necromancy is banned in every tract of civilization known to man, except for theirs," he argued. "They openly consult with the Fallen and worship the damned. To them, bringing the dead back to life is just... part of their *society*. They *enslave* them to put them to work. It's not unforgivable but it's... repugnant."

Anais pursed her lips and gave him credit for part of it. "Well, I will agree with your dislike of all things slave trade. Which brings us back to the good Ocsimmer. Shiverdines are just that – slavers. The living, however, less the damned."

That pulled him away from all the lessons he'd had about the 'Golden Sands' – and all the horrific stories he'd heard whispered about it from one priest to another. "A slaver? In Basion? Why?"

"Well, as it turns out, those 'freaks,' as you have said, have recently caught the eye of the Queen in a more... shall we say, constructive way, though still in parts full of the violence and death that you decry." Before he could ask what she meant, she went on. "In recent years, a particular style of gladiatorial combat has taken the Jewels of Sycio by storm – and while men fighting is not exactly a 'new' hobby or interest, the Sycians have taken it to a new level."

The news didn't set well with him, though it wasn't the first time that he'd heard of a new type of bare-knuckle brawling making the rounds. "What does that have to do with a slaver?"

"Combat needs combatants – and combatants from far off places fetch a pretty coin on those sandy shores. There's quite a living to be hand from it, from what I have heard."

"You're not suggesting that he's here to kidnap people, are you? You don't think he's the one responsible for the disappearances?"

"As easy as that would make your life and mine, no," Anais replied with a wistful little sigh. "While he *has* recruited some of the desperate – and a few retired souls willing to fight for causes that are less mercenary and are more entertaining – I've found nothing to make me think that he is our kidnapper."

Akaran frowned and took a drink of the sugary sweet wine she'd given him. "Then what's he here for?"

"While neither Basion City or Port Cableture is not what one would consider a major port of call for trade between Dawnfire and the Jewels, Cableture is often a place where pirates and other malcontents in the Alenic are brought to justice," she answered.

The truth was laid out right between the lines without her even saying it. "You're not suggesting that the Queen is considering getting into the slave trade, are you?"

"Suggesting? No," she demurely declined. "*However*, the pirates and privateers in the Alenic have not been offered the same rights and considerations in recent memory as even lowly criminals in the Kingdom are. Rights of citizenship and all that nonsense – with a significant disdain still held by the Crown after the Privateer Wars."

He had to take another drink to calm the heartburn building in the back of his throat. Criminals that didn't have the protection of the Queen's citizens being offered to a slaver? A Sycian slaver, at that? To be sent to fighting pits an ocean away?

And all with permission from the Queen. "That's... horrific."

"I must agree," Anais replied with a disgusted little shudder. "But there are levels of horror one grows accustomed to when one is considering the needs of society. Of course, as much as we agree that such is detestable, I am aware that you are bound by Queen's Law and your own morality is restricted when it comes to things that you may or may not be allowed to tolerate by sword point."

Meaning, he surmised, *that I don't have any right to throw him into a dungeon for doing what the law is allowing. Damn.* "Which brings me back to my earlier point: if you want me to go beat someone up, I'm not going to. Even if I think I should."

"Ah, but what I have is a way for you to change your tune and do us both a favor – your morals and my purse. What if I told you that I had reason to believe that aside from preparing contracts between Maiden Sanlain's Betrothed for inconvenient prisoners, he *is* allowing for the trafficking of assorted objects into the mainland that you and yours might find... problematic?"

"Problematic how?"

"You do take a dim view on artifacts that should be left in Agromah, don't you?" she asked with a smile as sweet as the wine and twice as threatening.

That, as she planned, was all it took to bait him into doing exactly what she wanted. She barely kept the smile off of her lips as he sat straight up and nearly dropped his goblet on the floor. "*That's* a crime that can have you punished by hanging."

"And here I thought you would be opposed to violence," she replied with a very faint purr to her voice.

"If you're aware of relics being trafficked from the Cursed Continent, then as a citizen of Dawnfire you have a solemn duty to inform an agent of the Crown at once."

Anais shook her head but the smile on her lips was bright enough to light up the room. "Ah, but there you're wrong – I am not a citizen of Dawnfire. I claim my home in the Free Cities of Ameressa. I'm under no such obligation to follow that decree."

Akaran pursed his lips and looked her dead in her eyes. "But."

He was hooked – and they both knew it. "But indeed. I am willing to. Having him removed from play would make me feel much better about where I lay my head."

"And why would that be? What would you get from it?"

"I mentioned that bigotry is not a flag that suits you. Unfortunately, there are others in this city that wear it with pride. If I show you what I have against the shiverdine, I expect that you will see to it that his influence in the city goes away. In turn, several people in assorted positions of power in Basion and places beyond will show some fondness in my direction," she answered with that same sickeningly sweet smile and purr. "Yours, too, depending on how you roll your dice."

He slowly rocked his cane back and forth between his hands as he digested her answer. The gossip was hiding something – there was absolutely *no* question of that – and it felt *wrong* to even consider helping her with it. Especially if it was just being done to curry favor somehow. "This feels awfully like an assassination attempt," he finally remarked.

"Of the character, not of the person," she elucidated. "Though if the latter happens, the tears I shed will be few in number."

"Why me, and why not the Guard? You could probably leverage Henderschott without much trouble."

"You assume I haven't considered that," the gossip dismissed with another annoyed wave of her little finger. "Please, give a lady more credit."

Akaran couldn't stop himself from rolling his eye. "Of course; I apologize. Doesn't answer the question though."

"Eh," she uncharacteristically muttered with as little care as she could. "I expect Hender would attempt to do something about the situation, but let's be truthful: Se'daulif is here on a diplomatic mission to establish a lucrative trade route to and from Sycio with Paverilak and Overseer Hannock. I wouldn't expect such charges to stick even if I tried. I'm sure he's offering more than just prisoner disposal; the Sycians, for all their faults, never pass up and opportunity to earn gold any way they can. But my failure? I do not imagine that the Order of Love would hit the same walls."

The priest sucked in air over his lower lip and smirked. "No, *you'd* expect that we'd act in defense of the Crown's *people* more than we'd be interested in acting in defense of the Crown's *purse*."

"Exactly," she smugly answered with that same wolfish smile. "It's not that I would expect Hannock or Paverilak to put the weight of the Queen's purse over the Queen's people, you know."

"Yes you would. What evidence do you have?"

"Enough, I believe, to be of interest. What say you?"

He couldn't hide his glare, but he couldn't argue the point. If she was right – and he was in possession of an illegal artifact – there was only one thing he *could* do. "I'm not going to promise that even if I do look into this Ocsimmer fellow that I'll be taking him out of play, as you said it. The law doesn't care for what people wish, only what people do."

Anais nodded in understanding and agreement, though she tried to act like it wasn't anything less than she had expected. "I suppose that's as much as I could want. Regardless if his influence is removed or not, as long as you put your best effort into verifying what I say to be true, I will put my efforts into helping you find Erine or her assistant."

"And either way, we agree to share what we know about whatever the fisk was that attacked us last night?"

"My good priest," she answered with a haughty laugh that cackled in his ears like broken glass, "why would I hide anything I know about that from you?"

Rmaci floated around between them and glared at the gossip with empty, bloody eyes and wished for all the world that the broker could see and hear her. "*Because you are a deceitful bitch? I'm* dead *and even I can see that much.*"

✳✳✳

Akkador East was not as dreadful as he'd first thought when he made it through the city gates nearly eight weeks ago. Compared to the snottiness of West Giffil or the holier-than-tho attitudes of Chiadon, it felt almost comfortable. The people here were straightforward and open with who they were and what they did. The aura of 'backroom deals' and 'quiet gossip' that permeated the other parts of Basion were banished by a plain, up-front, and otherwise honest attitude that could be felt radiating from everyone from the occasional lowly street merchant to the guards and the soldiers walking in the street.

The men and women in this distract had one job, and they knew it. They were fighters, warriors, mercenaries, and soldiers. These people were killers, and he felt more at home here than anywhere else in the city.

It was such a refreshing feeling that he even welcomed the gruff attitude espoused by a burly, grizzled man with a distinct lack of teeth and a crooked nose. His name was Jobbet Mafordin, and despite the unintended warmth Akaran felt from being around like-minded souls for a change, he'd be just as happy to never see him again.

For starters, he smelled. Terrible. To the point that Akaran's unwanted companion even had to remark on it. "*Rare is a time when I have been grateful you allowed for my nose to be burned away.*"

Don't you have somewhere else to be? he complained quietly.

"*A choice between mocking you or on my gutted stomach lapping at the blood and shit coated hooves of the damned with my blistered tongue? I'd much prefer the mocking.*"

He shuddered at the thought as she perched herself on top of an open door in defiance of any and all normal physics. It was just one more way to mess with his mind and he knew it. "You must be –"

"Busy," the filthy arms dealer snapped back, "I'm busy. What do you want?"

Going to be one of those *discussions,* Akaran groaned to himself. "To ask you some questions. That's all."

"Then go ask someone else," Jobbet snarled as he turned back to a small pile of rusty axes and dinged-up swords.

"Can't do that," the exorcist retorted as he dangled his sigil in front of him. "We need to talk," he insisted.

The armsman rolled his eyes and went back to sorting the weapons out. "Then talk fast. These swords don't sell themselves."

"You'd think that they would," Akaran quipped. "Those that need them don't often take a lot of convincing."

"But you make more coin by those that *don't* need them," the other man argued pointedly. "They're the ones that don't know the difference between good steel and bad."

The priest took another glance at the pile of battered steel and pulled back slightly. "If I weren't otherwise employed, I might wonder if you're selling weapons up to the Crown's Standards."

That just made the merchant bristle up more. "You'll find that all my wares are in compliance with royal mandates. Can't be selling anything that's not able to pass inspection."

"I wonder who passed the inspector."

"Someone with deep pockets," he chortled. The *odor* that wafted up as he laughed punched Akaran in the gut harder than the creature in the alley had and it was *all* he could do to keep from gagging even harder. "Ah. You're the one from Anais, aren't you?"

A feeling of revulsion that went away as confusion took hold. "I just left her estate. How did you know?"

"She has her ways," the merchant shot back with a grunt and a drawn-out sniff. "Said I might be seeing one of your sort sometime or other."

"*She did, did she? Almost like she has a plan,*" Rmaci pointed out from behind them.

"She says a lot of things," the priest noted. "Hard to say what is and isn't true."

Jobbet sniffed the air again and smirked. "When it comes from her, assume it is and bet that it isn't."

"Is that a warning or just idle commentary?"

"Is there a difference?"

The wraith dropped down beside them and shook her head vehemently. Little droplets of phantom pus and bloody oil jumped off of her scalp with every move she made. *"No. The answer is no."*

It was getting harder and harder to ignore her, but Akaran managed to trudge through. "She told me you might know someone I'm interested in. A man named Ocsimmer."

"Long as you don't confuse 'knowing' with 'liking,' then I'll admit to that much," the arms dealer replied slowly as he drew out the words distinctly. "I'll be assuming that the lovely Lady Lovic told you to come here and get proof of misdeeds?"

"This may be the most honest man in the city," the wraith quipped, more to herself than anyone else.

The priest just gave him a nod before he turned his attention to the other weapons hanging in the store. Nothing looked like it would pass an inspection, and all of it should probably just be scrapped. "She said you had dealings with him and that you kept records. I'd like to see them."

"Oh, I bet you would. You just wait right there," Jobbet grumbled as he went off to a back room in his shoddy, poorly-lit, poorly-kept hole in a wall of a shop.

Rmaci disappeared from view, then peered up at the exorcist from behind a rotten wood counter. *"Akaran?"*

I don't like it either, he thought back at her. The armsman's physical upkeep aside, there was just something...

"It's not that," she huskily whispered. *"I don't, of course, that's true. But I... I don't think you should be involved in this."*

Akaran arched his eyebrow at her and wondered if she was just trying to find a new way to mess with his head, or if she actually meant it. *Worried I'll end up dead and you'll lose your free ride?*

The corpse stood up and leaned forward over the grungy countertop. *"Worried because there are things worse than death, and this venture reeks of them."*

As the priest started to reply with what he felt was the wittiest retort ever given thought, Jobbet returned and interrupted their private conversation. "Since Anais sent you, then I'll tell you what she told me to say: that Sycian? He tried to get me to buy a couple of weapons he had. Swore they came from someplace special, and that you'd never find any others like them. I, of course, being an *upstandin'* citizen of the crown and all that, recognized trouble when I saw it and turned him down."

"I see," he replied as the choice words that the armsman used stood out like a sore thumb. He took the box but didn't open it. "You are aware that casting false accusations can have you tried as if you had done them yourself, yes?"

"Why would I lie to a man of the cloth? This is what I said he did, and I'll place my hand to my heart to prove it."

His reply didn't impress the exorcist, but it earned a happy cheer from his mental tormentor. "*I was wrong! The Abyss loves men like him!*"

Liars?

"*Fraudulent speakers of oath,*" she replied with a happy clap of her hands. "*His heart shall be stuffed into his mouth so he may not speak a lie once again, his hands placed over his mouth to hold the lie forever, and a bar driven through his skull and into his spine so that he may never remove turn his head to the truth again.*"

He gagged and couldn't hide it, so he made a show of coughing and squeezing at his leg for effect. *Fisk me...*

"*Not even with his dick,*" she quipped as she gestured at the dealer's stained and otherwise filthy leggings.

"Jobbet, I am serious," Akaran warned, "if you are lying, if this is falsified, it will not end well for you – neither in this world or the next. You need to know that. That said, what is this, anyway?"

"I mark the days and times I speak with others in my journal. Given the nature of my business, I like to remember whom I've armed in my travels. The box, now that's another story," he replied as he wrapped his grungy and calloused fingers around the box and took it back from the priest. He opened it and showed off a thumb-sized pendant on a silvery chain. "This little trinket? In all my days, I've never seen one like it. Thought it was too pretty to pass by. The weapon he was offering? Now I'm no priest but –"

Seeing it was all it took. If she'd been there, Anais would've been pleased to see how perfectly the plan worked. As it was, any objections Akaran had held were gone the moment he laid his eye on the reddish-gold symbol. "You got that from him? And he tried to sell you more? Do you so swear?"

Anais might've even been pleased to see the response that the wraith had. Rmaci's abject terror only served to reinforce the truth behind the signet. "*Akaran! The AURA from that thing! I DON'T like it. What IS that?*"

The one crest we were taught to both avoid and hunt for at all costs. There's only one recourse for anyone we catch wearing it. He stared down at the oblong bangle with a glare. It was in the shape of a perfectly-formed teardrop, like someone had allowed a piece of molten gold to carefully dangle from the edge of a smelter before they caught it and set a small diamond in the very center. It was a symbol of glory turned to pain; a reminder of an empire that once spanned a continent. It had once only been seen on the necks of royalty.

Now it was only seen in the possession of thieves, smugglers, and those that still claimed loyalty to a dead empire. Or more accurately, an empire of the dead. Having the crest of the Adelin Empire in your control was a surefire way to get someone brought before a military tribunal, or worse, an inquiry from the Order of Stara.

Or much, much worse – considering their history with the empire – the interest of the Order of Love. Which was exactly what the self-declared Merchant of Secrets had promised he'd offer, and no matter her motives, it guaranteed Se'daulif's fate if the armsman swore to it. Which he promptly did. "I swear, as Anais said."

"I don't care about her," Akaran snarled. "*Do you swear you got this from him?*"

"So sworn," Jobbet promised. "And the ledger shows –"

"Keep it," Akaran spat. "This is all I need."

The dealer exhaled in utter relief. "Then we're good? And you'll tell Lovic I held up my end of the bargain?"

He didn't bother to answer as all manner of dark thoughts and curses started to bounce through his head. After he stormed off, the wraith somehow managed to stay behind for her own amusement. Rmaci slowly drew a phantom circle over his chest and just quietly mused to herself one simple question:

"*I wonder if they'll use a knife or just rip it out...*"

VII. ENSLAVED TO LIES

The afternoon of Zundis, the 28ᵗʰ of Riverswell, 513 QR

Getting the Lieutenant-Commander to agree to let Akaran 'borrow' a pair of guards wasn't as difficult as getting past Seline. Henderschott made it clear: "If this is nothing, I'll order you to trial," and, in truth, that was more or less fair. The Manor, however, was a little less forgiving.

The headache started when Seline found him rummaging through his limited pile of belongings to dig out his tabard and heard his repeated complaints about not being able to keep a weapon on the premises. The blonde almost-beauty watched him fuss around from the door without making a sound, though he noticed her the moment she showed up. *No argument is a good argument*, or so he thought.

A thought she was quick to put to rest. "Where are you going with that?"

"Out. Found something."

Surprisingly, her reaction wasn't to yell at him. If anything, she straightened up and nearly dropped the blanket she was carrying as she scooted into his room and lowered her voice. "Something? About... about Liv or Raechil?"

"No," Akaran sighed. "Worse."

"What could be worse than what happened to them?" she asked as bewilderment filled her starry brown, green-flaked eyes.

One glance into her shining eyes and he damn near forgot what he was doing... and the fleeting feeling of warmth that he felt was dashed with a mountain of guilt about his last almost-lover. He shook the wayward thought out of his head and went back to digging until he found a small bag he'd been hunting for. "Stupidity. There are some stories that don't deserve being told."

When he started to move past her, she all-but jumped between him and the door. "I don't understand. What are you doing?"

"I'm being inventive," he answered with a grim little smirk as he hobbled his way past her.

Seline started to follow but a meek voice made her stop. She turned around and saw one of the Manor's oldest residents, and a woman whose name kept popping up when it was the least useful. "Do... don't. Let... let him go," the bedraggled, exhausted, white-haired woman half-whispered to her caretaker.

"Bistra! What are you doing out of your room?"

"Heard the... noise."

The healer looked at the older woman with her mouth agape. "But your room is upstairs? We barely spoke above a whisper. Surely he wasn't that loud?"

She gripped the old straw pillow she was carrying as tightly as she could. Her hands shook from the effort, or maybe they shook from something else entirely. "Not him," the older woman whimpered. "His noise. Noise... the noise around him."

Seline reached over and gently placed her hand on Bistra's and began to guide her back to her room through the dim, dusk-lit hallway. "Not sure it's wise to let him go. I should tell the Lady. He shouldn't be going back out into the city this late in the day."

"N... no," Bistra began to reply. "No. Don't. There... there is light in his darkness. Light in his... his shadows. It..."

"He is a priest, sweetie. Like you."

There was a moment where a flicker of her old life flashed in her eyes. Just enough to make Seline wonder if she'd gotten through to her just this once. Just enough to make her wonder if she had reminded the woman what, who, she used to be and be known as. That flicker faded to a cold dull ache in her mind as the healer watched. Still, it nudged a little bit loose. In just the right way. "I... he... not priests. Never... not priests," she lamented.

"Of course you were," the younger woman said reassuringly. "You serve the same Goddess, remember?"

Bistra nodded as she shuffled back to her room. "That's... that's how I know he... not a priest. We aren't."

The fact that she admitted that much in open conversation was a breakthrough in its own right, and the healer gave herself a moment to feel pleased with herself. "Oh? Then what are you?"

She shouldn't have. "Mur... murd..." the broken exorcist tried to say before she shook her head violently and shuddered. "His light... his light is angry," she added pitifully, as if that explained everything. "Don't stop. Don't stop him. Just..." Bistra whined with a frustrated tremor to her stutter.

Seline gently slipped her arm around the former priestess's shoulder and felt the poor woman shaking – in fear or anger or frustration, she couldn't tell. "Just what, Bistra? What's wrong?"

"His light... reminds me... reminds me of mine. Except... except..."

"Bistra?"

The poor, ruined woman looked at the healer with an ocean's worth of sadness in her eyes. Sadness, and terror. "His light is *scary*."

Akkador West was almost a city in and of itself. The people were friendly, the shops were legion, and there wasn't a street you could walk on that wasn't decorated with all manner of pottery, flags, carpets, and hucksters trying to convince you to buy their wares — legal or otherwise. That last part wasn't *much* different from the rest of Basion, but the merchants in West put a *lot* more effort into their work.

They needed to. The kind of garish and gaudy buildings they owned (or at least, rented at reasonable prices) each cost more crowns than the exorcist ever expected to see in his life. What was striking was how *kind* everyone was. Vendors were laughing and singing. Customers were clapping and laughing. Even laborers had smiles from ear to ear. There were children playing on their flutes and minstrels playing on their lutes and every other street was just another wonder of wonders.

It took him a few minutes to figure out why before one of the two guards assisting him took the magic away in a quick exchange with his partner. "Remember how it was before Hannock put his foot down?"

"You mean when he marched Hylene down here with him?"

"That'd be it," the first guard quipped back, "and the *talk* they had with the local blockmasters?"

The private's chainmail rattled as he nodded along. "Basically said, 'make the people feel welcome to spend coin, or you won't have any,' didn't they?"

That was Private Rocken. He was a few years older than Akaran, and had a little shuffle to his step. The other guard was a sergeant — he said his name was Marditt — and roughly the same age, though honestly, the two could've been brothers for all he knew. Both of them had their faces obscured by their copper-plated helms with half-visors, so aside from both of them needing to do a better job shaving, there wasn't much to say about them.

Of course, neither of them wanted to be there, though both of them had brightened up at the idea of arresting the shiverdine, if it came to it. "Right, that's it," Marditt replied. "So the locals gathered together, found some sods from the Guild of Songweavers, and made them teach half of the streeters how to sing. Damnedest thing."

And just like that, the magic was gone.

Still, it was vaguely impressive that the locals had pulled it off this well. *Give credit where credit is due I suppose*, Akaran mused to himself, *though I'm sure they're all secretly sad about the influx of coin the wedding is offering*.

Their tunes all collectively changed as the trio arrived at Shiedel Estate, a manor-house that *almost* could've put Ridora's to shame. The Estate was right in the center of the district, and it would've stood out even if it *hadn't* been built from a much lighter sandstone — opposed to the darker gray limestone that was used for much of the city outside of the religious quarters. Like the other stores and scattered houses, it had a fence and a yard in and of itself, with a three-tiered fountain sitting in the middle of it.

The fact that the second and third pool-tiers were held by a mix of nude male and female statues with shackles on their ankles said all that needed to be said about Se'daulif Ocsimmer. He didn't even bother to pretend to hide the nature of his trade, which was admittedly respectable. At least, to an extent. That said, he was still a shiverdine of Sycio, trader, slaver, and ultimately? Just another pain in the ass that nobody really wanted to deal with today.

It wasn't entirely illegal to own slaves in the Kingdom. It was frowned on, but not entirely, exactly, illegal. You could tell a great deal about how indebted a worker was to their employer by the look in their eyes, the clothes they wore, the way they bowed their heads when you passed. The manor's 'hosts' and 'assistants' that lead them through the carefully-tended grounds and into the manor's foyer?

If Akaran had grounds to do to Se'daulif what he *hoped* he had grounds to do, a few contracts of servitude were going to get dropped into a fireplace on the way out. It was a thought and a hope that didn't have to wait long. They were only kept waiting for a few minutes before the shiverdine made his appearance.

The wait was just long enough for the trio to start to feel disgusted by the sheer amount of *sex* put on display. There were paintings hanging from the walls depicting acts that Akaran had never *dreamed* of let alone *seen* before. A marble statue in the middle of the foyer displayed a woman as nude as she was proud of it; and while none of the peacekeepers were exactly prudes – there were limits.

For that matter, the servant-girls all had one thing in common with each other and it wasn't their shining personalities as much as it was how little they tried (or were allowed) to cover their upper-halves. It wasn't the first time that the Priest of Love had seen decadence like this (you didn't live near the Capitol without understanding the way that *certain things* worked), but seeing *so much of it* did not... set well.

"*Liar,*" Rmaci whispered behind his ear, "*it's giving you ideas and you know it. Would it help if I dressed up like that tonight when we have our time together? Cuffs and anklets? I can't say that I'm in as good of shape otherwise but...*"

He would've blushed if she hadn't gone to such great lengths to ruin the idea. Before he could deny anything she offered (or his stomach could upend itself over the other half of it), they were interrupted by the man of the manor – if you could call him that. "Friends, friends! There is no cause for this!"

Akaran took one long look at him before speaking up. He'd caught a glimpse of the slaver back at the Danse Festistanis without realizing who he was. Now? Now he'd never be able to forget him. Sycians were recognizable anywhere – the dusky color to their skin stood out from the paler tones on the mainland, but you could say the same for people from the Golden Empire of Matheia, too.

No, what set them off from any other people in the known world wasn't their skin, it was their eyes. From the mainland to Ogibus to Matheia, Atheia, and supposedly the islands to the south of the Golden Empire, rare was it to find someone that didn't have a blue or green or brown shine to their eyes. Magic would sometimes leave a practitioner with pale, glassy eyes. But Sycians?

"You're Ocsimmer, right?"

Se'daulif blinked his reddish-violet eyes at the priest and nodded. "But of course. So it must be that you have the wrong dwelling, I assume? I've done nothing to gain the interests of the Guard, let alone... a Lover? Is that what you are?"

Those haunting, red eyes with a black iris in the center? You couldn't hide that. It was theorized that there was a compound in the omnipresent dust that stained their eyes red at birth. Of course, it was also theorized it was a curse, much like the way that the Damian people had been forbidden to ever see the sun (or so they said). It could've been something else entirely. It was an immutable truth of their people, and it gave them away no matter what else.

None of it, as far as Akaran was concerned, mattered. "No," he shot back, "we're in the right place."

The slaver blinked in confusion again and nervously wrung his hands against the middle of his golden-brown cotton cloak. "Then I do not understand, my friends. Why is it that you are here; what is it that you want of me?"

"Talk to them," the exorcist remarked as he started to walk around the foyer with his eyes taking everything apart in his head. Rmaci, unseen and ignored by everybody else, did the same thing on the opposite side of the room.

"Uh, no. The L-Comm," Marditt said, "said that this was entirely your show. We're not here to talk."

Se'daulif turned to watch the priest – who was easily half his age, if not younger – pick up a vase worth more than his entire commission with the Crown and peer inside it like he'd misplaced a key. "Then what is it you are here for, hm? What is it that Se'daulif can do to calm your minds?"

"In that case, they're here to hurt you if you don't answer my questions," Akaran replied with a shrug as he set it back down.

"Uh, we're here to –" the sergeant quickly tried to reply before the slaver managed to get a word in edgewise.

"Do hurt or harm? I assure you, there's no cause for that!"

"For your sake I hope so, but for your sake, I don't think so," the exorcist replied with a frown as he pulled out the sigil he'd liberated from Jobbet earlier. "Do you recognize this?"

The slaver looked down at the golden signet and scoffed at it. "That? You have invaded my home over a bauble?"

"For one, it's not *your* home. It's being supplied by the Blackstone Trading Company, which somehow makes me think less of the BeaST than I already do," he pointed out. "Even though I assume they let you do the decorations. Understanding that, your arrangement with them can be easily revoked if I want to have it done. *Is this yours*?"

He poured his eyes over the pendant and crinkled his nose at it. "I swear to you, that is a design I've not seen before. Let alone have ever claimed as part of my stores."

"Do you know what it is?"

"A thing of tackiness?" the slaver asked. "It looks as if someone gave no care to refining an ingot of gold before they dunked it in bowl of rotten cherries and called the casting complete."

"*He's not wrong*," Rmaci quipped from the other side of the room. "*Not sure he's lying, either, for what it's worth*."

He is, just not a lot, Akaran thought back. "So you don't know what this is? Never seen it before?"

Se'daulif nodded his pudgy head. "I swear it, I do not. I prefer my necklaces to be wreathed with gems and not to be so disgraced by wearing simple..." he said as the thought trailed off to die on his tongue. "I... it has the air of being crafted yet is so basic that I cannot fathom a man bothering to adorn himself with it. My friend, I am Sycian; bearing the jewels of the sands is how we keep our souls close to our golden homes," he stressed.

Akaran pursed his lips and dropped the crest back into a pouch on his waist. "I have a sworn statement that says you were trying to sell this to a man in Akkador East. Jobbet Mafordin – that name ring a bell?"

"Bells, no, thoughts, yes. The lout attempted to sell me weapons for my trade, once."

"Oh did he? I thought he only sold armor," the priest asked with an easy lie.

The wraith arched an eyebrow at the blatant lie as Se'daulif fell into it. "Armor? If he sells that along with those dreadful weapons I would assume he gets no business."

Well, they know each other. "Did you buy any?"

"*Well played*," Rmaci purred as she started to feel her attention drift to a box in the corner.

"Buy any? Of that trash? Please, good sir, look around. Does it look as if I would soil myself with wares such as his? I daresay that my house would rot from even the hint of his shop should it find its way in past my doors." The slaver stopped and looked askance at the priest and his two guards before asking, "One would hope you at least stepped under the Falls before stepping across my threshold if that's where you've been as of recent?"

"So you don't deny knowing him?"

"I am a merchant that makes a living providing servants to the wealthy and passage to the poor. It is not uncommon for one such as myself to step into that district – and I assure you, his is not the only place I have explored across the bridge from West to East. Nor would I imagine that there are not far more many other souls that travel between that place and this day-to-day."

That was true, Akaran had to agree, but it missed the point entirely. "There are *four* Sycians in the *entirety* of Basion, and of those, one is a hunter and *might* be half your size soaking wet; not to mention he wouldn't be caught dead with that sigil. Another is a woman and the other arrived yesterday."

Se'daulif's mouth gaped slightly as he realized what the priest was getting at. "You cannot be so sure."

"The guards at the gate are keeping *very* good paperwork, shiverdine. So — tell me why someone would lie about you selling contraband in the city?"

Rmaci had the answer and she managed to get it out before the stuttering slaver could. *"Because that bitch sucked Jobbet's cock in exchange for him to lie to you?"*

"Men lie," the slaver retorted (as the wraith chuckled). "It is a thing that men do. Why do you believe a liar over I?"

Akaran rolled his head on his shoulders and cracked his neck with just enough of a pop that it echoed in the foyer. "Calling your accuser a liar doesn't mean you're telling the truth."

The Sycian took a few steps back as he watched the priest tighten his shoulders. "It is much harder to prove an innocence than it is to prove a lie. Do you have more than the man's word?"

"That," the exorcist replied, "is exactly why I am here."

"Then you've offered me no way to offer a dispute over your presumed truth. So should you have already convinced yourself that the words from my lips will be lies, what proof can I offer?"

"You can't," Akaran admitted. "So we're going to use other methods." When the slaver's eyes widened, the exorcist gently rapped the tip of his cane on the stone floor and smirked. "It won't be the same methods you use on your *staff*, I promise."

The promise didn't put Se'daulif into any kind of a better mood. "Then my friend, why have you not already placed me in chains if you are so sure my presence is a crime of whatever law you profess to claim?"

"Because I didn't find it on you," the priest replied as he gestured over to Rocken and Marditt. "Guards? Take him into custody, please." They thought about arguing the order for a moment, though for their sake, it was thankfully fleeting.

As soon as they had the shiverdine in hand, the trader immediately started to struggle. "I am a guest of the Overseer and the Merchant-Master! You must have grounds to place a man of a different nationality into chains — I am versed in the laws of your Queen's land!"

"Queen's Law says people like me have very *broad* discretionary abilities when it comes to Adelin contraband," he retorted, "of which you've been accused of. So allow me to make this clear: I'm going to rip this manor apart. I am going to open every door. Every chest. I am going to turn every jacket inside out. I am going to look inside the stuffing of your bed. I'm going to pull up the floorboards if I have to. But I am going to find out if you're lying to me or not."

Just outside the corner of the exorcist's vision, the wraith found something that took her attention. While he was grateful, he didn't care. She, on the other hand, did. *"Ah, Akaran?"*

"My friend, you've neither right nor cause!" Se'daulif protested as he struggled to get his arms free from the guards. "I am a guest in this city! Master Hannock himself will speak for me!"

"*Ah, Akaran?*" she called out again. She hopped onto an old stone clay chest that, at first glance, just looked like a stool someone had kicked under a table.

"Why would I believe a slaver?" the priest charged. "Why would I believe a *Sycian* over one of the Queen's *actual* citizens?"

The shiverdine looked more indignant than guilty, if there was any way to describe the look on his face. He was anything *but* a small man, and if the over-sized mound of muscle with a bit of a pot belly wanted to knock the younger man out? Well, there wasn't much that the two guardsmen could do. "If it's my profession you've angst with, then there's nothing of that I can say! It is an opportunity one such as myself has to take advantage of the systems that your own Queen has offered open!"

They knew it, too. "Alright big man, there's no reason to fight like this, let the boy have his say," Marditt grumbled. "Calm down or someone's going to lose their teeth."

A sentiment that the wraith agreed with, at least in part. "*Hey, dumbass,*" she called out — and this time punctuated it with a wad of phantom bile that flung across the room and at his head.

Akaran flinched as the blob stuck his cheek and bounced off into the silent ether. "What?"

"The Queen!" Ocsimmer desperately repeated, as if his objections actually mattered. "It's her interests that have allowed me to do business in this city for the last two years! I do nothing that I have not been allowed as a holder of citizenry in your Kingdom and as a gem in the hand of Dunesire Da'Keloth of Sharvastial!"

"*You don't have to try so hard,*" Rmaci scolded from across the room. "*Look here,*" she told him as she thumped the lid of the box with a bloody wet hand. "*I suppose it's too much to ask if you feel that.*"

Feel what?

The wraith rolled her non-existent eyes and hopped off of her gray perch. "*Just open the box. That Anais woman is lying to you about where that bauble came from but there's something here.*"

So he's lying too, he swore in the back of his head as he pushed past the slaver and walked right over to the box.

She hesitated before she responded, and rocked back and forth on her feet while she thought about it. "*In an odd way, I don't think that he is. But I feel that we won't like what's in there.*"

The lid of the chest slid off with a heavy 'thunk' onto the ground. The protests from Se'daulif grew louder as the guards had a harder time holding him back. *Should I be worried?*

Rmaci peered over his shoulder and into the box full of blankets, clothes, and little else she could see. "*I don't know. Be careful, would you now?*"

The blankets weren't anything of note. Two of them had the crests of the Jewels of Sycio embroidered on them, and he did idly check to make sure that nobody had thought to etch the Adelinic crest anywhere, too. When that thought resulted in nothing useful, he pulled another couple of blankets out before he found a sealed wooden box hidden below the bits of tacky fabric and furs. Though the box itself was hidden, the secret was what was written on it.

"What's in this box and why is there a binding spell written all over it?" he asked as he traced his fingertips over the runes carved all over the case.

The shiverdine forced the men holding his arms to turn around with him. "That? That I do not know."

"It's yours," he replied, "I assume, at least. Given that it's buried with your things. In your house. Though I don't know why you've covered it in purgalaito."

"No, no my friend, that is not a thing of mine," Se'daulif repeated. "I neither recognize the box nor… well, you must forgive me. Spells are not a thing that I know."

"It's a casket hidden in a box under blankets. You don't know what it is?"

"My friend, whatever in that box is not a thing that I know, as I said. And to as it is as you've said: I have been allowed to have this abode by the Traders of Blackstone. It must have been a thing left behind by them."

"In your room. Under your things," he pointed out, "under blankets with the markings of your people." He stopped and took a long whiff of one of them and gagged almost violently. "And they smell used. Recently used."

The slaver violently shook his head no. "The box was here too when I first arrived! I did not bring many things into this place that are here in the now! Speak of… of…"

Marditt cuffed the bigger man across the back of his head. "If the next words out of your mouth are gonna be for him to find out what happened to the last man that owned this place, then I'm gonna make sure you can't get away even if you wanted. We clear?"

The far-less-than-idle threat worked and Se'daulif did as requested. In the meantime, the priest went back to work studying the box in his hands. *Purgalaito for sure,* he mused. When no other answers seemed to be forthcoming, he looked up at the blistered and burnt corpse that had decided to lay belly-down on the table so she could watch. *Well. You want to do something useful?*

Her lips turned up into a smile that was more grotesque than normal. *"Are you asking me for help?"*

Sooner we get this over with, the sooner we can get back to you trying to torture me in my sleep, he suggested with a defeated sigh to match.

"Missing our time together? That's such a sweet thing to say."

It means I can lay down. Get over here and give me a clue what this means.

Rmaci delightfully chuckled at him before she began to read the inscription. She didn't last more than a handful of words before she disappeared and popped back into sight on the other side of the foyer. *"Ah, no."*

No?

"No," she repeated. *"Nor do I think you should open that."*

Why?

So far, there had been a few times when being able to speak silently with his personal haunt were helpful. There were other times when he did it as people watched him stare at apparent nothingness the air while he ran a gamut of facial ticks and angry body language was less so. "Priest? You alright?" Rocken asked as the silence everyone else was stuck with finally got the better of him.

The priest barely registered he was even there. Still, when playing with new magic... "Yeah, just... do me a favor you two. Take him outside."

"Eh?" the private asked. "Hender said we were supposed to keep a watch on you."

"Think Hender would be pissed if you got back to the barracks with your hair burned off?"

Marditt ran a hand behind his neck and plucked at a few loose strands of auburn hair that had gotten loose from his helmet. *"I'd be pissed."*

"Then you might want to step outside," Akaran cautioned. *"Don't let that fat prick get loose."*

As the soldiers started to march Se'daulif outside, the slaver managed to get out one last remark before they forced him outdoors. "My friend! I assure you, I am nothing of the sort!"

Once he was gone, the exorcist turned his full attention to the rune-inscribed box. "Alright you pain in my ass, talk to me. You've barely shut up since you realized you could manifest like this."

"That's a rude way to ask for my help."

"Do we really want to discuss manners right now and what is or isn't rude, considering how you like to throw fireballs at my face when I'm asleep?"

Rmaci sat on the edge of the table and idly picked at a flap of burned skin on her ribs for a moment before bothering to answer. *"I suppose you have a point. How did you realize I could read that?"*

"You're dead," he pointed out, "and you brag about how much knowledge the Abyss holds all the damn time."

"Your powers of deduction do not cease to astound me," she muttered as she walked over to the box once more, *"yet you deign to tell me that you don't recognize these words?"*

He shook his head and squeezed at the pouch of cocasa hidden under his vestment. "My head is pounding. Longer I look at this thing, the worse it gets."

"The words invoke a pair of maskings. An oath to Lethandria, and one to the Warden."

The contents of the box shifted as he tilted it back and forth in an attempt to study the hinges for signs of more mundane traps. "Leth's name keeps popping up recently. But the Warden? That's a surprise."

She traced a bloody fingertip that was more bone than skin under a line etched onto the dark wood. *"A request that what is locked away remains undisturbed by forces below."* The former spy licked her melted lips and moved back away from it. *"Were I more flesh than thought, I don't believe one such as myself could open it even if I wanted."*

"Makes sense," he mused. "He's Sycian."

"What does that have to do...?"

"Necromancy. It's what they do. I'm sure a ward like that is par for the course for them," he said as he pressed his thumbs under the lid. "You'd tell me if there was anything on this that said, *'Woe be unto mortal men that open, for your cock shall shrivel and wilt away,'* or some such – right?"

There was a very long moment where she just looked at him and smiled that grotesque, obscene smile of hers at him. When he didn't budge or rise to the silent bait, she let out a sigh he was certain he could *feel* and leaned back with a disgusting stretch and a yawn. *"No, I promise, nothing of the sort. The dead, yes, though most of the damned have few fun uses for those things. Most would prefer it not be attached upon arrival, should you catch my gist."*

The exorcist briefly shook from revulsion at the thought before he popped the lid open. The weapon inside was a delightfully twisted monstrosity in its own right: a mace with a leather-bound hilt and a shaft slightly longer than his forearm. The head was icosahedron-shaped with four flanges that flowed down from the top to halfway along the bottom curve. There were three twisted spikes between each flat protrusion to add to the pain the weapon was unquestionably made to inflict.

What it was made of, on the other hand...

"I've never seen steel like this," he marveled.

Rmaci blanched and scooted away like it was on fire. *"Because it isn't steel. I retract what I said; hang that man. Just to be certain. The Warden can sort his soul out if Purity doesn't."*

"What is it?"

She reached over and slid her etheric fingers along the hilt where someone had wrapped rotting hemp cord around the handle. *"Esth-atatic. Pitmetal. It's... harvested... in the Emberforge."*

"Pitmetal?" Akaran asked, then looked over his shoulder at her incredulous stare. "They have mines in the Abyss?"

The dead spy trailed her fingertip up the hilt then down his wrist until he flinched in revulsion and pulled away. *"We have everything in the Abyss. What – you assumed that in a place of fire and heat, of callous conditions and rocky cliffs, of cavernous pits and rotting holes that we wouldn't have ore? I'll assume you don't think that we have latrines, either."*

He fought with himself for a long minute before asking, "You do?"

"What else should we do with the souls of men who use the words of the Gods above to further their own ends? Speak offal, and be filled with it," she purred, and then pointedly (as he gagged) added, *"but that aside – that*

weapon is not for mortal men."

"I can't feel anything from it," he mused quietly to himself as he set the box down and started to reach inside for it.

"*Don't.*"

"It'll be fine. I'm protected by the Goddess."

She gave him a withering stare. "*Given my presence, one would argue that She doesn't do so very well — may I point that out?*"

The not-quite-a-threat was enough to encourage him to take a moment and send a silent prayer to the Lady above, and then as a precaution, he removed a small amber gem from one of his belt pouches and set it aside. A few seconds later, he cut open a small scratch on his left arm and rubbed the blood on the stone.

When Rmaci asked what he was doing, the answer was a bit of a surprise. "It's an imprint stone — old exorcist trick. Doesn't take magic to activate it. Just a bit of blood and a few seconds holding it. If something happens to me after I touch it, the Order will be able to see an imprint of my aura on the rock. Think of it like a very low-power absorption gem. Helps rule out if I got hurt before or after I touched the stone."

"*Oh really? And are you so sure it will work given your… our… condition?*"

"No," he admitted, "but it's better than nothing." One long, deep breath later, and he reached into the box and picked the mace up. The effect wasn't immediate — but it wasn't pleasant. It started with a dull throb up his arm, and his vision started to dim as a deep crimson fog appeared in the corner of his eyes.

It was just a heartbeat later when Rmaci let out a gasp of pain and doubled over. He watched her collapse, and then the room changed as the mace erupted with a dark flare. The shift only lasted a minute — but a minute was enough.

The gray walls morphed to yellowed bone. The table warped from a wooden frame and marble top to a flesh-covered blob. The rugs on the wall rotted in an instant. The air filled with snapping embers as cold steam began to roll off of Akaran's hands. Nearly everywhere they looked, words began to manifest along the walls and floors.

"*What did you DO?*"

He didn't answer; for that matter, he couldn't. Every ounce of his being felt like it was being consumed by resonating *joy* from the mace. It curled around him and through his skin. He kept his mouth shut tight for no other reason than to keep from giggling like a maniac.

When she realized he was completely hopeless, she looked closer at the words on the walls. They were written in every language, and somehow in no languages. As she tried to make sense of them, the inscriptions began to scream into her mind more than she was reading them.

Rmaci recited what she could out loud as Akaran struggled to work his fingers on the mace's hilt. "*He is Light. He is the End. He is Ascendant of the*

Descended. He is Light." As soon as she finished, she instantly regretted it.

The wraith howled in pain as small sickly green flames winked into existence on her arms and legs. They raced up and down her body and left rivulets of fresh scars in their wake until she could control herself and deaden her mind to the pain. *"LET GO OF THE DAMN THING YOU IDIOT!"* she screeched at the top of her lungs.

But he couldn't. He ignored her. Akaran focused on the head of the weapon and watched as the flanges started to turn and spin of their own accord with muted clicks and clacks. Each click made him giggle; each clack shot stabbing heat up his arm with embers that followed in their wake. Each twist made his body shake as streamers of blue energy began to radiate off of his skin.

Ice bloomed and wrapped both his hand and the hilt in an impenetrable shell. More spread from his feet. Embers turned to snowflakes, and the flames wreathing the spy were suffocated as the mana he was infused with went to war with whatever was in the weapon. "I... I feel it," he marveled. "It's... it's not... it has a name, I understand it..."

As he heard it chant it's name in his head over and over again, a wave of frost poured down his hands and swept over the room. When it reached the walls, the words caught fire and pushed back. The wraith watched as the room slowly froze over with wonder building up in her blistered, twisted face. *"What are you?"*

The battle between the essence of the warped room and the otherworldly – even for here – mana in his soul settled down as a new presence brushed it all away with a Word.

Except it wasn't just a Word.

It was a whisper on the wind...

...and with it followed a wave of warmth that was coated with raw *irritation*. Rmaci looked over his shoulder and caught a brief glimpse of the source and fell to her knees with her head bowed almost instantly. The spy quaked in fear as she humbled herself before the new arrival, though whatever she said was more blubber than actual words. Ice snaked around the priest and froze him in place, keeping him from turning to see whatever was happening behind him.

[*Mine,*] the whisper called out. [*He is mine – and* he *should* not *be touching* that, *nor should he be* here,] the decidedly feminine voice added before a not-unpleasant rush of heat pushed the two of them out of the vision. [*And where* you *go is up to you,*] Rmaci heard the voice say to her – and her alone, she was sure of it – before the otherworldly domain faded away.

Or whatever you wanted to call their shared nightmare.

Akaran dropped the mace into the box and stepped back, all color gone from his face, and his hands had been left a trembling mess. It was absolutely all he could do to keep from falling over and for another brief moment, you could see streamers of fog rolling off of his fingertips. "Moir... Moira," he croaked. "It likes the name. Likes it's better... better than the one it had."

"*Abyss... that was the Abyss but that was not the Abyss I know... was that you? Was that the mace? What was... no who... WHO was that with us?! TELL ME!*"

He shook his head and slumped back against the closest wall he could reach. "I don't... don't know what that was. The voice... sometimes the Goddess whispers. We're... I'm an exorcist," he said as if it explained everything, "I have to... see sometimes. See where things are hiding. Or what... what they are. Her... whispers help. In... prayer. Us... usually."

"*That,*" she started as she looked up from him from the floor, "*was* not *a* whisper! *And that weapon? WHAT IS THAT THING?!*"

"It... it said it was Moira," he repeated. "Heard it call out to me. Someone named it. Recently, too. It liked it better than its old name, the... the Mace of Rapturous Insanity." Akaran looked down at the weapon's box and tilted his head slightly as he thought about it for a minute longer. "Wonder where the 'a' came from."

The corpse fell forward onto her hands and bits of burnt muscle flaked off of her arms. "*Pretentious... but... but I...*" she tried to say before she gave up and looked up at him with a mix of horror and wonder etched into the bloody mess of her face. "*You aren't who I thought you were,*" she finally added, "*and I want nothing to do with you.*"

He closed his eye and sagged against the wall for another minute before responding. "I'm sure that makes sense to someone. Tired of nagging at me?" When he opened his eye and looked around, she was gone, and for a change, his leg had stopped throbbing.

That left him, the mace, and the glint of a few gold coins that had fallen out of a bag near the trunk that 'Moira' had been hidden in. Several prayers later, and all three left Se'daullf's apartment as quickly as he could get them out. The shiverdine, however?

A quick order later, and Badin was destined to have company in the dungeon before the day was over. Smuggling artifacts from the cursed continent of Agromah wasn't just a crime: it was just short of an act of war. One punishable quickly, painfully, and permanently.

The question was: an act of war ordered by whom?

***

"I don't understand what the big deal is! I'm allowed to go off-grounds!" Akaran protested a few hours later as Sergeant-at-Arms Telpid marched him into the Manor with one hand tight on the priest's sleeve. "I got back before evening prayers!"

"You know exactly what you did," Ronald gruffly replied, "and Lady Medias is pissed."

"For *what*? I didn't do anything wrong!"

The sergeant stopped cold in the hallway and gave him a disbelieving glare.

"Is that your official statement? A denial of any wrongdoing?"

Akaran quickly adjusted his tunic to make sure that the bulge hiding a few misplaced coins from Se'daulif's manor were kept safely out of sight before replying with a cool, "All I did was carry out permissions granted by the Crown. Nothing more, noth–"

"Permissions?" the guard scoffed. "Is that so? Which permissions do you mean?"

"By oath to the Order and the Queen," he replied curtly as they entered the foyer – and arrived in front of Ridora and Seline both, plus a few of the other caretakers. "I am honor-bound to uproot corruption wherever I find it. And by the *Goddess* did I ever find it today. I found –"

Ridora cut him off with a sharp wave of her hand and a barely-contained seething snarl behind her teeth. "It isn't what *you* found that concerns me. Frankly, my tolerance of your comings and goings at all hours was a mistake on my part and no doubt lead to this," she said as she gestured at a pile of books, bags, and other things laid out on a long table set between the staff and the priest.

"Did you really think we wouldn't find out?" Seline demanded to know. Her fists were balled up, her hair tied back, and her cheeks were flush with fury. "As paranoid as you are that the servants dig through your belongings?"

"Oh and the fact that you hid it for so long!" Lady Medias added. "Whenever we find whichever of my people that you bribed to aid you, I will personally see to it that they are banned from the city."

Akaran looked back and forth between the two of them, and it didn't escape his notice that the three orderlies behind them were armed. Nothing major, but there were swords present; and something about swords in the asylum didn't exactly set well with him. "What in the pits are you two talking about?"

"Be careful invoking the pits," the lady retorted. "You'll find yourself there soon enough if you don't change your ways."

"My *ways* are just fine," he spat back as he started to walk closer. Telpid stopped him with an arm across his chest and a sharp shake of his head. The priest just kept going until he realized that some of the books they had out on display were ones he had taken from the Repository. Only some, however; there were at least three volumes he didn't recognize at all. "You're upset about the books?"

She looked down at the stack and shook her head. "The books? Oh, as if I could be concerned. Honestly, for a man as lost in the mind as you are, it's been a surprise that you can keep up with them. I imagine that you can't, and that it's merely for show as it is."

Seline jumped in before while Akaran's eye went huge and his jaw dropped. "As far as the scrolls are concerned, we have already reached out to Templar Prostil and returned the ones you stole."

"STOLE?" he demanded even as the sergeant grabbed at his tunic to pull him back. "I didn't steal anything!"

"Her aid has a different view," the healer replied. "The reports on Appaidene and Bistra? You have no right nor permission to have them. And *why* do you?"

Akaran pursed his lips and only slightly lied through his teeth. "They were given freely, and as for the why – they were Livstra's recent focus. Assumed that if I was going to find a good reason for her to get dead, they'd be there."

Behind him, Ronald's own eyes narrowed as he quietly made a personal note for his handlers. All of his handlers. Even the bastard with the bone spikes.

"A matter that has been laid to rest and a matter you should have never had interest in. Those even aside – that's a dispute for you and Catherine," Lady Medias snapped. "It's the *rest*. *Look at this* and tell me how it is you think that you could be called immune to wrongdoing!"

He did as asked and gazed down at the pile of random junk. Well, not entirely junk. They'd found the bit of cocasa he'd bought off the grounds, but there was more than he'd put into storage. There was also a wineskin and a cup – which looked a little like one of the ones from the Danse at Comstead Manor – but there was a bunch of other things he didn't recognize at all. A few baubles, a couple of little wooden toys, and even an amethyst necklace. "So... you found... junk? You're upset with me because of... junk? What is all that stuff?"

"You deny taking it?" Ridora demanded.

"Taking it? I don't even recognize it."

Seline picked up the pouch of his painkillers and hefted it in her palm. "Where have you been getting the extra cocasa? There's more here than you've had access to."

That charge he couldn't deny, so he didn't even try. "I was given some gold as a gift. Same night I got into a fight with that inhuman. I needed some for the edge," he admitted as he held up a shaking hand. "You see this? I can barely hold my dick to piss. You two cut me back so hard that I –"

"At least you're willing to admit some of your shortcomings," the lady spat back with cold anger burning in her eyes. "You should admit the rest of them and clear your soul while you have a chance."

"LOOK at my hands! And my leg! How many times does it have to split open before you realize that yes, dammit, *I'm in pain and I need help*? You bloody twits aren't doing shit about it so what did you expect me to do? Drink a glass of water and go prancing out the damn door?"

The sergeant cuffed Akaran across the back of his head and the only thing that kept the priest from laying the guard out on the floor were the swords starting to come out of their sheaths across the room. "You will treat the lady with respect!" Ronald barked.

"Respect?" he thundered. "When they aren't bothering to show me a damn bit of it? Now what exactly are you two jabbering on about?!"

To her credit, Seline didn't flinch back once from the outburst. "Akaran. One of the maids found a loose floorboard. When she checked on it, we found all of these things hidden under it," she replied slowly before she added, "well, not all of them. Some were under the bedding, like the books."

He turned away from the sergeant and blinked. "All of that... in my room?"

"Some of those things belong to our other residents," she continued. "Which leads to one simple question: can you please give me, give us, one, just *one reason*, to not have you thrown from the Manor?"

Akaran's took that in with a surprising amount of grace and sagged down on his cane. "Throw me out? Are you serious? This is a joke, right, this has to be some kind of joke?"

"There is no joke here," the healer replied with the hint of a sad little smile.

"Nor any excuse," her lady responded with a thud of her fists on the desk. "I don't know how you made it around the grounds without being seen, but there is no explanation. I can only assume that you have been selling whatever you've been able to steal to buy more of that weed. *I warned you* that there would be consequences to –"

"Dammit, listen!" Akaran interrupted. "I *didn't* do anything! Okay, yes, the reports. I needed them. There's stuff in them that –"

Ridora interrupted him with another punch to the desk that made a small little wooden horse fall off and clatter onto the floor. "*You* needed to follow *our* rules. That is *all* you needed to do, and you have failed."

"We've talked it over," Seline added for her. "I am afraid that the Manor no longer welcomes you."

The priest stood there in stunned silence as he looked back and forth between them. "It no longer... are you... you're throwing me out?!"

"There is no need to pack your bags. That has already been done for you," Ridora flatly retorted. "What belongings you can't carry have been sent to Prostil's vault. You're *her* problem now."

Akaran started to lunge forward again and this time, the orderlies from the other side of the room stepped forward to block his path even as the healer tried to convince them to stand down. "RIDORA! SELINE! I didn't I swear I didn't!"

The lady turned her back on him and flicked her hand back dismissively. "I will hear no more of it. Sergeant, remove him."

Ronald shoved the priest against a wall as he started to lunge forward, caretakers be damned. That one final movement was enough to kill any control he still had over his temper, and the only thing that stopped the sergeant from losing teeth was a plea from the blonde-haired girl. "Please, don't," she implored. "I haven't given up on you. There is time for you to find your way back to the path of the Light. If you fight..."

Her superior scoffed as she made her way out of the room. "I've met many a man such as him, Seline. There's no path for them that goes places either of us should follow."

Akaran started to retort, again, but the healer moved across the room before he could do anything more than make a few uttered profanities. Her finger touched his lip and he realized that despite how pissed she was, she looked like she'd been crying. "Don't. Please."

That gesture was all it took to deflate his anger (even if for a moment), and he gave up struggling against the guard. "I didn't do it, and you two know it."

"What I know is that I failed," Ridora intoned from halfway up the stairway leading to her quarters. "I will do better with the next one."

***

Outside, on the balcony on the other side of the manor, another conversation was unfolding as the last vestiges of the sun set. Bistra leaned against the railing and stared down at the garden below, wisps of ratty white hair dangling loosely down her face. She stood and just listened to the world around her, and when she was content that nobody else was in the hall at her back, she called out a single name. "Annix?"

Nothing answered. Nothing would. It never did.

"I know... know you... you did... th... this. This is... is what you... you do."

Silence greeted her. As it always did.

"Didn't do it ri... right. Too noisy to do it ri... ght. You know... know that."

More silence came to her ears, but now it was quieter. Darker. Insects quit chirping. The balcony quit creaking. It was *offensively* quiet. Not to the morals, but to the *soul*.

"You think th... is will hurt him," she rambled as her voice started to crack ever so slightly. "You think th... this is your game. You... you poke and... and you poke... and you watch and... he hurt... he hurt you so... you want to... start hurting him... like you do. Like you... you do with me."

The silence *pulsed* with a faint hint of a laugh just beyond her hearing.

Bistra sniffled and looked up at the moons as they appeared in the starry sky. "He... he'll hurt. Others... others not watching. He'll hurt and... and... you... you know."

The moons dimmed from her sight as she felt long, thin, claw-tipped fingers creep up her sides. They caressed her back began to dig into her shoulders. The silence didn't need *words* to express itself.

She began to whimper but didn't let up. "I... I had light. Once. I did. You know... know I did. He... he doesn't. Doesn't have li... light. Has... shadows. You didn't... you didn't notice..."

The claws glinted in the darkness before they sank slowly, inch by inch, into her shoulders. They didn't leave a speck of blood behind. They cut deep though, just not into her flesh.

"You... you just made him go..." she softly cried out as she felt a familiar pain welling up in the corners of her soul. "You just made him go find his help in the shadows."

Annix's claws sunk in deeper and filled her with a searing again deep in her chest.

Bistra let herself smile for one fleeting moment as she taunted the monster with the last coherent breath she could give. "They *won't...* and *don't...* like... *you!*" she screamed.

She kept screaming until Seline came to find her.

VIII. FAILURE OF FAITH
Wundis, the 29th of Riverswell, 513 QR

"Right now, all I can offer are crowns. You won't be allowed to stay here another day until we can prove that you are fit for duty. Last night was a kindness, given your condition."

Akaran looked at her in shock. "You can't possibly think that I...?!"

"It doesn't matter what I think," Catherine replied, "only what I know. And I know that you're going to tell me how that mace came into your possession – and then you're going to tell me how you acquired the reports about the Auramancer Exorcist and... what was that poor girl's name? Appaidene?"

The door to her office slammed shut as Paladin-Commander Spidous and Catherine's assistant Karaj stepped inside. "How long it takes for us to decide you're worth saving is entirely up to you," he added, barely-simmering disgust burning in his eyes, "so I would choose your words as carefully as you can."

As he withered under their furious glares, someone else was having a day that just might've been worse.

***

"What do you mean, 'the BeaST *knows*'?!" Jobbet hissed through clenched teeth as he pulled the door of his shop closed tight. "There's no way for them *to* know!"

Donta smirked at him from across the room. "They know. What they know? Maybe more. Maybe less. They know you did it."

The armsman stormed over to his sales counter and dug a leather-bound tome from under it. The shoddy lighting made it hard to make out the numbers, or more specifically, the lack of them. "The page is gone."

"Page?"

"*The* page. The payment," he swore. "Someone... this can't be happening."

Anais's bodyguard shrugged and idly picked up a sword to inspect. "Lot of things happen."

"Yes, but you don't understand. Someone had to have come in and stole it and taken it to them," Jobbet seethed as he tossed the book across the room. "Do you know who they told?"

"Gistan. He works –"

The armsdealer cut him off with a disgusting snort. "Yeah. Know that fisker. If he knows, I'm dead."

Donta leaned against the doorway and shrugged. "Then go."

"Oh you think that might be a good idea? Of course I need to go."

The mercenary stood there and watched the other man walk back and forth, peer into his cabinets, and shovel piles of junk around for a few minutes before he spoke up again. "Doesn't look like you're going."

"You just told me!" Jobbet snapped back, before asking, "Why *did* you tell me?"

"You did your part. Anais returns her favors."

Suddenly, he felt like he should have been a *lot* less trusting. As his eyes narrowed, he pointed a shaking finger over at the messenger. "No. This is an extra favor. I know how she counts. What do you want from me?"

"Nothing," he replied. "Just that you go."

"That's what it's about? Me leaving?"

Donta nodded and moved away from the door enough that someone could easily open it. "Anais protects her own. You did business with her. You got warned. How you go is up to you."

The merchant looked around his dilapidated shop and took stock of the dozens of swords, daggers, and other weapons hanging all over the walls and stacked up on display tables. "I'm not going to have time to sell this. Won't have time to even *pack* this. Gistan will have the Guild on me before the night falls."

"Probably," the assassin agreed as he pulled a sack absolutely packed with crowns out from inside his frilled white cotton tunic. "This help?"

Jobbet stopped where he stood and felt his jaw drop. "You're... what?"

"Want to sell?"

"Well, yes, but –"

With a loud jingle, Donta rattled the bag again. "No time for another offer."

"I don't have time to do anything!" the armsdealer exclaimed as he threw his arms up in the air.

Anais's minion shrugged and chucked the bag of crowns right at the other man. "Then deal?"

Jobbet peered down into the simple leather pouch and the not-so-simple total all of the coins inside would have to add up to. "This bag... for what?"

"All of it," he answered with a gruff, almost barked, reply.

The merchant's eyes went wide as saucers as he fixed the mercenary with an absolutely shocked stare. "You're trying to buy my stock for ONE bag of coins?!"

"Candle's burning," Donta replied as he gestured at a timekeeping candlestick. Little marks on a piece of iron beside it helped guess at the time – and it was his guess that the dealer had less than three marks to go before his day got *much* worse. "Have time to negotiate?"

Jobbet looked at the coins, looked around his shop, and then looked back at Anais's messenger. "You're a bastard."

"You don't even know," the mercenary retorted. "Deal?"

"*Fisk you,*" the dealer hissed through clenched teeth – even as he clenched the bag even harder. "You come here. You tell me that I need to run. Then you offer to buy me out for this?!" he demanded before he dumped the coins out onto the ground.

Donta just stood there and watched him count it up.

When he was done, Jobbet sagged in defeat. "Not that this isn't… a fair price. Why does she want weapons? There's enough here to equip an army!"

"Needs what she needs. Still want to fisk?"

He knelt down and started to pick up the loose golden coins and sighed in defeat. "How do I know you didn't arrange for all of this?"

"You don't," the mercenary admitted, "take it. Or not. Your choice."

Jobbet stopped picking them up and gave Donta a nasty, hate-filled glare. "Some day, you asshole, someone is going to bury one of these swords in your chest."

He was wrong, of course.

It wasn't going to be one of those swords.

***

It wasn't long before Jobbet's assumption came true. The Guild was going to descend upon his holdings before the night fell, but they had a singular stop to make first. At least, Huntsmatron Elsith did, though the mercenaries she sent ahead to catch the arms-dealer continued on unabated. Though one of them – a Sycian by the name of B'tril – did at least stop long enough to give Donta a nod and a brief sign of respect as they passed each other on the street.

Relationships mattered.

The relationship between the Guild and their founding company, so many hundreds of years ago, was one that unequivocally did, at that. When the Blackstone Trading Company demanded a thing done, the Guild did it. When the Huntsmatron demanded a moment to speak to an asset, the asset would speak. Even if the employee of the asset had no desire to do so.

In fact, Donta'd have been just as happy to add her to the ever-growing list of bodies that he was hearing about. Her arrival meant another one. "For someone that had agreed to help me hunt down the people responsible for the recent carnage, your matron seems to be doing anything but."

"Does what she does."

Elsith stepped right in front of him to block him from going down the street.

"You do what you do. Though you've also been awfully busy as of late. I've been enjoying watching the F-F-G's twist in the wind," she said, pronouncing the letters as *effigy* in some attempt to be condescending and cute.

He debated forcing his way past, but he knew damn well that the sword on her hip would go to his throat if he tried. Might be a fun test of wills, but not productive. Yet. "They? Do what they do. I? Do what I do. She? Does what she does."

She must've realized what he was thinking, and very casually opened her cloak a little wider to show how many weapons she had available to use – and those were just the ones he could see. "It's what she's been having you do that's interesting. I asked her for help, but I'm wondering if I wasn't looking in the wrong direction."

"Don't care where you look," Donta spat back. "Have things to do."

"Oh I think you're very wrong there," she countered as a group of chainmail-clad guards stormed by. "It has not slipped my attention that the bulk of the bloodshed did not begin until after the pair of you made your arrival to our humble city."

He scoffed and looked up at the towering buildings all around them. In this district, there wasn't a shop or house to be found that didn't look like it couldn't withstand a siege. Petty and pointless designs built only to impress laymen that have never touched a blade before. "Humble?"

She smirked and followed his gaze. "Doesn't exactly stand tall, does it? You don't approach the city and be wowed by how tall it stands."

"Size in underworld? Doesn't matter," he countered.

"Just need cast a very long shadow," she said as she flicked a hand in the direction of one of the nearly omni-present shadows that the pit offered. "As our city luckily does... and as does the Guild."

Donta snorted and blew her off without a thought. "Blame her? Think we killed them?"

"Did she?"

"No."

The Huntsmatron offered him the faintest of cold smiles from her pink lips. "Then I don't think that I can believe you. Not all of the recent deaths and others have made much sense, you know. A few Aquallan refugees get killed after arriving – plus I lost one of my men. And, of course, not to mention Lexcanna, may whatever Gods that she followed offer her soul remorse."

He bristled up instantly and wondered if those guards might've been for him. "People die. Sense doesn't matter," he retorted quickly. If she wasn't just pulling names out of a hat, the day might just be getting worse if she could prove it.

"Not always, no," Elsith conceded. "But if you take it into consideration with what she's been after as of late..."

"She's after a lot. Money. Influence. Power. Same as you."

She shook her head and lightly stroked her fingers over the hilt of the shortblade at her waist. "Ah, no. I already have all three of those. Though, allow me to explain a little. First, she arrives in town and starts buying her influence anywhere she can get it. Second, she establishes a relationship with the guards at the gate, and then after Paverilak enhanced the security around it, I know she went out of her way to arrange back-channel entryway into the city."

Donta bit his tongue and picked the simplest answer. "Exits important to everyone."

"True," she agreed. "Yet she continues buying influence. Starts making an effort to get into the Repository. Even has you bribe a few people over in the Guild." She watched as the assassin froze in place and waved him down with a dismissive flick of her wrist. "Yes, I know. You aren't the first to try to exert control over my men. Half the city has at some point," she clarified. "And you've been careful enough that you haven't pushed anyone to doing something that would violate the oaths they took – which is commendable, and smart, because if you had, I'd already have you buried in the cliffside."

"Not afraid to die," he snapped. "Threaten someone that cares."

Which was a lie – he did. Just not for the reasons she thought, and not for the reasons she thought she had scored a victory over him with. "Soon after, both Livstra and Odern die. Related, we assume. Then she tries even *harder* to get into the relic pit that the Oo-lo's sit on. A few deals here, a few deals there. Those don't work, and Lex passes into the great hereafter. but that's not even the interesting part. Nor is that you managed to exert your own influence over the F-F-G."

The mercenary adjusted his hat and blocked what little light was coming down from overhead from blinding him. "This isn't interesting."

"Someone manages to smuggle a relic of Agromah into the city," she continued on, "a weapon just *dripping* with Abyssian magic and protected by *intensive* and *inventive* runes. All of that after two people who could have placed such runes made such a thing possible died."

"People die. Said that already."

Elsith ignored him and went on, counting down on her fingers with each pointed accusation. "Livstra and the F-F-G to smuggle, Odern to mask it, and Lexcanna who might have discovered it's existence in the city, given her Divine propensity against the damned. Oh, and not to forget Erine – there's few people who could've even had an idea how to obtain a relic of that cursed place, let alone arranged for it to be delivered into the city."

The worst part wasn't that she was wrong about what Anais had done – though that was bad enough – it was that it made *sense*. The only thing she hadn't offered yet was a motive, but with that many (and those many with connections), that wouldn't matter. "She didn't. I didn't. They weren't ours."

"I'm confident enough to say that *all* of them might not have been at your hand. Or hers. Just understand: I've seen enough killers in my life to know when I am looking at one." The Huntsmatron stepped right up to him and peered under the brim of his hat and into his navy-blue eyes. "Right now, I am *absolutely* positive that I am looking at one."

To his credit, he didn't flinch. It earned him a little bit of respect, if not a smidgen of the mercenary's honest admiration. "You are. But. Think we did it? For truth? You wouldn't tell me. You'd hunt me."

"Maybe I just wanted to see you squirm," she countered.

"Maybe you want something else."

Elsith sucked in a little air and smirked down at him. "Maybe I want to *remind her* that if she doesn't help me find the person responsible for the ones she *didn't* order – and *soon* – that Henderschott and his goons will have indisputable reasons to pack his dungeon. Do you understand?"

He glared daggers at her and debated dropping her then and there. If there had been even the slightest chance he could've gotten away with it, he would've. Which, he admitted, was likely why she had picked the middle of the thoroughfare to accost him. "Your job? It's done soon. I promise."

"No. No, it's *my* writ, but it's *her* job," the Huntsmatron countered. "Don't forget that," she added as she pushed past him and went on her way to catch up with the armsdealer that had her interest.

Donta refused to give her the satisfaction of watching her leave. Even still, he waited until she was long gone before he uttered a cold, simple, "I won't forget this."

That, he was right about. A few minutes of angry soul searching later, and he hatched a new plan to set in motion. Get Anais and her toady, Ettaquis, off to a safe place she had secured in Cableture. That would be hard, but it was the only way to keep her secure for the time being. She'd be followed regardless, and the move wouldn't hide her long. A naval base was not the *ideal* place for a marked woman to establish a sanctuary – but it would delay any actions Elsith might take by a few hours.

That, he wagered, was all he could hope for, unless they packed everything and departed right away. Given their benefactor's disposition towards his agents that failed to uphold their end their employment, it wouldn't change their fate all that much. If anything, it would be less pleasant than simply meeting the gallows.

His second move would be a bit more brutal.

Elsith had just earned herself an appointment with his blades, but the vampire that had been drawing so much attention in all the wrong ways was going to have to go first...

***

The *Drunken Imperial* was the last place that Akaran could think to go. He'd taken a shine to it over the last few weeks. The patrons were gruff, smelled foul, and he'd seen more prostitutes plying their trade in the not-so-hallowed halls than he'd seen anywhere else in his entire life, but... they were honest about it.

Nobody was playing politics. Nobody was angling for a score outside their means. Nobody pretended to be a saint or put on airs. There was the occasional con-man and thief, but you could spot those a mile away. The establishment had nice gentleman by the door that had a polite, yet firm way of keeping the most undesirables and aggressively deplorable souls at bay, and it kept things fairly peaceful.

It didn't hurt that he looked like he could pick up an ox one-handed.

For a brief moment, he debated placing a bet just on that. Could be enough crowns to afford a new shirt, at least. Wearing the colors of the Order just didn't suit his mood at the moment – but not enough to waste what few coins he had. The look on his face at the miserable little thought was enough to catch the attention of the barkeep, who, he had to admit, had a habit of giving him more attention than he wanted on a visit-to-visit basis.

"You look like a man having a bad day," Celestine – or simply just 'Cel' to her friends – pointed out. And, he had to admit, he was actually grateful just this once that she considered him as such.

The *Imperial*. The one place in the city where an exorcist could be treated as equally the detritus that called it home. "That obvious?" Akaran grunted as he settled himself down on a stool.

"You're missing your sigil, you've got a harder limp than normal, and your eye is either bloodshot from a bad batch of cocasa or you've been crying," she remarked with a pudgy finger pointing at each spot she mentioned. "Plus the black eye."

"You're good."

"You've been better," Cel countered. "What can I get ya, hon?"

He took a deep breath and looked into the anemic pouch in his hand. "I... I don't know what I can afford."

Her eyebrows arched so high that they almost disappeared into her hair. "Huh. No sigil and your credit with the Lovers has run out, has it?"

"I looked somewhere they didn't like," he muttered.

"You've looked a lot of places people didn't like."

He frowned and gave her a look that was equal parts irritation and confusion. "What's that supposed to mean?"

Cel gave him a wolfish grin that implied a hunger for something other than the barely-edible stew she had a habit of serving up. "That I may be a fat heifer, but I ain't deaf."

There were lines that even he knew not to cross. That was one of them, and he quickly sat up straight and began to offer a round of apologies as he (desperately) tried to figure out what he'd said *this* time. "Huh? I wouldn't ever call you, I mean that's not –"

Her laugh could've made the windows vibrate. He wasn't sure it didn't, though he visibly relaxed hearing it. "Aw calm your adorable boy-tits," she jovially quipped. "You didn't have to say it. Your eye goes to every other half-conscious woman in here but me. Just because you're not up for a trio of joy doesn't mean that I'm offended by it none."

"A trio of…?"

Cel hefted up her left breast with both hands and said, "Celiene," before she dropped it with a slight thump and lifted the other, "Celeia, and me," she answered as he looked on in utter bewilderment. "Who else you think?"

Akaran sat quietly, completely lost as if he should be offended, worried, curious about how she picked the names, or if he should just be apologetic. There was a brief moment when he wondered if Seline knew her name sounded a lot like… "You know," he said to interrupt his own thought, "look, I don't know what I can aff… you know, I should probably…"

"You ain't got many crowns and you ain't got a place to stay," she interjected as his thought trailed off. "That about right?"

"That's about right," he admitted with a sigh of defeat.

"And whatever's gotten you at a loss for both *probably* means your head ain't exactly firmly attached to your shoulders," she pointed out.

The exorcist ducked that comment and set his coinpurse on the counter. "I've got a handful of crowns. I can run a line of credit, maybe? I won't be…" he said as he sighed and slumped his head. "This will get resolved soon."

She nodded knowingly. "How long you on the outs for?"

"Until I see the errors of my ways," he grumbled sardonically.

Cel nodded and pursed her lips a little. "I'm gonna take a solid guess and say that you don't think your ways had any errors?"

"How'd you know?"

"You ain't the first young man I've seen come through those doors with that kinda weight dragging 'em down," she replied. "First priest in a while. Absolutely the first Oo-lo'er."

He grunted and idly flicked a loose crown across the counter at her. "Can we not talk about it?"

"We can not talk about that, fine, but the matter of credit? That's a different story."

"How different?"

She passed him a mug of something that wasn't entirely foul and rubbed her hands together. "Two nights. You get two free. We almost always have some scrap bread, too. The ale is free. For two days. Not a drop after. You've been busy, and busy gets rewarded around these parts."

Akaran took the mug reluctantly and peered down into the slightly-frothy contents. "I feel like I'm being accused of something else I didn't do."

"Aren't you the cripple-priest that's been going out and trying to deal with the bastard droppin' my friends?"

"Cripple-priest, huh?"

Cel smirked and poured out a glass of whatever she was trying to claim as beer for herself. "A few've taken to saying you're from the Order of the Stick."

All he could imagine from that was a crowd of people suddenly kneeling down to worship at the altar of a long, grizzled-looking stave, with him at the head of the flock. Crestfallen, he dropped his head onto the counter-top. "Goddess. Dammit."

She broke down into a throaty chuckle and swatted him across the back of his shoulder hard enough that he just knew it was going to leave a mark. She wasn't just built like an orc; she hit like one, too. "Oh it's not that bad. A lot of young men would want to be known for their sticks."

"A lot of young men would like to not have one," he grumbled as he utterly missed the point.

Not that she let him have that much luck. "For that, I hear you're in the wrong kingdom. How about Ogibus? I hear a lot of stories about those fishmongers."

"In all honesty, I'm not up for stories," he replied as he slammed the mug of ale back and held a little gag in the back of his throat. "Apparently, the normal punishment for a thief and a seal-breaker is to be sent off to the Grand Temple in chains until I am *penitent* for my behavior."

Cel pursed her lips again and frowned at the accusations. "Well those two things do sound rather serious, if you're putting them like that. Since you're here, I'm going to assume that's not the case."

"Oh, no," he countered, "they think that if I am forced to 'live among the people' for a few months, I will understand how good I 'have it,' even as broken as I am."

"Boy I don't know about you but that does feel like a bit of an insult," the innkeep answered after a minute. "Both to you and to someone like me. 'Among the people,' eh? I've seen enough of your folks through these doors to know that ya'll tend to like 'some the people' just fine when you need to get your *holies* holied."

It was almost impossible to let that slide – or not ask for names – but he lifted his cane instead. "The chains part was revoked since they don't think I'd be able to get far on this."

She crossed her arms and tightened her shoulders. "That absolutely *is* insulting."

"Ain't it just?"

Cel debated offering to go hit someone for him, or if she should offer him an opportunity he might actually take. "Well. The good news, I suppose, is that you came to the right place."

Akaran looked down into the mug and watched a lone bubble roll to the top of what was left. "Did I? Because..."

"Depends on what you stole and who from," she replied with a grin that was colder than anything he'd seen her wear before. "Sometimes we like thieves around here."

He scooted the mug away and shook his head vehemently 'no.' "I didn't *steal*," he countered. "I *negotiated* access to some documents."

"People that lose a negotiation don't always like the person that got ahead."

He didn't hide the snicker, and couldn't've if he'd even wanted. "I was left with the impression that this will take more than a couple of days. So if you have suggestions on long-term lodging...?"

The innkeep's eyebrows raised again. "They really kicked you outta *all* the temples?"

"Yes to the normal homes of the Lovers," he replied, "and I've been advised to avoid any Stara-based ones," Akaran added with a frustrated sigh. "With both Catherine and Ridora pissed, I don't think that the kindness the Order of Light had offered to show me is still going to stand. Then again, they might — piss off my people, their people may like me more."

"Well, the irritation of my enemy and all that I suppose," she agreed.

"Truthfully, if I've pissed off the Goddess, then I don't particularly want to grace the halls of the other Pantheon faithful. Piss off One, piss off Them all."

"Huh," she grunted. "Then aren't you just bent over a barrel. What are your plans?"

"I don't know," he admitted. "I... I don't. Whole life, I was told that I'd have a clear mission, told that I'd have backing and support. Told that if I did my job, I'd be taken care of. That's been shown to be a lie."

Cel nodded in understanding as she went to work cleaning a stack of plates piled next to her. "Well, you're young, so you've got time to learn that lesson and move on. Thing with moving on is that you have to move to other things."

"I guess. There's a couple of people I could talk to. The Odinal people liked me. Maybe that Lady Anais, whomever she is."

The innkeep dropped one of the dishes and quickly whipped her head back around to him. "Avoid her, boy. That woman and her cockpuppet of a minion. They are not people you want to get in bed with."

"At least it would be a bed."

"Well. You can find beds in places other than that," Cel replied with no little hopeful hint of encouragement, "so, maybe we can cut a deal?"

The priest tried to think of every possible stipulation that her offer could involve and liked almost none of them. "What do you mean?"

"If you've been kicked into the gutter by your folks, then you're not technically an *agent* of the Crown anymore, are you?"

"I... I guess not," he mused. "I'm suddenly... shit. I don't have authority anymore. That... I don't like that."

"Then we can do a trade for a while. Most of the city knows better than to fisk with a priest, former or otherwise. You may be getting *shunned* but most people out here ain't horribly dumb about things like that."

He pursed his lips and went back to nursing on the ale. "Hopefully. I've not made friends."

"Nah, wouldn't go that far," she gently disputed. "People know what the Guard is doing and when. They know when someone's trying to fix what the Guard fisked up. They know who, too."

"I'm just doing a job."

"You get your ass thrown out for doing it?"

Akaran grunted and finished the cup off. "More or less."

"Then I can give you a job, *if* you agree to a few terms," she replied slowly with the same wolfish grin from earlier.

He rubbed tiredly at his eye and felt a steady throbbing start up. "I just wanted a place to sleep tonight…"

"Just having a place to sleep tonight won't keep you from losing a place to sleep *tomorrow*," she deftly pointed out. "Or, day after, I should say. You're one of those fighting priests, so I'd act like it and start thinking ahead."

The fighting priest, as she put it, had to cringe at the rebuke. He took that moment to reach into his coat and pull his favorite-yet-hated bag of cocasa out. "I'm tired of thinking. I want to be doing."

Cel reached over and grabbed his wrist faster than she had any right to be able to move. "Rule one is that shit stays outside. Don't care if you partake while you're in the stalls or down the street, but if I catch you with it here, then it's gonna cost you more than a place to stay."

He sighed and pushed it back out of sight. "You know I don't get what the big deal with this stuff is. I feel fine taking it."

"You'd be the first and damn near the only," she retorted. "*Most* people taking it walk around buzzin' like a hornet nest is in their heads." The innkeep reached over and adjusted his tunic to hide it better and went on with her thought. "Go walk down the edge of the Overflow, closest to Naradol. See how they act. So. You don't do that *here* and we don't have a problem."

Akaran grunted and gave up trying to argue it all over again. The last thing he needed was to risk losing her offer of kindness. "Alright, alright. Fine. What's the job?"

"I need packages delivered. You don't look at them, in them, or otherwise open them, and we'll work out a deal."

"Packages," he repeated with a bland, dead look in his eye. "What does an innkeeper in the poorest part of the city have to do with packages that she'd need someone that would be able to dissuade other people from looking in?"

"What does a priest have to do with stolen documents?" she countered.

He bit his upper lip and couldn't hide his glower. "Fair."

"Doesn't pay much, but you'll get a place for now," Cel went on to explain. "Till you get back on both feet. I've got one that needs to go tonight."

"What is it?"

"You don't ask."

He tried anyway. "But I —"

"Doesn't matter about you," the innkeep interrupted. "*I* don't see anyone else offering you a job and a bed tonight, less you want to go hobble out to the Landing and see if they will let you stay without doin' anything either."

For a moment, he gave serious thought to the effort it'd take to walk all the way up there with the sun almost set and the day as long as it had been. He finally gave up and dropped his shoulders in defeat. "Where's it going?"

"I'll tell you after I get it together. Right now, you just sit back and enjoy some of this," she replied as she pulled a small stone platter out of the smoldering over behind her. It had bread and melted cheese on it, and in truth, was the best offer he'd seen all day.

He took one final swig out of his mug of ale and submitted to both the job and the offer of food. "I am gonna ask one thing."

"Careful..."

Akaran shook his head to ease her concerns and pushed the mug across the counter. "I'd always heard that the ale in the Kettering Province was great. But, and I mean this with no offense intended, every drink I've had everywhere is just absolutely..."

"Oh, I know," she agreed as she cut him off. "Like drinking muddy piss?"

He blanched slightly but nodded. "Wouldn't go that far, but... doesn't exactly live up to its reputation."

"Now *that* is a different story. What do you know about *pundja*?"

The priest gave it a brief thought and rubbed at his temple. "It's familiar sounding? It's um... fisk. A flower?" *Wasn't that in Bistra's...* he started to think before he stopped himself from saying it out loud.

"*Undja* is the flower," Cel explained. "The *blooded rose*. All the fiskin' rage with the ladies in waiting and their ilk. I'd expect that the city'd be covered in them if all things were normal."

"What isn't normal? The wedding celebrations or something else?"

"Something else," she answered. "See, now, the pundja is the stem, and that's the problem with the ale. The secret to the best brews in Basion is a handful of 'em thrown into a cask. Let 'em ferment for an extra week and you've done and got yourself a brew that'll knock the loincloth off your nuts. Just be careful not to get the thorns in the drink, 'cause boy, that hurts worse than a sunburned cootch."

Since the drink in his hand wouldn't knock a flea off of his ass, let alone a swath of cotton, he went for the obvious question. "Bad harvest?"

"Bad implies there was one," she retorted. "Some asshole-lickin'-scumbag went and poisoned the largest farm around a couple of years back. Now they can't get none to grow, no matter what they do."

Akaran felt the throbbing in his eye grow worse, but there was something about her story that started to nag at him worse than the pain in his head. "The blooded rose... it's called something else, isn't it? If not the flower, the plant?"

"Uhhh. Maybe? I don't diddy myself in those things. Plus, they've got thorns and... ow. You know?" she said as she busied herself with her hands in a cabinet well out of sight.

He ignored her and tried to focus on the thought picking at his brain. "No, I know it is. It's... that's right. *Crypt-bane*."

"Ah. Eh, that's a name, I guess. I like blooded rose, myself."

The priest shook his head again and bit down on his thumb as he struggled to think. "Cel? Do you know *why* it's called crypt-bane? Because… yeah. Yeah. I do."

"Nope," she replied as she handed him a burlap-wrapped package. "But I know that if the Overseer ever catches who did it, they're gonna get into a world o' hurt. And whomever brings 'em in is gonna make a mess of crowns."

"Where's the farm in question?"

"Northern Stairwall, I think. Just ask around there."

"Thank you. I need to go talk to them right now."

"No," she snapped back forcefully, "*you* need to deliver this package down to Raes at the *White Swan* down in Akkador East, or no place to stay. Whatever you're thinkin' you can't do a lot more 'till morning anyways. Go do this, and then come back and get some of this muddy piss brew down your throat. We can go on from there."

Akaran looked down at the tightly wrapped package and gave up with a slump of his shoulders. "I guess this counts as 'living among the people,' doesn't it?"

"It does," Cel agreed. "You know, one thing? Advice from a bat like me," she offered. Before he could ask, she went on and said: "Look around as you're out. I know 'bout your problems. Thing is, lots of folk hurt. Must of us have a bad back or our hands hurt. Ain't no shortage of people with canes. Pain ain't a new concept for the people of this world, you understand?"

"Well, no, but to lose… Her voice? Not be able to do Her will through magic? I can't… I can't *do* what I was trained to do and what I know to do now I'm not any damn good at."

She reached over and squeezed his hand reassuringly. "Magic ain't always snapping your fingers and making shit appear outta thin air. Magic is in what we do with each other, for each other. You're a priest; you know the lengths kindness can do for a soul in need."

He shook his head and focused on his fingertips like he could will some kind of divine light from them like he used to. "Yeah, but…"

"Besides," she added, "we can all do magic in our dreams. Now, you go deal with that package and I'll have a nice place set aside for you by the time you're back. Agreed?"

He, unfortunately, had to agree.

That didn't stop him from thinking about the trouble he was about to borrow, but he did agree. Outside, however, his tone shifted even as the headache not only grew worse, but grew to add someone to it. "Crypt-bane," he mused out-loud to absolutely nobody in particular.

Much the worse for his nerves when someone listened. "*Wherever your head is going I don't think I like it.*"

Rmaci's arrival didn't bother him anywhere near as much as it should have. To the point that this time, he didn't even bother looking around to find her or even feel much revulsion when he heard the tell-tale pitter-patter of bits of her ichor-covered phantom corpse dripping off of her body. "Was wondering if you were going to show up."

"*I don't want to be here,*" she groused as she pointed a flayed finger at his chest, "*but I don't like whatever you're thinking even more.*"

"That's a pretty profound change in tone from you," he remarked as he hefted Cel's package and went wandering off to its destination. "I thought you were enjoying all of this."

"*Before you touched that mace? There were a lot of things I enjoyed.*"

"I don't know how to respond to that, but, now that you're here, at least I can talk to someone about it," he returned as a distant crack of thunder overhead briefly interrupted his train of thought. "Crypt-bane is used as a natural deterrent to a few species of animated dead. They say it gets its color from absorbing the blood of the damned."

She looked down at the weeping gashes that dipped deep into her wrists and frowned in vague annoyance. "*As a member of the bloody damned, may I point out that I am not sad that they don't have any here? I lose enough of myself just by existing.*"

"You and a handful of other creatures, I'm sure," Akaran had to agree. "The Order of Stara and the nobility *loves* it. They think that if they put it out around their homes and funerals, it'll keep dead relatives or priests from coming back."

"*Does it work?*"

He shrugged as they walked on and paid no attention to the people listening to his one-sided conversation and ignored their 'he must be crazy,' looks. "It does more to discourage weak shades or other scavengers. It should've been all over the pyre you were thrown into."

"*Under, you asshole,*" she retorted with a nasty hiss. "*I was thrown under.*"

"Over, under, either way. If it helps, I plan on sending a rude letter to have the people that did it dismissed from service – or arrested, if I can find an excuse."

Rmaci's head wobbled back and forth a little. "*Can't say that it helps, but the suggestion is somewhat appealing. I'll accept it.*"

Normally, the absurdity of her approval would've induced a headache of its own, but he went on with his idea without giving her the satisfaction. "I can't think of a lot of reasons that someone would go out of their way to ruin a farm full of it."

"*Politics, economics, or even just spite? A ruined crop can ruin a farmer, or a merchant that makes a living on such things. I've done worse.*"

"Fairly sure 'doing worse' is why you fell into the Abyss, isn't it?" he taunted. "That aside, if it was just one or two, someone else would've planted a new garden of it and made a killing. There's something else, too. I can feel it."

The former spy mulled it over as they walked past a run-down store offering wilting flowers and a promise of 'bouquets that anyone would love.' Which, she decided, was also a lie. "*I saw you form the connection. That other exorcist in the Manor, what's her name? Bistra?*"

"That's her," he confirmed. "Tell me: what are the odds that the last thing she went to go investigate before she lost her mind is happening here, too?"

"*I don't gamble. It never pays in the pit.*"

Akaran stopped dead in his tracks and crossed his arms with a scowl in her general direction. "Okay. You know what? I'm going to ask you a question that's been bothering me since you first started poking around in my head and you're going to answer me truthfully."

His personal haunting chuckled in evil delight as she stretched her bloody body just to torture him a little more with the sight. "*What makes you think I'm going to do that?*"

"Because I may not be able to get rid of you, but Goddess help me, I can start focusing on every bad memory I've ever had," the exorcist warned. "Wanna know what a bunch of five-winter-old children singing, '*Oh Queen, Oh Queen, How Full of Glory Is Your Crown?*' sounds like? Because I remember. Or, maybe, I'll focus on Evalia. I know how much you despise her. You piss off every time I even give her a passing thought."

"*She murdered me. Set me on fire. She is WHY I am as I am! I'll speak the name of your murderer every chance I gain to make you feel the same the moment your soul crosses into the next realm!*"

"So, avoid getting murdered, got it," he taunted. Rmaci started to retort, but the priest didn't give her a chance. He closed his eye and focused on a room full of bored, snot-nosed, dirty, and otherwise disgusting children as they butchered every attempted 'note' before she cringed away and raised her hands in mock surrender. "*This may be the saddest attempt at torture I have ever experienced in either life.*"

"Wait until the chorus."

Her eyes reinflated in her skull long enough for her to roll them at him. "*You, you idiot, have lost your mind, haven't you? This isn't a threat, it's an absurdity.*"

He focused even harder and he could *feel* the choir of brats manifest in the air around him. Orphans and high-blooded children alike, the Sisters considered it an honor to the Order to host them every year. It was a mark of acceptance into the Order, a way for any child to open their hearts and sing to the glory of the Kingdom.

And it was absolutely horrific to listen to at best.

When the cacophony reached agonizing levels in his head, she gave up. "*You're a sick bastard. Ask the question.*"

Akaran opened his eye and squinted at her. "You've been dead for… three months? No, the better part of four? Almost that entire time, you've been stuck in my fisking skull. And apparently, stuck in Daringol's remaining mass, wherever *that* is."

"*I know where it is. It's close. Their screaming is getting louder as their ship gets closer. The Hullbreaker is soon to dock on these shores and the cargo she carries will corrupt the innocent and damned alike.*"

"Fine, whatever," he answered back dismissively.

"*Save the bravado, my boy.*" the wraith retorted. "*I know that just made your heart race. Darkness rises on the waves.*"

"And when it gets here I'll tell the Order what to do about it because *then*, at least, they'll believe me. It may take a few people dying, but eventually, they'll get off their high horses and *listen*."

Rmaci glared daggers at him. "*Maybe,*" she agreed, "*or maybe I'll take care of you first. Do go on with your thought.*"

There was an argument to be made for her being right, and the odds of Catherine sending someone to *purify* him at sword point weren't that low if and when the ship landed. He'd do the same, if he was in her boots. "As I was saying. You've been stuck on this side of the veil. How the fisk do you know anything about the Abyss? How do I know you haven't spent the last while pissing in my skull and saying it's rain?"

The spy blinked and studied his face before responding. "*Are you asking a damned woman how she became damned?*"

"Asking how a damned woman acts like she's had the run of the place when she's told me she's been in my head this entire bloody time," he countered. "You've been with me. *How* could you possibly know that shit when you won't leave me the fisk alone?" he demanded as another crack of thunder echoed off in the distance.

"*NEVER BEEN*?!" she screamed as she began to swell up to two, three times her normal size. The world began to shift around them as the street grew slick with blood and headless faces began to push out of the stone walls around them. "*I WILL SHOW YOU –*"

Akaran sagged down onto his cane and then backed up against a nearby wall as she ranted. A face turned to him and started to bite at his exposed throat when he hauled off and punched the wall with the back of his hand. "Just... don't," he sighed as his knuckles throbbed from the impact.

The wall – and the wraith – slowly went back to normal as the sound of utter *defeat* in his voice sapped the energy right out of her. "*What?*" The vision she pushed on him suffered the same fate, and faded away into the ether from where it came.

"Just... don't," he repeated. "The Order thinks I'm a thief, the Manor thinks I'm a hopeless addict, and now I'm running what are probably even more illicit drugs for an innkeeper that named her breasts. And I haven't even had the chance to take a nap yet, yet alone start to... cope. I'm not in the mood for your hedgewizard-level illusion tricks tonight."

She shrunk down the rest of the way, if not even smaller than normal. "*Saying it like that does something to take away from it being so special between us. Is that normally how you talk to a lady?*"

"You're a burn victim with a superiority complex who likes to talk down to people that are above you," the priest quipped back with a tired groan as he shifted his shoulders against the wall. "That's halfway to Dawnfire nobility, and would get you a title in Civa, but right now I'm standing in the middle of a street in the slums and I'm going to drenched from that storm and I just want you to answer the question."

"*Fine*," she huffed. "*Yes, I have been there. Yes, my essence has been fractured. Where do you think I go when I am not with you?*"

"Assumed you were resting."

"*What is rest?*" the spy asked. "*Here is an escape, and one that does not last for long. My hold on this reality is only as secure as the stability of your mind.*"

He blinked and rubbed at his overgrown goatee. "So... you're not all the way over."

"*We have a bond in the ether. As I stand here, I see the world as you see it. I also see through the veil at the same time.*" Rmaci paused for a moment and picked her next words carefully. "*I would say that there are other creatures that see the world such as I, though with loftier views of what is and what could be. The veil is thin, should you have the wherewithal to look in the right places.*"

"So when you're showing me that cell in my dreams...?" he halfway asked.

The wraith gave a simple nod before she clarified further. "*That cell exists in the next world. It is the last place I saw you, and you saw me, and it serves as a bridge.*"

"And you've been out of that cell," he remarked.

"*I made that cell,*" she explained. "*the moment I fell. I did not make it willingly. I made, and it was made, by me, for me, by death, by judgment of the storm. I didn't start there, and I don't end there.*"

"How long?"

"*What?*"

Akaran cleared his throat as curiosity battled sense. It was admittedly very rare to speak to a soul from the other aside, let alone have an extended conversation with one. He figured he may as well make the most of it since she was going to stalk him anyways. "How long have you been there?"

She wavered and looked up at the sky as a series of thunderclaps made her cringe with each distant 'boom.' "*Time doesn't matter.*"

"Of course it does," the priest argued. "It's how... how we explain everything. Our memories, our experiences, our lives. It has been ninety-nine days since Makolichi broke my knee. If I've counted that, you've counted the hours you've spent suffering."

"*Time doesn't matter because time doesn't exist. Not there. Not on the other side, either, so you know. A truth I can say is that there are three great torments in the eternal prison.*"

He mulled that thought over before he asked, "Worse than being burnt alive?"

"*Everything is worse than simply being burnt alive,*" Rmaci replied quietly, although wistfully pained. "*We do that, of course. The first torment is simple: we learn everything. All the secrets of all the worlds. All the secrets of time. I know things that you could never imagine. We learn them, and we're told of them, and we know that we know all of things of All.*"

The very idea of that made Akaran falter for a moment and he started to ask a question that he instantly regretted even thinking. "Even... no, no, it doesn't matter."

Her smile sent a chill down his spine. *"Even who your parents are? The thing the people who supposedly love you won't tell you?"*

"It's not important. The Goddess is my mother."

She just laughed at him. *"Even if She were, I could not tell you. That is the second torment – we* know *but we cannot* say. *It is an immutable rule,"* the spy added as she placed her hand on his chest and looked right into his eye. *"I know* everything. *Yet, for all the things that I wish to tell you to torment you with, for all the truths that would destroy your life, and for all the things that I know that you have the potential to be – no matter how slight that potential may be! – I cannot* express *it. I lack the ability. It is there in my head, here, on my tongue, but no sooner could you reach up and pluck the moons from the sky and wear them as a crown could I express the things that I know that would ruin* you," she promised as she explained.

Akaran rocked back on his heels and worked to digest that thought. It was fascinating, no doubt there, but he was regretting opening his mouth to start with. Even still... "Not... okay, not the answer I was expecting. So no way to force you to...?"

"There's one sure way to find out," Rmaci replied as she made a hanging gesture with her hands and hovered up off of the ground for a few heartbeats. *"I'm sure we can find a way that'll let you discover if I'm telling the truth or not, if you're willing to step off of that particular bridge."*

"What's the third? You said there were three."

"The third torment? We know everything. But everything is new." Before he could ask, she went on to explain herself unbidden. *"I know everything that's ever happened to me there. Every claw, every tooth, every lash, every ember and flame. Every scream,"* Rmaci replied as she curled up on herself as the memories rushed to her unbidden. *"When I slide back there next, I will lose the memory of what happened before it happens again. It's... it's all fresh. It's the first time. Every time. Time doesn't exist in the after because if it did, the horror would dull. It never dulls because it never happens a second time. It only happens the first time. Every time."*

He clamped a hand over his mouth as his stomach started to object to the picture she was painting. "So every time you..."

*"When I fade later tonight, I will walk from that cell in your mind to a cliff. I will be compelled to jump, and I will cry with every step I take because before I fall, I will **know** what is to come. I will cry because I know that I will land on the backs of three men who are lashed together with rusted iron cords, and tied to a bed of molten spikes. One spike will push through the center body, and it will punch through my thigh, here,"* she explained as she pointed at a spot on her leg, *"and exit through the other side. I'll push myself off, and then I will be compelled to kick that man until both his teeth and my foot break."*

"Rmaci, I..."

"*He'll scream,*" she continued. "*That scream will draw the attention of a monster. It'll look like you, actually, at first. It'll mimic you. I thought it was you, the first time. I'll think it's you later, too. It will offer to help me. Then it will take me by the hand, bring me in close like a lover, and soothe me with calming words and promises. Once I begin to believe that you've somehow come to save me, the monster will kiss me. Just a kiss.*" She gave him a sad, tired gaze that belied how horrific she was to look at, and then she pressed a bloodied finger to his lips to silence his objections. "*Then it will bite my lip off. It'll stomp on my foot, and break it again. I'll struggle and try to run, and it'll let me.*"

Akaran's shudder was less at the touch and more at the story she was telling. "Rmaci, please, I —"

She shook her head and quieted him a second time. "*No. You wanted to know. It will chase me until both of my feet are bloody. I'll run to a lake and think that maybe, just maybe, I can swim away. I'll get in the water. What's left of my skin will dissolve, I will scream; the water will get into my lungs. It will destroy them. I will thrash in the water, and the monster that looks like you will fish me out and break my legs with a hammer. It'll play with me, then throw me into the lake again when it gets bored. Ill float. I'll be pulled under. I'll be reduced to a bag of soggy bones, and then I'll make it back here. To you.*"

"That's... that's..."

"*And the* bitch *of it?*" she asked, "*The absolute bitch of it? That moment as I fall of the cliff? I'll forget. I won't know any of it. I will be crying as I jump because I know what's going to happen, and I will scream as I fall because I won't understand why I'm being sent to damnation instead of being rewarded for serving the Empress and the Goddess that she speaks for.* That's *a literal* damning *lie. That's a truth I can tell you,*" she finished.

The priest couldn't find the words to reply. He looked at her, truly *looked* at the bloody mess her wraith manifested as, and slowly, silently, dropped his head to his chest. There wasn't any way to say anything – nothing would make it better. Nothing could. By literal Divine edict, nothing was *supposed* to.

Knowing that did absolutely nothing to make it easier to cope with.

"*Hm? No witty comeback?*" she charged. "*No snarky little remark? No happy little cheer or bit of relief that now you know whenever I* let *you sleep that I'm off getting mine? That the Gods you serve have condemned me to torture without end and torture without understanding? That the glorious and wonderful and pristine and pure Cunts that look down on us from Their lofty thrones send* thousands *and* thousands *of souls into the pit every day, every hour? That the Gods you serve throw people that have done so much* less *than I into torments that will never, ever end? Nothing to say about that?*"

Akaran took a hard, long breath and shuddered as he exhaled. Finally, after a long, drawn-out moment of silence, he lifted his head and looked into her empty eyes. "You're a bitch, you're a liar, you're a murderess, and only the Gods know what else you've done."

"*Condemnation. Spoken like a true man of the cloth,*" she mocked. "*Don't you wonder why I'm here? Why I'm in your head?*"

"Assumed you wouldn't tell me even if you could."

"*You never asked,*" she taunted. "*I'm here because I am bound to you. You helped kill me. You saw me die. When Daringol swallowed you, I latched onto you because your guilt for how I died gave me a door.*"

He snarled at her and tried to shove her away. He only succeeded in stumbling through her vision and into another wall. "Then go back through it!"

"*I CAN'T,*" Rmaci all-but screamed. "*I am anchored here! I hear that damnable cluster of souls screaming for your name, I **feel** them pulling at me but I am anchored in **you**. They pull me towards their ship, the Abyss pulls at my essence every waking moment in this world, but I am stuck returning to you again and again and I will until you die and then maybe then I will claim that mass of souls and use what power it has to stay on this side of the Veil,*" she ranted. "*Until such a glory comes, the only escape I have from torment is when I am with you, you one-eyed **bastard**.*"

His second reply wasn't what she expected. In a way, it wasn't what he expected, and he knew without doubt he'd regret it sooner rather than later. He did it anyway. "Stay there as much as you can. Rest. Rest in my head, if that's where you get... peace."

She sneered and attempted to slap him. Nothing happened, even though he felt the gory mass of her hand pass through his mouth. If she did it again, all bets were off about the quality of Cel's ale. "*Now you're just insulting a dead woman because she didn't live the life* you *think she should.*"

"Shut up," he snapped as he took a longer breath and refused to look back into her eyes as another clap of thunder exploded in the background. "You can hide in my skull or my aura or my ether or... whatever it is you're fisking doing. Until I can figure something else out."

Rmaci's laugh was as cruel as it was disgusted. "*Oh isn't that adorable. I give you a sob story and suddenly you think that you can make a difference. We've already established that the only way that I'm going to find peace is —*"

"What part of shut up didn't you hear?" he demanded in a low growl under his breath. "I can't do much but I can give you a safe place for now. I don't care if you are a raging psychopath. I can't imagine that the pit made you any better of a person, so at least I can understand that damn much."

She narrowed her eyes and ran her tongue across her melted lips. "*If you think that I'm not going to drag you through the flames...*"

"I think I'm glad I'm not pit-bound," he snapped, "so shut up and let me do something to help."

"*You* think *you're not pit bound,*" she quickly countered.

That statement almost rocked him harder than the rest of the story. "Am I?"

Rmaci started to reply but suddenly stopped like someone grabbed her tongue from the inside and forced it still. Finally, she was able to reply with a simple, *"I can't say. We already discussed that. But there's nothing in the rules that say I can't make you wonder either way."*

"Fine," the priest grunted back. "Then shut up and enjoy the 'I'm not screaming in agony,' part of your day and let me go deliver this package before it gets any later. Or before we get drenched," he added as he gestured up at the clouds above.

"Careful. Helping the condemned can earn you the wrong kind of attention, you know," she cautioned.

"Compassion is a virtue."

"Yet the weight of regret will damn you all the same," she wistfully sighed just before another crash of thunder split the air. *"I do realize I've been dead for some time, as you understand it, but doesn't rain usually come with this kind of thing?"*

***

This was exactly the type of situation that Anais had been warning him against since they first stepped foot into Basion City, and for a moment, Donta was absolutely grateful she had taken his advice to move her base of operations into Port Cableture for the time being. It would take longer for her to find out about this, for one. And if he didn't live through it, she might be able to recover his body for their benefactor.

Not that he had plans to lose, but anything was possible.

The decision to head to Flynn's Landing hadn't been a difficult one. In fact, it was Donta's third trip. Like Akaran, he decided that it was an obvious place to look — if the missing are mostly vagrants, then you go talk to the vagrants. Except where the exorcist had actually *talked* to them, Donta had used Lady Lovic's purse and the spike buried in his hand to encourage answers.

He expected much the same on this visit, only with some more names to go on that his new 'contacts' in the Fleetfinger's Guild had provided. He had an idea where the nest was located, but the numbers involved? He'd seen two eating in the caves behind the Orshia Falls, but before he went back there, he was hoping for a more *certain* idea. Two could've easily been four, or five, or more. Vampires liked to make more of themselves. That was one of the immutable rules about their ilk, and why the Crusade of Suns had failed to exterminate their race entirely so many centuries ago.

On the upside, he was about to learn that it was at least three.

She'd waited until he had put the city to his back and was deep into the woodland between the Landing and the poorly-kept path that went up the south-western wall of the basin. It was hard to say who was hoping for fewer witnesses — Donta, or the woman with the dragon tattoo on her cheek.

They skipped conversation and banter. When the first blast of energy destroyed a branch as thick as a yardarm next to his head, he assumed it was the Guild making good on their threats. When she jumped down from the canopy to reveal herself, his next assumption was that the Dawnfire army had marshaled a spare mage to do the job instead. She wore steel chainmail dyed their typical red and gold, and had the pewter symbol of a Specialist-Major on her neck. None of that mattered when the next bolt of lightning from her hands dispelled any doubt as if the near miss was an accident.

When he charged her, she didn't flinch until the twisted bone spike in his hand lanced out and nearly took her throat out. That was when she *hissed* at him like an angry cat, and showed off both of her fangs before she scored his chest and left it blistered from an arc of golden lightning.

He howled in pain, and she worked to batter him back with multiple blats of electrical energy that left him dazzled and burnt. The battlemage-turned-vampire was faster than he was by far, and that was a problem. She had him beat on range, agility, and an argument could be made for overall lethality.

Donta had three things she didn't and it would make for a quick end to the fight. The next time that the assassin jumped into the canopy and vanished into the limbs above, he slumped back against a tree and waited. He didn't have to pretend he was exhausted for long; his ashen-haired assailant blasted the ground at his feet with a forking bolt of mana that would've blown his torso apart if he had moved to the left or right.

Instead, he flung his hat directly ahead and into her face as she fell from above to try and finish him off. The distraction, minor as it was, brief as it was, and seemingly pointless as it was, allowed him time to plant his right shoulder in her jaw with a sickening crack – and then to bury the spike jutting from his left hand into her face.

Except she moved at the last possible second, and the only thing the spur tore was her hair. Then, as she had done several times before now, she moved just a hair faster than he could and grabbed his arm in both of her hands. Pale yellow lightning cracked to life and if there had been any hair on his body, it would've stood straight up. Instead, all he could do was scream.

Scream as a coil of lightning wrapped around his left arm just below his elbow. Scream as it scorched his pale skin and incinerated his sleeve. Scream as it boiled away flesh and muscle.

And scream when she blew his arm in half.

He stumbled backwards and clutched at his ruined limb. If he'd been human, blood would have sprayed from the impromptu amputation uncontrollably. Instead, the only thing that pulsed from his devastated stump was a cascade of sand that covered the forest floor at his feet.

She held her left hand out at him, palm first, and stared him down as he tried to focus on anything but the pain. "You culled the hunter that saw him feeding. Why?"

"He… knew?" Donta managed to croak out.

"He did. He wants to know why."

"Then he…" the assassin grunted, "can ask."

The battlemage shook her head and ran the tip of her tongue over one of her fangs. "No. Why did you do it?"

Anais's bodyguard seethed in pain and gave her a hateful stare. "To make friends."

"Ah," she replied before she began to slowly circle him. "I assume you feel differently now. Meister does not need to friends with such... lesser beings... like you."

Donta didn't reply. Instead, he tried to see if he could recognize her in the dark. "So he turned you. Sent you to kill me. Because I helped him?"

The parasite shook her head no and planted her heavy leather boot on his hat and ground it into the dirt. "Annix gave me this gift years ago. He calls me when he needs me. You've interrupted his fun, and I've been sent to make sure you don't anymore." A ball of lightning began to race up and down her extended arm, building up strength as it oscillated back and forth.

A second later, and it would've turned his sandy blood into a pool of molten glass.

Instead, from luck, or fate, or divine intervention, a child – a little boy that couldn't have been more than six or seven years old – stumbled into the clearing and gasped in surprise. The vampire with the dragon tattoo on her cheek turned around with a snarl and prepared to unleash the blast at him, instead. Donta had other ideas.

The bodyguard lunged at her and swung his good arm in a wide arc. She had to dodge away to keep from losing her eyes, even as the spur sliced open her cheek. Her spell rolled off of her fingertips and missed. Instead, it slammed into a huge oak tree behind him and easily cut it in half with a deafening boom that sent a cloud of debris into the air.

By the time she could see past the smokey haze, Lady Anais's enforcer was long gone. She was able to follow the trail of sand for a few minutes before Donta managed to find a way to plug it. She ran her fingertips over the scratch on her cheek and licked the digits clean as she wondered when and where she'd be able to find him next. But now she had another, more immediate, problem.

Her Meister would not tolerate witnesses.

As the night stretched on, the peals of thunder Akaran had heard earlier were joined by a legion more.

IX. WHAT LIES IN VINES
Londis, the 30ᵗʰ of Riverswell, 513 QR

The day started like the steaming pile of crap he had taken next to the horses after waking up, and his feelings on the matter were intentionally in-eloquent. Cel hadn't been impressed with how long it had taken him to deliver the first package, and he didn't think she'd be interested in hearing how the delay was caused by a conversation with a damned soul occupying his aura. For that matter, he wasn't overly thrilled with it himself.

Rmaci, thankfully, had kept quiet most of the day. He didn't know if she was being hounded by the demons that had taken an interest in her in the other world, or if she was merely giving him time to himself to pick at his wounds without her help. Either way, Cel had expressed her displeasure by giving him a 'room' out in the stables — which did nothing to either improve his mood or give him a break from the waves of pain radiating from his knee.

Thankfully, the innkeep didn't have any work for him this morning. From what she grumbled out, she only liked to send packages in the evening — which didn't make him feel any better about their contents. But a roof over his head was a roof over his head.

And that, he was forced to admit, better than any other offer he had at the moment. The thunderstorm last night had been nothing but dry booms, but it had heralded a miserable misting of rain soon after dawn-break. Unfortunately, the question of how unpleasant the day was didn't factor into his goal — but it did make the damn stairs even slicker.

Surprisingly, it only took a few minutes to track down the name he was after — and luckily, it didn't take more than another full candlemark to find his farm. Nadler Alpaige owned one of three different farms that focused (or at least, used to focus) on growing undja for the city proper. Of the other two farms, one had gone out of business and sold their plot on the stairwall to the Blackstone Trading Company (who had done something else entirely with it), and the third had a plot of land on the slope that you could barely park a horse on – not that he'd know, now that Catherine had decided to confiscate his.

"You'll learn how much being honest in the Order is worth, one way or another," she had said. While she may have had some reason to be annoyed about the documents that he had made off with, thanks to Philanus, the rest of his punishment was being based off of whatever bullshit story that Ridora had fed her.

It didn't matter how much he denied any of it, either. They assumed that because he was desperate for more cocasa, he had to be guilty. His desire to go throw stones at the manor for a few hours was seconded only to his desire to find out more about the undja and whatever fate had befallen it.

That question was quick, if not uselessly, answered. "They died," Nadler replied.

And that was the extent of the conversation.

Akaran was able to pry out a few more tidbits that were only slightly more useful. The die-off had happened suddenly, and nothing he did managed to get them to come back. Whatever sickness had taken them out couldn't be identified by anyone from the Oder of Nature and even the local alchemists couldn't figure out what had happened.

Still, despite being as communicative as a rock, Nadler was willing to let him take a look at the single row of flowers that he hadn't torn out yet. While it wasn't the end-all-be-all clue he was hoping to find, it was a start.

Normally, they'd resemble climbing red roses. Now, however, the flowers weren't just dead, they were effectively calcified. The flowers had gone completely white, but it was the vines that proved to be the most interesting. Usually, dead vines tend to toughen up for a while and turn brittle. In this case, the normally brilliant green vines had gone completely gray and they were barely able to hold the dead bulbs. Effectively turned to stone, the few roses left on their stems dangled limply, though most of them had fallen loose and turned into hard rocks in the dirt.

General inexperience aside, it wasn't like anything he could remember seeing even in training – though that didn't mean that there wasn't documentation buried somewhere in the Repository.

Not that he was allowed to get in there right now.

Just because he couldn't get there didn't mean he couldn't get elsewhere. *Maybe another trade with Ledger Philanus, if he hasn't gotten his own permissions revoked.* He paused to give that an extra thought. *Of course, if they did, they may thank me for finding a roundabout way to get rid of him.*

Another hour digging around searching for answers didn't yield many. Extended searching did turn up a few more scattered clumps of other vegetation in the same state, which was equal parts good and bad. None of it to the same extent as the undja, and it was hard to explain why a lump of grass had gone bad in one area and a grapevine had gone bad in the other.

It gave him plenty of opportunity to gather samples, if nothing else.

It *also* stirred up an appetite for something other than Cel's stale bread.

That, in turn, started him on an adventure to find out how you could enroll in the, 'Work the field, earn a meal,' program that the BeaST offered. Granted, it was probably little more than cheerful slave labor as far as the Blackstones (and by relation, the Overseer) were concerned. Still, it was food.

He was busy doing just that (and had managed to smuggle an extra couple handfuls of grapes in his coat) when someone arrived to either give him a headache or a hand. It was hard to say which, but given the simmering fury in her voice, it was probably going to be more annoyance than assistance. "After everything we did, I *cannot* believe you'd steal from the Manor!" Seline charged, just barely an octave short of a screech.

Akaran looked up from the weeds and gave her an eyeful of disgust. "I can't believe you think I would," he grunted, "or that you'd hunt me down to give me another lecture after."

"Just... why?" she demanded as she trudged through the overgrown path. He took a little personal satisfaction watching her dress get pulled and frayed from one thorn-bush after another. "Why would you break into... I know you don't like the other patients but...?"

He shook his head and went back to foraging. "Again, I can't believe you think I would."

"How can't I? A doll from Appaidene. One of Divitol's spinning tops. I don't even want to know how you managed to steal a wineskin from Comstead Manor."

The priest stepped back from the bush he was working on and fought off the urge to chuck a pear at her face. "Easily: *I didn't*. I don't know how many times I have to say it, but I *didn't*."

Not that she noticed his restraint, or if she did, she didn't seem to care. "I don't suppose you want to tell me where the crowns came from?"

"I told you already," he retorted. "Some of it is part of my stipend from the Order. Some of it was a reward for helping out the Odinals," he explained – for the fifth time, at least – but made sure he left out where the rest of the coins had come from.

"That stipend is held by them until you need it. You don't keep it in your room."

"Okay that's not *entirely* true," Akaran replied as he lifted a finger for effect. "They keep it until I need it, but since I'd been spending some time down at the Imperial, I made sure to keep a pile set aside."

"But that's not the only place you got it, is it?" she charged.

His sigh was heavy enough to crush a boulder, and she again chose to ignore his discomfort entirely. "Can we just agree that hearing rumors is easier if you have something to barter with?"

Seline's eyes narrowed into slits as she pointed accusingly at him. "Barter with? So... oh. I see. You aren't just *taking* cocasa, you're selling it. That's what it is, isn't it?"

There wasn't any sense denying it. He'd be lying if he did – it helped grease a few wheels here and there, though damned all if it had given him anything actionable yet – and she wouldn't have believed him even if he'd put in the effort. "Did you just come here to insult me? Really? Because I've got better things to do."

"I came here because I care about you, you *fisking* moron. You think that I wanted her to toss you out?"

"I think that you believe I'm a liar and a thief. I think that you're pissed because you think I was doing it right under your nose. Since I wasn't stealing from the guests and wasn't doing it while you were watching, I really don't give a shit *how* you feel right now," he added with the same foul look in his eye. "Because, frankly, I can tell you how *I* feel, and I don't think you'd like to hear it."

She dropped part of her angry facade and clenched her fists out of frustration. "I didn't... we didn't. We didn't know Catherine would kick you out too."

"*You* didn't, I'll believe," Akaran agreed. "Ridora? Oh she knew. She had to. Catherine knew all about it before I even *got* there, which meant she had one of her little helpers go tell her everything she *thought* about me before she bothered to accuse me herself."

"She has to take care of the residents! In the years that the Manor has been treating its guests, nobody's *ever* stolen from them. Let alone stolen from them to fund their... their..."

The exorcist snorted and clutched the handle of his wicker harvest basket so tight that it started to splinter. "I'm going to assume you mean my supposed degenerate habits and hobbies."

Seline started to shoot back with an angry, witty retort, but she let it go before it fell out of her lips. "You're a sick man and you need help. I want to help. We want to help."

"I seem to recall telling you that if you want to start helping me, you can start *believing* me. Until then, the only thing – and I do mean the *only* thing you're doing – is finding new and exciting ways to piss me off even more."

"I'm not trying to piss you off! I'm trying to make sense of it!" she screamed loud enough for people the next several rows over to hear. "If, and I do mean *if* you are in the shape you suggest, then how are you walking? How are you stepping foot in any of the holy buildings in the city without... I don't know! Catching fire?"

Not that it wasn't a valid point, he admitted to himself, but it was one they'd already beaten to death. Repeatedly. With gusto. "We've established that I'm not being affected by things like that right now!"

Seline crossed her arms and tugged the tail end of her dress loose from an errant, poorly-growing stick. "No, *we* haven't. We've established that something has turned your aura and turned you into some kind of... kind of... *vessel* for powers we don't understand."

"And if you don't understand them then how exactly the fisk can you judge me when I say I'm doing and feeling what I'm feeling?" he shot back just as forcefully. "Tell me. I barely understand how I'm handling this! *Everything I know* has been wrong! Even that damn book that knocked me around in the library or that *horrific* vision when I grabbed Moira –"

"Grabbed… *Moira*?" the healer seethed. "You're grabbing women now, are you? No wonder your 'unrequited lust' from Toniki hasn't sent a single letter to check on you."

He flinched as the barb hurt worse than he wanted to admit. "Pissed I didn't try to grab you, is that it?"

She dropped her head to her chest and let loose with a guttural cry of frustration. "Give me a reason to believe you. Any reason. Just one. One reason, one *shred* of proof that you haven't lost your mind, and we can start. Please, Akaran. I don't want to think you're a liar. I don't."

"One reason? Okay. I can do one. I just found this shit," he challenged as he tossed a clump of gray vegetation at her. She managed to catch it before it hit her face, and internally, he was slightly pleased that it left a stain on her dress. "Any chance you've seen anything like this at the Manor?"

"What is… this is foul," the healer muttered as she lifted it up and took a deep sniff of the rotten thing. It didn't reek of mold or mildew, but it smelled like death. Raw, uncensored, baked-in-the-sun death. "Really foul."

"It is, isn't it?" he agreed. "From what I've been told, it's a sickness that's been spotted in a couple of different spots. It's wiped out the local crop of undja, and it's done a number on some moss outcroppings closer to the Falls. Lot of it down by the Overflow, too."

Seline shuddered and let the disgusting desiccated mass fall to the ground and stepped back away from it. "I know that if any appeared at the Manor, then Yannis – the gardener – would have it gone as soon as he saw it. The Lady is an absolute stickler for what she does and doesn't tolerate there."

"I'd be very interested to know if she's seen any."

"He, and why?"

"This crap? When it isn't a rotted pile of shit, the stem is called pundja and the flower is called undja. They're used for entirely different reasons when harvested – but more importantly, the whole plant is known as crypt-bane," he replied as he waved a hand around at the rest of the crops. "It's dying and I don't think it's natural."

The healer stared down at it for a few moments longer and carefully walked around it. "If it isn't dying by natural means, then…"

"Then maybe someone will believe me."

"That's not a lot and you know it."

"If I had a lot then you'd already believe me, wouldn't you?" he snapped back.

That was the one argument he had that she couldn't refute. Swear about, yes, refute, no. "Dammit," she sighed as she stuffed what little bit was still on her hands into a bag on her belt. "What else? What else do you know that you're not sharing?"

Akaran arched an eyebrow at her and looked at her in disbelief. "You mean aside from the voice in my head?"

"Is she sharing anything useful?"

He stopped everything he was doing and tried to deny it, but gave up and didn't. "Yes but... no," he finally mumbled. "That aside: I need you to promise me something."

"You're not in a position to ask for any promise," Seline pointedly remarked. "Or favors. Or anything. But I'll humor you. What?"

Akaran took a deep breath and tried to think of the least likely way to ask her without a blatant objection. "If you hear about a ship coming to port down in Cableture... the *Hullbreaker*... you get the piss out of this town. Grab anyone you care about and you run." He let the question linger before adding, "Up through the north, too. Don't go anywhere near Yittl, and stay near the clearest paths you can. Speed will be important. Don't stop until you hit another Lover shrine."

The insistent gravity in his voice made her second-guess the first quip she had, and she wavered slightly before she responded. "What? Why?"

"That voice?" he asked as he gestured at the side of his head. "She claims it's coming and claims it's loaded with the damned."

"You told me that once already."

"I did. When I thought she was a dream."

The healer let out a slow sigh as all of the pent-up anger she'd been carrying faded into concern and grief for him. "You don't now?"

He shrugged the thought off. "It doesn't matter. You've already decided. But I'm asking you regardless. Please."

She walked a few steps closer to him and tried to reach out to touch his face. When he recoiled away, she let her hands drop loosely to her sides. "Do you believe it? That it's real? She's real?"

"Sel... I don't... if I was losing my mind, wouldn't I know? If I was going crazy, truly crazy, wouldn't I know?"

"Does Appaidene? Does Bistra? Does Oda? You know, the screamer?"

"I don't know," he admitted. "But yeah. I believe she's real. I believe that the arin-goliath is still out there. I don't have faith that I banished the entire creature and I'm certain that it's coming here. After me, mainly," he replied with a sigh of resignation. "And I cannot do *shit* about it other than warn people I happen to think fondly of. They're not going to believe me and they're going to die and that's also going to be *my* fisking fault because *I* couldn't convince them."

"But you believe," she replied quietly, "and you think fondly of me?"

"Sometimes more fondly than others," he muttered. "Yeah. I do. Which means I'm probably going as mad as you think I am and I'm probably as damned as she's suggesting."

Seline looked at him – really *looked* at him – and watched frustration-born tears trickle down his cheek as he sagged against his cane, completely defeated and utterly crestfallen. "Maybe," she whispered.

He coughed and shook a few of the teardrops away as he straightened up against his cane and peered down into his basket. "Now if you're done making me feel even worse, thank you, then I'm going to go deliver this basket of crap to the field overseer and –"

"Or… or maybe not," she interrupted.

"Huh?"

She looked down at the ground again and started to fidget with a journal tucked into her belt strap. "I don't know what to make of this. It pisses me off. There's no explanation for it. None. I have no *fisking* idea what to think about this," she complained as she pulled the leather-bound book with a familiar title loose and handed it to him. "This. You're the one that found it but you didn't take it from her room and I wish you had because if you had then I could pretend it didn't exist," she swore as she handed it to him.

Akaran recognized it right away, though whatever reason she had to bring it with her was utterly lost on him. "*Against the Odds*? This is from Livstra's room. What's so important about it?"

"It's what's inside," she replied. "Don't even bother trying to read it, it's in some kind of code or foreign language or…"

He looked inside anyways and frowned almost as soon as he did. *Code* was an understatement. She'd written it in at least two different languages he *thought* he recognized, though nothing he could make out more than a stray 'owed' and 'paid.' "Why in the world would she write anything like… this? She's a healer, not one of the Queen's Diplomats, isn't she?"

Or as others knew them, the Queen's Corrective Diplomatic Corps. It was a fancy and polite name for the Crown's private band of spies, muggers, thieves, and assassins. The sarcastic accusation made the poor girl blink in surprise, because honestly, it wouldn't feel like much of a stretch. The Manor was known for housing people that knew things, but had lost the ability to keep them secret.

It would make sense if there was someone making sure…

The joke could've been all too real, and she choked on the thought. "I… I don't know. It's the only thing in her room that we found was written like that. Maybe… I don't know. There were other books missing. Maybe whomever killed her stole them and she wrote like this? Honestly? With the way that Ridora treated you? I was afraid to even bring it up."

"Think she's covering something up?" he asked. "Maybe trying to bury something other than my reputation?"

Seline pursed her lips as a slow wave of heartburn started to creep up her throat. "I think that she's in such a pissy mood she'd throw it at my face."

"It's not fun," he admitted as he flipped through the pages. "Still, you're trusting me with it?"

She sighed and let her shoulders droop a little. "Let's count my choices:

Take it to Ridora, piss her off. Take it Catherine, run the risk of it pissing Ridora off. Take it to Henderschott..."

"...and risk pissing Ridora off?" he guessed.

The healer curled her lip and made a gagging sound. "Ugh. No. Well, yes. But it'd mean I was stuck in a room with that human shithouse."

Her gagging was met with his surprised cough and a laugh. "What is with you two anyways? Were you two together at some point or...?"

She shot him a look that was viler than anything anyone had given him so far and he laughed again. "I'm afraid I don't know anyone else that would be helpful. You, on the other hand, I'm sure know someone. Or several someones."

Akaran flipped through it one last time before he dropped it into his basket. "Probably, but damned if I know who to trust with it," he answered. Before she could curse his paranoia, he went on to add a solution. "But! I know a way around it. Remember that invocation I read a few weeks back – the one in the Repository? Before the dance?"

"I remember you punched a priest," she retorted.

"Some spells have side effects," he replied with a shrug. "I wrote it down after. It's supposed to invoke the Goddess of Knowledge to unwind text and translate it."

"You can't use magic though," Seline quickly pointed out.

"No," he slowly agreed, "but it shouldn't be hard to find someone that can." A second later and a new thought dropped in his head. *I can't use it, but it activated. If Rmaci did... after I fell asleep... then I wonder... wait. I didn't activate that spell. I can't. I wasn't the only one there. Rmaci... thought she was a dream then but that was wrong. I can't use magic but she can manipulate the ether enough to manifest. Can she use it to do worse than just... pop up in my sight?*

Shit. That's interesting, bad. But interesting.

In the back of his head, a little voice chimed in. "*I can hear you, you know.*"

Before he could retort back at her, Seline rubbed at her temples and gave serious thought to taking the book back from him. "Just... please find someone trustworthy. I don't know what's in that book but it was hidden in her room. It could be something important about one of our residents. Or something that's supposed to be under seal of your Order. Or worse."

"I've just about had it with, 'or worse,' you know that, right?"

The healer had to nod in agreement with that before she turned and started to look around the farm for anyone close enough to eavesdrop on them. "I uh... there's... something else," she whispered just loud enough for him to hear. "I found... well. This I'd... I'd say that you aren't the only thief, but in all honesty Akaran, there's no way she could have gotten it. Please tell me you put it in her room. Lie if you have to. But please," she begged as she pulled a sigil out from her bodice.

There was absolutely no mistaking what it was or who should have owned it. That Seline had it dangling from her neck was one issue, but that she had it *at all* was another. "How – where – did you find *that*? You know what it is, right?"

"I know that Raechil used to have one in her room," she admitted. "Said it was a gift from her sister. Not the same one as this." The necklace was unique in design – a trio of silver chains braided around each other with a round iolate crescent (with just a slight curve along the bottom) that hung from it. The nearly midnight-blue gem had a pair of moons etched into the center of the disk, and a silver strip ran along the edge of downward-facing crescent.

"Her sister...? Kiasta? She's Erine's bodyguard, isn't she?"

"I guess? I never met her."

"I did," Akaran mused through clenched lips. "Cheerful woman... in the way that a sword is a fun toy for kittens."

She let herself smile at the adorable visual – then realized he wasn't laughing. Not only wasn't he laughing, he had set down his basket and was closing the distance between the two of them far too quickly for her comfort. "So, um... you know what it is?"

"Wish I didn't," he muttered. "Where'd you find it?"

"What is it?"

"Where, Seline?"

His reluctance to answer made her nervously wrap her fingers around the sigil. "Tell me yours I'll tell you mine?"

"I'm not sure you want to know," he replied before he gave in and explained what it was. "That's a Penumbra of Lethandria. Whomever had it last needs to be asked what they know about Erine's disappearance – because that belongs to a Mother Eclipsian."

Seline's fingers slipped off of the Penumbra as her stomach dropped. "How sure of that are you?"

He looked up from her chest and bored a hole through her head with the look in his eye. "If I didn't know you, I'd be asking with my hand around your throat while I looked for a nearby gallows."

The healer knew he meant every word of it, and Henderschott's old comment that he was the most dangerous man in the city made her heart skip a beat for all the wrong reasons. "Oh."

"Where did you find it?"

"Appaidene's room."

Akaran frowned and tilted his head quizzically. "That can't be coincidence."

"It needs to be," she pleaded. "She's completely mad. She can barely get to the chamberpot on time, let alone..."

"Except she had it with her, apparently," the priest pointed out.

The healer shook her head so hard blonde trusses fell down over her face. "Akaran, I don't know. I'm getting scared. First Liv gets killed, now she has a secret journal that can't be read. Then Raechil goes missing. Then you turned out to be a thief. Now a woman that can't even *talk* has the sigil of the missing

Priestess of Night?"

He shrugged and pointed a finger up to the sky. "If it helps, I'm not a thief," he lied as he casually omitted the coins he'd... *liberated* from Se'daulif.

"I don't know *what* you are," she sighed. "What did you tell Bistra, anyways? She's been wandering the halls and talking to the shadows in your room."

Bewildered, he rubbed at his goatee-turned-beard. "Nothing. I haven't talked to her since you had me watch over the bunch of drooling twits weeks ago."

Seline sighed and started to take the sigil off. "Quit lying to me, would you?"

"I'm not!"

"Yeah well, whatever you say."

The exorcist let that slide and felt his frown deepen even harder, if such a thing was possible. "More importantly – what's she saying?"

"Some mad bullshit about how your 'shadow' is all pissed off or something," she replied as she unclasped the necklace. "There's nothing in your room. There's nothing in any room. I've been looking."

All he could do was just sigh. And he did. Loudly, with gusto, and with his headache returning to agree with him. "I swear, whoever is talking to her, it isn't me. *I'm* pissed off, but my *shadow* isn't," he said as he gestured down at his shadow.

His shadow which, thankfully, didn't gesture back more than it should.

"I'm... okay. Fine," Seline replied as she took a deep breath to try to calm her nerves. It didn't help much, but... "I'm getting scared and losing my patience and don't know what to believe about any of this. So you tell me what's going on because of all the insane people I know right now you're the only one that isn't going to throw poop at me even though I think you're acting like a lunatic. Fair?"

He bit his tongue (hard) but let it go. "Fine. I can't do it alone. Will you help me?"

"You already got me to agree to look for dead plants and watch out for some sunken ship. What else do you want?"

"First, see if you can get Appaidene to at least gesture in the direction of where she found it," he replied.

That earned an uncharacteristic grunt from her. "I tried."

"Try harder," he stressed. "You do that and I'll work with the book."

She nodded and then handed the necklace over. "But what about this? What do you think about... this?"

As he held it in his hand, every thought and idea that he could come up with were bad. Universally awful. Exquisitely terrible. "There are maybe five things in this world that I know of that can cause crypt-bane to wilt like that. Two of them involve the Avatars of Fallen Gods and we'd know if they were here. One of the other three involves a breed of animate that hasn't been seen on this hemisphere since the fall of the Adelin Empire. The other two are the direct result of necromanctic acts foul enough that every other plant and small dog in this city would be long dead. So, if I guess at which of those, you'd call me a liar and the Order would call me an idiot. How about we don't do any of the above?"

"I've been calling you a liar," she pointed out.

"But I hate to give you a valid reason," Akaran returned. "So. If I figure it out, will you start trusting me?"

"Figure it out and you'll have a friend back. Trust is... maybe."

For some reason, that cut to the bone. "I don't have one right now?"

Seline's smile was as sad as it was faint, though in a lot of ways, it was the most honest thing he'd seen in weeks. "You don't have any friends."

But she was wrong.

He had a few friends – and one was almost here. Seline wouldn't welcome his arrival, but there was a chance he'd be her new friend too. And he was always going to be Akaran's *new friend*, no matter how far away or how long they'd known each other.

No matter how much the priest may have wished otherwise.

***

Port Cableture had an entirely different feel to it than anywhere in Basion. Generally speaking, it served two – and only two – distinct purposes. Basion was a place to live, a place to serve, a place to trade, a place to call home. Cableture was a place to trade, that was true.

It was also a place to plan a war.

That was about it. The only people that lived in the port city were the people that didn't have a choice. It wasn't a place full of flowers or shrines or amphitheaters. It wasn't a place for thieves or frauds – though there was a raging industry for prostitution. Then again, it sat in the middle of Dawnfire. A raging industry for prostitution was only remarkable when it wasn't present.

Yet for all the things it wasn't, it had a roaring boardwalk for taverns, tabernas, and wholesalers. It had a shrine to Aqualla, and a shrine for Stara, though fewer people visited the latter than the former. It wasn't a commerce *hub* in the sense of trading to people who would rush home with their newest trinket, but rather, to people who would march their newfound joys up the throat of Yittl Canyon to sell elsewhere in the city to the north.

In short, it had absolutely none of the things that Anais found useful.

To make it worse, while the port had more warehouses than it did people with common sense, it also had more soldiers than anything else. The 4th didn't bother to patrol it, because there was no point. Port Cableture was home to the 2nd Naval Armada, and you simply couldn't walk across the street without seeing someone wearing the red and rusty-green of the Royal Navy.

And sailors, she had learned, made for very poor informants when your interests were a day's travel inland. Still, the warning Donta had given her required her hasty exit, like it or not. Almost every single one of her plans had been upended in one single threat from the Guild – and until she could prove her innocent, that was the way it was going to stay.

A fact that made it all the more welcome when Adept Ishtva of the Basion Annex arrived at her new doorstop an hour ago. She'd made him wait a bit, as a matter of etiquette, and she stood with her back to him and her eyes firmly on the shipyard when she finally allowed him to come inside.

"You said you had good news?" she asked as soon as he stepped inside her room – ignoring every other formality he expected.

Which, all told, suited the mid-forty-something mage just fine. "I do. Good news requires a good trade, of course."

"The trade depends on the news, as always. You know better."

"Of course," he admitted. "I suspect you already know, but, the Repository has taken control of a very interesting relic."

She did – but the confirmation didn't hurt. It meant that the Order allowed him to see it, which meant that the Academy would know, too. It offered a little leverage with them, though not much. "Oh? There are many an interesting relic in this world. Do tell?"

The adept chuckled softly and found a place to sit down without bothering to ask for permission. "A matter of interest, for sure. As you requested to be notified, this one came from Agromah. It has *significantly* earned the concern of the custodians."

Anais smiled, though made sure that he couldn't see it. She flicked her fingers against the glass window dismissively. "Agromah is a long way away from here."

"Most things are, it seems. How *fortuitous* that the Lovers didn't have to trek out of the city to go get it. It was found practically on their doorstep. But you already know, don't you?"

"What would make you think that I know anything about a relic from anywhere?" she challenged with a cool, irritated tenor. "Let alone from that land of nightmares? That place, should the stories be told true, could rival Nia'valth's domain as a world of fright."

Ishtva had to nod. "So I have heard. Of course, I have heard a lot of things – there are advantages to working for the man that beds the Matron of the Guild. You're aware that they're doing their best to pin Odern's murder on you, yes?"

"As I've heard," the broker grumbled through clenched teeth. "Yet you're still here. If you thought it true, I wouldn't expect you to come running."

She didn't have to see his smug little smile to hear it in his voice. "Life takes us in interesting directions, and education is not always inexpensive. If you had Odern assassinated, then you could do the same to me if I ceased to be useful, too. My choices are to work with you and allow you to fund my research or to not work with you and run afoul of your temper. If you did have his books closed, then it seems that either option I pick could end the same way."

That was exactly the type of logic she had built her business around, though it pained her that he had seen through it so clearly. "If it makes you feel any better, I truly didn't," Anais replied – with an added sigh to reassure him. "I had never had any dealings with the man, and I do have suspicions for who brought his story to an end – but, no, my good Adept, I had nothing to do with it."

"You, maybe not," the mage agreed. "Your bodyguard? He's not long for the outside of a dungeon cell – or for the end of a noose."

That, however, was news. "Oh? Why would that be?"

"I can't begin to imagine you don't know, Lady Lovic," he retorted in a nearly mocking tone. "If I were you, I would take great strides to leave this province as fast as you can. Elsith wants your head for Odern and Livstra, and Gorosoch has been approached by the Lieutenant-Commander to hire magical assistance to bring your boy to heel for just about everyone else."

That wasn't just news. That was a man making a promise that someone else was going to keep. Anais turned around and studied his hazel-yellow eyes just to make sure he wasn't lying, and when she realized he was being unpleasantly forthright, the next question was easy to imagine. "Everyone else? Now this is news. Do tell."

"No, I don't think that I will," he replied. "Just because I like your gold does not mean that I am trusting of your endeavors."

"I suppose that's fair in and of itself," she admitted. "So – to be to the first point. The Repository has claimed the mace?"

His mocking tone was matched by his mocking little smile. "Tired of being coy? As you wish. Yes, they have. They have it, and they're utterly pissed about it. The fact that it exists has them riled up; the fact that it was smuggled into the city is another. I don't, for one moment, believe that it was brought in by a slaver, of all people. However, the truth is what is made of it."

Anais nodded at that and kept herself in check. It wouldn't do any good to show off how happy she was to get secondary confirmation – and from the man in charge of reporting new arrivals at the Repository to the Annex. "A great deal is being made of it, I'm sure. I have two very important questions, Ishtva, and the answers will dictate how much coin falls in your lap at the end of our business."

"You have but to ask, as always."

Knowing that it was there, however, wasn't all that she needed. Half a battle still left a battle, and her life depended on his next answer. "Where in that accursed cavern is it being stored?"

"Deep," he answered earnestly. "Into a section where I have no control, nor sway, nor way to access, if that's what you wonder. It has either been placed in the lower reliquary or the vault. Which of the two, I do not know; nor do I have knowledge on how to find my way around those sections, before you ask your other question."

The former was important; the latter didn't matter. "Close to what I was considering asking but not quite. So it is well and truly buried?"

Ishtva nodded in affirmation. "Shy of having dirt lofted over it? Yes. I imagine in the near future it will be covered in wards and enhanced runes. I have already delivered a request from the Maiden-Templar off to the Headmaster for assistance from some of our staff to help secure an unknown object with spellwork. I hate to assume, but…"

"As assumptions go, that would be a wise one. I have no doubt they recognized it for what it was without too much trouble. Have they been talkative about it, by chance?"

"No, though there was quite a commotion when it was delivered."

"I imagine so. I expect the priest lucky enough to bring it was well-rewarded for his efforts?"

The laugh that joined his response wasn't mocking. Or friendly. "Ah, no. The opposite."

"The opposite?" she asked as the implications of *that* statement put a cold chill down her spine. "I can't possibly think of a reason why…? Surely the Lovers reward their own when they accomplish a surprising task, don't they?"

"It is all a bit confusing, I will personally admit," he replied with a vague shrug. "However, now that the dust has settled, it seems that he abused the services of my counterpart with the Guild and made off with a few documents that he had no right to access," he explained. Then, a moment later, his eyes narrowed and he took a guess that was wrong in all the right ways. "Another one of your errand-boys, Lady?"

"We all keep quiet with who we do or do not do business with, you know that, Adept," Anais replied with a little purr. "Though I will honestly say, to deflect the accusation, that I have never hired him to root through their tomes nor asked him to abscond with anything from their shrine," she promised. *Though now I see I should have. Or found better ways to bribe Philanus.*

He nodded along though it was hard to say if he believed her or not, or how much. "Well, whatever reason he had aside, the word from the rank and file is that his commission has been revoked. He's no longer welcome on Order grounds. I wasn't left with the inclination to believe it was a permanent situation, but he's assuredly on the outs with his own people now because of it."

The look on her face would've earned Akaran's friendship on the spot, had he been able to see it. At the same time, news of his fate changed his value to her – in a very big way. "I… see. Well, the greed of men for knowledge excessive knows no bounds, and the bounds it does tend to be sharp to touch."

"A warning I should keep in mind?" the Adept asked.

"A warning we should all keep in mind," she countered as she casually strode over to the door with her pink gown flowing behind her like it was made out of water. "Thank you, my good Adept. I'll take all you said to heart."

Ishtva stood up and shot her a smile so cold it would've been at home in Frosel. "I am *an* Adept. I am not yours."

A chill that melted as she casually dropped a bag full of assorted gemstones into his palm. "Are you so sure?"

"I am sure that you should heed my warning," he insisted. "Whatever interests you have in this town, I would collect them quickly. Your manservant has made as many enemies as he has friends – and I don't think his friends would be all that sad if the 4th Garrison is able to hold him accountable."

"Accountable for what?"

Ishtva wavered and stopped before he could leave her temporary room. "You don't know? You really don't?"

"Adept, I have been in this port for not much longer than a full day," the gossip answered earnestly. "Given the sheer number of moving parts that make up Basion I have no doubt that I have at least missed one or two bits of notable news."

He had to agree, to an extent. "There was a massacre last night – at the vagrant camps. Someone tried to make it seem like it caught fire, but, no. Your man was last seen going in that direction. The Guard was willing to ignore what he did to the Fleetfinger's Guild, to an extent, but this? This cannot be ignored. It's not the first wholesale slaughter he's been involved in, and there are enough people in power to know it."

Her whole body began to pale as she struggled to concentrate on the illusion of health she projected, though he mistook her reaction – his assumption was that she was stunned he'd been caught. "What an interesting... development. I suppose it'll do no good to deny knowing what you're talking about?"

It didn't. "I'd leave, Lady Lovic," Ishtva warned again. "I do not know what you're after, or what he is trying to accomplish, but I would find either a way to extract yourself or find a scapegoat – and either way, I would do so quickly."

"Kind of you to warn."

"Education is not cheap," he replied with a faint little smile, "and the pursuit of knowledge may lead us on the same path again," he added as he left her room.

As he left, one of her other – and hopefully far more loyal – servants stepped into the room. There wasn't much to him, though there never was. It was one of the things that made him so useful. "M'lady, I can't say that I heard everything he said, but should I start helping you pack again?" Ettaquis asked hurriedly as he closed the door behind him.

She stared at her personal courier for a long minute before she gave up and sat down. "I don't know, though that conversation is problematic in far more ways than one," she seethed.

"What do you want me to do?" the athletic, short-haired blond courier asked.

"You? Little," Anais spat before she stopped and corrected herself. "No, no, I retract that. I have several things I need you to do," she replied as she picked up a quill, some ink, and a stack of parchment.

"Of course, my Lady," he replied with a slight bow. "As you're ready, when you're ready."

Not that she would've done otherwise.

But what she did do was lose herself in thought as she began to pen instruction after instruction. Orders to move assets, orders to cut ties with certain individuals, orders to transfer funds. Orders to do worse than that to a few unlucky souls – ones that she could have trusted to keep silent if her bodyguard hadn't gone off the rails.

*Donta won't crumble under interrogation, if it comes to it, but if they try to kill him – or he puts up a fight – they'll certainly come for me next. He was right to move me away from Elsith's immediate reach but he's exposed himself on a level I cannot abide. Named in a **second** massacre? How do I not know of the **first**?* she ranted to herself as she quickly covered the first sheet with angry strokes of ink. *He's been lying to me. The one thing, the only thing, I cannot abide.*

Well. He'll have to be removed from play. I can still use him for the short term, and I should be able to trust him to deal with that priest. Must find an urgent way to send him from the city. I won't risk bringing the wrath of his Goddess down on my head, assuming he hasn't forsaken Her, but I'm not opposed to having him trussed up and hauled off to another province by force.

Easy way to solve two problems at once.

Pity I can't blame him for the other deaths – but, no, that Huntswoman seems to be fixated on me now. No, simply cannot do it that way. I'm going to end up having to bargain with Rishnobia for another assistant. Dammit. I am in no mood to offer another pound of flesh for that.

The moment she finished the third sheet on her table, she passed the pile right to the unlucky boy and expressed her non-written wishes with a ferocity that he couldn't misinterpret. "Get this message to Donta, immediately, wherever he's at. I apologize for the long night, but he will need it before morning – take extra gold in case you have to replace your horse mid-way."

Ettaquis looked out the window with dismay as he realized how low the sun was in the sky. "But Lady, it's two marks away before sunset? Do you have any idea where he is?"

"Then ride quickly and carefully," she retorted. "I'd recommend taking a torch. For the other – no. Ask for a man named Raes at the *White Swan*, or Cel at the *Imperial*. He's mentioned that they are his current sources for all things underworld."

For all of his faults, he wasn't an idiot. She wouldn't have employed him if he was, but one look at the cool fury brewing in her eyes, and he decided not to argue the point. "Ah... uh. Yes, yes Lady. Your wishes be done."

***

It wasn't just her wishes to be done.

Once Akaran finished running yet another *errand* for the lovely Miss Cel, another courier had carried out another urgent missive. This one was marked from Henderschott, of all people, but his note was simply a scrawled warning written on the top of the letter. '*I'm only helping once,*' it read, and that was it.

Below that? Another statement written with such haste that it'd been folded before the ink had dried, which had smeared some of the words. '*Wherever that storm hit, you get there. You get there and you best be armed. That wasn't a storm. Was magestrikes,*' Badin had scrawled. '*Same strikes I heard before Lexcanna was murdered.*'

X. LANDING'S LOSS
Evening of Londis, the 30ᵗʰ of Riverswell, 513 QR

The smell. It's the one thing that Rmaci hadn't managed to replicate in his dreams (so far). He couldn't figure out why, and he didn't want to ask. Just in case, he rationalized, she'd find a way to do it.

She wouldn't need to, now. It was everywhere and he was already soaked in it without even being at the source. Burnt flesh, scorched organs. The acrid smell of charred meat. All of it had an undercurrent of death that floated in the air with all the subtlety of an avalanche. It hit almost the second he made it onto the small pathway leading to the Landing – but for the first time? It didn't slow him down.

Once you got over your first twenty bodies roasting in the pyre, the next three dozen apparently weren't that bad. Or maybe it was the cocasa deadening his senses. People said it would do that. Or maybe it was just knowing that whatever he was about to see wasn't going to be any worse than what the wraith had been tormenting him with (though she hadn't appeared since their last talk).

That was going to change sooner than later – but someone else beat her to the punch. "Whatever you think you're doing here exorcist, don't," the woman's voice called out from somewhere in the trees overhead.

Except, sadly, it wasn't just any woman. It was one woman in particular. One he'd had the pleasure to meet before – just once, thankfully – and who had threatened him with his life if he kept digging around in her affairs. Which was funny, in a way, because the only affairs she had that he knew of was being married to a researcher at the Granalchi Annex.

She was the wife of Headmaster-Adept Telburn Gorosoch, specifically, and the Adept joined her on the path with a smile that went from ear to ear as Akaran's day went from bad to worse. "In his defense, being in places like this is his job."

"He has no defense," Huntsmatron Elsith Gorosoch quipped back, adding, "his rank has been suspended. There is *no* reason for him to be here, and I am *more* than happy to assist the Guard in helping him be *elsewhere*."

Akaran took one look at the pair as they approached and immediately started to rub at his eyes with his hand. "Oh for fisk-all sake. Are we really going to do this?"

"I don't see any reason why I shouldn't," she said as she blocked his way.

"Because we both know I'm having a hard enough time lately without you sticking a knife up my ass?"

Her husband chuckled softly and waved them both down. "Now now, both of you. Maybe we should start by asking why we're all here? Questions instead of actions?"

"Please, husband," Elsith retorted. "He's here because of the dead. We're here because we're done, and honestly, I'd like to get back home."

"Yeah, I'm here because of the —" he began, then looked at her intently. "Dead? Plural?" A few moments later he realized he had to throw in an additional qualifier of, "*How many* dead?"

"See? He doesn't know," Telburn replied with a sad little nod. "Which leads to a different question: why are you on this path, hm? It only heads to the Landing, so you must have... had... some business there."

The exorcist rocked back on his heels and frowned. "I'm... I'm here because a friend said that the thunderstorm the other night wasn't one and asked me to come check it out."

Elsith flicked her tongue against the inside of her cheek and smirked. "Oh? Surprised to hear that."

"That I'm following a lead from a friend?"

"That you have any friends."

If looks could kill, she'd be the next soul on his ledger. "Oh for the love of all fisking —"

"Elsith, sweetie, there's no need."

She looked over at her husband with a loving, yet unfriendly, smile. "I'm sure I can find one. Who's your friend?"

"I'd rather not say at this point," he retorted, then after an encouraging look from the Headmaster, he slumped his shoulders. "Badin. The battlemage that Hender has locked up."

"A mage in chains suggested that a priest without his rank come investigate a storm that isn't?" she taunted.

Nobody could've argued that and he had to shrug in agreement. "Putting it that way, yes, it sounds suspect. However, between the smell in the air and the fact that neither of you look like you've slept lately..." he pointed out as he took note of the circles under her eyes and the ragged state of Telburn's normally well-shaven face – not to mention the mud on their clothes, the soot on their hands and arms, and a few unidentifiable dark stains on Elsith's green leathers. She wasn't even trying to hide her arsenal, including a dagger with a chain hanging from the hilt that looked oddly familiar.

Before he could ask her about it, Telburn interrupted his thought. "It has been a trying time in the city," the Headmaster admitted. "Research, the wedding, Odern. Other things," he went on to explain, and then with a slight smile and a squeeze of Elsith's hand, he offered, "many other, wonderful things."

She rolled her eyes and tugged her hand free from his tender, loving, and vaguely-obnoxious grip. "Oh, would you fisking stop."

"Sharing my love for you? I would never do such a thing," he retorted with a lofty smile and enough warmth in his eyes to thaw a glacier. "I'm sure that Akaran appreciates it, given his lot in life."

The priest looked at him, looked at her, and then rubbed his temples again. "Yeah. Sure. We can go with that."

"Not in the mood to rejoice in the love two people have for each other?" Telburn asked with no shortage of mirth.

"Is that an honest question?"

"Eh, fair."

The Huntsmatron, on the other hand, rolled her eyes again and made sure to distance herself away from both of them. "I suppose you expect to find something to play off with one of your delusional theories," she shot off at the crippled priest.

Akaran pursed his lips and nodded, then retorted with an equally pointed, "I'm guessing you're here because... you found evidence to support one of them?"

She clenched her teeth and dug her heels into the dirt path. "Nothing. Of. The. Sort."

"What my lovely wife means is that there has been... an incident," Telburn interjected with a faint cringe. "One, as alluded, that does not bode well for any soul. I believe you at least have a passing familiarity with the Landing?"

"Visited once," the exorcist answered, "and talked to a few people. Flynn's a nice kid. He helping or did the Guard chase him off?"

"He is..." Telburn started to reply as words failed him and his mirth died in his throat.

Elsith cleared hers and finished the thought for her husband. "They didn't have to chase him off."

"Oh, that's good. So is he..." the priest replied before he saw the look on her face and lost the color in his. "Oh."

"I'm afraid the Guard is, once again, at a loss," the mage added. "The damage the camp sustained is more than what a mundane person could do. Nor was it, I am sad to say, the result of any simple storm. Your friend was quite correct, I am – and I do mean this earnestly and honestly – quite dismayed to agree."

"You don't need to be here and you don't need to go there," his wife warned. "There's nothing for you here except sadness."

"Shit."

"You're still going to try to talk your way in there, aren't you?" she asked.

"If I lied and said no…?"

She curled her lips into a smirk. "Then I'd have my dear, loving, *wonderful* husband find a way to float you off the cliff."

He reluctantly nodded along in understanding. "Would've expected that if I had said 'yes,' more than the other way around."

"I don't deal well with liars."

The Headmaster agreed to that without any kind of hesitation. "No, that is one thing she assuredly does not do well with at all. As normal, she's also quite right. The camp has been destroyed, my boy. There's nothing to be seen except burnt bodies and mud huts someone attempted to use as kilns. I've rarely seen – no, I retract – I have *never* seen such a gruesome act of slaughter in my life."

Memories of what happened to Rmaci came back unbidden and he fought back a wave of disgust that boiled up in his throat. "Why is it every time I turn around it's a fresh horror…"

"You are the one who assumed the mantle of exorcist, boy," Elsith pointed out. "It's no-one's fault but your own."

"Fair. Fair. Listen, both of you, respectfully."

"That's a change," she quipped.

"Respectfully," the priest stressed, "I've had a really shitty week. In the process of this shitty week, I've run into a couple of things that I don't understand and I think that the two of you might be able to shed some light on but if you're already agreeing with Badin it means it's something I *didn't* count on and I need to go there to see if what's there works with any of the theories I've guessed at so far."

Telburn narrowed his eyes slightly. "Dare we ask what you've found?"

"Ask, sure, tell you, no," Akaran replied. "You'll be curious, she'll think I'm full of it, and you might end up agreeing with her to fling me back over the cliff – which, *for the record*, is a thought that's very nearly getting me to piss myself because I think you mean it and I have discovered that I am not a fan of high places."

"I do mean it," Elsith agreed, "and, truthfully, it's hard to argue with the way you're reading the situation. I do think you're –"

He cut her off with a short chop of his hand. "Okay, so, deal? I go and look, you two can follow me to make sure I don't piss off anyone that's not already dead, and if I'm *right*, I'll share what I've found and we can start working together. Or working more together, if you've still been looking at the stone like you promised."

"Oh, my boy, I've done more than look," Telburn replied earnestly and eagerly. "That relic is absolutely *fascinating* and I have learned a significant deal about it in the time since you passed it to me."

"Okay, great," Akaran quickly replied before he pointed at the huntswoman. "Elsith? Are you okay with this or do I need to find another path to get back up here after you pitch me back onto the stairwall?"

"*Huntsmatron Gorosoch* to you," she retorted with a glower. "Though I can tell you're serious. You've earned my attention for a short bit; don't squander it."

"Telburn?"

He let out a deep, tired sigh, though he gave in with a defeated droop of his head. "Where she goes, I go. While we're on the way, I can tell you what I've learned about the coldstone shard, if you like."

"Will it help me use magic again? Or help me find someone to do something about this damnable pain in my leg?"

"It might, albeit not in the immediate future. I haven't quite figured out a way to –"

The priest shook his head and started to hobble forward. The throbbing in his knee was growing atrociously worse the closer he got to the Landing, and he was beginning to think that it was something of an omen. "Then don't worry about it. Odds are good I won't understand it and, honestly, I'm too sore to try to comprehend advanced magical concepts."

"Not one to study magical arts?" the mage asked in mild surprise. "One would think that given your profession, you'd want to have a deeper understanding of how the currents of mana and the eddies of ether interact with the human mind and how we use our willpower, knowledge, and other affinity to use the base nature of it to better ourselves in our lives."

Akaran brushed it off as they made their way down the rough path. "I use it to beat bad things over the head. I don't care how it works, just as long as I can use it."

"You know," Elsith interrupted, "he's not entirely wrong with that approach."

"Intellectual heathens," the Headmaster lamented. "I am surrounded."

The exorcist made a point to ignore that even as his wife gave an amused chuckle. The rest of the (thankfully short) hobble the rough path went smoothly, though when they arrived, he wished it'd taken longer. The smell, like it always did, hit first. After getting into the Landing itself, he promised that he'd be the one hitting last.

Before the massacre, Flynn's Landing hadn't been anything worth bragging about. A collection of scattered wooden huts and tents, the Landing had been designated the local vagrant camp by the city Overseer – with help from Lieutenant-Commander Henderschott, of course. The arrangement, as Akaran had discovered a few weeks ago, was simple:

The vagrants would leave the city, they'd be given a level of protection and a chance to own land of their own once the wedding between Malik Odinal of Clan Odinal from the Midlands and Hylene Tessamirch of Basion's House Tessamirch concluded. It was the Overseer's way of keeping the city streets clean and proper for the outsiders. *An illusion of riches when the truth is anything but*, the priest mused to himself. Or at least as clean and proper as one could make the streets of a bustling city.

After the flooding, there had been talk of sending the Vahail refugees out here. Thankfully, someone decided that no, it would have been a bad idea – an issue with the lack of water for the watersculpts (and he still hadn't figured out what that was supposed to be). It mad sense, even if it made it harder to place the whining and soggy travelers, reasonably depressed as they were.

The level of protection received, apparently, was 'zero,' Akaran realized as he surveyed the damage. "Goddess," he called out breathlessly. "Shit."

Now, the camp was far from its former glory (if you could say it ever had any). The scattered tents had been reduced to burnt scraps and splinters. Everything was covered in soot, rubble, and a few stubborn embers that refused to go out. The mess looked like someone had visited a firestorm on the camp and then tried to blow it up. There was blood, too. You couldn't hide that much of it in the rubble even if you tried. It'd be gone in a few days, or the next heavy rainstorm – but the rest would linger.

There was a lot left to linger.

"Satisfied?" Elsith asked as he took a few measured steps into the rubble-strewn clearing.

Well, it used to be a clearing, he mused. *Little more than just debris now*, he thought to himself. Outwardly, he replied with a cold, flat, "That I'm going to kill whatever did this? Yes."

Telburn cleared his throat and moved closer to his wife. "That's a decidedly dark frame of mind to have."

"Should I give it puppies instead?" the exorcist shot back as he used his cane to turn a pile of burnt brush over.

The huntswoman moistened her lips and gave him a studious stare. "Huh. Maybe I was wrong about you."

They weren't alone in the camp, for good or ill. There were at least seven priests and priestesses of various ranking from the Order of Stara present, along with another five of the 4th's finest standing around and doing... not much of anything. To their credit, the locurats of the Order of Stara were at least trying to gather assorted bits and pieces of people (and they *all* tried to pretend they didn't know what those bits and pieces were).

As a result, none of their robes were entirely white. He didn't recognize any of them right away, which was both good and bad. They seemed to recognize him, which was probably bad, though after he walked closer to the largest structure still standing, he simply didn't care.

At least there isn't snow this time, he gloomily mused to himself as he worked his way through shattered logs and broken trees. Everything else about it was a very bad, very ugly memory of one of the first disasters he'd seen upon arriving in Toniki so many months ago. The difference this time really was just the lack of the cold – and the number of dead.

Outside of Toniki, the ice had kept the bugs away. Here, they were swarming everywhere. The constant humming of flies darting from one pink puddle to the next could drive a man to madness – and as someone teetering on that particular edge lately, he felt safe to make that observation.

Outside of Toniki, it had only been a handful of Dawnfire's finest. Here? "I'm going to kill whatever did this," he muttered again. Here, they'd be lucky if they could find matching parts for all the bodies. "And I swear, if I hear a dog..."

Before he got much further, one of the guards – a captain, by the look of the glorified sun-shaped pin holding his cloak to his chest – tried to block him. To her credit, Elsith interjected on Akaran's behalf and got the trooper back off. On the other hand, he almost wished he was being tossed off the cliff like she suggested.

"What does he have against dogs, do you suppose?" Telburn wondered as he listened to the boy.

His wife didn't reply – but she did watch.

The exorcist moved through the ruins quickly but intently. Evidence was abundant, but evidence of *what* was the question. The method to the murders was obvious; unless someone had lugged one of the Queen's Destroyers up from the 2nd Naval Fleet and then unleashed a broadside in the middle of the woods (an impressive feat, given the lack of water, among other things), then it was mageblasts. The question then became, 'what kind.'

You could tell a lot about a mage from the type of magic they used. In this case, it was easy to rule a few things out: there were no stones, no puddles of acid, no chunks of still-frozen balls of ice (*Thank the Goddess*, he screamed internally) that had been left behind. While the damage was explosive, there wasn't a lot of ash residue or signs that a fire had blossomed out of control.

It was likely set by the same person (*Or persons,*) he grumbled again, that had ripped the camp up. The rest of the damage? *Had to have been a mage. An instabilisist, I think. Non-elemental. Just... raw. Raw, that's the word. This is raw. This is blunt.* He looked at a blast mark on a tree as he hobbled past it. *These are... at chest height.* Akaran stopped and looked around at some of the other craters as he walked by and was happy with that deduction. *These weren't called down from the sky.*

Could've been a Kora'thi follower, I guess? Naturists can fling lightning. Doubt it though. Flynn didn't strike me as a naturalist. Just a guy trying to make the best he could for his people. A Melian follower would be much more likely, if this was a divinely-ordered attack. Though, honestly, the Goddess of Destruction isn't known to get off on wanton slaughter without just cause. The Fallen could've given strength to do this but if They had, the locurats over there would be shitting their prissy white robes instead of standing around with their thumbs up their holier-than-tho asses...

That wasn't an ideal thought to say the least, but it made sense. Very few people would relish in a disaster like this like a Melian Deconstructionist. He stopped and lingered next to a pile of glass-like rubble next to a crater on the ground. *Speaking of lightning...* thought as he prodded at it with the tip of his cane.

"If you're trying to figure out what caused it," the Headmaster called out, "then I can answer that question. You look a bit perplexed."

"Feel free to give a hint to the class," Akaran muttered under his breath.

The mage walked over and tapped at the same tree that his younger friend had been inspecting a moment before. "I may not need to – you came to the same conclusion I did, I can tell. Instabilisist?"

"Instabilisist."

"Correct. But can you tell what kind?"

The exorcist shook his head no. "One that had plenty of mana to draw on to do this much damage. Doesn't feel like it'd be from a Pantheon supporter. The Fallen wouldn't be this blunt, either, not without packing a message to go with it. Most of them don't play for subtlety."

"That is more your purview than mine, but yes, from what tomes I have studied of the Upper and the Lower, none of the Divine, on either side, care to act this directly without reason."

Akaran nodded and looked around the wreckage again. "How many strikes are there? I can see at least fifteen just from standing here."

Telburn nodded gravely. "At least. This was done by someone with training and the ability to focus themselves without necessarily making a plea to the Gods; that, my good boy, I will agree with. This was not an attack carried out by some neophyte."

"I don't know," Akaran mused. "Us neophytes can get into a lot of trouble if left unattended..."

"Yes, well," the mage agreed, "every rule has an exception. What our spellcaster of interest used was very refined in their crudeness." He bent down and scooped up a piece of the glass-like rubble and held it up for the priest to see. "Do you know what this is?"

"Melted glass?"

"Close," Telburn affirmed, "but it goes by another name. Geomancers often call it *forked-rock* or *split-sky* stones. They are the natural result of lightning strikes."

The priest pursed his lips and looked down at the fused soil, rock, and melted sand. "So. A sparkcaster mage," he realized. "Well. At least we know it wasn't Badin."

"Badin?"

"The battlemage that Henderschott thought killed Lexcanna," he replied before he quickly turned around and stared at the knife on Elsith's waist. "Hold on."

Elsith, for her credit, was busy arguing with the captain to let the priest stick around – against her better judgment. Judgment that was, quite promptly, immediately called back into question. As much as he appreciated her sticking up for him, she happened to turn around in time to see her cloak move away from her hip again and to show off the dagger he'd seen earlier.

That she was armed was expected, but there was a chain and a badge dangling from the hilt that he thought he recognized. She protested when he came over and grabbed at the blade (and the Headmaster started to object when it looked like Akaran had tried to grab something else). She reached down and slapped his hand away, which didn't dissuade him in the least. "Not to be rude, but where did you get that?"

"You *are* being rude, you disgusting little roach," she snarled as her hand dropped to it. "And you're going to wish I had thrown you off the cliff."

"WAIT!" he said as he backtracked – literally and figuratively – and pointed right at the knife. "That's battlemage's dagger. Where did you find it?"

Elsith narrowed her eyes and slid her hand down over the leather-wrapped hilt. "How do you know it's not mine?"

He shrugged and rattled off three key points. "For one, it's filthy. Looks like it's been laying in mud. Given the state of... well, this..." he said as he gestured around the site, "I thought you might have picked it up. I don't think you're the type of woman that lets her toys get dirty without cleaning them off right away. For two," Akaran continued before she could comment, "unless it's a trophy, that didn't come from the Guild. That chain and badge? That's –"

"Yes, I know," she snapped as slapped his hand away again. "A designation for Specialist-Majors. The 5th, specifically. How did you know?"

The exorcist shrugged his shoulders. "I spent three weeks traveling with one. He used that damn thing to do everything from cutting up meals to picking his teeth."

"So is it his?" she asked with a sudden dark glint in her eyes before she pulled it loose and handed it over. "Please tell me you know."

Akaran took one glance at the emblem and shook his head. Like the rest of the knife, it was dirty, dinged up, and covered in equal parts mud and blood. "No. This is the 5th Garrison's sigil. Badin served in the 13th." As she cursed vehemently under her breath, he looked it over a few more times. "Where did you find it?"

"Near the other entrance to the Landing," her husband answered for her. "There's two or three paths that lead here, and that was hidden under a body."

"Show me?"

Those two words set a series of events in motion that, in short order, he'd pray he could take back. Those two words caused the Huntsmatron to roll her eyes and lead him through the debris-strewn slum to another path leading into the Landing. If it was possible, this path was even rougher, with just a pair of wooden posts and a roughly carved archway showing the entry into what was once Flynn's territory.

Elsith pointed a scorch mark on a tree, and a disturbed pile of leaves on the ground. "Found it here. No corpse, but, looked like someone stabbed him and let him fall. Probably one of the ones roasted in the pile."

"But they left the weapon?" Akaran asked.

She pointed towards an arrow embedded in a tree a few feet away. "Someone shot at the attacker. Guessing whomever did it came down the path, stabbed this guy, and before he could get his knife free, got distracted. Then it must have fallen out of the body or the killer dropped it on the way to the Landing, and couldn't find it after," she guessed.

The priest pursed his lips and nodded in agreement. "You said he?"

"Or she," Elsith replied.

He looked at the scorch mark on the tree and sucked on the air. "Victim took a blast to his chest after he got stabbed, didn't he?"

"Looks like it," she admitted. "I've seen my fair share of killers before, Lover. Whomever did this enjoyed it."

"Yeah," he said after a minute of peering down the pathway. "Then again, you almost have to."

"True. Maybe enjoyed is the wrong word. Rejoiced in, perhaps?"

"Better word, like it less," the priest quipped. "Any other bodies down this way?"

She shook her head and stretched her neck with a wince. "We didn't look far. I've sent word for a couple of my men to come look through the woods. I saw evidence of another fight down that way – but to be truthful, the focus has been here in the village."

Akaran balked at the thought. "But you've been here for what, almost a day?"

"Since the first light," she growled. "We *assume* this happened last night. If I didn't have runners searching for... well, doesn't matter for who. Hard to say when we would have found it if I didn't have people scouring the woods."

"Don't judge her harshly, young priest," Telburn interrupted. "I'm afraid that you haven't yet had the pleasure of seeing what passed for their meeting hall."

The glimpse he'd taken on the way from one path to the other was all he really wanted, but he had a feeling that the mage was about to make him take a much closer look. "So if there was a fight there and one here..." he started as he looked down the path and then into the village. "I'm gonna guess whomever got into that fight let it roll into the Landing. Can you ask a few of the guards to go give it a patrol?"

"There's no need," the huntswoman replied. "We looked and found what we could."

"You found something?"

"I didn't say that. I said we already looked."

"You said you found what you could," he retorted.

The golden-haired woman gave him a dirty look. "What we do or haven't done doesn't matter. You asked to look around. Either look, or leave."

Akaran looked down the muddy path and sighed under his breath. "Okay. Telburn. Elsith. Can we come to an agreement?"

"My name is Huntsmatron –"

He lifted his hand and cut her off. "Elsith. Your name is Elsith, his is Telburn, and we're all too tired to get ourselves hung up on titles when we'd all rather go kill what did this."

"I'm not a fan of drawing blood, myself," the mage interjected as he stepped in between them with his hands open and pointed down in a gesture of peace. "Though I understand that I am alone in that thought. I'd much rather find a way to ensure that as little blood flows as needed, and I want to ensure that innocent blood never flows onto the ground again."

"Fine," Akaran snapped. "Look – we can do this one of two ways. Either we spend an hour fisking around up here while you watch me flounder around like a newborn kitten rolling through one puddle to the next, or..."

"I don't know," the huntswoman sadistically purred behind her husband, "that sounds like it might be a lot of fun."

Telburn reached behind his back and gently took her hand in his. "As too would a bath and pudding. Hear the boy out?"

She 'harrumphed' in response as the exorcist went on. "*Or*," he stressed, "if you two want to go home and eat... pudding?" he asked as he *strongly* considered asking for some himself, "...then you two can tell me everything you've found out and we can get on to the business of execution."

"*You* have no business in executions," Elsith countered, "given that you have no authority to so much as piss on a gravestone."

"*Currently*," the priest countered. "I'll get my permissions back."

"But if you do anything now, then you will be just as guilty as the person that did all this," the mage countered with a jovial – but firm – tenor to his voice. "I have to agree with my lady in this case."

Akaran began to brush them off with an insult, but managed to check himself at the last possible second. Then again, the crunch his back teeth made was enough to earn a smirk from the hunter and a sympathetic wince from her husband. "Look. You hunt killers, and you study magic," he replied as he nodded his head at them in turn. "I've spent my whole life training to study magical creatures that *are* killers, so even if I can't go kill it myself maybe I can give *you* an idea of what to study and *you* an idea of what to hunt? Please? Or am I going to have to wander back up here in six candlemarks after you two have gone to bed and twist my ankle trying to dig around in the dark?"

Telburn turned to face his wife and the two of them exchanged looks back and forth for a few moments. "The ground truly is unpleasant. If he comes back after dark, a twisted ankle would be among the least of his injuries."

"If you're arguing on his behalf, that's the wrong stance to take."

"It's not nice to mock the lame."

"My love?" she countered, "How often has anyone ever considered me nice?"

"I don't," Akaran agreed.

"See?" she pointed out.

The mage gave a long-suffering sigh and ran his fingers through his hair. "We allowed him come this far, and he may have a point. Neither one of us recognized the arm."

"I recognized the arm," Elsith countered, "it was the other part that was the problem."

The casual way she dismissed a presumably dismembered arm made the exorcist's eye twitch. "Attached to a body or other?"

"Oh you had to let him hear that, didn't you?" she scolded the mage (even though it wasn't his fault). "You may as well show him."

"Show me? Where is it?"

Telburn stepped back and began to wave his hands in an intricate design in the air. Brilliant blue light began to radiate out from his fingertips as he sketched out a glowing door at chest height to his wife. "We're putting that knife in here with it," he said as he glanced over at her, "no offense to our unexpected companion but if he happened to notice it, it's hard to say who might else give it an unwanted glance before we get home."

She rolled her eyes again but muttered something that sounded like an agreement as she handed it over. "As long as I get it back once we're inside."

"Should we deliver the arm first?"

"You should show it to me first..." Akaran muttered.

"Yes, yes," the mage chided as he finished his spell. The glowing translucent door he drew in the air opened down the center to reveal a dim gray pocket of ether that just hung in the air. "You know, other people are more impressed when they see someone open a portal to the other realms than this. You've truly seen a great deal for a man your age, haven't you?"

The exorcist stared into the formless void and shuddered hard. "Haven't seen one of these up close. I didn't realize they were so easy to open."

With a smug smile, the Headmaster reached into the void and began to rummage around. You could just barely make out his hand as it slipped into the crackling portal, and a slow stream of granite-colored fog trickled out down the lower lip. "They aren't, but years of study has its own rewards."

No matter what you called them, the 'pockets' that the Academy had developed didn't set well with the Order – with good reason. The mages had found a way to secure physical objects somewhere in the World Between Worlds. Seemingly at whim and will, they could then open the small doorways back up and pull out whatever they had stored inside from anywhere else in the world.

There was talk about the Army experimenting with using the method to transport siege equipment from one place to another. Expensive talk (very, very expensive talk) but the rumors had been percolating around the Order for the last couple of years. The very idea that a Garrison or one of the Queen's Companies could build a fleet of siege towers and battering rams at the Capitol and then disgorge them a continent away at will? It thrilled the Holy General with delight.

As much as she loved the thought, it filled the Brothers with dread.

There were things on the other side of reality that liked to pull physical objects from this world into their domain to corrupt them – and what came out the other side was never what was sent through. Not that it stopped the

Granalchi, and Telburn was all-too-happy to show off the trick. The only thing that kept the Lovers (except the General, of course) from petitioning to have the practice stopped was that they hadn't found a way for living beings to survive in whatever dimension the mages were busy exploiting.

A problem exemplified by the dead arm that the Annex's chief instructor pulled out of the gateway before the portal shrunk close and sizzled shut. It was, without a doubt, an arm. It was, also without a doubt, very dead. Yet, as bad as that was, it was not bloody. It was so not bloody, one could be excused for not thinking it was real at all.

But, as Telburn held the floppy limb up by the wrist, there was no dispute as to if it was some kind of illusion or wooden toy. It was flesh and bone, at least, even if not flesh and blood. "Oh," the priest mused quietly, "oh I don't think I like that."

"It does pose a bit of a quandary," he admitted.

"The lack of a torso attached to it is a concern," Elsith added. "Though I think even you can see the issue."

"I was wondering why you were so upset over an arm... I mean, I realize that I've only seen a few chopped off in my life but still...."

As Akaran gently took the limb from Telburn, the Huntsmatron continued on. "We found it at the other battle sight. Just that arm, no evidence of a survivor. I assume whomever it belonged to ran away."

"Or was vaporized," her husband added.

She gave him a dirty look and scoffed menacingly at him.

"Careful, Headmaster," the priest warned. "I think your plans for pudding are at risk."

"Think his plans of having a son are..." Elsith muttered under her breath, just loud enough or the mage to hear.

As he turned and started to focus his attention on his loving, dedicated, *kind* love of his life, the exorcist focused on the arm. It looked familiar, but most arms do. What wasn't familiar was the material inside it – or specifically, what was pouring out of it. It was flesh, muscle, bone, and as he tilted the limb down, he realized what it had for blood:

A steady stream of reddish-gray sand.

That's oddly familiar, he mused, even as he struggled to remember why.

As he held it, it began to trickle down from the stump and all over the ground. Bits of fused glass fell to the dirt with it, leaving him stupefied. It wasn't uncommon to have creatures from other worlds ooze something other than 'normal' blood, but it was another to have something mimicking a human to this extent not be filled with a substance that wasn't at least *wet*.

"If you think that's bad," the Huntsmatron called out, "turn it the other way and squeeze the wrist."

The way she said it was the exact opposite of 'comforting,' but curiosity got the better of him. As soon as he did what she suggested, a thin bone spike jutted out from the center of its palm with a disgusting, grating, *'shhhk'* sound.

It stuck out at least an extra foot, and as sturdy as it looked, he had a strong feeling that it would be enough to survive in a sword fight.

"To be fully honest with you both, I've never seen anything like it," Telburn admitted. "I assume it must be some kind of construct, but what kind? I do not know. That sand… it doesn't feel… I don't think that this is the plane it originated from."

That comment earned a nasty, violent curse from the priest. "It's not. Oh, dammit. I know where it's from."

"Do tell?"

"I don't know where the *arm* is from, but I know where the *sand* is from," he clarified as he stuck a finger into the stump and wiggled it around the stiffening tissue inside. The smell that answered his errant probing wasn't as bad as the deathly odors around him, but it wasn't going to settle his stomach any.

Telburn started to ask, though a single glance into the exorcist's eye told him exactly what he needed to know. "I gleaned a bit about your condition… you mentioned that you had encountered water from the supposed River of All Souls?"

"I did."

"There's only one place that those waters flow through."

"Three," Akaran countered. "They start with the Origin."

The mage nodded his head slowly. "And should the lore that the various Orders prescribe to be true, it travels from one plane of the Divine to the next."

"It does," the younger man replied, "before it goes elsewhere. Before the purity within gets filtered through the thoughts, memories, and sins that fill the Veil."

He took the arm back from the exorcist and looked into the glassy, burnt wound. "An arm stuffed full of sand from the World Beyond? *Remarkable*. I daresay I was right about it being a construct, I suppose. But who could build such a thing and give it life?"

"Are you positive it had life?" the priest asked before he pointed at the Huntsmatron. "You need to get this to the Repository. Tonight, honestly. Now, ideally. I'm as reasonably certain as I can be that if you two can't identify what animated it, then it has to be some kind of necromancy. I'm not even going to pretend to hope that someone destroyed this village in an attempt to make a full person and stopped at just the arm."

Elsith walked over and tugged at the spike. "I'm positive that it belonged to a walking, talking asshole. You recognize the owner?"

He shook his head no. "Looks familiar. Do you?"

"Unfortunately, yes. There's been several people that have gotten killed lately by a weapon leaving a single deep puncture wound – I've been keeping an eye on the man doing it. We couldn't figure out how until now."

"Is that the one that Henderschott asked me to prepare a couple of Adepts to help him apprehend?" Telburn interjected.

"That would be," she confirmed. "Well, Donta's not using it now. Less people at risk of a bad death tonight, I imagine."

All of Akaran's thoughts stopped cold as his jaw dropped and eye went wide. "Donta? Lady Anais's bodyguard?"

"And apparent assassin," the Huntsmatron added. "You know him?"

"Know her. Met him once."

"Do you happen to know where he might be?" she asked with an eager, sadistic little smile. "The Overseer would like a word."

Telburn handed the arm off to his wife and began to work his magic again. The portal reappeared soon after, though there was a bit of strain in his eyes from the effort. "He may not be able to get one. Thorough, given the sand and the lack of blood... Akaran, have you ever seen...?"

"No," he sighed. "Though that doesn't mean much. There are stories of necromancers using anything from leaves to burlap for stuffing. I mean it's possible that it's some kind of warped geomancy, perhaps? I nearly got killed by a monster that was a skeleton wrapped in ice so...? I'm..." he took a moment to compose himself as he rubbed a grain of sand between his fingers and watched it sparkle in the light before it winked out of existence. "It's dissipating the longer it's out of the body. Or... limb, I guess."

"It is," the mage replied. "I planned to test it extensively but I don't think there's a need now, if that is what it is. Otherworldly substances do not last in this plane without an anchor. That's what makes the bauble of yours so unique."

He took a ragged breath and shuddered hard enough that he almost looked like he was having a seizure. "It's one thing to animate a creature. Or make a construct. It's another to make something that can pass for human and fill it with material from outside of this world to power it. You understand why that's *bad*, right?"

Even if Telburn didn't, Elsith did – and in a hurry. "The Guild was founded upon hunting down monsters not of this world. I don't need someone capable of making them walking around my city." Before the exorcist could follow that with a quipped reply, she shrugged in his direction. "We have a long history. It's not all mercenary work."

"No, that assuredly it is not," her husband agreed. "Akaran? I hate to agree but this may need to go to one of your former bosses rather than returning to the Annex with me. As much as I realize that you're on the outs with them, do you think that you would be willing to accompany me there? I imagine that they may have questions about the discovery and would like to have some kind of *assurances* that this wasn't one of my experiments gone wrong."

"I can't promise that they'll agree with me, and honestly, I wouldn't blame them for asking." His reply elicited a sharp gasp of shock from the older man, but the priest dismissed it quickly with an added, "Not that I think you did."

"Then we should go. Right away, don't you think?"

"I do, but... not yet."

"Why?"

Akaran looked over at the one person present in their circle that hadn't said a word since they arrived. Her silence said it all, and the ruins she stood in front of almost begged him to go take a look. When she turned around and looked at him with her dead eyes, he could see the blood streaming down from them and over her cheeks like a stream of uncontrollable tears.

"Because something tells me that I haven't seen the worst of it yet."

And he was right.

But for once, the worst of the dead had answers.

XI. EMBERS OF HONESTY
Evening of Londis, the 30ᵗʰ of Riverswell, 513 QR

Of all of the ramshackle buildings in the Landing, the camp had been built around an old barracks of some kind. The one time that Akaran had visited, it had all the trappings of an old Garrison outpost, stone walls and all. It had served to be the safest place for the destitute from the elements, even if not the most comfortable.

Now, it looked like it had served as an oven.

There wasn't a single hut or tent left standing, but whomever had gone after the village had given extra attention to the Landing's hall. A formerly overgrown trussed roof had collapsed straight down into the building and the walls had been blown out from their bases. Only a rough third of the structure was still upright, mostly around the doorframe and a quarter of the rear wall.

"You really shouldn't go in there," Telburn warned from several yards away. "That's where the bulk of the victims were found. Since it was burned once, I have come to understand that the prevailing thought from the locurats is to have it burned once again."

From a corner of the hut, half-hidden in shadows, Rmaci looked up from the carnage and shook her head. "*No. Not like this.*"

"You mean they aren't being consigned to the pyre?"

"Ladjunct Risson was through earlier," the mage explained. "Well, I should say, 'Acting Upper Adjunct of Stara,' Risson. He is convinced that simply sanctifying the ground and having a prayer said over them will be enough."

Akaran frowned as the shade in the corner growled in open anger at the older spellcaster. "Did anyone think to talk to Maiden-Templar Prostil about it? Or Spidous? Or anyone with... experience?"

"*Udju* Risson is perfectly capable of making such a ruling on his own," one of the Stara-aligned 'helpers' retorted as she gingerly laid a bundle of clothes and other things into the wreckage. "A consultation with the Order of Love was not needed."

The exorcist gave the Stara follower a sideways glance. "You do know why the Kingdom put rules on burial methodology, right? Or is that too much to ask from a locurat?"

"To force people like us to devolve ourselves into ashes so that people like you have less to do is my understanding," the woman replied with a hefty sniff from her petite nose, "and given how often tales of the exploits of your Order cross our ears, and as much as you ask us to listen to your disgraced Lady, one could assume that it does little but ruin our robes."

"*Bicker later,*" Rmaci pleaded from the shadows. "*Please, Akaran. Please, listen to them.*"

"Listen to who?"

The locurat must have thought that he meant her – which was reasonable – and replied with a cold, "Listen to the pointless complaints you make about the rest of us looking down at you when you should be looking up at us," she snapped as she stormed away from the ruins.

"*Listen to them,*" the spy begged again as she crawled across the wreckage and gestured at the air.

"I can't hear anything and you know it," Akaran replied in a hushed whisper.

She looked up from one of the more intact corpses and tried to cradle a half-burnt head in her bloody hands. In the shadows, it was hard to tell where she ended and the other bodies began. "*Then look. LOOK at them.*"

It was odd to get that much encouragement from... well, anyone... but Rmaci specifically. Still, as she tried to dig through the ruins without any kind of luck, he started to prod around himself. It was a blessing and a curse to finally get to look at someone's remains in person. On one hand, he hadn't missed the experience.

On the other, there was only so much faith he had in Henderschott's reports. Starting with the obvious that had been left out of almost every story he'd heard so far: what was *missing*. It was to be expected that bodies that had been torn – or blown – to pieces would be short on blood. These seemed to have less than you'd expect, and while blood tended to pool or otherwise cause a body to bloat, these chunks of meat had little of that.

He was happy, or as happy as he could be, to note that most of the bodies were either intact or only missing a few parts. That didn't mean that they looked any less like someone had covered the ground with black powder, lit it from a safe distance, and promptly (presumably) left. It just meant that most of the victims had fewer places to bleed out from.

As he circled the decimated hall, he found a corpse with less explosive damage than the rest. Nestled against the back wall and covered by a few errant support beams, it was devoid of wide-scale bruising, bloating, or other discoloration. Once he pushed more of the broken debris away, he saw a pile of shrubbery desiccated just like the crops on farm at the stairwall. He knelt down (and ignored every stabbing pain his knee offered) and ran his hand over the cold, pale body. There wasn't anything obvious that stood out, just a hole in the neck where the killer had sent a blast of mana through it.

Elsith heard him cursing his knee, and idly came around to help him up. "You know, I've traveled across most of Dawnfire. Spent some time in the Midlands. Trekked down to Matheia once or twice. You know what this reminds me of?"

"No, what?"

"There's these insects. Or they say they're insects. They look more like something you'd deal with," she said as she helped him stand up. "Nasty creatures. About the size of your chest – winged. They look like giant versions of bloodbeaks."

Akaran blinked slowly. "Giant... bloodbeaks?" he asked with a disgusted and vaguely-horrified shudder. "What does that have to do with anything?"

"Well," she started, "they have an odd relationship with another creature in the jungles, the *dashan-borer* beetle. The beetles take the exsanguinated bodies of smaller animals that the giant bloodbeaks – they call the evil things *tentricials* – and fill them with this nasty gunk and their eggs. The body gets hard, doesn't break down like normal, and it helps protect the dashan spawn. Like a rock cocoon"

"That's... really disgusting," he replied as he looked down at the poor old woman's discarded corpse. "Still not seeing what you mean."

The Huntsmatron pointed down at the body. "Well, look at her. No sign of bleeding around her, even with that hole in her neck. No blood all over her clothes. Nothing on the trees."

He felt the piece click into place in the back of his head before the words even left his mouth. "It's almost like they've been drained," he replied before his eye went wide. "Like... like they've been drained."

"Exactly it," she said. "I swear, boy, if I find out someone's smuggled a clutch of tentricials to my city, I am going drown the entire damn basin. You just watch."

"Watch... watching..." he mused aloud as Rmaci lifted herself out of the wreckage and leaned through the rubble.

Her face was covered with concern, her shoulders were slumped, and the constant mocking tone to her voice was long gone. She looked as defeated as the exorcist felt, and that was saying something. "*They're screaming.*"

They? he quietly thought back before the answer hit him across the cheek. *Oh shit. Please don't tell me some of them didn't cross.*

"*I won't tell you. You should already know.*"

We've been through this...

The wraith sighed and gestured into the ruins. Akaran brushed past Elsith to follow her back into the rubble, though it took him a few moments to navigate it with his cane. "*Look around,*" she repeated. "*Look closer. If you could see them, you'd know.*"

If I get any closer, I'm going to end up face first in someone's stomach.

"*If you don't, you're going to hate yourself,*" Rmaci argued. "*It's here, and you're missing it. You know it. You know you're missing it."*

The priest looked around again and didn't see anything else out of place. *Missing what? Whomever did this cleaned up after themselves.*

She shook her head and gestured down at another corpse; one that belonged to a young woman with reddish hair. She'd been pretty in life, but now, her upper body had been scorched with flame and perforated with heavy wooden splinters. *"Not that well. Look. Look, and ignore them. They* won't *believe you, but it's in front of you. This is battlemage work. You hunt them. I used to employ them. An instabilisist was here. A sparkcaster."*

We figured that out already. What am I missing?

"That dagger," she replied as she pointed at Elsith's hip. *"Go get it."*

Confused, he did as she asked and was able to cajole the Huntsmatron into handing it over. The spy's ghost appeared next to him and tried to catch the dangling badge with her finger to no luck. "Hey, Elsith? You have any idea where the 5th is stationed?"

Before the Huntsmatron could reply, the Captain – the same one that had objected to his presence earlier – spoke up for her. "Lowmarsh. You find something of theirs?"

"You expect me to?"

"They've been having a tough time of it lately," the soldier admitted. "Number of sods decided to get up and walk out. The whole of the 4th has been told to keep look for any deserters."

"Really?" Elsith asked. "Do, tell me more," she said as she walked past the ruins to focus on this new development.

She wasn't the only one to focus. *"Who do you know that was in or around Lowmarsh in the last few years?"* the wraith asked the priest.

I can't think of many? I spent time there training, but... everyone in the Order does. The ruins in Sebbidule there are haunted as little else. We train there. It taught me how to look at creatures like... well, like you, no offense... without throwing up.

"So happy you think so little for how I look," she retorted with a bloody snarl. *"But no, you daft man. There's someone else you know."*

No... no I can't... he mused to himself as he struggled to come up with a name. When he did, it was shock – though it shouldn't've been. *No I can. Bistra. She was there.*

Rmaci nodded her skinless head. *"She was. There was a reference to her time up there, yes?"*

That she was looking for someone from... from the 5th. A major.

"A specialist," the spy pointed out.

"A battlemage," Akaran uttered out loud. "She was looking for a battlemage."

Off to the side, his sudden outburst took Elsith's attention again. "Who? What are you talking about?"

"What did she hunt? What was she after?"

I don't remember... he sighed as he dug into his tunic for another piece of cocasa. The third of the hour or not, his leg felt like it was about to explode.

She shook her head violently and stepped up to stand right in front of him. Rmaci grabbed at his cheeks and only barely managed to keep her frustration in check when she couldn't quite touch him. "*You do. Think. You* saw it. *It was on the paper. You ignored it because you're in pain. I saw it. So you saw it.* Remember *and you'll know.* Remember. *I can't tell you. That's a rule. You remember the rules.*"

He slammed his eye shut tight – both to concentrate and to block her from his sight – and focused on remembering the report. *That report... had several entries. Last one was... 17ᵗʰ of Deepfrost... 510 QR... Lithdis, I think? Scribe Penneltuk of Sebbidule recorded... written by Hunter... fisk, I can't...*

"*Those things aren't important. You're seeing it. You're not remembering it. Look,*" she implored as she made a copy of it manifest in the air. It was hazy and wavy, with only the details he remembered being clearly visible. "*In the corner,*" she said as she tapped at the edge of the paper and a red ball of wax.

For all of his efforts to focus on it, little appeared – just a crescent moon in the red wax. A single moon hovering over what appeared to be two mountain peaks. *No*, he realized, *that's two moons. I've never seen that sigil. Two moons, two mountains.*

"*I've been stuck in your head long enough to know damn well that you've seen that,*" the spy retorted. "*You just can't think past that pain in your knee.*"

Then spell it out for me!

"*I already* have," she insisted. "*It's right HERE.*"

As she tapped lower on the scroll, he bent in to read (and remember) more. *Okay – she completed an exorcism. Found a wiped out village... Squistal. That's right. In 508. That sounds familiar. The target... I don't know. Someone had spilled ink all over the bottom of it. Couldn't read it.*

"*No,*" she agreed, "*but you remember the rest of it. She did what? What did the Auramancer Exorcist do? That's her title, isn't it?*"

Akaran rubbed at his eye and wracked his brain. *She went all over Lowmarsh looking for a battlemage...* he replied as more reports manifested in the air near the wraith's face. *...before went after a solg and subsequently went mad. Then after she was found, she ended up in the Manor.* He shook his head and watched as the reports faded from view. "Why would a battlemage from an exorcism go missing and show up *here* the better part of five years later in the middle of a bloodbath? Recruited by.... I don't know. The League? One of the Fallen? That makes next to no damn sense."

Her face lit up and she began, literally and otherwise, to glow. "*Wrong word. Right idea. Wrong word. Look at that body. Listen to those screams.*"

"I can't hear them," he complained loudly.

"*If you could you would know.* LISTEN," she demanded as her voice grew so loud it felt like someone was shoving a tornado in his ears.

Desperate to get her to stop, he went back to the corpses again and started to push them aside. As he worked at a frenetic pace – muttering under his every breath – both the Headmaster and the Huntsmatron began to express their quiet concerns over his well-being as the Stara worshipers stopped gathering the dead and started to back away from the hall. "I can't hear them," he repeated. "If they're crying, I can't. You know I can't."

"*It's* there," she replied with her melted lips suddenly right next to his left ear. "*It's front of you. What would one of you idiots hunt that could convince a battlemage to go rogue? What would be able to jump off buildings, move that fast?*" she demanded.

A lot can do that. If you're as deep in my head as you claim then you'd know that already.

"*I do know that, you half-blind* imbecile," she hissed. "YOU *know it,*" she added as she stepped back in front of him and gestured like she was trying to choke him to death. "*Quit thinking about your damn knee and LOOK.*"

The nastiness, the anger, and the raw... frustration... in her voice made him come to a stop. "My leg is killing me and my head is absolutely pounding. I am doing the best I can, you fisking pain in the ass. If you want to tell me something then *tell me.*"

"*No, you're damn well* not," she swore right back at him. "*You keep asking people to trust you and you don't even trust yourself to know if you're going mad or not and if you don't trust* you *then you sure as piss aren't going to believe* me *so you need to do the one thing that everyone else around you needs to do with you and that's to* pay the fisk attention *to what's going on.*"

The sheer vehemence in her rant made him take a step back. "All I can see right now is you standing there trying to push my sanity over the edge," he retorted before he gestured at the onlookers and continued to argue with her in a hushed tone. "If they didn't think I was mad already they probably do now, to make it worse."

"*Let them think what they will. What can jump that high? What can punch that hard? What can use magic and do both of those things at once? What would need to hunt people on a regular basis – and have an easy way to hide the bodies? What fits the profile? Come on Akaran,* think. *Listen and* think. *You're brighter than this!*"

"I don't see it," Akaran repeated again, this time without trying to keep his voice down. "I can't hear them, and you *know* I can't! *Dammit!*" he shouted as he swung his cane at her. It passed through her effortlessly, but knocked a chunk of stone free.

Several feet away, Elsith started to walk over but her husband caught her by the wrist and made her wait. "If you can't see, then I can bring you a light," he quipped as he cast a small spell and willed a ball of light into his hands. It floated over and helped to illuminate the wreckage, much to the priest's quiet gratitude.

Akaran sunk back to his knees and looked closer at the wound on the two closest corpses to try to find whatever insanity Rmaci was preaching. As he moved around, he started to cast a shadow – and decided to whine about it for good measure. "Great, and now I can't see because of the shadows. Couldn't have found this at noon, could I?"

"*Because of the shadows,*" she repeated in his ear. "*You can't see it because it doesn't like the light. A city covered in shadows would be a perfect home.*"

Most things we hunt don't like the light.

Rmaci shook her head and moved over to wrap the ball in her hands. Telburn frowned as his spell suddenly dimmed – a fact that the priest noticed too. "*This isn't* light," she flatly returned. "*This is a* spell. *Spells aren't light. Spells aren't the source of light that it doesn't like because it's* not *light. LOOK. It's not LIGHT that it doesn't like! What makes LIGHT?!*"

"It's not bothered by magelight but it doesn't like light?" the exorcist asked aloud as he began to wave his hand around the ball once he let it go. "It doesn't mind torchlight but it has to stay in the shadows the rest of the time," he mused as he looked up away from the wreckage and into the giant glowing answer hanging overhead. "It's like there's something wrong with the su…" Akaran looked into the sunlight and felt his jaw drop.

"*Yes.*"

"No. It… no. It can't."

For one moment in time, the entire world felt like it had collapsed around him. All he could see, all he could think, was how *stupid* he had been. How stupid *everyone* had been. All he could *hear* was her voice as she hovered nearby. "*Yes,*" she whispered. "*Yes.*"

His shout echoed through the ruined clearing as the color drained from his face. "It… are you *fisking shitting me*!? HERE!?"

The wraith started to pace around him in a circle like the ruins weren't even there. "*It walks in shadows. It hides from light. It attacks in the dark. The night – that's what you missed. That's the clue. That's what ties it together. You know, don't you? You see it. You can't hear it, but you can see it.*"

Akaran shook his head and dropped down to his good knee (even as the bad one sent a howl of pain through his body that made tears well up in his eye). *No. Not fisking possible. They don't come this far north! They aren't on the mainlands! It's a rule!*

She cleared her throat and gestured at her skinless, dripping form. "*I'm the ghost of a Civan spy that nobody else can see except you. I think there's a lot of rules that have been broken lately, yes…? And that's a lot of bodies for something that doesn't exist.*"

He barely managed to even register her comment as the shock wore off and the world started to come back into focus. *That explains it. Everything. No, not everything. What happens to the feed? Bodies should be everywhere. Their souls should turning up every…* "Turning. FISK."

"*That's the right word!*" she crowed. "*Turning!*"

"It didn't recruit a battlemage. It *turned* one."

"Hey. Cripple," Elsith called out as he paced back and forth. He'd nearly tripped over the same corpse three times now, and while watching him have a meltdown was entertaining, he was doing it so intently that she had lost faith in his ability to do so safely. "Are you okay? Tel, should we do something?"

The headmaster, for all his wisdom, was just as inclined to agree. "I think that may not be a terrible idea, my love. I think the scene is too much for –"

Akaran whipped his head around and gave them both a *stare* that chilled them to the bone. "No, don't. Not yet, please," he half-begged and half-ordered like a maniac. "It's... shit shit *shit*."

"*What happens when they die?*" his nightmare – his *older* nightmare, not to be confused with the new one unfolding around him – pushed.

Well, they become infected by the curse... it gets in their souls and... he ranted quietly before turning back to her. Before he *looked* at her. Before he looked at her like he was seeing who she was for the very first time as a very familiar twinge in his knee demanded attention. "It infects them."

Rmaci shook her head so violently that part of her cheek ripped open. "*No! Not the right word! That's* not *what happens and you know it! What happens when* they *die?*"

"Infected. Infected," he rambled. *It would hurt it would last it would drive them insane until they changed and...* "Doesn't possess the body. Turns the body after it infects the ether."

"*The soul, not the ether. Those are the wrong words*," she argued. "*What happens when one of* them *dies?*" she demanded as she knelt down and shoved an etheric hand into the pile of rubble.

His mouth went dry as he watched, and dryer as he bent down and mimicked her gesture. When his fingers hit the charred remains, he knew where the missing went and how they'd gone undetected for so long. "ASHES. They turn to *ashes*. It turns them after it feeds, kills them, they go to ash. No souls. No lingering wraiths. No bodies."

She looked up at him with a strange glow in her empty eyes. "*Where would you dispose of ashes if you didn't want them found?*"

If I couldn't get near the Pyre? In the water. Or in a garden. Or anywhere nobody's gonna pay attention to a new cloud of dust and dirt.

The wraith let him sort that one out for a moment before she gave up on him and pointed out the obvious. "*What did you just find in the gardens? What feeds on the blood of the damned – your words?*"

Life drains wherever they go. It's feeding, turning, and then killing its progeny. Dumps the ashes at the Wall of Gardens," he replied as another thought hit him. "Wiping out the blooded rose isn't intentional. It tries to feed but it can't so it dies. Or gets poisoned. The other crops... they just get poisoned. It's why it's so fisking popular – it absorbs latent magic. Perks up when it senses it, but it doesn't work around things that are parasitical... it just starves out."

"*Then what?*" she demanded. "*What else does it* do?"

"Bistra. It goes back to her. Seline said the darkness found her once and never let go. She's always talking about shadows."

Rmaci nodded along. *"And fangs. You've heard her. She's been telling everyone all along, and nobody has believed her."*

He looked around the ruins and away from the crumbling hall. "Why here? Why this? If it's been stalking her all along... it had to know that this would get attention."

"The one that did this isn't the one stalking her," she pointed out. *"It likes hiding. It wouldn't have done this. But what do you do when you're getting annoyed by people poking around in your business when you're otherwise busy?"*

"You go get help. Or you make a distraction."

"It makes its own help. It doesn't have to go anywhere. Whatever started in Lowmarsh turned the mage she was looking for – and called it here."

Akaran rubbed at his goatee and ignored the fact that he was smearing bloody remains across his chin. It didn't go unnoticed by the locurats (or the husband and wife team staring at him in vague concern), and one of the priests gagged so hard you could hear it across the clearing. *Why? What would it need help for? Why would it need to destroy the Landing? If its been hiding all this time, why do something like this?*

"As you said: a distraction," the spy answered. *"Someone's been getting closer to figuring it out, and it wanted to cover it's tracks."* She pauses and looks at him, her flame-ravaged face as serious as it ever gets. *"Who spent the most time treating Bistra?"*

The name of the book he'd found in the Manor flashed back into his mind. "Liv. Livstra. It started with her," he said aloud. Off to the side, Elsith tensed up as he invoked her name.

She nodded along. *"It did. That woman must have been close..."*

That doesn't explain Odern. What could he have to do with the poor woman?

"Bistra? Hard to say. You know so little about him; maybe he was a friend of hers. Maybe he was a friend of the healer's. What was it that lecherous mage over there said?"

"That he liked dice, I think," the exorcist muttered as he gave a studious glance over at the headmaster. A glance, it should be noted, that made the Granalchi suddenly feel incredibly uncomfortable.

The wraith crossed her arms and the gnarled muscles on her forehead furrowed as she frowned. *"A mage that plays dice? I can't say I'd be particularly interested, but if he owed a debt, then he might owe a favor to someone. Maybe Liv asked him for help...?"*

That was where Seline's discovery came in – and suddenly he wished he'd brought her clue with him. "The Gambling Mind," he replied as the connection snapped into place. "That's it! He owed her. He helped her and got killed for his trouble. If it took one mage..."

"It could take another. What was he, exactly? Some kind of defensive

instructor? Is it so outside the realm of possibility that a creature that could kill him couldn't overcome the threat posed by one of the Queen's so-called 'battle' mages?" Rmaci asked, spitting in disgust at the title. *"Specialists. Not a one could stand to the Empresses' Firestormers."*

The Huntsmatron interrupted the former Civan's complaints – not that she could hear them, but she interrupted them all the same. "The Gambling...? What do you know about her?"

Akaran blinked and looked over his shoulder. "About who? Sorry, didn't hear what you –"

She stormed over to him and grabbed him by both shoulders. As he protested, she shoved him away from the pile of rubble and just barely kept herself from wrapping her hand around his throat. "You keep your damn voice down and you tell me what you know about her."

He stumbled back and nearly fell onto his ass, with his cane the only thing that saved him from both world-class embarrassment and suffering alike. "WHO?"

"You just said her name!" Elsith hissed at him. "Livstra! The Gambling Mind!"

"I have a book she wrote, called that, I don't –"

Her eyes went as wide as saucers. "You found it? *You* have it? I need it. Where is it?"

The priest took an extra step back but she grabbed him by his tunic before he could get far. As he worked to get her to let him go, he snarled his reply. "Okay, talk. What am I missing here?"

"Missing?" she scoffed. "What are you *missing*? Livstra *ran* the Fleetfinger's Guild, *you moron*," she hissed. "If you have evidence that Odern owed her, then that goes a long way to explain why she had him killed. What proof do you have?"

"None that she killed him," he replied as a new idea boiled to the forefront of his mind. He looked over and called out to Telburn. With a quick question. "Headmaster – do you know who Odern worshiped? Did he have any ties to any of the Gods?"

"Ties? He had a habit of visiting the Shrine of Covered Moons," the mage replied with a frown. "Though he is far from the only Adept to do so. There is a measure of back and forth that the Academy engages in while trying to stay neutral to the various –"

Akaran blinked quickly and halfway covered his mouth with his filthy glove. "Lethandria. Erine. He knew the Mother Eclipsian."

"So did half the city? What of it?"

He shook her off as she loosened her grip. "Everyone is connected. Shadows. Fangs. *Oh Goddess*. Why?" he muttered over and over to himself as he walked back into the rubble of the hall.

Rmaci flickered back into existence beside him and placed her hand on his back. *"It's the most adorable thing to watch when you finally start to get a clue*."

The priest took a deep breath and did something that few people ever saw him do in person – he reached into a pocket on his belt and pulled out a simple silver coin with a casting of a woman's face in the center. "Lover, Matron, Mother," he began as he spoke down at it with his voice just barely above a whisper, "I know I can't channel Your will right now but please, please, tell me what I'm missing. I don't understand what I'm supposed to see to tie this together, please, answer me, I beg..."

"Prayer won't solve your problems boy, believe me, I know," the shade interrupted. *"The Gods gave us free will, didn't they? And a mind to solve the problems we're faced with?"*

"Some of us more minds than others," Akaran sighed in frustration as he slipped the coin back into his belt. "Why now? Why would it go from hiding and killing in quiet to cover its tracks to mass murder and... it wouldn't do this if it was looking for me... I haven't been here in weeks..."

She flicked her split tongue against her sagging lip. *"But it would if it was looking for someone else,"* she crooned. *"A lot of people have been looking for answers. Not just you. You got it's attention when you stopped it from feeding on that Anais bitch..."*

So the son of a bitch set me up at the Manor, he thought back at her. *I didn't steal that shit.*

"Yet you were there, and it recognized you as a threat," Rmaci pointed out. *"Maybe it didn't want to risk another murder on the Manor grounds. Wanted to get you away so it could have you killed at leisure."*

He frowned as he followed her thought through. "Maybe it couldn't get close enough to do it again? The wards. They wards were replaced after I broke them, and it can't get close again?"

"No," she pointed out, *"because that blonde girl just told you the auramancer is talking to the shadows in your room. I think that maybe it just likes to play with its toys and thought you'd be a fun one to send spinning around. Pay you back for punching it in the face,"* she suggested with a little smirk and giggle.

Before he could comment, Elsith interrupted his conversation, one-sided as it appeared to be. "Okay, that's it from you. You're acting like a deranged fool and I think you will be better sent somewhere you can't hurt yourself."

Telburn, for his credit, stopped her before she could grab the priest by his shoulders with a hand on hers. When she started to object, he silenced her with a short shake of his head and a gesture at the flickering ball of light still levitating in the center of the ruins. Every few seconds, it dimmed like someone was walking past it. "My love, I don't think he's talking to himself. Remember, suspension of rank aside, he *is* an exorcist."

"You're suggesting he's seeing something and talking to it?"

Her husband focused on Akaran's eye and watched where it went – and when the magelight flickered. "I suggest, as a man of magic myself, that sometimes the ether doesn't ripple in the same way for everyone who can otherwise sense it."

Elsith watched him pace and slowly slid her hands down to the blade at her waist. "Are we in danger?"

"My love, we stand in the middle of a massacre. I would say yes, but…"

"But?" she pressed.

Telburn watched Akaran idly rap his cane against a chunk of burnt stone and narrowed his eyes at the exorcist. "…I have this odd feeling that whatever danger *we* are in pales in comparison to whatever has gained the attention of his thoughts."

He was right, and he'd understand *how* right in the very near future.

The wraith, however, was far from done 'helping' in her own way. "*So it couldn't get past the wards, and had one of the residents… so you have it's attention, yet you aren't involved in the Landing. However, we both know someone that has been moving in the land of the undesirables that you've had involvement with.*"

Akaran looked up from one of the bodies and frowned. *Anais? I stopped it from feeding on her…*

"*Yet she has her own muscle, despite her efforts to recruit you to do her dirty work.*"

The camp wasn't the target, he realized as he turned around and looked at the bag that the Headmaster had dropped the arm in. "Donta was. Donta was the target, that arm belongs to him, and the 5th's mage went after him and decided to wipe out the camp to cover their tracks."

"*You know what it is,*" Rmaci needled. "*You know it has help. You know what's it been doing. You* know. *You know, and you know these people are* screaming. *They weren't all dead when they burned.* You *can't hear them but I* can," she ranted as she glared raw hatred at him and the bloody cracks in her charred flesh began to catch fire all over again.

"I don't need to hear them," he snarled. "I know. I know what it is. For the love of the Goddess, *shit*, I *know*."

The wraith flickered in and out of sight. For a brief moment, she looked… human… before soft skin turned darker and more inflamed than ever before. "*Now tell me what the fisk you're going to do about it.*"

Akaran took a breath and walked out of the ruins to try to compose himself. A few gloomy thoughts later, and he drove his cane into the dirt hard enough to leave a divot in the soil. *There isn't a soul on this planet that's going to believe me*, he snapped over at her.

"*You're wrong. Bistra will.*"

I can't get to her. Wouldn't do any good if I could. Nobody else will.

"*So you say with such finality. This world is full of things that go bump in the night; what makes you believe that the existence of vamp –*" she started to challenge before he cut her off.

You don't understand, he cautioned. *The Crusade of Suns reduced them to nothing. Obliterated their race, as far as anyone could tell. They were believed lost to time until... fisk. I don't remember. Four hundred something. They pop up time to time in Matheia since then.*

She narrowed her eyes and gave him a petulant stare. "*We are far away from the Golden Empire.*"

We are, the priest agreed, *and that's the problem. There was more than one Crusade of Suns*, he explained, *and the fact that you don't know anything about it is part of why they don't exist here anymore.*

"*Your riddles do little for my patience*," she warned.

The Sisters of Love have an agreement with the Crown, Akaran explained, *and it's really simple. We are protected from persecution, we're given land, we're given authority to make sure something like the fall of the Adelin Empire never happens again.*

"*And in exchange...?*" she asked.

In exchange, we make sure that those bloodsuckers never touch foot in the Queen's territory ever again. If there's been one operating here for years...

"*...then you've failed,*" the spy finished.

Worse than failed. We'd be at risk of losing... we'd lose just about everything, he quietly admitted. *One or two dead? Understandable, if it was covered up quickly. Dozens? A massacre like this? ALL of this? Catherine will be lucky to run out of the city with her head still on her shoulders from the wrath that General Fire-Eyes herself will rain down, let alone whatever the Queen decides to do. Nobody is going to believe me because nobody is going to* **want** *to believe me.*

Rmaci crossed her arms and sent a cloud of embers into the air. "*So what are you going to do? How are you going to prove it?*"

I'm going to drag that thing out of the shadows and see what the sun does it.

The vehemence in his answer seemed to mollify her to a small degree, and it did put a smile on her twisted face. "*I'll help. But before that?*"

The exorcist looked down at the bloody mess near his feet and felt a deep, cold rage build up inside his heart. Instead of answering her, Akaran turned to face the married couple and laid out the only truth that they might be willing to listen to. "Okay. Both of you. I don't have any answers that you're going to want. I don't have answers you're going to believe. But I will. I beg you. I will get down on my knees and *beg you* if you do a couple of things for me."

"Given the shape of your leg," Telburn started, "I don't think that kneeling would be a great idea."

"Might be fun to watch," his wife offered.

Akaran stared them both down until the jovial smiles fled their lips. "Please."

"I'm inclined to agree with my wife that you may not entirely be of yourself, my friend. What are you asking?"

He gestured at the pile of corpses and pieces of people before responding, with all of the solemnity he could muster, "Have these bodies taken down to the Pyre outside the Ellachurstine. Don't leave a scrap behind up here. And please, *please*, ask Catherine or Spidous or *someone* to come here and sanctify this massacre. Someone that can establish not just a blessing but put down a Ward of Defiance and an *il estapasaiage* ward."

That request drew the ire of the *locurat* and her merry band of tenders. "The pyre?" she demanded with a sharp rise to her voice. "With all respect due to the Headmaster and his bladed companion –"

"His *wife*," Elsith hissed through clenched teeth.

"Ahem. With respect to his *wife*," the locurat corrected in the most respectfully disrespectful manner she could manage, "I've listened to your ramblings long enough. There's no need for that. They've already been burnt. We'll bury them in accordance with the Queen's Law and bless their souls as we do. There's no reason for the extra effort."

"Two months ago, Adjunct Risson promised me that if I ever needed aid, the Order of Stara was to provide it," Akaran retorted with only a brief glance in their direction. "This is the aid. The Everburning Pyre needs to be used for these bodies. We can write the favor off if you do it."

"That was when you had standing with the Harlot's servants. I am sure his mind has changed by now. If you're too unstable even for them, then why should we follow your request?"

"Because you will regret it if not," he warned through clenched teeth. "That's why I'm not asking you, I'm asking her."

Rmaci allowed herself a fit of mocking laughter as the locurat's cheeks flared red. "We'll regret it? Are you threatening me? Huntsmatron, I'd ask that you exercise your duty to the crown and remove this man from this disaster."

Elsith looked at the enraged priestess – and then looked closer at the source of her anger. "Was that a threat or a promise?"

"Promise."

"Harm by you or other?"

"Other," he replied before he succumbed to the look she was giving him. "Potentially both."

She pursed her lips and tilted her head slightly as the locurat continued to fume. "I see. You understand I think you're both a fool and a madman, yes?"

"Figured."

"You truly think that this is warranted?"

Akaran took a deep breath and gave her a pleading stare. "Elsith, I've got fifteen crowns to my name. I will give you all of them and my cane if it'll hire you to have these bodies moved. I don't care if I eat or not tonight, but *please*, get these consigned to the flames properly. There will be a *problem* if not. Not the kind I can deal with right now, and not the kind *you* want to deal with while the wedding is going on."

Telburn took that moment to clear his throat and interject himself back into the conversation. "In times of trouble, my love, I tend to lean towards the advice of experts. Magic was involved with this, and I am beginning to assume that our good friend has cause of his own to think that it may not have been human in nature. As such, his experiences may eclipse our knowledge; painful as it is to admit."

"Human?" he scoffed. "Not anymore. Used to be."

"*You hope it used to be human,*" Rmaci cautioned, "*Or at least, you hope that whatever sired the monster that did this once was.*"

He ignored her. Or at least, he tried very, very hard to ignore her and all of the myriad ways that her statement could make things so much worse. "Will you, please?"

The Huntsmatron gave it less thought than he expected and didn't even try to negotiate terms with him. "As you ask. But I do want those crowns," she warned.

While the locurat began shouting at the mercenary at the top of her (apparently impressive) lungs, Akaran turned his attention over to the Headmaster. "Fine," he replied as he dug the coins out of his pocket and handed them over. "Telburn? Whatever you're doing to get my magic back?"

"Yes?"

"Get it done faster."

The mage blinked and took an involuntary step back. "That almost sounds like an order, my boy – both an intensity and a tone that I'm not sure I am comfortable being addressed with. Why now? Why so... demanding, I should say? I realize that this situation is poor at best, but you can surely stand to maintain a level of composure, can't you?"

"Because nobody's going to believe what I'm hunting until I can prove it. I need Her touch to prove it. So I need you to hurry up so I can hurt it a lot."

"Hunting things now, are you? I believe that's a job of the Guild," his wife chimed in as she counted out the last of the crowns.

"Trust me, Elsith," he sighed, "you're gonna get a Writ the size of which you've never seen if I'm right."

"I've seen many writs in my time, little lost priest."

"Not one that's going to pay like this," he promised. "Gorosoch? I need an absorption gem."

Of anything the Adept was expecting to hear, that was at the very bottom of the list and his surprise caused his busy eyebrows to almost go to the top of his head. "Those, my boy, are *not* cheap. You are asking for something outside of your pay, even if you had the blessing of the Lovers with you still."

Akaran gave him a short shrug and slightly understanding nod. "Yeah. I need one anyway."

Telburn glanced over at his wife and probed the inside of his cheek with his tongue for a moment before responding. "You just bartered the last of your crowns away for the bodies. You have little that I can be interested in that you're allowed to say. Outside the Order or not, that seal, as you have pointed out –"

"Necrosia," the priest interrupted as the locurat and her minions wandered away. "That's how he did it."

"Excuse me?"

Rmaci stopped trying to dig around the bodies and gasped in complete shock as he explained in ways that he really shouldn't explain anything. "You wanted to know how Usaic hid his efforts to create the coldstone, right? You wanted to know how a rogue wizard figured out a way to manifest an object from beyond the Veil without setting off every auger and scryer on this side of the planet, right?"

The mage straightened himself up and studied the priest with more interest than he'd shown anything else in the glade. "That... that would be pertinent information, yes."

"Fine," Akaran shot back. "Necrosia. I'm not telling you how. I'm not telling you that you have permission to do it. I'm not giving you the spell. I will give you the *idea* because I *need* that damn stone."

He lifted his finger and lightly chastised the priest. "A word is not an idea unless it is couched within other thoughts, my boy. Necrosia is a dangerous word, of course, though you and I both know —"

"He enslaved a demon and made it use necrosia to summon another entity. An *arin-goliath*. The *arin* was able to absorb the stray ether he was leaving behind in his wake. That's half of how he hid."

"*You were not to say that,*" the wraith warned. "*Be careful of the cracks you place in that particular box.*"

If you're not lying about Daringol, he's going to get acquainted with the arin sooner than later, Akaran thought back at her with a disgusted grunt. *I'd rather him start to understand their nature before it shows up on his doorstep.*

A hint of a smile flickered across her twisted lips, or at least, he thought it was a smile. "*That's decidedly duplicitous. Playing him against me, voiding your constraints to get what you want under the guise of saving lives to justify it to yourself. That is an* impressive *bout of self-rationalization. The pit would come to adore you if you ever changed sides.*"

While she expressed her twisted admiration, the duo listening to him tried to make sense of it. "An Adept summoned a demon? My love, isn't that forbidden?" Elsith asked.

"He was outcast from the Academy," the priest clarified. "There. Now you know. I need a stone so I can track down the thing that did this. Please?"

"I... I am fairly certain you just broke an oath," her husband replied.

"No, I disregarded an instruction. Didn't swear to anything, but just because *I* didn't doesn't mean that *you* won't. So, swear it."

The Headmaster tilted his head and frowned. "That I won't...? Are you suggesting that I've somehow offered a promise to you?"

"Yes," Akaran retorted. "*You* aren't going to do *shit* about what I just told you because *you* know what would happen *to* and *by* the Academy if word got out that a Headmaster was dabbling with the forbidden school. And, in the middle of this bloody mess, you're bright enough to know what could happen if you started blabbing it to other people. So you're going to say an oath avowing that you know better and won't. Aren't you?"

Telburn wavered on the threat as he worked his way through the priest's twisting logic. "You are also bright enough to know that the only way to keep a secret between two people is if one of them is dead and there are more than two of us standing here."

"*That isn't entirely true*," Rmaci intoned. "*Contrary to popular belief the dead do, indeed, tell tales.*"

"Not in my line of work it isn't."

Neither the mage nor the mercenary could argue his assessment. "That does... that does open doors to other lines of research, however. Research not forbidden."

"Okay," he quickly returned. "Gem? And oath?"

The Headmaster clucked his tongue. "It's customary to agree to terms before giving away your side of the offer."

"Fisk customs. Gem? Please? Say the oath on your own time, just say it at some point so I don't earn any more of the Goddesses' wrath?"

"You are completely insane and single-minded, aren't you?" Elsith interjected.

The priest gave her a little shrug. "Starting to think so."

"Honest, too," she mused. "You know, if the Order doesn't take you back once you put away that stick... come see me."

Her job offer slipped his notice as he held his hand out towards the mage. "*Gem?*"

"You are... most insistent," Telburn grumbled before he let loose with a frustrated sigh. "Almost sound like my daughter. *Fine*. I will have one delivered to you *but* we will be speaking about this again. Since I assume you need it sooner rather than later, I promise, you'll have it before the moon crests, if you aren't asleep by then."

"Fine. Thank you. I won't be. Also, your daughter sounds nice. I'm staying at the *Drunken Imperial*."

His wife rubbed at her temples. "She's an absolute terror."

The mage reached over and draped his hand over her shoulder. "She learned from her mother."

Elsith made a point to ignore that particular remark and instead, turned her ire back to Akaran. "You better be right about that writ, exorcist. You better be right about whatever you've been going on about. I think I like you, but I am not convinced you are to be trusted. I mean, you didn't make me swear –"

"The Guild has hunted necromongers and demon-scryers since the Sons of Veritas first captured Arch-Duke Belizal's bride at the end of the Adelin Civil War and the rise of the Empire of the Damned. You'd sooner dance naked in the Court of Necrohol for the Duke's amusement than tell the world how to create an *arin* and we both know it," he ranted. "Listen: I promise that I'm right," he swore, "and I promise you'll be mad at me when you figure out why. That said, I promise you'll get a writ. I promise it'll pay."

"I'll hold you to that," she cautioned.

Rmaci walked over and hovered right behind the Huntsmatron as she peered at a spot on the back of the woman's golden-blonde head. *"How much do you think the Order will pay them once you can prove you're right?"*

How many crowns do you think Catherine has buried in the vault? He shot back as he put the Landing to his back and started his trip back to the city.

***

As the sun set over the city, Sergeant-at-Arms Telpid had an entirely different problem that he was intent on handing off to someone else. As luck would have it, Seline ended up being just that person – and she was so bedraggled, run-down, and *sore* that she couldn't have given less of a shit about it. Nor did expressing that in as many words seem to do any good.

"M'am, I don't know who he is or what he wants," he complained. "He showed up half an hour ago. I tried to toss him off the grounds, and every time I do, I find him at another entrance."

She looked down her pert nose at him and took slight offense that after the day she had, he managed to look so prim and proper in his garrison uniform when she looked and felt like she'd been on the wrong end of a vulture all day. "Aren't you the man the Lady employs to have people like that thrown off the cliff if they become troublesome?"

"Yes, but..."

"But what?" Seline demanded. "Listen, Ronald. I've had Appaidene screaming her head off over her doll all day. I've had Benjin throwing *actual* shit at the wall for the last three hours and Divitol keeps taking his swaddlecloths off and keeps trying to stick his dick in the mouth of the boar's head in the dining hall. So, in all honesty, you either throw him off the cliff or I throw you."

Telpid swallowed nervously and looked over his shoulder as a loud 'thunk' and a matching 'thud' echoed down the hall. "That's the problem. He's got someone with him that could throw both of us over without breaking a sweat."

She threw her hands up in the air and let out a tired little scream from the back of her throat. "Are you *serious*? Are you telling me that you're standing there, with a *sword on your hip* and you're afraid of two people trying to get us to *answer the damn door*?"

"Sel, please," he begged. "Come see what this guy wants. It's not worth the headache to argue about it."

"Oh, there's no need," another voice intoned as a plump figure in a garishly orange vest rounded the corner of the hallway to confront them. "I'm here now."

Telpid started to draw his sword before the overweight intruder wagged his finger at him – just once – and convinced him that discretion might be the better part of valor. Still, he tried to speak up and salvage whatever authority he pretended to have. "You aren't allowed in here! I told you to wait in the foyer and –"

"– and, simply, I grew bored," the other man interrupted with a droll tilt to his voice. "You, serving girl, I assume? I need to speak to someone in charge around here. It's very important."

"I am a healer," she seethed as she gave him a withering look that could've (and should've) floored just about anyone else.

The bemused smile that popped up on his lips made Telpid cringe and retreat to the edge of the hallway like the coward he was. "Ah, good. I hope that a healer is more useful than this fellow here."

"Oh you won't have to worry about him after this, I promise," she snarled as she reached up and tied her loose blonde hair back into a bun. "The manor is not open to guests, and you will be leaving. *Now.*"

"I'm sure that you allow people to come speak to your residents as needed," he returned as his smug little smile stretched from ear to ear. "I assure you right now, it is very badly needed."

"Contrary to what you may have seen so far, there is a way to gain access into these halls," she retorted, "and you have assured yourself through your actions that you won't... oh."

Behind the interloper, another man – bigger, (much bigger) and dressed like a border stable-boy – pulled one of the Manor's orderlies limply along behind him with one hand tightly wrapped up in the neck of his white tunic. "Boss, this one got rude. Sorry."

The 'boss' of the mountain of meat looked down at the dazed helper and sighed in vague annoyance. "Manners in a Manor. You'd expect them to be better. You're forgiven, Austilin, of course. You must do what you must. Set him down somewhere? Carefully?"

Seline swallowed nervously and reached over to pick up a small clay vase sitting on a table lining the hallway. "What... what do you want? Nobody else has to get hurt."

"No, someone does," the pudgy – no, *bulky* man, she realized – clarified. "That's why I'm here and why I need to speak to one of your esteemed residents. I'm looking for Akaran? Akaran DeHawk? Claims to be some kind of 'not-nice' priest? An exorcist, I think they say. One eye, poorly-kept hair."

She kept her grip on the pottery but rolled her eyes as her shoulders sagged. "Why am I not at all surprised. Of *course* you are."

He cleared his throat and adjusted his vest with his left hand. "My dear, as much as I would love to have an extended conversation with you about it, I am afraid I have manners quite pressing to attend to and I've come such a long way to see them through. Where is he?"

"It won't do you any good even if I knew. He's little more than a cocasa addict at this point. Matter of time before he's dead in a gutter somewhere, if he's not already. Ridora threw him out a week ago."

Austilin's boss narrowed his eyes and took a single step closer with what felt like the weight of the world following his movement. "I don't think you understand, my dear. You're going to take me to him."

"He's not here. I don't know where he is," she repeated.

"That's unfortunate. This is a matter of life and death."

She shook her head vehemently and backed away even as Ronald cautiously moved to help the borderline-unconscious orderly. "I don't care if it's a matter of wine and women. He's not here, I don't know where he is, and you need to leave before I call –"

"Specifically," he interrupted, "yours," he said as a dark patch of skin on his cheek began to smolder... and move of it's own accord.

XII. DREAMS OF DAMNATION
Late Evening of Londis, the 30th of Riverswell, 513 QR

The Pyre of Everburning Flame was a fixture in any city where the Order of Stara was present. The original meaning and use had been lost to time; some scholars assumed it was part of a ritual to show the light of the Origin, or to represent how eternal the light of Stara herself was. Others guessed that it was just a way for humans to always have some source of fire to keep the dark at bay. A few, sometimes branded heretics (especially in Dawnfire, where worship of the Queen of Flame was at odds with worshiping Her sister), suggested that it was done in honor of the First Fire to show humanity how to survive on their own.

Whatever the reason then, the fall of the Adelin Empire gave it a new task and duty in the now. While demons and unholy dead had stalked the land since the dawn of time, they had only once before done so in numbers so great to cause the fall of a nation – an event that had only occurred a scant five decades before the collapse of the Adelin. The Orders of Light (in one of the very few instances in their collective histories of 'attempting to defend against the damned') determined that two nations falling was at least one too many.

As a result, they prayed for guidance from any that would answer.

They received a reply, though they'll never admit Who gave it to them.

The response was simply that if the souls of the departed had no remaining flesh with which to anchor themselves to, and the tainted from the lower Abyss had no shell to seep in to? Well, then the spirits of the dead would have nothing holding them from crossing over. Or staying over, depending.

So it came to be, by Order of the Queen in 286 Q.R., that anyone that passed away in the Kingdom was to be purified by flame. For anyone near a Temple of Stara, what was once called the 'Brazier of Everburning Flame' became the 'Pyre of Everburning Flame.' Anyone not neither either would have to be scrubbed from the world by way of bonfire – though most people were of the opinion that if nobody saw what they did, maybe they didn't *need* to burn their family in the end.

It was ill-advised to ignore the law, but that never stopped anyone.

From a hilltop a mile away, Akaran watched the flames creep ever higher and try to lick at the top of the marble dome with each body loaded into it. His thoughts were not on the beauty of the brass bowl or the craftsmanship that went into constructing the four pillars that stood twenty feet overhead. He didn't care about the procession of locurats and the undlajunct presiding over each corpse as they were carried up the steps and ceremoniously slipped into flames – one into the north side, then the south, then east, then west, and then repeated for every person (or piece of a person) that had to be submitted to purification. He didn't care about the prayers, or care that Elsith had taken it upon herself to personally watch over the disposal after his warning.

"I don't know what I'm supposed to do about this," he sighed as he looked away from the flames and at the two moons overhead. The moons and the pyre were really the only two things he could see clearly in the dark. The only other source of light anywhere near him was a flickering torch he'd swiped from a lamppost on the way up the hill.

Rmaci, blunt and more irritated than normal, snapped back at him as the stench of burning flesh wafted past his nose. "*Hunt them. Kill them.*"

"That's rather obvious, isn't it?"

"*Not obvious if you don't know what you're doing.*"

He scoffed at her and took a drink from the flagon sitting next to his hip. After leaving the Landing, he'd stopped by the *Imperial* for a chat with Cel and a few minutes alone with the *Gambling Mind* journal that the Huntsmatron was so interested in. The innkeep had been nice enough to give him something a little stronger than just cocasa to deal with the stress of the day once Telburn's courier arrived and let slip everything that the priest had been up to.

To say that it gave the ale a nasty aftertaste was an understatement, though it was unpleasantly familiar from his trip to Toniki. Nastier than normal, at that. "There needs to be a full sweep of the city," he mused. "Priests at every intersection. Everyone here checked. Examined."

"*Not quite everyone,*" she replied. "*I think we'd both be happy if we avoided that particular intrusion. You aren't their greatest friend at the moment and honestly, I'm not what one would consider a fan myself.*"

"Again. The intrusion *again.*"

"*As you say,*" she answered with a sigh and a forlorn look down at the pyre. "*You're aware that if that had been done correctly at my passing, I may not be here. I may have been cleansed and been able to ascend. As I should've.*"

"Or you may have been in the pit with no escape," Akaran pointed out. "How much of your damnation was caused by faulty faith and bad acts compared to the anchor that Daringol cursed you with?"

The spy blanched and looked away from him, almost like she was ashamed. "*Regardless. I'll have peace. Soon.*"

"The *Hullbreaker* is almost here, isn't it? How soon?"

She let a smile dance over her face. It never ceased to grow worse each time she showed a genuine one. "*Too soon for you, not soon enough for me.*"

The priest cast a side-eye in her direction and took another drink. "A vague answer. Want to give me a little more with that while you're being helpful today?"

Instead of the bullshit answer he was expecting, acquiesced. "*A half-turn of the moons. Three, if the weather changes. A solid wind in the right direction and the rest of my soul may be on land before the full week is out.*"

"Shit."

Her body flicked out of his sight and reappeared sitting directly across from him with her back to the pyre. "*You know, of a man of your education – and don't claim not to have one, I have seen inside that skull of yours – one would have expected that you might have a deeper grasp of language than to say that word every time someone gives you a truth you don't like.*"

Akaran snorted and took another swig of the ale as he felt the effects start to kick in. "There's at least two vampires running around the city that I can't do anything about. I'm watching what we're *guessing* is twenty-six people turn to ash. I've been disavowed from the Order, and you just told me that there's a ship full of wraiths on its way."

"*Well yes, I can see how you'd find that a bit glum, but still –*"

"I'm sorry. Should I take on airs and say, 'Alas, m'lady of the House of Perdition, it is such a great preponderance of fates that I am now cursed to comprehend both the knowledge of my impending doom and the loss of innumerable lives to either fang or rotted flesh. It is with great regret that I see no hope and have few options to consider to move forward with anything but a dismal attitude.' Is that better?"

The wraith pursed her bloody lips and dropped her pathetic indignation. "*Well. No, I suppose not.*"

"Good," he grunted as he took another drink. "Shit."

She matched his curse with another sigh – an impressive feat for someone that didn't need air – and reluctantly offered an agreement. "*Shit indeed.*"

"I don't know what I'm going to do about this. But…"

"*But?*"

"But you, I do," he finished.

Rmaci's smile returned and she snorted in bemusement. "*Come up with a way to rid me, have you? You forget that I can hear what goes on in your mind. Can't say that I've noticed any grand schemes lately.*"

"I know," he admitted, "there's no doubt that you can listen in and piss me off. And at the moment, I can't lay a hand on you. Can I?"

"*No. You have no power over me out here. Any more than I do over you. Annoying each other is our limit for now.*"

He nodded and started to smile as a deep, cool wave began to rush out of his stomach and through his body. "That's what I thought. So do you remember when I asked Cel to give me the special brew? I mentioned a couple of people?"

"*You know, speaking of women that I'm not particularly fond of in your life, did you have to add my* murderesses *name to your lips? Have I not suffered enough as of late to your tastes?*"

"Did you think to ask what was in it? Or were you too pissed that I talked about Evalia?"

The wraith grimaced. "*You're speaking in circles. I* just *said that hearing her name — let alone having to tolerate you* thinking *about her — was enough to drive me to distraction. When* you *end up dead, I promise I'll make special care to come by your spirit and whisper my name in your ear every chance I get, should the opportunity arise.*"

Akaran yawned and made sure he was comfortable. Then, as she watched in bewilderment, he began to roll up his pantaloons up and over his right knee. "Well... see, you gave away your game earlier," he replied as he yawned again. "Shit. That's hitting hard."

"*What are you doing?*"

He took a long breath and pulled a straight, polished knife free of his belt and watched it glint in the light of the torch at his side. "We need to be on equal footing. Hah. Footing. That's funny."

Rmaci twitched as she saw the flames reflect in the cold steel. "*You intend to kill yourself? Dive headlong into the Abyss with me?*"

"No. But this might do it anyway," he admitted. As she watched and grew more and more anxious, he placed the end of the knife into the lantern and let the flames slowly heat the blade. "Three questions. I need you to be honest with me. Please."

"*I have never been anything other. Liars suffer great torments, and I've no desire to add to them,*" she replied as he rolled the tip of the knife in and out of the small fire. "*Though I may decline to answer.*"

"What's his name?"

"*Who's?*"

He took a deep breath and kept working the weapon back and forth. "The demon. The one that wears my face. Down there."

The wraith stopped moving and worked to puzzle out the request. When she came up with absolutely no idea whatsoever, she finally caved and asked. "*Him? Why would you want to know...?*"

"Because that offends me," the priest retorted. "That's *my* face. Nobody's allowed to use my face but me. So what's his name?"

She flickered out of sight and returned a few moments — and several yards away — later with all of her bravado gone. "*It'll do you no good. He's not like me. He's not like a damned soul. He doesn't want out — that's his* home. *He's where he* wants *to be. He'll never come out and bother you or stalk this world; he is content.*"

"Home's where the hurting is, I guess," Akaran replied. "Okay. So. What's his name?"

"I... I don't know if I can say."

He plunged more of the knife into the flame as it finally started to glow a little on the tip. "Well... you told me you know everything. So, if you know everything, and all the secrets, you have to know his name. You also told me that you can't tell me most of it 'cause you're somehow *blocked* by... you know what? No. I'm not gonna try to figure that out. I'm not that sober."

"No you most definitely are not," she retorted with an indignant sniff. *"Once again I am grateful for my inability to taste or smell whatever it is that's in that jug. What* are *you drinking?"*

"Painkillers. Lots of them."

Her eyes went wide and she dropped down to all fours on the grassy knoll. *"Why are you... what are you doing with that knife?"*

"Really... really hoping... you'll answer... the questions quickly. His name?" he pushed as his voice slurred.

She swallowed nervously and looked away from the priest. *"It's Sala... Salassellaki. Salassellaki. He doesn't call himself that. He says he's you. But I know his name when I'm not there."*

"Salassellaki," he repeated. "Goddess, I'm glad I asked that first. Another couple of drinks and I dunno... dunno if I could... say that. Whew. Okay."

Rmaci oozed forward across the ground until she was close enough to look up into his eye. *"You're not a man of verbal tricks, Akaran. Don't try to suggest you're capable of doing them now, inebriated as you are now."*

"Oh. No. No trick," he quickly replied. "Just hurt. So. Other questions: why did you help back there?"

"Why? Isn't it obvious?"

The exorcist shook his head and took another draw off of the ale as the knife started to shine. "No. Apparently, see, I'm stupid. I never realized. I should've. Vampires. Infestations. Infections. I should've. I'm smarter than that. I should've known."

"One would doubt that often. Still, it's hard to see what lies beneath the surface unless we know where to look."

"Ohhhh that's so fisking true. *Fisking* true. So why? Why help? I'm dumb. Tell me. Please," he implored, "while I can understand. Before this gets worse."

She looked up at him again and then quickly turned to face the pyre. As she stared at the flames, he watched the skin on her back began to turn crispy and blackened. *"They're not screaming now. I can't hear them anymore."*

"They were at the Landing."

"They were," she whispered. *"I couldn't... see all of them. Most... most were past me. But I... I heard. I felt them. Even the ones that were past."*

Akaran took another look at her and then down to the knife. "Let me guess. The vampire wounded some of them. Chucked them into the hut before torching it? Let 'em roast?"

She didn't answer right away. *"Five. Not all were of age."*

"So you want to help me."

"*I want it dead,*" Rmaci spat back. "*When the* Hullbreaker *arrives, I will hunt it down and rip it to shreds. I shall lift it to the sky and let the people of this misbegotten Kingdom watch as I take power and desecrate the corpse of that monster for my own personal amusement.*"

He smiled, though he refused to let her see it. "Then you'll be stuck with it. You'll absorb it. You'll get to listen to it laugh about the people it burned alive. Is that what you want?"

"*It enters my mind, and I will subject it to horrors that only the Abyss could dream of matching,*" the gory wraith shot back.

"If it doesn't take you over," he countered. "That's how it works, ri… right? A strong soul? It fights for supremacy? Forces it's way to the top?" he asked before he took one final drink from his flagon. He felt his words start to slur already, which was going to force him to speed up. "What's to say you… you survive and… don't get stuck in the cart? You kn… know. With the other mad souls?"

Rmaci twisted her top half around to look at him and snarled spitefully. "*If you think that there is a chance that I will allow myself to submit to such wretched vermin as one of those cockroaches…*"

"I think I… I can't risk that," Akaran retorted. "Last question: did you know? Did you… before we got to the Landing?"

"*Know what it was? How could I? I saw what you saw, I've seen what you've seen. If I had known before I would've told —*"

"Would you have?" he challenged. "Really? If you had… had known? Would you have curled up beside me and said… I mean, said, '*Dearest Akaran, who I torture every day, there is a vampire lurking in this city?*' Or would you have held onto that? Just… just until you were convinced that I… I couldn't… couldn't do anything about it to… to torment me even more?"

The wraith's face crumbled and scrunched up, the movement causing bits of teeth to fall out of a hole in her cheek. "*Of course I knew! I know everything there is! We discussed this. It is a curse of perdition.*"

"But if you *knew…* then you *knew…* that some of those innocents? They… they were going to be thrown into a fire. Bur… burned alive like you were," the priest argued. "As pissed off… pissed as you are, I… I think you would've tried to stop that," he slurred and stuttered.

"*Of course I would've! I am damned but I am no monster!*"

"So you knew," he slowly replied, "you just didn't *act* until *I* knew. That means their deaths are on your hands, doesn't it? Because you could've acted to stop it. I didn't think you wanted to be weighed down by any more sin."

Rmaci lunged at him and pressed her wet, bloody face against his as she hissed out her reply. "*How dare you! Their deaths are* not *my fault,* not *my sin! If I had kno… if I could… if…*"

"If you had known… you would have. Which means you… you didn't know," he answered in a slurred, measured, pointed tone as he began to feel his consciousness begin to fade, "which means you… you've been lied to… by… the same entities that... damned you. Does... doesn't it?"

She slid away and felt her mouth flop open as he twisted her logic around. "*Knowing... that I know... that was to balance... the great suffering... all the things I know, all the pain I know that's to be visited and revisited upon me and others I know I...*"

"No, Rmaci," Akaran whispered as he pulled the glowing knife from the lantern and placed the tip to the side of his knee with a pained hiss and a sizzle of flesh, "the Abyss. It... it only let you know... things that hurt you. It let... let you think you'd know the rest," he added before digging the blade deeper into his skin. "Ohhhh shiiiiit this is gonna be awful."

She watched as fresh blood welled up around the knife and a little wisp of smoke escaped from his leg. "*What are you DOING?*"

"Getting answers," he replied as he pulled back – and suddenly jammed the heated knife right into the underside of his knee. His sharp scream went ignored by the locurats below, and nobody noticed that he passed out.

***

When he came to, only a few minutes had passed in reality – though where he woke up was far from the waking world. Rmaci's dungeon, the horrific construct she had created in the World Between Worlds, had seemingly manifested in part on the hillside. If anyone else could've seen it, it would've been terrifying. As always, he was locked inside the stone cage with rusty iron bars. Outside of the cell, what would've normally been more bricks and loose mortar was just open air and the rolling grassy hill.

As always, Rmaci was outside of the prison. Though instead of appearing as the living, attractive, demure woman she had been before she'd been set on fire, she hung onto the outside of his cage as the bloody naked mess he saw her outside of his mind. She kept thrusting a clawed hand inside the cage to try to catch him and drag him forward – and she was howling in rage. "*WHAT ARE YOU DOING YOU FOOL?!*"

Akaran looked down and saw himself. Actually, he saw two of himself. One of him was laying on the grass with his eye closed and body crumbled on the ground. The steel knife was buried in the back of his knee and flesh continued to sizzle as blood poured down around it. "Finding... a way... to end this," the second version of him uttered in a daze.

Rmaci managed to catch his 'dream' self by his naked chest and pulled him to the cage bars. He grimaced, but didn't otherwise react. "*This isn't the dreamscape! This isn't your world! Where are we, what have you done?!*"

"I thought you were the one in my head... knew everything," he groaned as his dreamed-knee began to glow red and blister. "And... and it is my world... sorta..."

She dug her claws into his dream-flesh so hard that his skin ripped and bled. "*ANSWER ME! WHAT DID YOU DO?!*"

"Larochi and belistand," Akaran groaned back at her, as if that answered anything.

In a way, it did. The spy let him go and took a step backwards as she blinked in confusion. *"Midwives give that to their charges. Given that you are as far from pregnant as a man can be, and since a man cannot be..."*

"See, the thing... the thing is," his dream-self slurred, "I needed... to be able to... not hurt... and have some control. Look... look in my head. Toniki. Before... before Mako... Makolichi. Before it broke my knee. What did I do?*"*

She curled her lip up and snarled at him as she did just that. A short scene played out in front of her: he was serving drinks to two women. The image was hazy, but she could make out one of them all-too clearly and howled in rage as she saw her: Evalia Wodoria, Commander of the 13th Garrison.

The woman that had set her on fire.

The woman that drank from a mug that the priest had spiked with belistand and larochi so that she would pass out. The plan was to leave her unable to follow him to confront the demon and the wraith that had killed her husband. The demon that was, in part, responsible for Rmaci's presence on this plane. The mixture of painkillers and ale that had knocked her out cold. *"You... drug the bitch so... now you've drugged yourself... why? What purpose...?"*

Dream-Akaran looked down at his 'real' body and willed it to move. "They... gave this to me a few times. When they... they tried to fix my leg at Gonta. See... I'm an idiot. I never... thought it through. Until the Landing. It doesn't put... it doesn't... really stop the pain. And... I woke up. A lot. Woke up as they worked," he explained as he watched himself sit up and slowly work the knife back and forth in his knee. From the ground, real-Akaran sluggishly gave the knife a short, sharp tug and a scream before he crumbled back to the grass.

For the first time since she'd started haunting him, the wraith actually covered her mouth with her hand and looked vaguely *ill*. *"You're... you... put yourself in this state to... cut on yourself?"* She stared at him and with a wave of her hand, made the cage bars melt away. *"If you wanted to* suffer *all you had to do was* ask," she added with a heap of indignation.

Every time that real-Akaran roused up to cut a little deeper, dream-Akaran vanished from sight. On the third cut-and-scream, the dream-vision clutched his leg and sank down on the ground. "I... I took a guess. You... you gave the game away."

"I what?"

"The Landing. You... you made things appear," he explained. "Things... I could see, could remember. You did it with me... awake. Sure you've... show me things, pointed them out. I didn't... didn't think you were just in my head. But you showed me... that I could see... through you. Get into my head through... through your head."

"This was your intention? To force yourself asleep so you could do what? Subject yourself to me here, subject yourself to a knife there? You somehow expected to be in this... whatever this state is?!" she demanded.

He gave her the faintest of smiles and flickered out of view. Real-Akaran roused up and pulled the knife free of his leg and watched as an oily substance began to seep out. "No, I didn't expect... the cell," he admitted. "Kinda... didn't expect to... see myself but... that's... it's what it is," he groaned, "and what it is... is pain. Oh this hurts in ways I can't explain to you."

Rmaci looked down at her fleshless, bloody, burnt body and then back at him. "*I would think otherwise.*"

The dream-priest pursed his lips and nodded. "Okay, I suppose... you would. So... let's... let's talk. For a minute... because honestly... I dunno how much longer... longer I have."

"*Before you pass out entirely? I'm* not *letting you out of this dream. Once that weed puts you to sleep the rest of the way I'm going to show you what* real pain *is,*" the wraith snarled, "*since you seem so intent upon inflicting it on yourself.*"

His dream-self shook his head and vanished. On the grass, Akaran picked up the gem he'd set aside and held it tight in his shaking, sweating hand. "This isn't... this isn't going to end..."

"*I'm sure it will feel that way. It will. But it's going to feel like it won't,*" she hissed, "*I promise.*"

"I mean... not the way... not the way you want," he groaned as he slowly took the gem and pushed it against the ragged gash in his leg.

"*I want you dead. Anything after that is just a bonus,*" Rmaci shot back. "*And now what be-maddened bullshit are you doing to yourself?*"

He didn't answer; he just shut his eye and screamed through clenched teeth as he wedged the chunk of dark crystal into the wound with a rough, agonizing push. "Is it? Is it a bonus?" he asked as his dream-self reappeared next her.

The spy flinched away but slapped a bloody hand across his face. The blow actually connected against his dreaming form, and left a bloody mark across his cheek. "*You'll be dead. I'll be free. I'll have a legion of souls at my call,*" she swore.

Akaran touched the bloody spot on his face and felt a smile start to grow on his lips. "Then what? How do you think that ends?" he asked as the fog of the drug faded from his unconscious mind.

"*How does it... end?*" she demanded incredulously. "*It* won't *end. I'll have the wraith and it will spread and we will –*"

"What? You will *what?*" he challenged.

"*We will... we will exist,*" Rmaci finally answered after a few moments of unexpected confusion. "*We will carve a niche for ourselves in this world and –*"

"– and be hunted," he interrupted as he started to rouse up on the grass again. With tears pouring down his face and blood freely pouring around his knee, he pushed the gem even harder until it split the gash open even more. "You'll be hunted."

The wraith bristled up and grew another few feet taller. "*We will survive.*"

The real world around them started to fade as the pain in his leg began to ebb, and her dungeon started to solidify around them. "No you won't. You'll be tracked. You'll be searched. You will be uprooted. Each body you possess will be burnt to cinders," he responded flatly as the slur in his voice faded as he began to succumb to the effects of the root. "I suppose there's even decent odds you'll feel each one."

She inflated a little more, but his tone made her furious facade start to crumble. "*We will* escape. *We will hide!*"

He forced himself to give the gem one less press before the real world faded entirely as a pitch-black oil and discolored pus replaced the blood coming out of his knee. "*You* will live in fear for the rest of your miserable existence in a rotting shell," he countered. "Be it a day, a week, a month, a year, or even a decade. You'll survive, alright, running and dying, feeling your spawn get destroyed and banished."

"*We will have an army!*"

"Then it won't even take a month," he spat as the real world vanished entirely. "Imagine how fast word will spread. A demon is consolidating power through Dawnfire. It's raising an army of the damned to take over the world," he growled as he gave her a look right in her dead eyes. "You really think that *humanity*, fisk the *Kingdom*, is going to risk another Adelin Empire?"

That was enough to shatter her bravado. With it, the walls of the dungeon began to crack and crumble to show a pitch black void beyond, even as she tried to argue against the truth in his words. "*We will be... numerous. We will spread.*"

Akaran wrapped his hands around his knee and watched as it mended itself together in the dreamscape. "You *might*, *might* weaken the Queen's control enough that the Civans will finally get their way," he countered. "You *might* distract her long enough for the Empress of Flame to break the borders. You'll get your wish; the Kingdom *might* crumble and let the firebrand clear the Queen from her throne."

Rmaci lit up at the idea – both literally and figuratively. The cracks in the wall erupted with orange flames and the cracks in her skin began to shine with ominous yellow light. "*In its fall, we shall become legion. We shall spread. We will exist.*"

"You're really not thinking this through, are you?"

"*From the man that thought it would be wise to nearly kill himself before diving into my domain? I do not think you are in a position to cast disparagement on me.*"

The priest snorted and gave her a cruel little smile as the last of the pain in his leg faded away. "Don't forget your history, spy."

"*What does that mean?*"

"The Civan Empire was *founded* on the backs of the people that fled the fall of the Adelin. The backs of the people that fled a demon uprising," he pointed out as her face crumbled into the first real look of fear he'd seen from her since she'd died. "You really think that they'd do anything *but* hunt you down, shell by shell, and roast each and every single person you inhabited to burn to cinders?"

As her face fell, the wall behind Akaran did too, though nothing came into focus from the black void beyond. "*It will be different!*" she shouted. "*I will show them – all of them! – how strong the true wrath of the wraith can be!*"

"The truth 'wrath' of that wraith animated dead squirrels and cried for its father every time I got close enough break a vessel," he snarled. "You'd be responsible for the deaths of dozens. Hundreds, maybe. Thousands if you broke out of the city. Goddess knows how many if you give the Civans a path into the Kingdom," he admitted, "but you're so focused on making *me* suffer that you forgot what would happen to *you* assuming that you don't lose yourself in the process."

Rmaci lunged forward and hovered in front of him with bloody froth spilling out from her cheeks and out of a hole in her throat. "*I will not lose myself! Never again!*"

"No, you desperate bitch, what you'll *do* is beg. When you end up back in the Abyss – and you *will* – you'll be held accountable. Every body you steal, every soul you take, and every death you cause, you *will* be held accountable" Akaran spat back. "Worst part about it? Daringol didn't have a choice. It was *made*. It was *cursed*."

"*I was made to be like this! I didn't have a choice!*" She grabbed him by his neck and thrust her thumbs all the way through his throat. There was pain, short and sharp, but it ended and the wound repaired itself as quickly as he grabbed her wrists and pushed her away. "*YOU TOUCHED ME! HOW?*"

He stood up as she began to shrink. She returned to her normal size, and then as he planted his feet on the ground and the rest of the walls crumbled away into the blackness all around him, she shrank even more. "You had a *choice*. You got murdered. Desecrated. That part, no choice. What you've done after that? Live in my head? Torture me? Torment me? That's because you *wanted* to. Planning on killing more people just to survive? It's because you *want* to. Because you think that it's your only way out of this mess you're in."

"*YOU'D DO IT TOO! IF IT KEPT YOU FROM THERE, YOU'D DO IT TOO!*" she screeched at the top of her burnt lungs.

"Maybe I would, if I was desperate enough," the exorcist admitted as the blackness all around them began to shift gray, then to a muted white glow. "Maybe not," he added. Then, before she could retort, he lunged forward and grabbed her by her throat and *lifted* her up off of what had been ground. "You've spent so long in my head. Let's see what's in yours."

Rmaci grabbed at his wrists and struggled to absolutely no avail. "*What are you doing? WHAT ARE YOU DOING?*"

"You gave the game away, you vile creature," he snarled as he repeated himself. "You *showed me* that you can make whatever I remember appear, interact with me, make it as real as anything gets in this place."

"*What of it? What are you doing?! Answer me!*"

"You know how you made the report show up back in the landing? You *saw* it but you *showed me* how to focus on it enough to *see* it and *interact* with it."

"*Because I am in your soul! Your mind! I have control over here!*"

"You've had control long enough," Akaran growled, "but this is *my* head and if I can focus on things and make them appear because *I* remember them, well guess what?" he demanded as he squeezed her throat even harder.

All around them, a metal *chink-chink-chink* sound started to fill the void. Rmaci looked down and saw silver chains begin to manifest in the air around his wrists... and then slowly appear from the fog below to wrap around her legs. "*I... I have control... here!*" she repeated desperately as she kicked at the phantom bonds.

"If you're in *my* head, and this is *my* dream, then anything I want to do in here I can, *right*?" he countered with a deep, rumbling growl that made the empty void quake with every word. "Want to know what I remember, you deceitful piece of shit?"

Her burns faded as her body healed in his grip. No longer appearing as a tortured, twisted soul, no longer bearing the scars that showed her as the victim of a fire that claimed her life, she hung limply in his grip like a child as he stared down into her face. "*Please... please don't...*"

"I remember how it feels when I channel Her ire," he whispered, "and I'm fairly sure She's as pissed as I am."

Rmaci's face paled as she lost all strength and all semblance of command. "*Akaran... please don't...*"

"You've been living rent-free in my head. Time to see what's in yours. **ENLIGHTEN**!" he shouted, the Word pouring out of his every fiber and into the dreamscape without constraints.

The off-white fog faded as the wraith melted away into nothingness. He blinked, and when he opened his eye again, the fog was gone – replaced by an ending dune sea of pristine white sand that stretched to nearly every direction. To the north, the sand ended at the foot of a pure white marble wall that stretched from horizon to horizon. It stood so tall that there was no way to see over it unless you were miles away, and he had a sinking feeling that it wouldn't even appear unless you were meant to see it at all.

Or, as he assumed, unless you willed yourself here against all odds.

That idea was confirmed as a portion of the wall fell in on itself to reveal a gargantuan gate of pure gold and hinges of pure platinum. A pathway of tumbling blue stones rolled out from under the bottom of the edifice and trailed all the way to his feet as two lines of molten copper flowed forth to frame its edges along the eternal sands.

Infer, he realized as he stared in wonderment. *The Upper Elemental Plane of Flame, and home of Illiya Herself. With her professed allegiances, I'm sure that's what it is*, he mused to himself before pausing to wonder why it was *here* in the Worldly Sands and not beyond Pristi's Gate on the Heavenly Mount. *A question for people smarter than me*, he finally admitted to himself, *though not one I'm gonna ask. Of all the realms that I'd be welcome in... that won't be one.*

Neither was Rmaci, he realized in very short order.

A warm wind blew out of the gateway and washed over him. It took the throbbing from his leg and calmed the ache in the back of his head. The world behind the gate started to come into view, but there was so little he could see beyond a wall of rainbow-hued fire just inside the gateway that he gave up trying. Instead, he noticed a pile of sand swelling up a few feet away from the molten pathway.

A moment later, and he heard the scream from under it. The former spy burst forth from the sand and crawled onto her hands and knees until she was free of it. The few moments she had enjoyed free of wounds was gone as quickly as it appeared, and coarse grains of sand poured out of every hole, blister, and burn on her body.

Her agony was exquisite and her screams unceasing. They grew in intensity as she looked down at her body and saw the horrific, twisted shape that she was in like she was seeing it for the first time. "*It was my first time,*" she admitted from beside him. "*This... my arrival. Past the Veil.*"

Akaran looked over and realized that she was still with him – naked, unburnt and unbroken – even as her past self struggled to pull herself free of the sands. "How long were you here?"

"*Asks someone that still believes in time,*" she sighed under her breath.

Her past self shook the last of the sands free and shambled towards the gateway. With every step she took, blood and charred skin littered the ground behind her. None of it lasted; the gore sank into the sand and vanished with each fresh step she took. When she reached the golden gate, the doorway didn't move as much of an inch, let alone open.

Instead, two massive, molten, humanoid figures with skin the color of polished bronze stepped through the wall of flame. They walked through the golden bars of the gateway like it wasn't even there to stare down at the cowering lost soul at their feet. The bronze behemoths shrugged their shoulders and unfurled mammoth wings made of flame that blocked the way into the elemental world beyond.

Rmaci's memory threw herself onto the ground at their feet and begged. She pleaded. She cried. She demanded to be let inside. She screamed and begged for help. She struggled as the sand started to swell over her legs again.

Through all of it, they stood guard over the wall and refused her entry.

What felt like hours of pleading went by before one of the guardians thrust a silver-tipped spear into the sand and fished through the shifting dust. A short bit later, and it pulled the squirming body of another lost soul from the ground and deposited it at their feet.

"I recognize him," Akaran realized as the soul stood up on shaking feet. He had a hole in his ribs and looked much the worse for wear. "That's Elder Ronlin, from Toniki. Hirshma's brother."

"*I killed him,*" the wraith admitted. "*Well. I had Yothargi kill him, but in the eyes of the Divine, an order carried out is much the same as an act itself."*

His soul was joined by another, and another. Some were pulled from the sands and dropped at the divine being's feet, while others slowly took form from silvery clouds and stepped out of thin air. *"[Your victims,]"* one of the guardians intoned. *"[Some righteous. Some less.]"*

Rmaci's soul argued with them as the silent shades of her actions in service to the Civan Empire formed a circle around her. She claimed she only did what she had to. Claimed she killed because she needed to. Murdered to further the goals of the Empress, the woman who was said to be the mortal mouthpiece of the Goddess of Flame. She demanded to be let in because she did no different than anyone else at war.

The guardians disagreed.

They offered no dispute or argument to explain themselves. They allowed the shades a chance to say their own piece, and each one damned her for stealing their lives. Each time they condemned her, a black mass in her chest grew in size. Slowly, it began to eclipse her torso and spread down her arms and the top of her thighs.

After the last shade cursed her, the guardian on the left brushed them all way with a sweep of its wings. The souls pulled from under the sand fell back and through, while the others simply disappeared. *"[You are unworthy,]"* it intoned.

The other one drove the hilt of its spear down onto the blue stone pathway so hard that burning blue chips flew into the air. The path began to recede as quickly as it had appeared as the guardian passed judgment down on her. *"[You are wicked. Wicked has no place in the home of the pure.]"*

She screamed in anger and desperation and tried to rush past them. The pair of Illiya's emissaries caught her arms and drew her away before the leading Herald took its spear and thrust it through her collarbone and into the suddenly-churning sands at their feet.

Her cries of agony, desperation, and fear were swallowed up by the Worldly Sands along with the rest of her body. As she sank, Akaran and her current self dropped through the sands and to somewhere else beyond. The air was the first thing that changed; no longer was it warm and inviting.

It was cold. Cold, bitter, harsh. Cold wind lashed at his skin and burning embers snapped at his face. The empty blue sky disappeared and was replaced with nothing but darkness. Darkness, and a cloud. Except it wasn't just a cloud, it was a storm.

A raging, horrible storm that both paradoxically was only one small point in an eternity of darkness, but as they fell towards it, it became eternity itself and the unfathomable maelstrom was all they could see. He heard the name it had been given at the dawn of time echo in his ears in Rmaci's memory, although neither of them uttered it. It blossomed in his soul with such force that he could *see* the words in the clouds as much as he *heard* them echoing in his mind.

For I am the Entrance of Agony, the Fall of the Heavens.
For I am the Eye Unblinking, the Mouth Unfilled.
For I am the Storm of Sin, the Reckoning of Insanity.
For I am the Nul'kotak, the Unceasing Dark, the Abyss.
For I hunger.

He screamed as a lone eye opened in the center of the eternal storm and *looked* at them. Memory or not, reality or not, the eye of the storm *looked* at him and for one agonizing moment, found him lacking. "Oh. My. Goddess," he whispered as he saw a sight no mortal should ever see.

It was the last sight Rmaci had seen before she entered the pit.

As they plunged into the swirling clouds with streaks of red lightning, he went blind again. When his sight returned, he recognized exactly where they were – only it was different this time. He pushed himself off of the recreation of the cold stone floor of her former cell in Gonta's Keep.

The wraith left his side and appeared next to herself in the cage. Her memory clutched at the cage bars and whimpered in pain, while her current self refused to do anything more than stare at the ground. "*This... this is where I will wait.*"

"Wait for what?"

"*The Heralds of Illiya damned me, but it is the Warden who will pass sentence,*" she explained. "*I will be pulled before Him and have my fate decided.*"

Akaran looked around the cell and took a deep breath of sulpheric air. "When does that happen?"

The shade gestured at the walls as the bricks and stonework began to crumble. "*When He wishes. Not before,*" Rmaci answered as hulking figures pushed their way into the dungeon. They shoved at the stones and brickwork as the rocks stretched in an impossible fashion around questing hands and monstrous faces pressing in on them from behind. Behind him, a heavy thud heralded the arrival of a cloven-hoofed demon just at the top of the stairwell.

More howls and screams came from the corridors beyond even as faceless, naked creatures of stone-scraped flesh ripped themselves out of the floor inside her cell. The memory screamed in terror as the first one grabbed her leg and pulled her close. Rmaci's shade cowered behind the exorcist and started to cry as the scene began to play out.

The cell doors themselves twisted away from their moorings and stretched out to wrap twisted, sizzling bars of suddenly burning iron around her arms. As more demons crawled into the dungeon, the priest looked around in disgust and wrapped his hand around her hand. "Yeah, we're not doing this," he muttered as he shut his eye and willed the two of them to go... elsewhere.

Elsewhere was better.

Elsewhere was much better.

The cell and the demons within disintegrated as he retreated to a safe place in his memories. The gaseous void beyond it crackled and crumbled away in turn, leaving nothing but a soft white light. Slowly, a few shapes appeared in their sight; a floating tree here, a starfish wiggling happily on the sand beside Akaran's thigh there. The sound of waves lapping on the shore. The sound of birds in the distance, chirping with musical tones that weren't quite right.

They were better than right. They were perfect. As was the sand, and the water, and even the starfish. The tree in the bay was perfect, too, as if it had been created and placed there solely to be seen. For all he knew, it had been.

"*This isn't... this isn't one of mine,*" Rmaci's shade marveled.

"I know. It's one of mine."

She looked around the beach with her eyes wide as a soft ocean breeze brushed dirt from her face and dried her tears. "*Where are we?*" she asked with a whisper as she tried to turn around, but suddenly realized she couldn't.

"Don't," he warned. "When I came here, I was told if I turned around I couldn't leave. I don't know what's back there and I don't know if you could see it even if you tried."

The spy stayed quiet and watched as the waves crested and settled one after another. An errant bit of spray splashed across her leg and she drew back away from it like she expected it to burn. "*Where?*"

"I don't know, honestly," Akaran admitted, "but I have guesses. You'd already left Toniki by the time Daringol attacked, but between it, the dogs, and that damned ice monster, they got lucky."

"*What do you mean – lucky?*"

He ran his hand down his side and let his fingers dance over a scar across his stomach. "I mean that dying sucks but I guess there's worse things to happen than waking up on a beach after," he replied.

Rmaci looked down at the scar and then up into his eye. Her soft green eyes were wide, and were filled with a dawning mix of rage and disbelief erupted across her face. "*You... you died and this... this is where you came? While I... how? How did you come back?*"

He carefully reached over and brushed a strand of hair away from her eyes. The shade recoiled again and scrambled across the sand until she was too far away to reach. "I wasn't all the way gone, I guess. I don't know. Magic. Magic and a pissed-off little girl." The priest looked around the length of the shore and shrugged after a moment. "Surprised I don't see her here. I guess my thoughts are a little off."

"*You drag me... drag me through my memories of rejection and damnation and... you mock me by... showing me this?*" she hissed as she dug her fingers into the sand as even more tears welled up in her eyes. "*You are as foul as the demons of Frosel! WORSE, if such a thing is possible!*"

"One, I got tired of seeing inside your head," he retorted, "and two, I wanted to show you what you're missing."

"*I knew that cruelty lurked in the shadows of your mind,*" she snarled, "*but this is beyond the pale. You will suffer for this, I promise, I will –*"

"Wait," he interrupted as he lifted both hands in surrender, "just wait. Hear me out." As she stewed, the priest took a deep breath and started to explain himself as best as he could. "You're dead, and there's nothing I can do to fix that. Even if I could, I don't know if I would."

She quit playing idly in the sand and hissed at him again as rage boiled up so hard that he could see the veins sticking out from her forehead – and saw as her healed visage started to crack and turn gray again. "*I knew you were happy I was dead, happy I was consigned to the Abyss,*" Rmaci charged.

"No," he responded firmly, "I wasn't. That said: you earned your spot in perdition. You murdered, you lied, you cheated, you stole. You know it, I know it. I saw Illiya's Heralds cast you out and I listened to all those you did wrong by confront you. By my count, the Crown could've ordered your execution years ago if you'd ever been caught. *Most* Crowns, not just Dawnfire's."

"*I did what was needed!*" she screamed at him. In the distance, a pair of birds chirped back and continued to chirp until she slowly down onto her laurels. When she relaxed, they quieted themselves. "*I... I thought I did what... what I should...*"

"And you were wrong," the priest sighed as he shook his head. "Thank the Goddess that it's not my job to judge."

"*Bullshit,*" Rmaci snapped, "*your very calling has you doing just that.*"

He bit down on his lower lip and nodded after a moment. "Fair. I don't judge where people go, just if they get *expedited* on going there, I guess."

"*Pretty words to comfort your soul. Tell me, how does it feel knowing what happens to me when I'm not with you? How does it feel knowing what happened to me after I burned? Or the jailer you killed after he defiled me? He's burning too, you know. I've seen him. We talk on occasion.*"

A wave of revulsion welled up in his throat and threatened to spoil the pristine landscape if she had offered any further details. "It's not my place to say what happens, and if it is or isn't just. That's up to the Gods."

She sneered at him and gestured at the ocean beyond. "*Such a pretty way to say that you get yours and damn the rest of us.*"

The priest shrugged and followed her gaze to the waves. "Who's to say that I'm getting this? You seemed to think that I'm pitbound when I go, so... who knows. Maybe I earned this before I pissed off Istalla and killed your rapist and watched you burn and started making deals to get cocasa in my stomach," he sighed. "I don't know, and I don't think you know."

"*I know a great deal, you sniveling little wannabe-holy man,*" she grumbled under her breath, "*and I know I've spent my life dealing with deluded assholes like you.*"

"I'll take your word for it," Akaran answered. "Your *life*, which you no longer have, may well have been spent that way. The rest of it doesn't..."

"*Doesn't what? I feel as if we've already discussed what happens* after."

He took another deep breath and looked out towards the ocean as he tried to collect his thoughts. "We have. Between us? I don't like your after. I know, I know, you like it less," he added before she could cut him off, "but you have a choice. I get it – you think you can run forever and not be punished. Maybe you can. Maybe you can spend until the end of time surviving as the core to the *arin-goliath*, spread over the world, and outwit the Gods. *Maybe* you can, or *probably* you don't and you end up worse than what you've got now. It's safe to say that there's *worse* in the pit, isn't there?"

For a change, she was silent. All she did was look down at the sand and carefully scoop a little up in her hand. As it trickled through her fingers, he watched her shoulders slump in defeat.

"You didn't have to tell me that there were souls still bound to the world, back at Flynn's. You could've left them there. For that matter, you could've left them there and rolled through with the rest of the ones trapped in Daringol's essence when it finally shows up. Gotten a head start on your new army," he told her, "and you know it. Except, you didn't."

"*They were burning,*" she whispered, "*and it wasn't right.*"

"No. It wasn't. It's not. You could've let them suffer anyways. For *that* matter, you helped *me* in Toniki, too. Remember why? It was in your letter you left me."

Rmaci hung her head in shame. "*Because the darkness left unchecked could do more harm than not,*" she admitted, "*but that was then. Things are different now.*"

"The only thing different *now,*" the priest pointed out, "is that you're trying to find a way to keep from spending eternity getting torn to shreds."

The shade refused to look up at him. "*As if you would do different.*"

Akaran gave that a moment's thought and nodded. "From what I've seen? That storm? That... Nul'kotak? I'm not gonna dispute your desperation or say that I'd do much better," he agreed, "then again... looking around..."

"*Looking around, you may not need to,*" she spat with a little vehemence in her voice. "*Knowing this awaits you when I rip your heart out through your ass makes the idea of killing you less appealing.*"

He gestured over his shoulder. "For all I know there's a mountain of snakes ready to crawl up my ass back there and I wasn't allowed to see it because someone wanted to get my hopes up," Akaran retorted. "The point remains: you worked to stop Daringol once, albeit in the *literal* least amount of effort you could've possibly put in it *and* you just went out of your way to help a bunch of murder victims cross over instead of suffering in silence for Gods-only-know how many years. *You* did those things *and* you've gone out of your way to help me figure out *what* has been adding to the pile of victims around town as of late."

Rmaci looked up at him with tears pouring down her cheeks and tortured guilt burning in her eyes. "*So? Just because I'm damned doesn't mean I can't do the right thing!*"

That was what he was waiting for her to say. "I'd have wagered that being damned meant that you'd have an absolute predication *against* doing the right thing."

"*I'm DAMNED, you insufferable fool,*" she hissed through clenched teeth, "*but I am* not *some wretched shit-born Abyssian*! *I still have control*! *I still have agency*! *I am still my own person*!"

"Until you surrender to Daringol or someone bigger comes along and supplants you as the core," he quickly argued. "For all you know, there's some demented spirit on the ship you keep threatening me with that's already managed to establish itself as some kind of super-wraith ready to turn you into something as insignificant as that log out there," he added.

The spy rolled back on her heels and shook her head vehemently. "*No. I would know. The core is ripe for the taking.*"

"So you can take it and strip *those* souls of *their* agency," Akaran countered. "Kinda surprising, given how you felt about Se'daulif."

She looked away again and he watched as she slowly clenched her fist in the sand. "*We do what we must to survive.*"

It was his turn to shake his head. "That's my point. You did those things *without* thought to your survival. I doubt a vampire is going to be any threat to you if you can get the rest of the wraith pulled together," he said as he strung her along. "You're doing things because you don't want to see more harm come to pass than has to, aren't you?"

"*I am no monster, no matter what those... those... those* things *claim*!"

"Those things?" he asked. "You mean the Heralds? The creatures responsible for carrying out the direct word of the Divine and personally responsible for ensuring that Their will be done? You're going to argue with *eternity* if you're a monster or not?"

Rmaci looked out to the never-ending ocean and started to shake. More ember-filled cracks appeared down her back and shoulders as she listened to him. "*I hate you.*"

"I'm not fond of myself, honestly," the priest admitted. "So you're damned, but not a monster, and you don't want to go back to the Abyss but you're willing to do anything it takes to keep from going back there, though you're not willing to see innocents get hurt because you don't think they should suffer? That about it?"

"*Succinct,*" she sighed before adding, "*you bastard.*"

"If only there was a way out of it," Akaran replied as he scooted closer. As he moved, he realized that the ocean was getting harder to see, and the birds were getting quieter – and a familiar pain was returning to his leg.

The spy glanced over at him and let her eyes fall to his knee. "*I think our time here is about to end, isn't it?*"

He followed her gaze again and bit back a curse as he realized the healed visage of himself in this dreamscape was starting to show what the reality really was. "Sooner than I want," he agreed, "so let's hurry. I'm going to offer you a deal. You can take it or not. It's up to you."

"*A deal? You truly are in a dream, aren't you? Detached from reality as much as my soul has become.*"

"You don't want to burn anymore, I don't want to chase down Daringol the rest of my life – no matter how long or short that may be – and you're not interested in evil for the sake of evil. That tells me you've got a choice to make."

"What choice could I possibly have? If I consign myself to the Abyss, then – as you put it – I burn. If I kill you, I burn as you enjoy this lovely beach. Or I take command of the nesting wraith and spread and... and do what I must to survive. I would assume you'd be against most of those choices, and not be in a hurry to tell me to pick one." She paused and looked back at the ocean. *"Though I'd not fault you for wanting to hurry and return here. This is... this is wonderful. Where are we?"*

"I *think* we're on the shores of the Grand Palace of Love," Akaran answered. "Niasmis. It's Her realm. I read a few things about it in the study at the Repository."

"It's pretty. I do like it here."

"Like it enough to come back?"

The spy looked over at him with a blank look in her tired eyes. *"A jester now, are we? Even if you could grant me passage from the Abyss, my pledge was to Illiya. Should you have forgotten in the drug-fueled haze you seem to be in, those two Goddesses have a tendency to argue with each other."*

"They do," he agreed, "which works in your favor, I think."

Rmaci lifted her head and squared back her shoulders as she tried to make sense of the talkative fool. *"The moment I can wrap my fingers around your throat..."*

"You won't do a damn thing, because you're gonna like this offer," the priest retorted quickly. "Illiya decided you weren't worth saving. *However*, the very *Word* of my Goddess is that we are to offer aid and help those who ask for it to ease their suffering because we *all* deserve Love and we *all* deserve a chance at grace." He gave her a faint, if not slightly-reassuring little smile. "Damned or otherwise."

"Are you...?"

"I'm giving you a way out," he answered. "I don't know if it'll work. I know that the Goddess offers a path. Repent and pledge your loyalty, and... well."

"And well? That does not offer one much relief."

Akaran answered with a short shake of his head. "I'm not saying it's a great choice. But it's a choice."

She curled her toes up in the sand and sighed tiredly. *"A choice? How can you say that's a choice?"*

"It's better than your other options, isn't it?"

That argument was utterly irrefutable and she simply sat there in silence for a long time before she responded. *"If She refuses? If I... what? If I offer my service to Her? Is that what you're asking? I offer and then She says no?"*

The priest shrugged his shoulders and matched her last sigh with one of his own. "Then you go back to your cell, I guess."

Rmaci flinched and stared down at her hands so intently it was like she was trying to burn the image of her fingers healed and whole into her mind. "*No. No, I'll answer to the Court of Infer again. Illiya will condemn me to the Emberforge for turning traitor, if not worse.*"

"Where will you be condemned if you try to lead an army of the damned?" he asked. "Who's in charge of that department?"

She shuddered and tried to give him a truthful answer. When she couldn't, she surrendered the argument with a simple, "*I am truly damned.*"

"But you've got a choice," he repeated.

"*I need a guarantee.*"

Akaran choked on air and bit back a laugh. "Do you really think you're going to get one? That's the point of faith, Rmaci. Did you get a guarantee that you'd be released from the Abyss after you serve some time there? Because I didn't hear one offered."

She flinched again and refused to meet his gaze. "*I had faith. See my reward for it.*"

"Faith, but fisked up the actions," he countered. "You can't even deny it – you were literally cast down for it."

"*What makes you think I'll do better this time?*" she asked with a dejected sigh of utter frustration.

"Not a damn thing," he admitted. "Right now you're trying to run away from your problems, not that I blame you. Truth is?" he remarked with a shrug. "I'm not gonna lie; you're gonna have to prove yourself. I mean, you had to prove yourself to *me* and I'm not some eternal all-powerful entity that could crush both of us between Her fingers if She wanted."

Silence reigned between them again as the waves gently lapped at the shore. "*That doesn't fill me with hope, you know,*" she finally confessed.

"I don't deal in hope, you know that," he retorted. "I deal in... well. I deal in things like you."

Rmaci took a deep breath and scooted further away from him. "*You should want to banish me. Why are you trying to keep me from the pit?*"

"Because you showed kindness when you didn't have to. That tells me that you aren't perfect, but you're not entirely evil," he answered. "If you're not evil, then maybe you deserve a second chance. And if you aren't evil, then do you deserve to suffer? I don't know, but..."

"*...then you would rather see me helped than see me buried?*"

"I'd say burned, but."

She grit her teeth and clenched her fingers into her palm. "*Insults, now?*"

Akaran narrowed his eye and pointed a finger dismissively at her. "You wanna tell me with a straight face that I'm not allowed a few after everything you've put me through recently?"

She didn't respond to that, not directly, though her shoulders slumped again. "*Even if I say yes, what is it I can do? I am trapped in your head. I cannot leave, and I cannot pull myself entirely from the Abyss, nor can I part myself*" *from the arin-goliath."*

He stretched his leg out and grimaced as the first flicker of pain returned. "You'd be wrong."

"As often as you claim that nobody else knows what's going on with you I would like to think that you would understand that –"

"Are you willing to help hunt that vampire?" he interrupted.

That wasn't what she was expecting and it completely made her mind choke. *"I..."*

"Yes or no?" he pressed. "Are you willing to help me or not?"

She looked at her hands again and for the first time, he saw teardrops fall from her eyes. *"I... I have no choice. Do I?"*

"Oh, no, you do," he disagreed. "It's all about choices. Are you willing to atone for your sins? Are you willing to turn to a *different* light and find a *different* path that *might* save you from punishment?"

"I'm damned if I don't, aren't I? Or don't you so claim? That does not sound like much of a choice." As she spoke, cracks began to appear in her flesh. Her clean skin started to char in little flecks and spots. A long, smoldering crack formed on the side of her neck.

"You're the one that's been pitside," he countered. "I don't know what your path to salvation is gonna look like, but just about anything else is better than going back to your cell, isn't it?"

Images of her cell flickered in her emerald eyes as more cracks appeared on her skin and her old self started to burn away. The thought of the cell was horrifying, of that there wasn't any doubt. *"There are worse places to be than on the shores of Frosel. Pray you never learn."*

The memory of the Ocean of All Souls started to turn a pallid gray and dark blotches began to appear in the sky. *"One more thing, if it helps," he added. "That fun we had in the atrium? When I touched Her statue and tripped Her ward?"

Rmaci cringed and curled up on herself as she remembered the feeling of Niasmis's *irritation* that flooded his body and through her essence. *"Yes? That was an exceptionally uncomfortable experience."*

He smirked. "I'm glad. 'Trespass against Love and Love will trespass against you.' That's the threat behind it."

"Leaves little to the imagination," she admitted. *"Almost impressive."*

The exorcist grinned and pointed back over his shoulder. "If She didn't want you around, there's no reason that it shouldn't have sent you screaming back into perdition. Take that for what it is."

She sat back and watched her arms skin disintegrate into burning embers as the sand at her feet blurred and melted into one giant piece. *"I... I saw Her. Or saw someone that was supposed to be Her... I... I think. When you touched that damn mace. Is She always that... radiant?"*

"Don't know," he admitted after a moment. "Haven't seen Her. Just hear the whispers She puts on the wind."

"That wasn't a whisper."

"She doesn't usually ask me to speak softly," he returned.

The spy looked over at him and felt her eyes widen as she realized how much blood was coming out of the side of his knee. *"A sentiment I have noticed in practice,"* she remarked before adding, *"That much blood? Are you going to live to see this offer to fruition?"*

He ran his hand down his leg and cringed at the sight of how much blood came back on his fingers. "Your call, Rmaci. There's not much longer to decide."

"Why? What did you do?"

"Solved the problem," he grunted as the pain in his leg started to creep through, "one way or another. Choose *now*."

"I..." she started as her lower half began to fade to embers and ash. The sky cracked and crackled, the ocean lost cohesion, and blades of grass appeared in the sand all around them. *"I accept. I offer my help and... I turn my soul to you. To... to Her. Please, I don't want to go back to the pit. If... if this will save me..."*

He grit his teeth as burning, ripping pain blossomed in his leg and more grass appeared around them. "It's only going to save you if you work to save others," he countered harshly. "Will you? Will you work to undo the harm you've done and the harm you've planned?"

Rmaci's upper body blistered and caught fire. Skin gave way to scars and charred muscle. Pain, all-too-familiar pain, rushed over her in a wave. *"If I... I must. I will. PLEASE."*

That was what he needed to hear.

The only question was if someone else was listening. Akaran lunged over and grabbed her wrist before it faded away with one hand, and her face with the other. She screamed in surprise as a glint of blue in his eye flashed and raced down is arms before he even said the word. "Goddess if this'll work in my head then let it work in my body – EXPUNGE!"

"WHAT –!" she screamed as a brilliant lavender light rushed up her arm and pale streamers of blue light whipped under what was left of her skin all the way to the back of her eyes. The same light erupted in his bloody knee as everything in the dream world lost cohesion. As a cascade of blue sky fell around them to reveal the cloudy night of the real world, her body broke away in a shower of brilliant embers and black shadows.

She screamed once more as she exploded into nothingness.

And just as suddenly, the embers twisted in the air and spun back around his hand. The embers, the ash, the shadows, and barely-controlled magic burst into flame. He had less than a heartbeat to realize what it had just done. "Oh. Fisk," he muttered before it was *his* turn to scream.

The fire swelled and erupted into a fireball that blossomed around his hand and spread up his arm. The magic traced the same path back as it did as it left, and a gout of flame briefly lanced from his eye and down his chest before it flared as bright as the sun from the side of his knee. The blast – and his shout of pain – obliterated the dreamscape like a giant glass globe right before the fire in his eye blinded him entirely.

The feel of the grass under his back was a massive downgrade from the comfort offered by the beach, dream or not. The pain in his leg? Absolutely worse than in the dream, and a lot bloodier. He rolled onto his side and clutched at it as he felt the crystal start to dislodge from under the skin.

It was hot to the touch and slick with blood – among other things. He let loose with a curse that had to have been heard all the way down to the pyre, if not all the way up to the heavens as he plucked the stone free. A small crack in it (that hadn't been there before he had passed out) scraped his thumb as he unceremoniously tossed it aside and drew fresh blood. His next several minutes were spent laying on his side and flexing his leg.

Not to mention uttering every profanity he knew.

Sometimes they weren't even uttered.

Before he could begin the process of bandaging his leg up again, a pair of voices – both familiar, though one was harder to place than the other – piped up just a few feet away. The exorcist hadn't heard them coming, though there wasn't anything he could've done about it even if he had. "Told ya I heard him scream," the first voice said.

Akaran turned his head over and tried to see the speaker and tried to push himself up to a sitting position when he realized who it was. "Ce... Cel? Cel what are you doing...?" A gloved hand from his blind side pressed firmly against his shoulder and forced him (only somewhat) gently back down.

"Even if you had not," the woman holding him down replied, "the devastation he's inflicted in the ether would have been enough to find him." He recognized it before he could pull around to see her. For a moment, every painful thought and feeling he had went away as one of the last people in the city he expected to see ran her other hand down his leg and stopped just before she hit his knee. "Though it seems he didn't direct his efforts solely against the ether."

"Oh piss on me, that's an ugly gash," Cel grumbled as she caught sight of it. "Now I've seen and done uglier but not to nobody I wanted to see stand up again."

"Of that I'm most certain, and the usual methods to patch it up won't work if all I've heard is true," the other voice intoned, "though we'll have to deal with it quickly. It looks as if his solution was going be... oh. I suppose that worked."

"Oh?" Cel asked.

"Bandages and even more belistand," the other woman muttered under her breath. "I'm left with the distinct impression he had no plan to move from this spot until morning, if he was lucky."

The priest groaned and tried to move out from under her grip, which only made her tighten it. "I've had... worse ideas... if that makes you feel any better."

She quietly scoffed at him. "There has been very little that has made me feel well as of late, as I suspect you know. What you've done is brash, dangerous, and potentially exceptionally harmful to yourself," she scolded, "and through damaging yourself, risky to others."

"But did it work?" he groaned as Cel started to wrap a tourniquet around his thigh.

"If you were tryin' to kill yourself, no, you're here with us," the innkeeper retorted. "Whatever else you were trying to do, damned if I know."

"The gem," he croaked as fresh tears welled up in his vision. "I need it."

Cel's companion tightened her grip on his chest and shook her head as her face finally came into focus. "I think that would be an atrociously foul idea. What possessed you to do that?"

He looked up at her and gave her a weak smile. "Possession."

She drummed her fingers on his chest and withheld the first remark that came to mind. "Someone will be along soon to get you to a place where you can rest. Cel, do you know somewhere nearby...?"

"I do," the innkeeper replied after giving it a moment, "though his people ain't gonna like it if they find him there."

"Then I hope he's smart enough not to stay there for long," her companion scolded. "Though I imagine that it depends on how long it takes for his knee to heal."

"Oh this thing ain't gonna heal for *weeks* if he doesn't get a proper mage on it," Cel retorted. "Only truth I can assume is that he's taken a likin' to walking around on that stick."

Before the other woman could reply, Akaran looked up at her and bit back a ragged cry as the innkeeper bound the gash with a rough bandage. "There's a lot of people looking for you, you know that?"

She nodded, and her long dark hair flowed down off of her face and over her shoulders. "More people than you know – which should tell you much, given that I risked myself to come find *you*."

A quiet sobbing cry from yards behind his head called out once, painfully, and simply, "*What did you do to me*?" that went entirely unanswered.

"I'm... I'm glad you're alright," Akaran managed to choke out as the innkeep tightened the bandages around the gash in his leg.

It was hard to tell who he was talking to. It didn't seem to matter. "You should be pleased with yourself. Not many learn how to be awake in their dreams; far fewer still figure out how to use magic in the realm of the Grand Dreamer," the raven-haired priestess intoned.

"*What did you do to me*?" Rmaci's voice interrupted again. "*What... what am I now*?"

She looked down into Akaran's blue-gray eye and sighed. "The *Uncrested Wave*. Be there tomorrow evening. I don't care how you get there, just be there. When you arrive, ask to speak to Bantia. She hides her face in a hood. Tell *no one* why you're there."

"I don't... I don't think you're giving me a choice, are you?"

"No. But you'll be pleased – I have a gift for you."

"What is it?"

"What good is a gift if it isn't a surprise, hm?" she returned. "Just be there. And I need you to remember something very, very important. Do you think you can do that, even in your haze?"

The exorcist gave her a little nod as Cel finished tying up the bandages on his leg. "I hurt too much to forget. I promise. What is it?"

"You are being watched, you are being judged. Goliaths fall; do not risk being under one when they do," she warned with a deathly serious look in her almost-mahogany colored eyes.

Rmaci crawled out of the darkness and placed a healed, whole hand on Akaran's shoulder. He glanced up and caught a glimpse of her newest manifestation – half-healed, half-burnt, but where burning embers crackled in the cracks of her skin, the gashes had been sealed with thin slivers of perfectly blue ice. "*I've given enough threats to know one when I hear one.*"

"I don't think she was talking to just me..." the priest mused.

As the spy recoiled in surprise, his newest benefactor looked down her nose at the two of them. "I wasn't," she replied.

"*Oh*," was all the wraith managed to croak out through half-healed and half-frozen lips.

"The *Uncrested Wave*. Tomorrow evening," the woman repeated firmly.

Akaran ran his tongue over his suddenly dry lips as he finally caught a good look at her in the light. She looked as regal as she had the first two times they'd crossed paths, and weeks of hiding from the garrison hadn't diminished her aura in the slightest. "I promise."

Cel pushed herself up off of her knees and grunted in pain as she eyed the spirit nervously. "Boy, you best tell me she's with you and that you ain't been summoning demons in my barn."

His best friend's lover gave him the first real smile he'd seen all evening. Coming from Erine Rrah, the Mother Eclipsian of Basion City, the speaker for Lethandria? The woman tasked to speak for both the Goddess of Night and Her daughter Nia'valth, the Grand Dreamer? It was even more terrifying than he was sure she meant it to be. She gestured over at the wraith. "I'll be holding onto *that* for the time being."

He shook his head and feebly reached over towards the bloody gem in the grass. "No. I need. She stays with me."

"No, she doesn't," Erine snapped. "Your preceding reputation was apparently well-earned. Using magic in the realm of the Dreamer without offering a tithe? I see why the Frostborn have no care for you. Her service will be mine for the time being."

"Yeah well," he grumbled, "the Order of Frost are a bunch of stuck-up assho–"

"They are Pantheon-ordained. The Dreamer is not, and cares less for your opinion on the matter than the cold ones," she scolded. "Your pet comes with me."

Rmaci looked up with one eye smoldering, and the other covered in frost. *"His... pet? You deign to call me his...?!"*

The Mother Eclipsian gave the wraith a withering stare that made the spirit blanch. *"You* are in no position to argue. We've met once before, don't you recall?"

The wraith didn't rise to the bait. She didn't need to. The last time they'd encountered each other, she had been tormenting Akaran in his sleep – and Erine had plucked her out of his dreams like she was an irritating gnat. *"I don't understand what's happening... I... what do you want from me?"*

"You seek to turn from perdition to places other, don't you?"

"Yes," the wraith said with a weary sigh. *"Through him. Through his... whatever She is. However She is. Not you. Not yours."*

"And therein is how you are mistaken," Erine warned. "To pass through the Dark to the Light, you must first trek through the realm of Dusk to the Dawn."

"But –"

The priestess of the Goddess of Night crossed her arms and allowed a cloud of shadowy magic to radiate off of her fingertips. "There are other options for your future, should you wish to explore them," she warned coolly.

Rmaci shut up and dropped her head. Akaran looked over at the innkeep as she slowly stood up. "You're being quiet."

Cel shrugged after she stood. "What am I supposed to say? She's magic," she said as she gestured her thumb over at the priestess, *"she's* obviously magic," she added with a nod towards the wraith, "and you're bleeding all over the hill. Only complaint *I've* got is that you took all the belistand I gave you instead of rationing it *like I told you*, you idiot."

"That's enough," Erine scolded. "There's work to be done that can't wait any longer," she said as she twisted her fingers in the air and summoned a shadow that swallowed her and the innkeeper whole.

After they faded away, the priest rolled onto his back and took a long, ragged, painful breath as he tried to unpack everything that had just happened. "I'm... I'm tired."

"I don't think she cares."

"She doesn't," he agreed as he dug into his belt pouch and pulled out a small glass vial halfway full of a white, chalky powder. "Though I'm so fisking glad they didn't look for this."

"If you kill yourself now, I swear..."

Akaran shook his head and popped the top off of the vial. "Just need to sleep. Dreamless, dreamless sleep."

The wraith began to feel an odd pull and *pang* deep inside her chest, and it was matched with a pulsing red glow just under her skin. *"You're going to miss me,"* she taunted.

He brought the vial to his lips and gave her a teary smile. "Not as much as you're going to miss me."

Rmaci looked down at her new body and began to fade away as the Mother Eclipsian called her back to the absorbtion gem. *"Well,"* she sighed. *"Shit."*

XIII. OF RAPTUROUS INSANITY
Madis, the 1ˢᵗ of Firstgrow, 513 QR

Port Cableture wasn't large enough to support districts in the same way as Basion City did. That wasn't to say that there wasn't a residential area, or a merchant's square, or two lines of warehouses – one line that stored supplies for the 2ⁿᵈ Naval Armada and one that held wares destined for Basion or elsewhere. It had all of those things, and no shortage of inns for weary, sea-sick travelers to find a place to stay that had solid ground attached.

It also had a few buildings that towered over the rest of the Port. One of them housed the Office of Oceanic Divinations, an offshoot of the Granalchi Academy tasked with everything from weather forecasting to effects the ocean may have on the ether itself. Beside it (and two scant stories lower), a slightly-less-than-a-tower-sized building housed dignitaries and envoys that may arrive to the area from anywhere in the southern hemisphere.

Pelloic's Tower of Hospitality, as someone more full of himself than not had named it, was a building of nearly five stories of apartment housing. Each story effectively was a miniature manor house in and of itself, complete with servants to attend any visitors and guards to protect against the unwelcome. Guards, it should be noted, who were worn out from trying to keep up with all of the demands of the Odinal delegation.

Guards who were not at all happy with the way that a mixed group of Lovers and Hunters stormed the Tower with weapons drawn and malicious spells that hovered in the air over their heads. Paladin-Commander Spidous reached the door on the third floor first, but Huntsmatron Elsith was right behind him. They switched places with practiced ease, and as the moons lit the port with all of that silvery glory, she wrapped a gloved hand around the doorknob and whispered a quiet spell.

The result was anything but.

Her glove turned red and the iron door handle matched the color almost instantly. Spidous gave her a curt nod and uttered a Word of his own that summed a shimmering wall of translucent light in front of his body. The handle melted and the edge of the door exploded inwards to shower the apartment with slivers of burning wood and bits of molten iron.

The Paladin-Commander went through the threshold first. His cloak whipped at the air at his back as he drew his sword and charged through with an edict on his lips that you could hear from a block away. "Lady Anais Lovic and Donta, surname unknown: By Order of Maiden-Templar Catherine Prostil and Overseer Hannock, you are commanded to surrender before the Crown on charges of Consorting with the Dead, Necromancy, and Murder of the Queen's Lowest!"

Elsith followed right on his heels with a pair of daggers almost instantly in her hands. "By Writ of Investigation and order of Lieutenant-Commander Randic Henderschott of the 4th Garrison, you both are ordered detained for questioning in regards to the murders of Instructor-Adept Odern Merrington, Lady Livstra Oliana – otherwise known as Liona Reanage – and Priestess Lexcanna Jealions!"

More shouting erupted as the pair – and a handful of garrison soldiers, Hunters, and a pair of exorcists followed in behind them. Along the street, members of the 4th swarmed down alleyways and detained anyone that looked even remotely suspicious. A bellowing shout of, "They're not here! FIND THEM!" reverberated on a magically-enhanced shout that *everyone* on the street could hear.

Yet for all of their effort, they failed to look *up.* "[Lost control/lost plan,]" the black, multi-legged, oddly furry mote of a demon ridiculed.

From a window at the very top of the Office of Oceanic Divinations, Anais scowled down at the swarming mass of weapon-wielding thugs and sighed. "I did no such thing."

"[They would say otherwise/They act on otherwise,]" Rishnobia trilled beside her.

She clenched the windowsill so tightly that her fingers left impressions in the pale sandalwood. "They aren't important. Let them play soldier, for what good it'll do them."

The mote shook its head, which was an impressive feat for something with no real neck to speak of. "[They do not play/They hunt you both.]"

"As I said: let them. They won't find a damn thing. All of my belongings and the like are elsewhere. There is no evidence to trace my steps, even if they should try."

"[Don't deny to me/This is a setback,]" it scolded.

Much as she hated to agree, the blasted thing was right. "It is. Dangerous games get played, dangerous results come at times. It is an unexpected change of station, but not one I haven't prepared for."

Rishnobia blinked at her as it tilted its entire body around like a quizzical cat. "[I see failure/Master will too. Your plans are lost/His plans now endangered.]"

"No, to either," Anais retorted. "You worry too much, little demon. It does you little good."

"[I exist for my Master's wishes/You were risen for the same,]" the vile creature retorted. "[If plans are set/I must know them.]"

"You must, must you?" she scoffed. "Fair enough. Donta, of course, is the immediate issue. This is *his* fault. I will arrange to have him found and be removed from the city posthaste, and you can do to him as you wish. I will need a new bodyguard, of course."

The mote laughed at her. She *hated* it when the little cretin *laughed* at her. "[You become exposed/Demand new favor? Lost more than station/Lost your feeble mind. No assistant/No help. Fail to deliver/Fail to survive. He raised you once/Pray he doesn't again.]"

"Now that's unnecessarily cruel of you," the broker chastised. "Not to mention it's entirely incorrect. You address me as if I haven't done as tasked. What I need now is his next set of instructions – though to be honest, I do feel as if my time in this particular puddle has come to an end and I think it is best if I was allowed to find my own way clear of this... well. The Kingdom, I think, may be a wise idea."

It laughed again and jumped up on the sill to block her view of the scrambling guardsmen and the heated argument erupting between Elsith and Spidous below. "[Completed his wishes you claim?/Run scared as a bitch,]" Rishnobia snarled with fangs exposed. "[You have completed nothing tasked/You only risk his wraith.]"

"That's entirely untrue, you offensive little courier," she snapped back as she walked away from the window and turned her back to him. "What he seeks is not hard to find – hard to reach, yes, but not hard to find. It's there. It *is* in the Repository."

The demon jumped out of the window and hovered right behind her back with its eyes suddenly huge and brimming with shining dark light. "[It's there?/ Found it? Demand to be told/Demand to know now!]"

"You forget what it is our red-robed ally wished of me. He wanted eyes to seek for his goal." Anais waved her hand in front of her face and relaxed as the glamour around her faded away. She stared into a nearby mirror and smiled with cracked, lifeless pale blue lips and with a shine on her all-white iris-free left eye. Her skin had no sign of the pale pink she let the outside world see; it was a cool, mausoleum-gray that almost shone like silver in what light the window offered.

But it was her right eye, her empty eye, that took what passed for Rishnobia's breath away. The eye was missing, and a thin, partial tendril, of a still-attached optic nerve still attached moved around in the socket as if it was looking for something on its own. "It only took one."

In one of the furthest depths of the Repository, a small iron box began to glow. Inside, what Akaran had thought was a strip of leather slowly unwound from the Mace of Insanity's Rapture and a small bump at the end swelled up and pushed through a crack in the lid. Once free of the box, the root of Anais's eye coiled itself like a snake and the eye began to swivel around the room.

It was full of blossoming red wveld-weed flowers and dangling vines hung from the rafters. It was a large room, one of many, one buried so far underground that it seemed impossible for the plants to find light to survive. But they didn't need the sun.

They just needed the relics.

As it took note of assorted gems, swords, skulls, books and more, it eventually focused on a caged bush brimming with red flowers and blooded-roses. Nestled in the center was a hardened clay urn with gold bands wrapped around it. The lid was made from a hefty chunk of solid silver, yet the bottom edge was scorched and stained.

As the Mace continued to glow, the urn did the same.

The mace's glow turned a sickly green, and the urn began to match. Her eye slithered across the stone floor and hid itself in the dirt under the urn as a series of runes began to take on a dull, amber-colored glow on the front. As they activated, the plants in the room reacted immediately. More flowers blossomed. More vines sprouted. Withering bits of green brightened and the grip the wveld-weed had on the cage tightened like a lover's fierce embrace.

Anais's eye took one last look at the plaque nailed to the wall below the cage and all the way in Port Cableture, she smiled. "You did say he wanted the 'Urn of Xabraxis,' yes? The 'The Hold of Abyssia, Bride of Belizal, Duchess of the Abyss, the Grand Consumption?' That *is* what my benefactor wanted, wasn't it?"

All Rishnobia could do was laugh in delight before it disappeared into the ether. Word would reach the Man of the Red Death soon enough. Then, she assumed, she would be free.

Hope was always a wonderful thing to have.

Even if misplaced and misguided.

***

Torchlight from the Pyre worked its way up the hill with dawn eagerly chasing right behind – along with a pair of souls on a mission. One of the two, the bulkiest one laughed at a joke he'd just made at his companion's expense. She, however, was in no mood to laugh – and with every forced step she took she grew angrier by the minute. "You still haven't told me your name," Seline snapped.

"I told you as much as you needed," he replied slyly. "What matters is that you are my new friend. Do you need to name me to know me?"

"No, sir, I do not," she snapped back. "I am out here because you made me at threat of –"

He stopped halfway up the hillside and gently squeezed her wrist. He hadn't let go since they left the Manor, and his grip was tighter than a vise. "Would you prefer to be my friend or prefer to be otherwise? Otherwise can very much be arranged, if you request, though I would hate to do so."

She flinched at the threat and tugged at his grip again, to no avail. "Why me? Why do you think I know where that idiot is?"

"I assumed that was obvious."

"It's not. It's not obvious why you think he's out *here* either, and why you decided to drag me along after you came up with this idea."

He shrugged and waved the lantern he was carrying in front of them. "The latter is because I fear he may be in need of medical attention. As a healer, that means I need you because he probably does."

"And the former?"

"Because you called him an idiot," he answered honestly. "In my time dealing with the boy, that's usually a sign you've gotten to know him."

Seline bristled and stumbled as he gave her a not-so-gentle tug forward. "I have *not* gotten to know him on *any* level. He's just... just... he's an idiot. What more do you want?"

He chuckled and focused on the dim light of embers up ahead, and the shadowy lump laying beside them. "I want what all men of power want, my dear. Though I'll settle for him," he added as he pointed up the hillside. "Though if he's dead, I'll relinquish my interest in him fully back to you, of course."

"Of course you will becau..." she started before she followed he gaze to the man-shaped lump, "...oh shit. He's dead, isn't he."

Her *new friend* lumbered up the hillside and stopped beside the barely-conscious, bloody, and *leaking* body. "No, though it seems I was right to bring you."

Akaran looked up at him with a bleary eye. His hands trembled as he tried to hold onto the empty, dripping flask on his chest, but his blood-soaked fingers couldn't quite gain purchase on it. "Oh. They didn't tell me... tell me I'd see things. You're not here, but. Hey. Hi."

"Oh, I'm here," his rotund friend grumbled disapprovingly. "Did you do this to yourself or did someone help?"

"Do... do I look like... the kind of man that needs help?" he croaked out. When he tried to pick the flask up again, the bigger man reached down and swiped it out of his fingers.

"Yes," Seline hissed as she tried to figure out where the blood was even coming from. "By the Pantheon, you *idiot*, what did you do?"

"See what I mean? You do know him," the other remarked.

He rolled over to his side and vaguely gestured down at his ruined, bloody, and oddly oil-slick knee. "To... told you... felt like... something was... in there..." he answered with a weak laugh.

The healer followed the gesture and didn't bother to hide her shock. "What did... oh dear Goddesses! Your leg!"

"It's out... doesn't hurt so... so bad now. It... it's out. See?"

The other man looked down at the puddle of blood and *other* things by his leg as he swung the lantern down closer to it. "I do. What is it?"

Akaran barely shook his head back and forth. "Don't... know... don't touch it... it's..."

"Squirming," the traveler grunted. "Disgusting."

Seline stopped rooting through the pouches on her waist and looked up, alarmed at the use of *that* particular word. "It's *what*?"

"Squirming," he repeated as he took a step back. "It's moving. Oh, Akaran. What did you manage to do this time, hm? I thought we covered this once."

The healer looked down and watched a tendril of what she had first thought was blood poke up and probe at the wound on his leg. It coiled back as silver dust on the wound sparkled and snapped at it. "Where did... that came from YOU?"

"Here, knee, it was... told you there was..." he tried to explain before he forced himself up on his elbows. "Wait. Still squirming? I got rid of... rid of all of it. She left."

She reached for it, but the priest flailed wildly at her and knocked her hand back. "Hey!"

He vigorously, violently shook his head and pushed her back limply. "DON'T! DON'T TOUCH!"

"It's squirming," her companion replied with a sneer. "I assure you, I won't let her touch it unless I absolutely must."

"'Course you won't," Akaran retorted, "you aren't here. Neither are. Must be... the powder. I'm tired."

"No you idiot, no, we're here," she sighed as she watched the puddle of black ooze bubble on the grass.

He shook his head again and dropped back to the ground with a pained groan. "*You* can't be here because he's here and he *wouldn't* be here because my luck hasn't been that bad, no... it... it hasn't been that bad. It's not that bad."

"Oh my boy, it's only going to get worse. I need to claim a favor from you. It's rather fortuitous that you owe me so many."

Akaran chortled as he stared up at the clouds in the night sky and put a bloody hand on his forehead. "Hah... fever... asking for a favor. Fever favor? Neither... nobody cares nobody should you two aren't..."

"Go get some of guardsmen," Seline ordered the larger man in the ugly orange vest. "We're going to need help getting him back to the city."

"I have an aversion to going to find guardsmen," he retorted.

"You'll have a bigger aversion to carrying him."

The priest lifted his head a little and looked at her with his eye half-closed. "Carry? I'm fine. Ground soft, smells so good. Sky is so pretty."

"The sky is pitch-black and cloudy," she snapped.

"Clouds don't... sparkle and shine," he countered. "See? *Shiny*."

She rolled her eyes and knelt down several inches away from the twitching puddle of bloody gore and put her hands on either side of the gash on his leg. "You apparently do," she muttered before she turned her attention back to the man that had brought her here. "*You.* Go get some guards. Or go get that big bastard that was with you earlier. We're... fisk. The Manor. Or the Repository. Repo is closer and –"

"No."

Seline looked up at him and blinked. "What do you mean no?"

"I mean 'no' to the Manor, and any place with a name as lofty as 'The Repository' will not welcome me to it," he retorted. "You have a place, yes? Upper Naradol, third house down from the *Nightgale's Roost*?"

The healer felt the blood drain out of her face (again) and her hands went numb from surprise. "How do you know that? Who are you?"

"I like to learn about my friends before I meet them," he answered with a dismissive shrug.

"Before you...?"

"I made it my business to learn a great deal about the Manor before I visited it," he explained. "Oh, and you should have a talk with your surgeon about Who it is he takes council with, you know that, yes?"

She rolled back on her heels and tried to get her fingers to work again as she looked at him in an all-new light. This was not a simple drug-dealing or debt-collecting thug like she had thought he was, and for that one moment, she began to wonder if her life wasn't in more danger than the idiot she was supposed to tend to. "No and... *who* are you?"

He sighed and then it was his turn to roll his eyes. "You're going to be insistent on that, aren't you? Are you sure you want to know?"

"I'm sure you just volunteered my bed for this bloody and... well, *bloody*... fool," she exclaimed with a frustrated (yet terrified) snap. "So either give me your damn name or get out of my sight."

"Feisty," he replied with a grin. "I see why you two have gotten close."

"We. Have. Not."

He dismissed that out of hand. "Either way. My name is Riorik. I assure you, I'm a friend."

"Real-you is... is not... a friend. Real-you is... a pain in... in the ass..."

Riorik smiled down at him and bowed his head ever-so-slightly. "Well, they do call me the Hobbler, so there's much to be said for that," he retorted with a little grin. Then, to Seline, he said, "I'd like you to be my friend, too. However, we are going to take him to your place and treat him there, 'less you'd wish you discuss the nature of my nickname."

The healer looked at him, looked at Akaran, and looked back at him as feeling started to come back to her hands as the initial bout of terror finally faded. "Shit. Fine, fine, my place. This stuff though... we need a priest."

"I'm a priest!"

"We need a *functional* priest," she grunted.

"I'm... functional," he offered as he rolled his head around on the grass.

"That... that powder. Really good."

Seline fought back the urge to scream and saw the knife he'd used on his leg laying haphazardly a few feet away. "No, you know what, no. I'll just scrape it up and –"

Akaran grabbed her wrist again and squeezed as tight as he could. "NO! No fake-Sel, no fake-thief. NO TOUCH. Bad so bad it's bad it's *arin* it's... the screaming stopped, it's quiet now, do you hear the screaming anymore?"

She looked down at the offensive oily mass beside him and felt her eyes go wide (*Again*, she noted with quiet irritation). "Oh my Goddess. That's... but it's not real... we didn't think it was... no. No, that can't be, because if it is then we were wrong and if we were wrong..."

Riorik walked back over and took a closer look at the puddle of inky gore. "Rather offended you call her by name and I'm just 'fake-thief,' you should know."

"Step away from that," she cautioned.

"Oh, my dear," he started as he bent down with an extended finger. "I see what it is now, which means that – sadly – I truly do need a favor from him," he finished. He let his finger hover over the puddle and watched as a disgusting little tendril snaked up from the mass of blood and pus. It wrapped around his finger and then his hand. The tendril quickly crawled it's way up his arm and plunged into a dark blotch on the side of his neck she'd first assumed was an old scar. "I seem to have it myself."

A lifetime's worth of nausea roared in Seline's stomach at the same time as she made the conscious decision to *never, ever*, remember the sight *ever* again. Akaran, however, reacted even worse and tried to fight her off of him before she could force him back down. "You both have to get to a temple right now. *Right now*."

"Ah, no," the pudgy stranger replied firmly as the blotch on his neck *roiled* under his skin.

On the grass, the priest had his own comments for it. "Oh no. No. I just got... got rid of one wraith," he groaned as his knee began to bleed again. "I'm... no. Not dealing with... no. *Not you*. No. No I... I refuse. It's my hallucination. Not yours. Nope. *No*."

Seline pointed a shaking finger up at the bigger man and gave him the same scowl she was known using to quiet even the most rambunctious of the Manor's residents. "You *have* to get to a temple. If that's what I think... if that's what *he's* thought it is, then a temple. Now."

On anyone else, that look would've worked. On Riorik, it only made him smile. "Again, no. Nobody touches me but *him*."

"He can't touch anyone!"

"Wanna watch?" Akaran asked. "I can touch myself and –"

Blessedly, the club-wielding thug interrupted him before he could finish the thought. "I am afraid you don't understand the gravity of this situation. *It* won't shut up, and *it* wants me to find *him* and I think *it* wants me to kill him."

The healer lunged for the knife as he bemusedly watched her go from panic and disgust to panic and protection. "You're here to kill him!?"

"Ah, no. I would rather not," he answered honestly, "though your reaction is most adorable for a woman that isn't close to the boy."

"Then *why are you here*?" she hissed through clenched teeth.

"I'm here to have him help me get rid of this thing before I go mad," he replied. "So. I will go get 'that big bastard,' as you put it, and have him come help. He's down by the pyre but I don't think it would do anyone good to scream right about now, do you? Oh, and his name is Austilin, by the way, and he's very sensitive about his height."

Seline glared daggers at him – and pointed the bloody knife at him to punctuate her stare. "I won't let you harm him."

"I already gave my word that I wouldn't."

"Who are you that I should believe that?"

Riorik poked at the inside of his cheek with his tongue (or that's what she hoped was making his face move) as he thought about how much he should answer, and decided that maybe, given her apparent like for the idiot, to be completely truthful. "The Guildboss of the Fleetfinger's Guild of Weschali Province. Moving soon, I think, to someplace warmer, if not more in the shade. That aside, if you can't trust a thief, who can you trust?"

"Oh please don't ask that," Akaran groaned as the healer felt her arms start to sag again. "Don't ask if... if can trust him. Because can. But won't admit that."

"First thing he's said of importance," the master-thief retorted before he turned and left with a few choice muttered curses under his breath.

Once she was certain he wasn't going to turn back around and kill them both, Seline dropped the knife and cupped the priest's bloody cheek in her hand. "You... what did you do?"

He swallowed hard and reached down to touch his knee. She swatted his hand away before he could and then gently entwined her fingers in his. "It hurt. So tired of the hurt. I removed hurt."

"How did you manage to get through the pain?" she whispered before she wiped some of the bloody mess off of his face he'd managed to smear across his forehead.

"Never... never underestimate the power of... bad mood and... painkillers," he quipped as he felt himself melt under her touch. Or maybe melt under another wave of pain from his leg. It was hard to tell, even for him.

Seline shook her head and tried to take stock of the poor boy, gash aside. "I can't believe you," she said with a frustrated little chortle before she saw the flask that Riorik had tossed aside and then noticed a little glass vial next to his arm. "No. No, I can believe you. That's the problem," she grunted as she leaned in and sniffed at his mouth.

"Hey, that... that tickles."

The healer ignored the brief protest and sniffed at the vial and then at the flask as her face brightened with rage. "You smell like... belistand, larochi, and... and..." she said before she gave a little bit of the powder left in the vial a taste with the tip of her tongue – right before she promptly spit it out all over the grass. "*Bonsev*?! *BONSEV*?! People DIE from that!"

Akaran flinched at her outburst and gave a counter-argument that did next to no good at all. "Die... die from knives. If I... had to pick..."

Instead of giving him the remark he deserved, she rocked back onto her heels and looked at the awful mess he'd made of himself. The cut was bad enough. The blistering skin all around it was worse, and the fact that he seemingly had ripped off at least one bandage and then had rubbed a box full of silver and Gods-only-know what else into the wound didn't help matters any either. "I suppose I should ask if you think you got it all out, or am I going to have to go digging?"

"No digging," he pleaded, "but torch it. Burn it."

"I am not setting your knee on fire. I don't care how it hurts right now."

He took a breath and shook his head 'no' again. "Sulfur. Silver dust. Basil," he replied. "Pack... pack it in and ignite it. Only... only way to be sure."

"What's that supposed to do, hm?" Seline asked with a sigh as she pulled out an extra bandage and the start of a wet herbal compress from her belt. "Stupid, stupid boy. You're feverish."

"Gonna... gonna make me scream," Akaran admitted.

"I imagine it would. What else is it supposed to do, hm? You hack yourself to bits and then set yourself on fire? Whomever taught you how to bind a wound... I swear, I'll cut them apart myself..."

"It'll clear... clear. Cleanse," he explained. "Can't... can't magic. Use... old solutions," he said before he pointed at a small bag he'd brought with him to the hilltop. "In there. Just... give it here."

She grabbed it and peered inside. "You brought it with you?"

"Couldn't... couldn't risk this. Not working."

The healer bit back another curse and tried to take stock of everything in the sack. Silver, sulfur, amethyst, different herbs and who knew what in vials and pouches. She couldn't even imagine where he could've found the supplies, let alone how he planned to use them. "What did you do, Akaran? I need to know."

"I... I was right... and... and I proved it," he answered as he began to drift off again. "Seline?"

"Yes?"

"If... if you're real. Please. Bistra. Protect her."

She leaned over him again and gently patted his cheek to try to get him to focus. "Why?"

"Because the fangs... her fangs. It's real. All of it is real," the exorcist croaked out before the pain – and the drugs – sent him blissfully back into an empty dreamscape.

He woke up to scream after she lit the mixture.

If smell could bother them, they didn't show it. Even if it did bother them, it was worth putting up with. Madam Pramidi's House of Hides in Lower Naradol was the premiere tannery in the city, and pulled in gamesmen and non-mercenary hunters from all over the region. The proprietor, Olea Pramidi, had almost made enough to retire and sell the entire facility off to the Blackstone Trading Company.

But, almost two years ago, things had changed. Since then, business had slowed to a trickle. Very few people knew why. The wretch tied to a long table had an idea, though his consciousness faded an hour ago when his host had poured a ladle full of molten silver into his mouth. The gurgling scream had been exquisite, if not short-lived.

Which was fine. The tannery was a transitory place – in more than one way – and not the place for extended entertainment. That suited Sherril just fine; as much fun as it was to drag out a few screams, she didn't quite share her Meister's interests in torment. "Word spread quickly," he wheezed from over his toy's naked chest. "They've almost forgotten about the earlier demonstrations."

"They think you did it," the battlemage replied as he ran a single clawed finger down the prisoner's stomach.

"Maybe. That will change. Soon."

Sherril grit her teeth and braced herself for whatever barb he was preparing to throw her way. "Will it? Or won't it be better to blame that foul creature you had me attack?"

Her Meister looked up at her with a single acorn-brown eye that bored right through her. His other eye had marbled over, though he'd never told the battlemage why. "*Kill*, my *charianne*, not *attack*. You failed."

His pet name for her service raked over her skin like hot coals. She was no charwoman, and his insulting addition to the word? She looked down at his victim and fought the urge to grab at her hip where her knife used to be. "You said no witnesses."

"I said *discrete*. It was not time to slaughter freely," he snarled. "You are saved from my table *solely* because they do not seem to know *what* you are. There will be time to elicit that terror, but *not* until my glory is complete."

"Glory? Meister, she is but a simple woman."

He picked up a small fleshing tool and raked it down the bare skin of his plaything's thigh. It drew a sharp outpouring of dark, rancid blood down the length of the cut. "No. She is more than that. She is the curse that claimed my heart. She will pale as a replacement, but she will exist in Zilyph's shadow."

Sherril leaned over the twitching body and looked right into his eyes. "The other murders have drawn too much attention. Kill her and leave."

"If there's too much attention you are the one that brought it on us," he spat. "Though if I had truly not wished to risk a failure to keep the action quiet, I'd have done it myself. There was a chance you would disappoint me, though the result could have been worse."

The rebuke set her back. "Meister? I don't understand your plan for her."

"It is simple," Annix replied as he drew another long cut into the body. "The only way for her to be as I wish is for her to *submit*. Not die. Not break. Submit. Give herself. Accept that there is no fate for her but the gift I offer."

"Like you did to sway me."

He looked up from his victim and gave her a withering stare. "Nothing so menial," he spat. "You were willing to be more once you saw what awaited you if you didn't. She is not."

The memory of how he made her beg, how she had been strapped to a table much like this one, sent a cold shiver that threatened to make her heart race. Not that it could, but the nagging feeling was still there. "If she's not, then is there a point to risk discovery? You know how they'll react if they suspect."

"They react to what they're shown. That you have educated them that no gathering is safe? That is how they will react now." Annix carved another curve into the flesh before him in silence, then added, "It is a deeper fear you have unearthed than I expected. Their response to be from the others was muted. This is not."

"The others made them angry. This made them scared."

"Yes. As such, you deserve... more," her Meister purred. "There's a girl the next room over. You are welcome to her."

"A girl?" she asked with a blink and a quick lick of her lips.

He nodded as he drew a fifth cut across the squirming sod he was working on. "Fresh. Priestly, at that. Still in her whites," he answered with a smile. "I know you prefer them that way."

She shivered and licked her lips again as her fangs started to descend. "Your kindness is appreciated."

"You work towards my plans, you deserve a reward. It is better than the alternative, is it not?" he asked as he dipped a finger into one of his victim's gashes and swirled it around inside his gut.

The shiver was replaced by a shudder. "Yes... yes, my Meister. It is," she admitted. Before he could remark further, she changed the conversation around. "It surprises me that you bring them here. The tunnels are safer, aren't they?"

"Safe is a concept that grants no concern to ones such as us. The tunnels are a place to rest, a place to play. Yet here? Passerbys give no thought to the smell of death in a studio such as this," Annix replied with a wave at a stack of leathers in the corner. "If I need one to wake, then they wait here as they grow into what I need," he continued before pointing at a second pile and curled his lip into a smirk. "There is one waiting there as we speak. With the arrival of so many waterlogged wretches around the falls, the cover this room offers has become more useful than ever before."

She glanced over at the pile and bit her lip. "A new? You found need for another?"

"Concerned of your future, my charianne?"

"No... I... I did not expect more kin."

He flicked his tongue against the edge of his upper fangs and shook his head. "It is not a matter of kin. It is a matter of necessity. Tell me, don't you wonder how I move so freely? How I step into that house of the mad without a care to be given?"

"No, Meister," she admitted honestly. He moved how he wanted when he wanted. The night offered plenty of opportunity for her, and she assumed it was no different for him. "You did not see fit for me to know."

"I didn't," he agreed. "Yet, as we move to the end of my game, there may be a time when you need to gain the same access as I."

Sherril furrowed her brow as her eyes darkened. "I may? Surely you are capable...?"

Her Meister nodded in bored agreement. "Once I have her submission, I will have no need for that place. I would see it destroyed."

That made more than a little sense. He was not one to part with secrets, she'd learned, unless he had a need to expose them. "I see. You will wish I carry out your will?"

"I may," Annix admitted. "I may do it myself. It cannot be ignored that you have your own methods of ensuring that what is lost cannot be found."

Have me destroy the building to remove any trace of what you did, you mean, the battlemage quietly retorted inwardly. "Of course. Your wish is my will, my Meister."

He purred his satisfaction as he put the finishing touches on his sired creation-turned-victim on the table. "Good woman, good. It's no secret that they use magic to defend those grounds. I know you've felt it as I. Though, I imagine, you've felt it worse. The difference in age, of course."

"Their Gods do not care for us," she said with a dismissive flip of her hand. "The feeling is mutual. As you have taught, there is only one God that matters to such as us. The Shunned One, the Enshackled One. Nithcanthious."

"As it is, for truth," the elder vampire agreed. "Such a shame that Nithcanthious' so-called Council is so... painfully ineffective. Our peoples could be spread around the world by now, had they the courage shown by the First Sire. Instead they hide so far to the south that we are all but forgotten."

"But being forgotten is a benefit itself, isn't it, my Meister?"

"Mayhaps. Yet if we were still feared as we once were, we wouldn't need to hide in dilapidated houses of skin and shit as this one. That aside," he said as he switched the subject again, "I have found a magic that allows us to blend with the balance between worlds."

Annix reached under the table and pulled out a Penumbra of Lethandria and placed it on the chest of the tortured vampire as it rolled its head lazily back and forth on the bench. "I've seen that design before, rarely but at times. That belongs to the Order of the Cloaked, doesn't it?"

"So it does," he acknowledged. "You see, my little mage, without darkness, light has no meaning. In a home that cries out to the Goddess of the Mad, darkness exists. It is the nature of things."

Sherril tilted her head and frowned. "I don't understand what you mean, Meister. We can't stomach the light, and the light permeates that place. It's not a shrine to the Fallen, occupancy aside."

"No. The light *shines* on that place, but not by choice, only by nature," he argued. "Darkness, however, broods where Madness reigns. It too is nature, nothing more, nothing less. Nature, however, can be bent. A bull eats grass, a fox eats a rabbit. Yet in captivity in a pen, they eat as they are given should they hunger enough. It is within the knowledge of our weaker, former selves that we can claim our own birthright. As the sentient races grow crops and grow feed for their livestock, we can in turn plant seeds of a more elemental nature to grow from."

The lecture didn't help, no matter how many flowery words he used to try to get his point across. "I still don't understand, Meister. Darkness is just... *darkness*. It's shadow. It doesn't have a seed."

"Ah, but it does," Annix countered. "*We* are the seed. *We* are creatures born of darkness, and darkness we spread. As seeds, it is ours to grow – and ours to cull," he replied as he straightened the sigil up and tapped the center of it with a single outstretched claw.

The runes he'd carved into his unholy brood's chest began to glow faintly before he finished chanting the first word of his invocation. It barely sounded like a language, and whatever tongue he was speaking in made her stomach roll as he continued. Nausea was not something she'd felt in a very long time – and she hadn't missed it.

As she clutched her stomach, the crest began to radiate all the colors of the rainbow. It's shine started to blind the battlemage and a ray of particularly brilliant white etched a small burn across her throat. Steam began to rise from Annix's arms, though he didn't stop chanting or even give a hint that the burns erupting on his flesh hurt at all. His victim, however, had no such restraint.

The doomed and damned creature struggled violently against the ropes holding it down. It screamed wordlessly around the gag in its mouth and bucked under the elder's hands. As her Meister continued to chant, the bloodied parasite caught fire under the medallion.

The fire spread rapidly. The Penumbra fell through skin and disintegrated ribs with ease. The fire raced across its flesh and consumed muscle, flesh, and bone alike. As soon as its heart was destroyed, the entire body arched up so violently that its spine cracked in half – and the rest of its body burned away in a cloud of orange embers and thick black ash.

As the surprisingly little smoke left behind from the inferno spread through the room, Annix smiled down at the sigil. No longer glowing with brilliant reds, blues, and yellows, the icon simply throbbed with a wave of *darkness* so intense that looking at it felt like looking into the mouth of the Abyss itself.

"Harvest the seed of darkness," he intoned, "and we may hide where it grows. By the time that light can banish the shadows, we have come and gone with impunity. All we need is a soul to grant us passage by quieting the Gods for a time – and nature allows us to do the rest."

Sherril cupped her mouth over her hand and marveled at how simplistic, yet how cold, the act was. For a moment, she wondered when *her* turn to charge his spell would be – though she decided to compliment him instead (just in case he might entertain the idea sooner than later). "That's... that's ingenious, my Meister. I assume that's why you tolerate that fool of a sergeant?"

He glanced up at her with enough disgust in his eye that she cringed. "Oh, never. I wouldn't trust him to do more than advise when those that may notice us happen to be about," he retorted dismissively. "No, my dear. Sometimes to plant a seed, you need someone that has lost a crop. That aside – I do have a task for you."

The battlemage quickly dropped to one knee and bent her head to the ground. She took a heartbeat to brush loose ash away from her face before she replied, far more earnestly than she really needed to, "In your service, I do as you ask."

Annix barely even noticed her genuflection. "In twenty-eight days hence, that pathetic wedding will take place. Every five days prior, I wish for an Odinal or a Tessamirch to die. I will allow you to pick them; do aim for ones of importance. The act will be enough to give birth to a riot, and that will remove the concern of being found for the time being."

"That many bodies – done public – will gain attention. They may identify what we are if we lash out."

"Yes – though for more. The Guard will be shown to be powerless. The Overseer will beg for peace and claim the couple love each other truly. The fools in the Order of the Harlot will be tasked to protect the wedding – which will preempt their efforts to defend one of their own, should they suspect my goals as I grow closer. They'll be embarrassed, exposed," he explained with a smile. As he wiped the ash over his pale skin, he continued on. "I will hurt them for what they did with blood and their own failure."

Sherril licked her lips at the thought. "Ruin a wedding as you take revenge for your murdered bride?" she asked with a cool smile and a happy shiver down her spine. "It would be my pleasure, Meister. But tell me, please, if you so will, who is it that you found to plant your seed?"

"Ah. That was but a stroke of luck, and not of my machination," he admitted as he held the sigil up and peered closely at a detail only he could see. "A child of light that was turned to a mother of the dark in her own right. A woman none can hear, a woman non can understand. A woman lost in her mind, which allows the nature of the void to reign when the natural order itself was stolen from her."

As the vampire spoke, Appaidene looked down at the doll in her hands as she sat in the Manor's atrium. She chirped at it, held it, crooned at it. She told it a story that she made it promise that it couldn't tell anyone else. A story of how a man once came to her in the dark, and offered her a baby. A baby he'd made of cloth, of wool, of padding, and of hair so beautiful that it could've come from a queen.

It hadn't.

It came from an Eclipsian.

EPILOGUE
Lithdis, the 2nd of Firstgrow, 513 QR

Even in hiding, there were some things you couldn't take from the Mother Eclipsian. Darkness offered comfort, but so do velvet-covered couches and down-filled pillows. Wine offered some delight, and darkness made hangovers easier to deal with the next day. It made sense then, in a way, that her exile offered at least a few creature comforts – though if someone finally got around to giving her a bath in the moonlight, it wouldn't be rejected.

Sadly, the arrivals in her wine-cellar-away-from-home offered none of the above. However, there were decent odds that given enough time, Riorik may have offered. "I am reasonably sure I told you to come alone," Erine grumbled from her couch. With only one small glowing lightstone in the ceiling illuminating the entire room, it was hard to tell that she was wearing much more than a thin gauze gown that did little to leave anything else to the imagination.

Or maybe that was the intent. "You told me to come alone, in a hurry, and after I healed up. You get one of the three," the exorcist countered.

"I wanted you, and I normally get what I want," she countered with a sigh as she swung her legs off of the couch and sized him up. A day's rest hadn't done him any good, and his caretakers had forgone even finding him pants. "Though I was expecting to see you wearing... more than a tunic."

A cane, yes, pants, no. The Master Thief of Gonta, yes, and Seline, of course. Despite objections from the latter, of course, though she felt that if she let Akaran out of her sight for even a minute, he'd find a way to make her stitch his leg back together. "A woman of my own soul," Riorik purred in that way that could (and frequently would) make your skin crawl and your heart swoon at the same time. "Mother Eclipsian Erine Rrah, I presume."

"Yes, and of all the things I am after, your heart is not one of them, Master Hobbler," she replied with a brief nod of her head and as little interest as she could possibly convey. "Though do you prefer Lord Dallidon?"

"Rare have I ever been called either in full, m'lady. Though I can see now that my reputation precedes me. I'm impressed."

"I'm not," Seline grumbled as she helped Akaran lean against the wall. She looked worse than simply disheveled, and it was a wonder anyone had let her walk down the street without coming to her immediate aid. "Mother Erine, I'm grateful to see you safe but whatever you want with him, it has to wait. He can barely stand. Asshole made us bring him here, and I want to get him back into bed."

He tried to flex his leg, but her bandages were wrapped so tight that all he managed to do was wiggle his foot and make his cane creak. "Honestly? I *can't* stand," he said as he pointed towards the chair by the fire in a quiet request to sit.

A request that was either missed or ignored. "Because you're an idiot," the healer retorted.

"Because he did what was necessary," the priestess interrupted. "Though in the worst way I could have ever imagined someone taking the effort to do."

Against the wall, Akaran shrugged the best he could. "The power of a bad attitude and a sharp knife," he quipped. "But that's not the point. What do you want from me?"

"Whatever it is – it can wait," Seline interrupted. "Mother Eclipsian, I have to ask: do you know what happened to Raechil? She disappeared at the same time you did."

The priestess' irritated bravado faded instantly and she strode over so elegantly that it looked like she floated across the floor. The blonde woman guessed the answer started to cry even before Erine took her hands in hers. "She did not disappear, I'm afraid."

Tears flowed freely down the younger woman's face as she shook her head. "No. Please no. Don't tell me she's dead."

"I'm afraid she isn't."

Riorik rubbed at his chin and frowned. "It is never a good sign when someone is sad to admit that a soul *hasn't* crossed over to the ether."

"Her soul has, I believe," the Eclipsian gravely replied. "Her body has not."

"I think I know where this is going and I don't think I like it," Akaran said as he developed a foul taste in his mouth.

"Nor should you," the Eclipsian agreed. "Seline, I am sorry. Both Raechil and Kiasta were taken. One was turned, and forced to feed on the other. I am not sure which was which."

She blinked away a few of her tears and rubbed her eyes tiredly. "Turned? Turned how? Raechil would never...? She couldn't harm a fly. I've seen her *refuse* to harm a fly!"

Erine turned away from her and looked at the exorcist with a look of mild disbelief in her eyes. "You didn't tell them?"

"I take it you know," Akaran replied with a little grunt.

"Tell us what?" Seline asked.

"I didn't think they'd believe me, honestly," he added.

The priestess gravely nodded her head and sighed as she made her way back to her couch. "They may not."

"Tell us *what*?" the healer stressed again, though with less confusion and more irritation in her voice.

Akaran and Erine shared a knowing, pained look. "Healer, Hobbler," she started, "what he's about to say is true. I offer my word as the Speaker of the Moons – he does not lie to you. It will not be easy to stomach, as some truths are not at times."

Seline moved closer to the thief, of all people, and crossed her arms defiantly. "If you don't tell me *what* you two are hinting at, I'm gonna take *his* club and beat *him* over the head with it," she growled back with a gesture first to Riorik and then to the exorcist.

The exorcist cringed and lowered his head. "I know what killed Livstra. Fairly sure it killed Odern. Mostly sure it's responsible for the missing vagrants, and it had a minion wipe out Flynn's Landing. I'm not sure who else it claimed. I heard about a dead hunter, but..."

"Lexcanna," Erine added. "It came for me, too, for reasons that I do not understand. As well as Raechil and her sister."

"Oh, you don't know?" Akaran asked as he pointed at an empty spot on the priestess' neck. "I think I do."

Seline's eyes went wide and her fists clenched. "You know but you haven't told anyone?"

"I just figured it out before I had to go digging," he retorted. "Give me a little time."

"You're out of time," she spat. "Who is it?"

Riorik cleared his throat and edged between the healer and her charge before she could march over and punch him. "Yes, I'm very interested in knowing, myself. Something has drastically upset the balance of the underworld in this province and I am here to restore it... among other things."

"*Your* problem is not *that* problem," Erine countered. "However, *his* problem affects us all."

"Let me ask, first," he started as he reached into the lone pouch on his hip and pulled out the sigil that Seline had given him in the vineyard a few days prior. "Is this your Penumbra? I notice it's missing."

Erine took one look at it and hissed sharply. "That isn't mine, but I know who it belonged to, and when she was slain. Mine is missing because it was stolen when that damned thing attacked me... and I know *damn* well how long it's been killing at whim. I just did not know it was *here*."

Seline looked back and forth between them and made a little, 'oh' sound in the back of her throat. "What was it doing in the Manor? How did it get there?"

"A question worth answering," the priestess agreed. "Akaran... you're hunting something that's been making a name for itself in certain circles. The Order of the Cloaked has a very *vested* interest in seeing it cast from our shadows to rot in the light. The Cloaked... even the Circle. Your Order too, though that, I assume, is a given."

"It's name is Annix, isn't it?" he asked.

"Annix?" Seline asked. "I know that name."

Erine nodded and frowned. "Yes. I did not know it was here, but I know that it has made many, many enemies over the years. Slay it, and you will gain friends in places you didn't know were places."

He pursed his lips and gave her a little nod. "I like making friends. Fisk the Circle, though."

"Humph. You've yet to warm to me, however," Riorik scoffed.

"I'm not your friend," the priest countered.

"Of *course* you are," he countered. "You're too useful to be otherwise."

Akaran ignored that and tried to work his leg a little with a groan before he looked over at the healer. "Seline? The same thing that's been killing it's way through the city is the reason for Bistra's nightmares. For how long, I don't know, but I'm gonna take a guess and say it's been for a while."

"I don't see how? The Manor is warded, you can attest to that."

"Liv can attest for how well it isn't," he disputed.

The priestess of Lethandria peered at the amulet and tried to discern if anything had been done to it. "There are ways to circumvent magic with other magic. Most creatures wouldn't know, but Annix would."

Seline frowned and tapped her foot on the floor. "I *know* that name," she repeated. "I saw it in one of Liv's journals once. She was able to coax it out of Bistra... it was... something in her nightmares. She had tried to condemn it? Excise it, I think?"

"Oh, he is a nightmare. Of no question that," Erine agreed. "A physical kind, one not welcome in the shadows. Nor welcome in the light. This Bistra woman – a resident of the Manor? I assume an exorcist?"

"That's right," Akaran replied.

"One would assume that it didn't want its name known. Given the nature of Bistra's former occupation, what would Livstra have done once she learned the name?"

The exorcist pursed his lips again and frowned. "She would've gone to the Repository and looked for it. If she had any reason to think there was truth to it, that is."

An angry light flashed deep in Erine's eyes. "You have motive."

"I've got everything."

"Not everything," she disputed. "You have another problem that needs to be addressed."

His jaw clenched and he felt his shoulders tighten up again. "What now?"

"You still didn't tell me what it is you're rambling about," Seline interrupted. "Who is Annix? Just tell me!"

"Annix," Akaran said before he took a deep breath, "is a vampire."

She didn't respond – at first. Then, slowly, her face cracked. A little smile curled up on the corner of her lips and she placed her fingers over her mouth to stifle a laugh. "A... a vampire? Do... do you take me for a fool?"

Riorik, however, was far less bemused and it took everything in his power not to hold himself still. "Are you serious, priest? That's a dangerous accusation to make even on the best of days and today is not one of the best of days."

"Told you they wouldn't believe me," he grunted at Erine. "Let me explain."

"A joke like that? I don't think you can," the healer quipped.

Unfortunately, he could. "Before she became a resident of the Manor, Bistra tracked down and killed a vampire. It was covered up, because the Order... well, *because the Order* is all I can to say. She killed it. Or at least, she killed one. The other has been after her ever since. It followed her here to Basion, and it's been hiding – and feeding – ever since," he explained. "I don't know how it's getting into the Manor. But I'm gonna say that Livstra figured out that it's been terrorizing that poor woman, and it killed her for it, and I'm betting it killed Odern for the same reason."

"You haven't seen it. You don't know for sure. That doesn't... maybe someone got angry with Liv and Odern and..."

"Then I got into a fight with it," he went on over her objections, "and that pissed it off. Not enough to kill me, but enough that it wanted to get rid of me. So it set me up, and got Ridora to toss me out. All the meanwhile, a few other people have started getting in the way... probably because I've been asking questions," he added with a sigh. "So now we have a mountain of bodies and the Goddess only knows what it plans to do with Bistra, but I am *also* willing to bet it's going to do it sooner than later."

"You got into a fight with some battlemage from the Midlands," she said, "someone trying to stir up trouble. That's all," she tried to counter.

"It jumps higher than a human, it's obviously sentient, it punches harder than most, it drains its victims, and plantlife that feeds on the aura of the damned are having their own auras siphoned off when they're left around the dead this thing is piling up. It also managed to twist a former army battlemage into an ally – I'm sorry Sel. There is *one* type of creature that can do this. Two, if you count an actual Fallen God, and if *that* was the case, well..." he said as he let the thought hang in the air.

By the time he finished, she had sunk down onto a nearby barrel with her head in her hands while the thief stood in stoic, stunned silence. "A hard truth to hear, as I said," Erine wistfully pointed out.

"The crypt-bane was what should've tipped me off," Akaran continued. "It's a vampire."

"I... I must admit, that's an uncomfortably detailed argument you're making," Riorik finally spoke up after several very long, very quiet, very stunned moments.

"One I shall confirm," Erine replied with a tired sigh.

Seline took a very long breath and swallowed nervously. "If this is true... everyone is danger."

"Everyone's *been* in danger," the Eclipsian returned. "We only now understand how. If you were to research the vault of the Order of Love, I suspect that you'll find his name featured prominently alongside this Bistra woman's."

Akaran nodded in complete agreement and rubbed at the back of his stiff neck. "If only I had access."

She shot him the faintest flicker of a smile. "Oh, you're soon to."

"Uh, no? I've managed to successfully piss everyone with an inkling towards the light, present company included," he said as he gestured over at Seline.

"I'm... I'm not pissed," the healer meekly interjected as she stared down at her hands. "I'm just confused. And a bit scared, if you want me to be honest."

"You're pissed."

"I agree with the priest," Riorik chimed in. "You've been pissed at him since I had a chance to meet you."'

"You're not helping," Akaran countered before she could offer a suitable retort.

The thief affixed him with a toothy grin. "Give me time, and I'm sure I will."

Erine cleared her throat and waited for the grumbling between her three guests subsided. "This is only fitting now, I suppose. You bring answers and you return a Penumbra to the Night, and I give you a gift in return. To be fair, I didn't expect this wealth of information, so this is far more of a favorable trade than I had planned."

"I thought you mentioned a gift," the exorcist responded, "though honestly I wasn't sure if I was dreaming it or not."

"I did," she confirmed, "and with it, you will find your path back to the good graces of those with good grace."

"Good, because they're not gonna take my word about Annix."

"No, but they'll take it about something else. Follow?" she asked as she stood up from the couch and beckoned him towards a different room. He cast a pathetic look over at Seline until the healer rolled her eyes and helped him follow her.

The wine cellar gave way to a hallway that plunged somewhere under the city. Finally, it lead into some long-forgotten storage room buried deep beneath the streets. A cloaked figure that nobody but the Eclipsian seemed to recognize stood by an old wooden door, though the guard wasn't half as interesting as the wardmarks scrawled into the wood. Most of them were in a language that the exorcist simply didn't understand, though a few of them seemed similar in design to ones used by the Order of Love.

Once inside the dimly lit room, everyone's eyes went to the figure sitting in the middle of the closet-turned-cage. He was hooded, forced to sit in a simple wooden chair in the middle of a warding circle that stretched from wall to wall. His hands were tied behind his back, and someone had taken the effort to secure a heavy steel collar to his neck – and then chained it to the ceiling.

That wasn't entirely right, Akaran realized.

His *hand* had been tied behind his back.

"Oh, now *this* is unexpected," the exorcist mused.

Erine smiled coldly. "As it turns out, slaughtering most of the Fleetfinger's Council makes one very unpopular in certain places. A few friends of mine were only too happy to take advantage of his current *discomfort*."

Riorik had his club in hand before she could even finish the sentence. "Though it makes one popular in others. Akaran? Thank you for bringing me here," he silkily purred. "The gift may be yours but I think I'd rather have it for myself. Call it a repayment of one of the favors you owe me."

"This one is beyond your skills, Master Hobbler," the priestess intoned as she gently placed a hand on her shoulder and guided him back from the prisoner.

"Do not mistake me as some −" he started to snap before Akaran quieted him with a voice as hushed and gravely as the thief had ever heard.

"It's not human, Riorik," he warned. "This one isn't yours. I'll owe you one later. You'll get your fill."

The thief curled his lip in a sneer as he looked at Erine's naked, pale-skinned, waxy prisoner. "Not human? I suppose that does present a challenge but one has to learn somewhere."

"Not this one," Akaran repeated. "You know, I thought something was wrong with you the first time I saw you, Donta," he said before he glanced over at the healer in the corner. "Think I told you that, too. First trip through the city?"

She didn't respond. Neither did the assassin.

He walked over and pulled the hood up off of his face. Donta had seen better days; deep scratches on his face had given way to reddish-gray sand-covered clumps and exposed bone. It looked like someone had tried to bash the side of his skull in, which wasn't too far from the truth. "I have some questions for you. What was that weapon Anais gave me? Why did she want Se'daulif locked up? What did an inhuman monstrosity like you do to piss off a vampire?" After a moment of silence, he asked the other, and patently obvious question: "What in the pit, exactly, *are* you? Who made you? Anais?"

Anais's mercenary looked up with bloodshot eyes and croaked out a simple, "Go... rot."

The exorcist frowned and pulled the hood back down as he addressed Erine. "Has he been this stubborn the entire time you've had him?"

"One would assume he lost his tongue with his arm, except for all the ways he's found to use it to disparage my lineage."

"Kinda expected that," he muttered. "Though... is *she* here? She can do it."

Erine's smile returned, though the sheer amount of eager *delight* behind it even gave the Hobbler chills. "Yes. I expected you may want to see her before you left."

Chills or not, the thief crossed his arms and almost pouted (though he'd never admit it). "Oh? You don't think that I, a man with the reputation I have, would not be able to coax it from this one-armed... whatever he is... yet you expect someone else can? I am insulted."

Seline timidly cleared her throat and sized the prisoner up. "He's... it's not human? But I've... I've seen him in the daylight? He's not a vampire? Are there more things in the city that...?"

"Oh, my dear, there's always things in the cities that you don't want to know about," Riorik not-exactly-reassuringly remarked. "Plus, given you know about my particular *condition*, I recognize that this may not be the easiest day for you."

She shook her head and tried, ever so desperately, to make sense of this. All of this. Any of this. "I'm not... I'm just a healer. This isn't..."

Akaran gave her a sad but understanding nod but otherwise ignored her quiet little breakdown once he turned his attention back to the thief. Erine slipped a cracked purple gem from her robe and carefully passed it to him. "Hobbler? I'd like to introduce you to someone. Meet..." he staid as the gem began to glow and the shadows in the room started to coalesce around a shape in the corner, "...meet the Burned Woman."

Her voice echoed from everywhere and nowhere at once. "*Oh. A title now? I think I could learn to like that one. It is better than others I've had.*"

Seline's jaw dropped and she pressed herself against the far wall of the storage room as Rmaci moved into the light. "Oh. My. Goddess. Who are... who is...? What is...?"

The wraith strode out of the shadows in full and displayed herself in all of her new half-burned, half-healed, ice-and-ember wreathed glory. She bathed in the horrified stare from the healer, and displayed herself almost obscenely at Riorik's mixture of fright and excitement. "*She isn't the brightest, is she?*"

"Told you I wasn't losing my mind," Akaran muttered over at the healer.

Her face crumbled even further as she started to sink down to her knees. "That's... oh no. I was... you were... the whole time?"

"*The whole time.*"

"I helped set her world on fire," he said with a sigh as he waved her towards the prisoner in the middle of the room. Rmaci laughed and faced Anais's bodyguard as the snapping embers around her ignited into a blaze that bathed the room in an unholy red and orange shine.

"*Now it's my turn.*"

End:
Saga of the Dead Men Walking: Insanity's Rapture

Insanity will have it's Reckoning in 2021... but for now, if you enjoyed this Rapture, can you leave a review? Those little stars directly equate to sales AND they help me write better stories in the future. Just a click and maybe a few words would mean the world to me! ~J

http://www.amazon.com/review/create-review?&asin=B08P61MNVN

COMPENDIUM OF THE DAMNED, THE DIVINE AND ALL THINGS IN-BETWEEN

4th Garrison
The garrison that oversees the security of Kettering Province, Basion City, Port Cableture, and others.

5th Garrison
Currently assigned to protect the Lowmarsh provincial region.

7th Garrison
Currently assigned to protect the Ummasil Provincial Region.

13th Garrison
Formerly under the command of Evalia Wodoria, the 13th was in charge of protecting the peace in Weschali Province.

2nd Naval Armada
The Armada tasked with maintaining the peace along the southern shores of Dawnfire. Its home base is in Port Cableture.

Abyssia, the Bride of Belizal, Duchess of the Abyss, the Grand Consumption
During the Fall of the Adelin Empire, Abyssia was one of the worst Daemons unleashed by Arch Duke Belizal. Known by many names, survivors described her as a towering, perfect woman with skin so black she appeared almost as a silhouette. It was said that she was the essence of the pit itself, and that she could ingest objects great or small and return them as twisted versions of themselves. The Sons of Veritas hunted her after the war ended, and rumor has it that she was captured at great cost… but where she was imprisoned? Some

say in the darkest caverns of the world, others say she was captured by the essence of the Heavens. Yet some say she fell victim to her own flames, and her ashes were placed inside an urn for safekeeping.

Adelin Empire
The source for much of the woe in the world. At the height of the Adelin Civil War, the then-Emperor made a deal with a demon to end the war and let his people live eternally. He was granted his wish. The fall of the Empire was not swift, nor bloodless – though his people still walk the cursed continent to this day.

Adept Ishtva
A liaison between the Granalchi Academy and the Order of Love, stationed at the Repository of Miral.

Agromah
The Cursed Continent where the dead walk and Arch Duke Belizal has held sway since the fall of the Adelin Empire.

Aqualla
The God of Water and Waves.

Avaritisha's Palace
One of two realms ruled by Avaritsha, the Fallen Goddess of Lust. In Her palace, you can find delights beyond delights, and servants that will cater to your every whim...

Basion City Districts
As a city of many interests, Basion's territories have been broken down into eight individual districts, including Chiadon, Akkador West, Akkador East, Upper Naradol, Lower Naradol, Piapat, East Giffil and West Giffil.

Berserkers of Odinal
Elite warriors and soldiers of Clan Odinal.

Bistra Enil
The Auramancer Exorcist. Once considered one of the Order of Love's best, she suffered a mental breakdown and was admitted to Medias Manor in 510 QR.

Blackstone Trading Company (BeaST)
The premier merchant organization in the world. Their tendrils are everywhere, and in everything.

Brother Steelhom

Akaran's favorite mentor, teacher, and confidant in the Temple of Love. A Paladin-Commander in his own right, his name continually appears atop documents detailing the events during the Age of Misfortune, in a place named New Civa. Why, or how, is anyone's guess; there is an odd form of chronomancy that has taken root in the Temple Archives...

Central Indexiary
Located within the Repository of Miral, the Indexiary is the go-to resource to record where, well, records are kept.

Charianne / Charwoman
An antiquated term for maids and maidens, it was used in a derogatory faction by Elvish nobility towards their human servants. The elves may have died out, but a few people use the word as a slur still – including one that found a way to change it to refer to someone even lower than that.

Covorn, Lord of Hate
The God of Hatred, and considered by some as the Father of Sin. Is presumed to be the Lord of the Abyss, second only to Gormith himself.

(The) Crown's Standards
The Queen requires that any and all weapons, armors, ores, agricultural yields, leatherwork, metalwork, and assorted other works meet a specific criteria for use by her armies, guards, agents, or goods sold bearing the Crown's seal.

Crusade of Suns & the Second Crusade of Suns
The first Crusade was carried out by a united front of Kingdoms and Empires to eradicate the influence and existence of vampires across the globe. The second Crusade was a more clandestine operation carried out by order of the Queen to purge the Council of Nith from the southern mainlands.

Damian
A subterranean race of human and elf crossbreeds, their influence was effectively destroyed when they were cursed by Zeborak, the son of Belizal, to never see the sun again.

Danse Festistanis
A celebration observed for "Unions of Great Importance." Typically only attended by the high and mighty of the Kingdom. Smaller dances sometimes pop up that everyone can attend.

Daringol / arin-goliath
A 'nesting wraith,' a spirit that absorbs and commands other spirits from a central, and frequently insane, core soul. Daringol was the result of magic gone

bad in the mountains around Toniki – and while weak individually, the entire being was a nightmare in its own right. Akaran believed he banished it, but it found a way to sink in… and found a way to infest a ship on the waters of the Alenic.

Darvol
The racist head of the Woodmason's Guild.

Dashan-borer
An insect native to the lands held by the Golden Empire of Matheia. They place their spawn inside dead (or hopefully dead) bodies and excrete a substance that hardens the corpse as the spawn gestate.

Days of the Week/Months
Starting with the first day of the week, Wundis, Londis, Madis, Lithdis, Pridis, Staddis, and Zundis, the day of rest. The year begins with the coldest month – Deepfrost – and continues with Hearthbreak, Greenbirth, Riverswell, and Firstgrow as spring arrives. Warmbreath and Highsun continue, with Hossun cover the summer as Lastgrow, Darksink, Harvall and finally Coldset closes out the year.

Donta
A mercenary, assassin, and non-human with the ability to read the thoughts of his victims if he spikes their minds with his claws.

(The) Drunken Imperial
A tavern in Lower Naradol run by Celestine 'Cel' Navarshi.

Dunesire Da'Keloth of Sharvastial
The ruler of Sharvastial, one of the Jewels of Sycio.

Eberenth, Goddess of Knowledge
She who knows All.

Elder Ronlin, Hirshma's Brother
One of two elders of Toniki. Ronlin was murdered by Rmaci's husband, Yothargi.

(The) Emberforge
The home realm of Charnac, the Lower Elemental God of Fire. Considered one of the worst places to spend eternity, many a blacksmith offers a nod to the realm – a respectful gesture to avoid ending up on the wrong side of the hammer.

Episturine
Guardians of the Upper Elemental Plane of Ice. An Episturine is responsible for Akaran losing his ability to use magic.

Esth-atatic
Pitmetal, harvested in the depths of the Emberforge.

Expunge
Like Expel and Expulse, Expunge can banish an unholy spirit or destroy a demonkin. Unlike the two, Expunge is designed to break apart any anchors that an entity may have in the physical world (such as in cases where a spirit has taken over an inanimate object). It provides a much stronger force than either Expel or Expulse, and uses more of the spellcaster's energy.

Firestormers of Civa
The Imperial Army of Civa enlists experts in fire magic from the Order of Flame to serve as magical support, much akin to the Specialist-Major Battlemages of Dawnfire.

Fleetfinger's Guild
The Guild of Thieves. You can find them operating in every province in Dawnfire, with some established halls greater than others. In Basion City, each district is managed by a representative of the FFG. Prior to her death, the Basion FFG was overseen by Livstra Oliana, aka Liona Reanage, the Gambling mind.

At the time of Akaran's arrival to Basion, The district representatives included: Bantia, Rodric, Yuchin, Aldeina Hessmage, The Gambling Mind Liona Reanage, Raes, Hammer, and Celestine 'Cel' Navarshi.

Flynn's Landing's
A territory granted to a large group of vagrants and homeless to get them out of Basion City for the duration of the wedding between Clan Odinal and the Tessamirch family.

Frosel
The Lower Elemental Plane of Ice, ruled by the terrifying Fallen God, Zell, the Brineblood.

Gaundant
A plant with small yellow-and-brown spotted flowers. The petals are a hallucinogenic. It's addictive, but when mixed with alcohol, can result in a feeling of immense euphoria.

Golden Empire of Matheia
A large, and extremely wealthy, Empire located south past the Alenic Ocean.

Golden Sands of Sycio
The north-eastern continent of Sycio is covered in a vast, rolling desert. The Golden Sands are inhabited by a multitude of small nomad tribes, but primarily by the seven Jewels of Sycio along the Golden Shores.

Golem
A semi-sentient animate, usually crafted by an elementalist.

Gormith, the Warden
The God responsible for judging the damned – and controlling the denizens of the Abyss. He is not evil, only eternal, and *dislikes* souls that escape their assigned perdition.

Granalchi Academy
The overarching guild of mages across all of the known land. Over the centuries, they have set the rules of magic and established the sciences built on understanding them. If anyone says otherwise, they're wrong.

Grand Palace of Love
The Heavenly realm of Niasmis, the Goddess of Love.

Grand Temple Promenade
A huge plaza of merchants and more that sits outside of the Grand Temple of Love in Dawnfire.

Guild of Songweavers
The semi-secretive guild of all things bardic through the Kingdoms. Why musicians need secrets has never been fully understood.

Hall of Sea's Song at Vahail
A temple for Aqualla, served by Tidesinger Quinchero. On the 18th of Riverswell in 513 QR, the Hall was obliterated by a flood caused by the destruction of a dam. Rumor has it the Hall was under siege by a necromancer at the time, and the dam was destroyed to protect the relics stored within.

Headmaster-Adept Telburn Gorosoch
The Granalchi Adept who oversees the Granalchi Annex in Basion City. Is the husband to Elsith Telburn.

Heaven's Wing (tavern)
A tavern run by Bantia of the Fleetfinger's Guild.

Heavenly Mount
The home of the Pantheon.

(The) Heralds of Illiya
Guardians that watch over the gateway to the Upper Elemental Plane of Fire, and home of the Illiya, Goddess of Flame and Matron of the Civan Empire, Infer.

High Priestess Lexcanna
The former Upper Adjunct of Stara (or known to outsiders simply as the High Priestess) in Basion City. Murdered in the middle of Riverswell, 513 QR.

(The) Hullbreaker
One of the Queen's warships. It departed Gonta in early 513, and promptly fell off of the map, despite carrying a cargo of precious metals..

Hunter Levandarious
A Huntsman assigned to assist Bistra Enil in 510 QR for an exorcism in Stovannahsburg.

Huntsmatron Elsith Gorosoch
Controls the Hunter's Guild of Basion City.

Il estapasaiage Ward
A ward used by the Order of Love. This ward channels divine energies to help guide souls towards the veil, and to ease their passage into eternity.

Imprint Stone
A stone used by Order of Love exorcists, clerics, templars, paladins and others. It works as a very light absorption stone – you merely need to squeeze it, and it will receive an imprint of your aura. Just in case someone needs to know your condition prior to a potential... accident.

Instabilisist
A mage that doesn't use any of the specific schools of magic, just someone that channels raw ether to typically explosive results.

Instructor-Adept Odern Merrington
Formerly in charge of teaching defensive magics at the Granalchi Annex in Basion, his murder set off a series of bloody events....

Jeitee Ovokon
The gatekeeper for Thesd Estate.

Jewels of Sycio
The seven grandest cities of Sycio, each located on or near the Golden Shores.

Jobbet Mafordin
An armsdealer of both questionable ethics and quality.

Kiasta Lamar
Sister of Raechil Lamar, she is, or possibly *was*, the bodyguard of the Mother Eclipsian, Erine Rrah.

Lady Anais Lovic
A merchant of secrets, a broker of information, a woman sent to Basion City to discover the location of the Urn of Xabraxis by her 'benefactor' and his minion, Rishnobia.

Leaguesman's Hall
Manors and small fortresses granted to supporters of the Luminary of the Missian League. Often used as seats of local governance.

Ledger Philanus
A liaison between the Hunter's Guild and the Repository of Miral.

Lord Avager at Avager Hall
A minor official of the Blackstone Trading Company.

Lord Riorik Dallidon, the Hobbler
The Guildboss of the Fleetfinger's Guild of Gonta, in Weschali Province. He likes making friends wherever he goes.

Lowmarsh Province
The provincial region on the northern part of Dawnfire, and shares a border with the Missian League. It's a moderately-temperate region, but the constant flooding from the Equalin Mountain range has left it a giant marsh that is only barely inhabited with small villages. That said, the fact that it's a border region has given it a great deal of importance. However, given both its remote distance and its closeness to people that actively worship the fallen, it's come under scrutiny and interest by powers of all kinds. Among other locations, it is the site of the villages of Kellspout, Swampnest, Squistal, Grimedeep, Stovannahsburg.

Madam Pramidi's House of Hides and Olea Pramidi
The House of Hides is the largest tannery in all of Basion City, and is located in Lower Naradol.

Maiden-Templar Catherine Prostil
The current caretaker of the Repository of Miral in Basion City.

Maiden Sanlian Esterveen
Provincial Maiden of Kettering Province.

Mattanic
A school of magic taught by the Granalchi Academy that covers such subjects and arts as conjuration, teleportation, and telekinetic movement.

Melian Deconstructionist
Priests in the Order of Destruction. Capable of both destroying and growth, they are often seen as world-builders... and kingdom-enders.

Missian League
A loose arrangement of city states located on the northwestern border of Dawnfire and the southwestern border of Civa. They're headed by Luminary Cobliver, who is an open worshipper of Neph'kor.

Mother Eclipsian Erine Rrah
The high priestess of the Goddess of Night, Lethandria, in Basion City.

Nadler Alpaige
A farmer that owns and operates several tracts of land on the northern stairwall of Basion City.

Necrosia
The school of magic otherwise known as necromancy.

Neph'kor & the Circle
The God of Rot and His followers.

Nia'valth, the Grand Dreamer
The dual-Goddess of daydreams and nightmares.

Nightgale's Roost
A tavern in Upper Naradol.

Nithcanthious, the Shunned One, the Enshackled One
A demi-God, and the first vampire, child of Covorn, the God of Hate. He rebelled against His father in an attempt to gain control of the Abyss. When that failed, as an act of spite, he turned himself into a creature that would offend both the living and the dead. As punishment, the Warden Himself

entombed him in a burning red sun overhead of Covorn's realm – so that every time the Lord of Hate peers up, He is forced to see His failure cast light over His realm.

(The) Nul'kotak
The Grand Storm. The entrance to damnation. Said to be a portal, it is rumored that it is the soul of the Abyss itself. And it hungers.

Ocean of All Souls
A mythical landscape in the Heavenly Realms. It is said to connect all of the realms of the Mount and to be part of the River of All Souls.

Office of Oceanic Divinations
A subset of the Granalchi Annex. They work to monitor the currents of the oceans and rivers of the world, to help understand weather, and warn the various water-dwelling military and economic interests of the Kingdom of impending natural concerns.

Oh Queen, Oh Queen, How Full of Glory is Your Crown
A lovely song that the Crown makes a pointed request to hear performed every year at the capitol. The Order of Love is asked to provide vocalists to help perform it – of all ages.

Order of Love
Followers of the Goddess of Love, Niasmis.

Order of the Cloaked
Followers of the Goddess of Night, Lethandria.

(The) Origin
The first God. The Faceless One, the Grand Eternity. The creator of all, yet worshiped by none.

Paladin Faldine
A paladin of the Order of Love currently assigned as a bodyguard to Overseer Hannock's interests in Basion City.

Paladin-Commander Spidous
The current Paladin-Commander of the Repository of Miral.

Parl, Enth-Blade of Odinal
The chief advisor to Malik Odinal, of Clan Odinal.

Betrothed Paverilak

Maiden Sanlian Esterveen's Betrothed in Kettering Province. His job is to ensure that the various civil and economic aspects of the province are managed and run without interruption. He's also a bit of a drunk and is far from well-liked.

Pelloic's Tower of Hospitality
A boarding house/manor/tavern in Port Cableture that serves as a brief waystation for people arriving to the Kingdom by sea.

Penumbra of Lethandria
A sigil held by Mother Eclipsians of the Order of the Cloaked. It marks them for their rank.

Pristi's Gate
The entrance to the Heavenly Mount, guarded by the Goddess of Purity.

Privateer Wars
A prolonged set of naval engagements between Dawnfire, Sycio, K'pina and Matheia that ran between 503 and 510 QR. Sycio exits the entanglement in 507, and resumes normal trade relations with Dawnfire by 508.

Pundja, Undja, Crypt-bane, the Blooded Rose
A flowering vine with red blossoms. It absorbs Abyssian magic and wards away lesser spirits. The few that have ever spoken of it claim that it makes them feel as if they are being pulled into the root system....

(The) Queen's Corrective Diplomats
A pretty name given to the organization that carries out quiet orders issued by the Queen to quiet others.

(The) Queen's Destroyers
A designation given to the fastest ships in the Queen's navy. Fastest, and the most lethal.

Raechil Lamar
Sister to Kiasta Lamar, was (or presumed still is) one of the aids assigned to Medias Manor.

Reports: Interests in Exposed Auras & Updates on Disabled Assets
A pair of reports buried in the vault of the Repository tracking and detailing injuries sustained to exorcists in the Order of Love suffered in the line of duty.

Report: Residents of Unknown & Questionable Origin
A list of all current and former residents of Medias Manor.

Repository of Miral

The Repository serves as a library, a vault, and a pit of secrets for the Order of Love. Not much is known about the inner workings of the outpost, but it is just that: a military outpost. One of the most heavily guarded locations that the Order of Love directly owns, it is believed that any record of any encounter the Order has eventually winds up buried somewhere in the sprawling hallways and chambers underground.

Request of Spiritual Remittance

A leave of absence granted to exorcists, paladins, templars, and clerics of the Order of Love when they find themselves too taxed by the battle against the forces of the damned to continue on.

Ridora Medias

The Lady, and founder, of Medias Manor.

Rishnobia

A vile little demon, and a known associate of the necromancer known only as The Man of the Red Death

River of All Souls

Also known as the River Solindal. It flows from the feet of the Origin and through the entirety of eternity.

Rmaci

A Civan spy who worked tirelessly in Toniki to uncover the secrets of Usaic's work. A liar, a thief, an adulteress, and a murderess to boot – she came to a very bad end in Gonta. Her current plane of residence is believed to be Frosel, the Lower Elemental Plane of Ice.

Sebbidule

Desolated ruins in Lowmarsh. They serve as a natural gateway and anchor point for lesser damned. Instead of sanctifying and pacifying the area, the Order of Love adopted it as a training field for new recruits and trainees in the arts of exorcism.

Sergeant-at-Arms Ronald Telpid

A man of many managers. Assigned to help protect the grounds of Medias Manor, he soon became a confident of Lady Livstra – and soon after, was inducted into the Fleetfinger's Guild. However, his allegiances eventually ended up... elsewhere.

Shiedel Estate

A series of houses around a singular large manor currently rented to/occupied by the shiverdine, Se'daulif Ocsimmer.

Shiverdines
Slavers from the desert kingdoms of Sycio.

Shrine of Covered Moons
A shrine and place of worship to Lethandria.

Sire Elverich
A watersculpt, formerly from Mardux.

Solg (Abyssian)
A monstrous vile creature from the Abyss. They are not… subtle… in their methodology.

Specialist-Major
The rank given battlemages in the Queen's army.

Tentricals
A truly disturbing subspecies of bloodbeaks. They're rumored to be as large as a man's chest, and can drain a cow in a single feeding.

Testaments of Geshalda
One of the holiest books of Geshalda, the fallen Goddess of Greed.

Tev'alin
A toxic mineral found in the dankest regions of Lowmarsh province. It comes from a soft, gray stone and is a powerful analgesic.

(The) Sands
The World immediately beyond the Veil. The sands expand for eternity, with only the Abyss behind them and the Heavens in front of them. Known for nothing but bright blue cloudless skies and sand that is abrasive (if you are destined for damnation) or soft (if you are destined for heaven). Other than that, for all that mortal men know, the Sands are a great nothingness.

Thesd Estate
One of many estates, manor houses, and waypoints used by the rich – or at least the passable – nobility and those who wish to be considered as such.

Tidesinger Quinchero
The priest formerly in charge of the Hall of Sea's Song in Vahail.

Uncrested Wave

A taberna in the Chiadon district of Basion City.

(The) Urn of Xabraxis, aka, the Hold of Abyssia
An object of legend thought lost to time. Supposedly, it holds the remains of Abyssia, Duchess of the Abyss.

Usaic
An ice-elementalist exiled from the Granalchi Academy. His efforts to create a magical stone born of the elemental plane of ice itself accidentally unleashed the frozen wraith known as Daringol, the iced-over demon Makolichi, and untold suffering on the village of Toniki and areas around.

Ward of Defiance
A ward used by exorcists of the Order of Love to warn off the dead – or those that seek to use the powers of the Fallen – from the site of a calamity. It's the magical equivalent of a sign reading, *'You may have won the battle but you will not win the war.'*

Warmaiden
One of the bodyguards assigned to nobility or other individuals of power in the Odinal wartribe.

Watersculpt
A water-elementalist capable of channeling any water-based liquids into works of art or temporary tools. They are, almost entirely, Aquallan worshipers in some way.

(The) White Swan
A tavern in Akkador East. Serves as the home base for Raes, one of the FFG Bosses in Basion.

Yothargi
The former husband of Rmaci, a Civan Spy. What he didn't know was that he was just a cover, and any feelings she had for him were accidental at best.

THE SAGA OF THE DEAD MEN WALKING
Available in Digital and Print!

Year 512 of the Queen's Rule
The Snowflakes Trilogy
Book I: Snowflakes in Summer
Freshly minted by the Order of Love, a young exorcist is sent to the edge of the Kingdom of Dawnfire to deal with a 'small, simple haunting.' Between a winter that won't end, a girl that doesn't belong, and people being eaten in the woods, only one thing is for sure: he's over his head, and utterly out of luck.

Book II: Dead Men in Winter
As the search for the Coldstone continues, new allies enter the fray in the mountains around Toniki, and in the streets of the City of Mud. But new blood only means new bodies, and Makolichi seeks to provide those in excess...

Book III: Favorite Things
It's time for Usaic's Tower to ascend. Truths will be revealed, blood shall be spilled, and suffering shall become legendary. But it's not just the living who should fear the Coldstone being set loose. For though the dead will rise, the damned had best be ready for Who comes next...

Year 513 of the Queen's Rule
The Auramancer's Exorcism
Book I: Insanity's Respite
Beaten, broken, and battered, Akaran is sent to the Safest City in the Kingdom to recover from his battle against Makolichi, Daringol, Rmaci, and the rest. What he expects is peace and time to heal. What he finds instead is that insanity knows no bounds and offers no respite...

Book II: Insanity's Rapture
As Akaran's worst nightmare comes true, he realizes that the only peace to be had is through the mind of one of the most insane souls he's ever encountered. The problem? He set her world on fire, and now she thinks it's her turn.

Book III: Insanity's Reckoning (Release date: TBA)
Pity the instruments of madness, for they answer to the one that calls down Love.

Origins of the Dead Men Walking
Year 510 of the Queen's Rule
Blindshot (Release date: TBA)
A self-professed Merchant of Secrets enlists the help of the Northern Hunter's Guild to trek to the Cursed Continent of Agromah to recover a relic lost to time. In this land of the dead, what chance does a blind man have against a demon

king?

Year 512 of the Queen's Rule
Slag Harbor (An Interruption in the Snowflakes Trilogy)
After battling Makolichi in Gonta – and before facing him down for the final time in Toniki – Akaran decides to leave Private Galagrin behind in the City of Mud to make sure that nothing got missed in his sweep. What he finds is more than just stray shiriak; it's an answer to an unasked question...

Year 513 of the Queen's Rule
Lady Claw I: Claw Unsheathed
Who's to blame when a young girl is accused of murder? Did she do it, or did her father? And when she's cornered and the claws come out... does it matter?

Year 516 of the Queen's Rule
Fearmonger
Years after Toniki, a grizzled Akaran serves as a peacekeeper to the Queen – and nothing wants the peace to be kept.

Year 517 of the Queen's Rule
Blindsided
Stannoth and Elrok couldn't be any more different. Trained mercenaries in the Hunter's Guild, they absolutely hate each other – but they don't have a choice but to work together.

WELCOME TO A WORLD WHERE GOOD THINGS HAPPEN TO BAD PEOPLE AND THE GOOD PEOPLE ARE QUESTIONABLE... ...AT BEST.

Good things come to those who wait, but I'm impatient as the fires in the Abyss are hot (or cold, depending on Frosel). I'm working on the next book as fast as I can (I promise!) and I've got some stuff for you.

Please be sure to follow me on social media to find out where I'm going, what I'm doing, how I'm doing it, and the occasional stupid meme just to laugh. Plus, get some random business insights on the self-published side of the coin AND see what I'm doing when I dress up for charity purposes.

There's also a newsletter you can sign up for!
You can expect free stories, character information, special promotions, extra information about the World of the Saga, and more! Be sure to visit and subscribe (it'd mean a lot to me if you did)!

Firstly though, I need your help.
If you enjoyed this boxed set, could you take the time to leave a review? As odd as it sounds, there's more to marketing than just a few ads. Reviews help me write better stories, they let me know that you read the whole book, and truthfully? There are ad platforms and editorial services that will only pay attention to a specific book if the author has a certain number of reviews. I know it's a lot to ask but if you have a few moments to spare, it'd mean more to me than you'd know.

Link
http://www.amazon.com/review/create-review?&asin=B08P61MNVN

Dead Men Emailing Newsletter
http://email.sagadmw.com

Amazon.com:
https://www.amazon.com/author/sdmw

Facebook.com:
https://www.facebook.com/sagadmw

Website:
http://www.sagadmw.com

Goodreads
https://www.goodreads.com/author/show/14201900.Joshua_E_B_Smith

Instagram:
https://www.instagram.com/sagadmw

Printed in Great Britain
by Amazon